# GRAVEN IMAGES

# GRAVEN IMAGES

## Classic Stories of Ghastly Paintings and Dreadful Effigies

Edited by Chad Arment

COACHWHIP PUBLICATIONS
Greenville, Ohio

*Graven Images*, edited by Chad Arment
© 2022 Coachwhip Publications edition

Cover: Frame © Modify260 / Sculpture © mw_listing

CoachwhipBooks.com

ISBN 1-61646-533-6
ISBN-13 978-1-61646-533-9

# CONTENTS

# SKETCHBOOK
# (SHORT STORIES)

# La Vénus d'Ille
## PROSPER MÉRIMÉE
### 1837


Γλεώς ἤν δεγώ, ἔστω ὁ ἀνδρίας καί ἤπιος,
οὕτως ἀνδρείος ὤν.

                    *Λουκιανου Φιλοψευδης*


I was descending the last slope of the Canigou, and though the sun was already set I could distinguish on the plain the houses of the little town of Ille, towards which I directed my steps.

"Of course," I said to the Catalan who since the day before served as my guide, "you know where Monsieur de Peyrehorade lives?"

"Just don't I," he cried; "I know his house like my own, and if it were not so dark I would show it to you. It is the finest in Ille. He is rich, M. de Peyrehorade is, and he marries his son to one richer even than he."

"Will the marriage take place soon?" I asked him.

"Soon? It may be that the violins are already ordered for the wedding. Tonight perhaps, tomorrow or the next day, how do I know? It will take place at Puygarrig, for it is Mademoiselle de Puygarrig that the son is to marry. It will be a sight, I can tell you."

I was recommended to M. de Peyrehorade by my friend M. de P. He was, I had been told, an antiquarian of much learning and a man of charming affability. He would take delight in showing me the ruins for ten leagues around. Therefore I counted on him to visit the outskirts of Ille, which I knew to be rich in memorials of the Middle Ages. This marriage, of which I now heard for the first time, upset all my plans.

"I shall be a troublesome guest," I told myself. "But I am expected; my arrival has been announced by M. de P.: I must present myself."

When we reached the plain the guide said, "Wager a cigar, sir, that I can guess what you are going to do at M. de Peyrehorade's."

Offering him one, I answered, "It is not very hard to guess. At this hour, when one has made six leagues in the Canigou, supper is the great thing after all."

"Yes, but tomorrow? Here I wager that you have come to Ille to see the idol. I guessed that when I saw you draw the portraits of the saints at Serrabona."

"The idol! What idol?" This word had aroused my curiosity.

"What! Were you not told at Perpignan how M. de Peyrehorade had found an idol in the earth?"

"You mean to say an earthen statue?"

"Not at all. A statue in copper, and there is enough of it to make a lot of big pennies. She weighs as much as a church-bell. It was deep in the ground at the foot of an olive tree that we got her.

"You were present at the discovery?"

"Yes, sir. Two weeks ago M. de Peyrehorade told Jean Coll and me to uproot an old olive-tree which was frozen last year when the weather, as you know, was very severe. So in working, Jean Coll, who went at it with all his might, gave a blow with his pickaxe, and I heard *bimm*—as if he had struck a bell—and I said, 'What is that?' We dug on and on, and there was a black hand, which looked like the hand of a corpse, sticking out of the earth. I was scared

to death. I ran to M. de Peyrehorade and I said to him,—
'There are dead people, master, under the olive-tree! The
priest must be called.'

"'What dead people,' said he to me. He came, and
he had no sooner seen the hand than he cried out, 'An
antique! an antique!' You would have thought he had
found a treasure. And there he was with the pickaxe in his
own hands, struggling and doing almost as much work as
we two."

"And at last what did you find?"

"A huge black woman more than half naked, with due
respect to you, sir. She was all copper, and M. de Peyrehorade told us it was an idol of pagan times—the time of
Charlemagne."

"I see what it is—some virgin or other in bronze from
a destroyed convent."

"A virgin! Had it been one I should have recognized it.
It is an idol, I tell you; you can see it in her look. She fixes
you with her great white eyes—one might say she stares
at you. One lowers one's eyes, yes, indeed, one does, on
looking at her."

"White eyes? Doubtless they are set in the bronze. Perhaps it is some Roman statue."

"Roman! That's it. M. de Peyrehorade says it is Roman.
Oh! I see you are an erudite like himself."

"Is she complete, well preserved?"

"Yes, sir, she lacks nothing. It is a handsome statue and
better finished than the bust of Louis Philippe in colored
plaster which is in the town-hall. But with all that the face
of the idol does not please me. She has a wicked expression—and, what is more, she is wicked."

"Wicked! what has she done to you?"

"Nothing to me exactly; but wait a minute. We had
gotten down on all fours to stand her upright, and M. de
Peyrehorade was also pulling on the rope, though he has

not much more strength than a chicken. With much trouble we got her up right. I reached for a broken tile to support her, when if she doesn't tumble over backwards all in a heap. I said, 'Take care,' but not quick enough, for Jean did not have time to draw away his leg—"

"And it was hurt?"

"Broken as clean as a vine-prop. When I saw that I was furious; I wanted to take my pickaxe and smash the statue to pieces, but M. de Peyrehorade stopped me. He gave Jean Coll some money, but all the same, he is in bed still, though it is two weeks since it happened, and the physician says that he will never walk as well with that leg as with the other. It is a pity, for he was our best runner, and, after M. de Peyrehorade's son, the cleverest tennis player. M. Alphonse de Peyrehorade was sorry, I can tell you, for Coll always played with him. It was beautiful to see how they returned each other the balls. They never touched the ground."

Chatting in this way we entered Ille, and I soon found myself in the presence of M. de Peyrehorade. He was a little old man, still hale and active, with powdered hair, a red nose, and a jovial, bantering manner. Before opening M. de P.'s letter he had seated me at a well-spread table, and had presented me to his wife and son as a celebrated archeologist who was to draw Roussillon from the neglect in which the indifference of erudites had left it.

While eating heartily, for nothing makes one hungrier than the keen air of the mountains, I scrutinized my hosts. I have said a word about M. de Peyrehorade. I must add that he was activity personified. He talked, got up, ran to his library, brought me books, showed me engravings, and filled my glass, all at the same time. He was never two minutes in repose. His wife was a trifle stout, as are most Catalans when they are over forty years of age. She appeared to me a thorough provincial, solely occupied with her housekeeping. Though the supper was sufficient for at least six people, she hurried to the kitchen and had pigeons killed and a number broiled, and she opened I do not know how many jars of preserves. In no time the table was laden with dishes and bottles, and if I had but sampled everything offered me I should certainly have died of indigestion. Nevertheless, at each dish I refused they made fresh excuses. They feared I found myself very badly off at Ille. In the provinces there were so few resources, and of course Parisians were fastidious!

In the midst of his parent's comings and goings M. Alphonse de Peyrehorade was as immobile as rent-day. He was a tall young man of twenty-six, with a regular and handsome countenance, but lacking in expression. His height and his athletic figure well justified the reputation of an indefatigable racquet player given him in the neighborhood.

On that evening he was dressed in an elegant manner; that is to say, he was an exact copy of a fashion plate in the last number of the *Journal des Modes*. But he seemed to me ill at ease in his clothes; he was as stiff as a post in his velvet collar, and could only turn all of a piece. In striking contrast to his costume were his large sunburnt hands and blunt nails. They were laborer's hands issuing from the sleeves of an exquisite. Moreover, though he examined me in my quality of Parisian most curiously from head to foot, he only spoke to me once during the whole evening, and that was to ask me where I had bought my watch-chain.

As the supper was drawing to an end M. de Peyrehorade said to me: "Ah! my dear guest, you belong to me now you are here. I shall not let go of you until you have seen everything of interest in our mountains. You must learn to know our Roussillon, and to do it justice. You do not suspect all that we have to show you, Phoenician, Celtic,

Roman, Arabian, and Byzantine monuments; you shall see them all from the cedar to the hyssop. I shall drag you everywhere, and will not spare you a single stone."

A fit of coughing obliged him to pause. I took advantage of it to tell him that I should be sorry to disturb him on an occasion of so much interest to his family. If he would but give me his excellent advice about the excursions to be made, I could, without his taking the trouble to accompany me.

"Ah! you mean the marriage of that boy there," he exclaimed, interrupting me; "stuff and nonsense, it will be over the day after tomorrow. You will go to the wedding with us, which is to be informal, as the bride is in mourning for an aunt whose heiress she is. Therefore, there will be not festivities, no ball. It is a pity, though; you might have seen our Catalans dance. They are pretty, and might have given you the desire to imitate Alphonse. One marriage, they say, leads to another. The young people once married I shall be free, and we will bestir ourselves. I beg your pardon for boring you with a provincial wedding. For a Parisian tired of entertainments—and a wedding without a ball at that! Still you will see a bride—a bride—well, you shall tell me what you think of her. But you are a thinker and no longer notice women. I have better than that to show you. You shall see something; in fact, I have a fine surprise in store for you tomorrow."

"Good heavens!" said I; "it is difficult to have a treasure in the house without the public being aware of it. I think I know the surprise in reserve for me. But if it is your statue which is in question, the description my guide gave me of it has only served to excite my curiosity and prepared me to admire."

"Ah! So he spoke to you about the idol, as he calls my beautiful Venus Tur; but I will tell you nothing. Tomorrow you shall see her by daylight, and tell me if I am right in thinking the statue a masterpiece. You could not have arrived more opportunely. There are inscriptions in it which I, poor ignoramus that I am, explain after my own fashion; but you, a Parisian erudite, will probably laugh at my interpretation; for I have actually written a paper about it,—I, an old provincial antiquary, have launched myself in literature. I wish to make the press groan. If you would kindly read and correct it I might have some hope. For example, I am very anxious to know how you translate this inscription from the base of the statue: 'CAVE.' But I do not wish to ask you yet! Wait until tomorrow. Not a word more about Venus today!"

"You are right, Peyrehorade," said his wife; "drop your idol. Can you not see that you prevent our guest from eating? You may be sure the he has seen in Paris much finer statues than yours. In the Tuileries there are dozens, and they are also in bronze."

"There you have the saintly ignorance of the provinces!" interrupted M. de Peyrehorade. "The idea of comparing an admirable antique to the insipid figures of Coustou!

'How irreverently my housekeeper
speaks of the gods!'

Do you know that my wife wanted me to melt my statue into a bell for our church. She would have been the godmother. Just think of it, to melt a masterpiece by Myron, sir!"

"Masterpiece! Masterpiece! A charming masterpiece she is! to break a man's leg."

"Madam, do you see that?" said M. de Peyrehorade in a resolute tone, extending toward her his right leg in its changeable silk stocking; "if my Venus had broken that leg there for me I should not regret it."

"Good gracious! Peyrehorade, how can you say such a thing! Fortunately, the man is better. And yet I cannot bring myself to look at a statue which has caused so great disaster. Poor Jean Coll!"

"Wounded by Venus, sir," said M. de Peyrehorade, with a loud laugh; "wounded by Venus, and the churl complains!

'Veneris nec præmia noris.'

Who has been wounded by Venus?"

M. Alphonse, who understood French better than Latin, winked one eye with an air of intelligence, and looked at me as if to ask, "And you, Parisian, do you understand?"

The supper came to an end. I had ceased eating an hour before. I was weary, and I could not manage to hide the frequent yawns which escaped me. Madame de Peyrehorade was the first to notice them, and remarked that it was time to go to bed. Then followed fresh apologies for the poor accommodations I would have. I would not be as well of as in Paris. It was so uncomfortable in the provinces! Indulgence was needed for the Roussillonnais. Notwithstanding my protests that after a tramp in the mountains a bundle of straw would seem to me a delicious couch, they continued begging me to pardon poor country people if they did not treat me as well as they could have wished.

Accompanied by M. de Peyrehorade I ascended at last to the room arranged for me. The staircase, the upper half of which was in wood, ended in the centre of a hall, out of which opened several rooms.

"To the right," said my host, "is the apartment which I propose to give the future Madame Alphonse. Your room is at the opposite end of the corridor. You understand," he added in a manner which he meant to be sly—"you understand that newly married people must be alone. You are to one end of the house, they at the other."

We entered a well-furnished room where the first object on which my gaze rested was a bed seven feet long, six wide, and so high that one needed a chair to climb up into it. Having shown me where the bell was, and assured himself that the sugar-bowl was full and the cologne bottles duly placed on the toilet-stand, my host asked me a number of times if anything was lacking, wished me good night, and left me alone.

The windows were closed. Before undressing I opened one to breathe the fresh night air so delightful after a long supper. Facing me was the Canigou. Always magnificent, it appeared to me on that particular evening, lighted as it was by the resplendent moon, as the most beautiful mountain in the world. I remained a few minutes contemplating its marvelous silhouette, and was about to close the window when, lowering my eyes, I perceived a dozen yards from the house the statue on its pedestal. It was placed at the corner of a hedge that separated a small garden from a vast, perfectly level quadrangle, which I learned later was the racquet court of the town. This ground was the property of M. de Peyrehorade, and had been given by him to the parish at the solicitation of his son.

Owing to the distance it was difficult for me to distinguish the attitude of the statue; I could only judge of its height, which seemed to be about six feet. At that moment two scamps of the town, whistling the pretty Roussillon tune, *Montagnes régalades,* were crossing the racquet court quite near the hedge. They paused to look at the statue, and one of them even apostrophized it aloud. He spoke Catalonian, but I had been long enough in Roussillon to understand pretty well what he said.

"There you are, you wench!" (The Catalonian word was much more forcible.) "There you are!" he said. "It was you then who broke Jean Coll's leg! If you belonged to me I'd break your neck."

"Bah! What with?" said the other youth. "It is of the copper of pagan times, and harder than I don't know what."

"If I had my chisel" (it seems he was a locksmith's apprentice), "I would soon force out its big white eyes, as I would pop an almond from its shell. There are more than a hundred pennies' worth of silver in them."

They went a few steps.

"I must wish the idol good-night," said the taller of the apprentices, stopping suddenly.

He stooped and probably picked up a stone. I saw him unbend his arm and throw something. A blow resounded on the bronze, and immediately the apprentice raised his hand to his head with a cry of pain.

"She threw it back at me!" he exclaimed. And my two rascals ran off as fast as they could. It was evident that the stone had rebounded from the metal and had punished the wag for the outrage he had done the goddess. Laughing heartily, I shut the window.

Another Vandal punished by Venus! May all the desecrators of our old monuments thus get their due!

With this charitable wish I fell asleep.

When I awoke it was broad day. On one side of my bed stood M. de Peyrehorade in a dressing-gown; a servant sent by his wife was on the other side with a cup of chocolate in his hand.

"Come, come, you Parisian, get up! This is quite the laziness of the capital!" said my host, while I dressed in haste. "It is eight o'clock, and you are still in bed! I have been up since six. This is the third time I have been at your door. I approached on tiptoe: no one, not a sign of life. It is bad for you to sleep too much at your age. And my Venus, which you have not yet seen! Come, hurry up and take this cup of Barcelona chocolate. It is real contraband chocolate, such as cannot be found in Paris. Prepare yourself, for when you are once before my Venus no one will be able to tear you away from her."

I was already in five minutes, that is to say, I was half shaved, half dressed, and burned by the boiling chocolate I had swallowed. I descended to the garden and saw an admirable statue before me. It was truly a Venus, and of marvelous beauty. The upper part of the body was nude, as great divinities were usually represented by the ancients. The right hand was raised as high as the breast, the palm turned inwards, the thumb and two first fingers extended, and the others slightly bent. The other hand, drawn close to the hip, held the drapery which covered the lower half of the body. The attitude of this statue reminded one of that of the *mourre* player which is called, I hardly know why, by the name of Germanicus. Perhaps it had been intended to represent the goddess as playing at *mourre*. However that may be, it is impossible to find anything more perfect than the form of this Venus, anything softer and more voluptuous than her outlines, or more graceful and dignified than her drapery. I had expected a work of the decadence; I saw a masterpiece of statuary's best days.

What struck me most was the exquisite reality of the figure; one might have thought it molded from life, this is, if Nature ever produced such perfect models.

The hair, drawn back from the brow, seemed once to have been gilded. The head was small, like nearly all those of Greek statues, and bent slightly forward. As the face, I shall never succeed in describing its strange character; it was of a type belonging to no other Greek statue which I can remember. It had not the calm, severe beauty of the Greek sculptors, who systematically gave a majestic immobility to all the features. On the contrary, I noticed here, with a surprise, a marked intention on the artist's part to reproduce malice verging on viciousness. All the features were slightly contracted. The eyes were rather oblique, the mouth raised at the corners, the nostrils a trifle dilated.

Disdain, irony, and cruelty were to be read in the nevertheless beautiful face.

Truly, the more one gazed at the statue the more one experienced a feeling of pain that such wonderful beauty could be allied to such an absence of sensibility.

"If the model ever existed," I said to M. de Peyrehorade, "and I doubt if heaven ever produced such a woman, how I pity her lovers! She must have taken pleasure in making them die of despair. There is something ferocious in her expression, and yet I have never seen anything more beautiful."

"'C'est Venus tout entière à sa proie attachée!'" cried M. de Peyrehorade, delighted with my enthusiasm.

But the expression of demoniac irony was perhaps increased by the contrast of the bright silver eyes with the dusky green hue which time had given to the statue. The shining eyes produced a sort of life. I remembered what my guide had said, that those who looked at her were forced to lower their eyes. It was almost true, and I could not prevent a movement of anger to myself when I felt ill at ease before this bronze figure.

"Now that you have seen everything in detail, my dear colleague in antiquities, let us, if you please, open a scientific conference. What do you say to this inscription which you have not yet noticed?" He pointed to the base of the statue, and I read these words:

CAVE AMANTEM

"Quid dicis doctissime?" he asked, rubbing his hands. "Let us see if we agree as to the meaning *of cave amantem!*"

"But," I replied, "it has two meanings. You can translate it: 'Guard against him who loves thee,' that is, 'distrust lovers.' But in this sense I don't know if *cave amantem* would be good Latin. After seeing the diabolical expression of the lady I should sooner believe that the artist meant to warn the spectator against this terrible beauty. I should then translate it: 'Take care of thyself if *she* loves thee.'"

"Humph!" said M. de Peyrehorade; "yes, it is an admissible meaning: but, if you do not mind, I prefer the first translation, which I would however, develop. You know Venus's lover?"

"There are several."

"Yes; but the first is Vulcan. Why should it not mean: 'Notwithstanding all thy beauty, thine air of disdain, thou wilt have a blacksmith, a wretched cripple for a lover'? A profound lesson, sir, for coquettes!"

The explication seemed so far-fetched that I could not help smiling.

To avoid formally contradicting my antiquarian friend, I observed, "Latin is a terrible language in its conciseness," and I drew back several steps to better contemplate the statue.

"Wait a moment, colleague!" said M. de Peyrehorade, catching hold of my arm; "you have not seen all. There is another inscription. Climb up on the pedestal and look at the right arm." So saying, he helped me up, and without much ceremony I clung to the neck of the Venus with whom I was becoming more familiar. For a second I even looked her straight in the eyes, and on close inspection she appeared more wicked, and, if possible, more beautiful than before. Then I noticed that on the arm were engraved, as it seemed to me, characters in ancient script. With the aid of my spectacles I spelt out what follows, and M. de Peyrehorade, approving with voice and gesture, repeated each word as I uttered it. Thus I read:

VENERI TVRBVL . . .
EVTVCHES MYRO.
IMPERIO FECIT.

After the word 'Tvrbvl' in the first line it looked to me as if there were several letters effaced; but 'Tvrbvl' was perfectly legible.

"Which means to say?" my host asked radiantly, with a mischievous smile, for he thought the 'Tvrbvl' would puzzle me.

"There is one word which I do not yet understand," I answered; "all the rest is simple. Eutyches Myron has made this offering to Venus by her command."

"Quite right. But 'Tvrbvl,' what do you make of it? What does it mean?"

"'Tvrbvl' perplexes me very much. I am trying to think of one of Venus's familiar characteristics which may enlighten me. But what do you say to 'Tvrbvlenta'? The Venus who troubles, agitates. You see I am still preoccupied by her wicked expression. 'Tvrbvlenta' is not bad a quality for Venus," I added modestly, for I was not too well satisfied with my explanation.

"A turbulent Venus! A noisy Venus! Ah! then you think my Venus is a public-house Venus? Nothing of the kind, sir; she is a Venus of good society. I will explain 'Tvrbvl' to you—that is, if you promise me not to divulge my discovery before my article appears in print. Because, you see, I pride myself on such a find, and, after all, you Parisian erudites are rich enough to leave a few ears for us poor devils of provincials to glean!"

from the top of the pedestal, where I was still perched, I promised him solemnly that I would never be so base as to filch from him this discovery.

"'Tvrbvl,'—sir," said he, coming nearer and lowering his voice for fear some one besides myself might hear him, "read 'Tvrbvlneræ.'"

"I understand no better."

"Listen to me attentively. Three miles from here at the foot of the mountain is a village called Boulternère.

The name is a corruption of the Latin word 'Tvrbvl-nera.' Nothing is more common than these transpositions. Boulternère was a Roman town. I always suspected it, but I could get no proof till now, and here it is. This Venus was the local goddess of the city of Boulternère; and the word Boulternère, which I have shown is of ancient origin, proves something very curious, namely, that Boulternère was a Phoenician town before it was Roman!"

He paused a moment to take breath and enjoy my surprise. I succeeded in overcoming a strong inclination to laugh.

"'Tvrbvlnera' is, in fact, pure Phoenician," he continued. "'Tvr,' pronounce 'tour'—'Tour' and 'Sour' are the same word, are they not? 'Sour' is the Phoenician name of Tyr; I do not need to recall the meaning to you. 'Bvl' is Baal; Bâl, Bel, Bul are slight differences of pronunciation. As to 'Nera,' that troubles me a little. I am tempted to believe, for want of a Phoenician word, that it comes from the Greek νηρός, moist, marshy. In that case, it is a mongrel word. To justify νηρός I will show you at Boulternère how the mountain streams form stagnant pools. Then, again, the ending 'Nera' may have been added much later in honor of Nera Pivesuvia, wife of Tetricus, who may have benefited the city of Turbul. But on account of the marshes, I prefer the etymology of νηρός."

He took a pinch of snuff in a complacent way, and continued:

"But let us leave the Phoenicians and return to the inscription. I translate it then: 'To Venus of Boulternère Myron dedicates by her order this statue, his work.'"

I took good care not to criticize his etymology, but I wished in my turn to give a proof of penetration, so I said:

"Stop a moment, M. de Peyrehorade. Myron has dedicated something, but I by no means see that it is this statue."

"What!" he cried, "was not Myron a famous Greek sculptor? The talent was perpetuated in his family, and it must have been one of his descendants who executed this statue. Nothing can be more certain."

"But," I replied, "on this arm I see a small hole. I think it served to fasten something, a bracelet for example, which this Myron, being an unhappy lover, gave to Venus as an expiatory offering. Venus was irritated against him; he appeased her by consecrating to her a gold bracelet. Notice that 'fecit' is often used for 'consecravit.' The terms are synonymous. I could show you more than one example if I had at hand Gruter or Orellius. It is natural that a lover should see Venus in a dream and imagine that she commands him to give a gold bracelet to her statue. Myron consecrated the bracelet to her. Then the barbarians or some other sacrilegious thieves—"

"Ah! it is easy to see you have written romances!" cried my host, helping me down the pedestal. "No, sir; it is a work of Myron's school. You have only to look at the workmanship to be convinced of that."

Having made it a rule never to contradict self-opinionated antiquarians, I bowed with an air of conviction, saying:

"It is an admirable piece of work."

"Good heavens!" exclaimed M. de Peyrehorade, "another act of vandalism! Some one must have thrown a stone at my statue!"

He had just perceived a white mark a little above the bosom of the Venus. I noticed a similar mark on the fingers of the right hand. I supposed it had been touched by the stone as it passed, or that a bit of stone had been broken off as it struck the statue, and had rebounded on the hand. I told my host of the insult I had witnessed, and the prompt punishment which had followed it.

He laughed heartily, and, comparing the apprentice to Diomede, wished he might, like the Greek hero, see all his comrades turned into white birds.

The breakfast bell interrupted this classical conversation, and as on the preceding evening, I was obliged to eat enough for four. Then came M. de Peyrehorade's farmers, and, while he was giving them an audience, his son led me to inspect an open carriage, which he had bought at Toulouse for his betrothed, and which it is needless to say I duly admired. After that I went into the stable with him, where he kept me a half hour, boasting about his horses, giving me their genealogy, and telling me of the prizes they had won at the county races. At last he began to talk to me about his betrothed in connection with a gray mare which he intended for her.

"We will see her today," he said. "I do not know if you will find her pretty. In Paris people are hard to please. But every one here and in Perpignan thinks her lovely. The best of it is that she is very rich. Her aunt from Prades left her a fortune. Oh! I shall be very happy."

I was profoundly shocked to see a young man appear more affected by the dower than the beauty of his bride.

"You are a judge of jewels," continued M. Alphonse; "what do you think of this? Here is the ring I shall give her tomorrow."

He drew from his little finger a heavy ring, enriched with diamonds, and fashioned into two clasped hands, an allusion which seemed to me infinitely poetic. The workmanship was antique, but I fancied it had been retouched to insert the diamonds. Inside the ring these words in Gothic characters could be discerned: 'Sempr' ab ti,' which means, 'Thine forever.'

"It is a pretty ring," I said, "but the diamond which have been added have made it lose a little of its style."

"Oh! it is much handsomer now," he answered smiling. "There are twelve hundred francs' worth of diamonds in it. My mother gave it to me. It is a very old family ring—it dates from the days of chivalry. It was my grandmother's, who had it from her grandmother. Heaven knows when it was made."

"The custom in Paris," I said, "is to give a perfectly plain ring, usually composed of two different metals, such as gold and platina. The other ring which you have on would be very suitable. This one with its diamonds and its clasped hands is so thick that it would be impossible to wear a glove over it."

"Madame Alphonse must arrange that as she pleases. I think she will be very glad to have it all the same. Twelve hundred francs on the finger is pleasant. That other little ring," he added, looking in a contented way at the plain ring he wore, "that one a woman in Paris gave me on Shrove Tuesday. How I did enjoy myself when I was in Paris two years ago! That is the place to have a good time!" and he sighed regretfully.

We were to dine that day at the Puygarrig, with the relations of the bride; so we got in the carriage, and drove to the château, which was four or five miles from Ille. I was presented and received as the friend of the family. I will not speak of the dinner, or the conversation which followed. I took but little part in it. M. Alphonse was seated beside his betrothed, and whispered a word or two in her ear now and then. As for her, she hardly raised her eyes; and every time her lover spoke to her she blushed modestly, but answered without embarrassment.

Mademoiselle de Puygarrig was eighteen years of age. Her slender, graceful figure formed a striking contrast to the stalwart frame of her future husband. She was not only beautiful, she was alluring. I admired the perfect naturalness of all her replies. Her kind look, which yet was not free from a touch of malice, reminded me, in spite of myself, of my host's Venus. While making this inward comparison, I asked myself if the incontestably superior beauty of the statue did not in great measure come from its tigress-like expression; for strength, even in evil passions, always arouses in us astonishment, and a sort of involuntary admiration.

"What a pity," I thought, on leaving Puygarrig, "that such an attractive girl should be rich, and that her dowry makes her sought by a man quite unworthy of her."

While returning to Ille, I spoke to Mme. de Peyrehorade, to whom I thought it only proper to address myself now and then, though I did not very well know what to say to her: "You must be strong-minded people in Roussillon," I said. "How is it, madame, that you have a wedding on Friday? We would be more superstitious in Paris; no one would dare be married on that day."

"Do not speak of it," she replied; "if it had depended on me, certainly another day would have been chosen. But Peyrehorade wished it, and I had to give in. All the same, it troubles me very much. Supposing an accident should happen? There must be some reason in it, or else why is every one afraid of Friday?"

"Friday!" cried her husband, "is Venus's day! Just the day for a wedding! You see, my dear colleague, I think only of my Venus. I chose Friday on her account. Tomorrow, if you like, before the wedding, we will make a little sacrifice to her—a sacrifice of two doves—and if I only knew where to get some incense—"

"For shame, Peyrehorade!" interrupted his wife, scandalized to the last degree. "Incense to an idol! It would be an abomination! What would they say of us in the neighborhood?"

"At least," answered M. de Peyrehorade, "you will allow me to place a wreath of roses and lilies on her head:

*Manibus date lilia plenis.* You see, sir, freedom is an empty word. We have not liberty of worship!"

The next day's arrangements were ordered in the following manner: Every one was to be dressed and ready at ten o'clock punctually. After the chocolate had been served we were to be driven to Puygarrig. The civil marriage was to take place in the town-hall of the village, and the religious ceremony in the chapel of the château. Afterward there would be a breakfast. After the breakfast people would pass the time as they liked until seven o'clock. At that hour every one would return to M. de Peyrehorade's at Ille, where the two families were to assemble and have supper. It was natural that being unable to dance they would wish to eat as much as possible.

By eight o'clock I was seated in front of the Venus, pencil in hand, recommencing the head of the statue for the twentieth time without being able to catch the expression. M. de Peyrehorade came and went about me, giving me advice, repeating in Phoenician etymology, and laying Bengal roses on the pedestal of the statue while he addressed vows to it in tragicomic tone for the young couple who were to live under his roof. Towards nine o'clock he went to put on his best, and at the same moment M. Alphonse appeared looking very stiff in a new coat, white gloves, chased sleeve-buttons, and varnished shoes. A rose decorated his buttonhole.

"Will you make my wife's portrait?" he asked leaning over my drawing. "She also is pretty."

On the racquet-court of which I have spoken there now began to be a game which immediately attracted M. Alphonse's attention. And I, tired, and despairing of ever being able to copy the diabolical face, soon left my drawing to look at the players. There were among them some Spanish muleteers who had arrived the night before.

They were from Aragon and Navarre, and were nearly all marvelously skillful at the game. Therefore the Illois, though encouraged by the presence and advice of M. Alphonse, were promptly beaten by the foreign champions. The native spectators were disheartened. M. Alphonse looked at his watch. It was only half-past nine. His mother's hair he know was not dressed. He hesitated no longer, but taking off his coat asked for a jacket, and defied the Spaniards. I looked on smiling and a little surprised. "The honor of the country must be sustained," he said.

Then I thought him really handsome. He seemed full of life, and his costume, which but now occupied him so entirely, no longer concerned him. A few minutes before he would have dreaded to turn his head for fear of disarranging his cravat. Now he did not give a thought to his curled hair or his fine shirt-front. And his betrothed? If it had been necessary I think he would have postponed the wedding. I saw him hurriedly put on a pair of sandals, roll up his sleeves, and, with an assured air, take his stand at the head of the vanquished party like Caesar rallying his soldiers at Dyrrachium. I leaped the hedge and place myself comfortably in the shade of a tree so as to command a good view of both sides.

Contrary to general expectation, M. Alphonse missed the first ball. It came skimming along the ground, it is true, and was thrown with astonishing force by an Aragonese who appeared to be the leader of the Spaniards.

He was a man of about forty, nervous and agile, and at least six feet tall. His olive skin as dark as the bronze of the Venus.

M. Alphonse threw his racquet angrily on the ground.

"It is this cursed ring," he cried, "which squeezes my finger, and makes me miss a sure ball."

He threw off his diamond ring with some difficulty; I approached to take it, but he forestalled me by running to the Venus and shoving it on her fourth finger. He then resumed his post at the head of the Illois.

He was pale, but calm and resolute. From that moment he did not miss a single ball, and the Spaniards were completely beaten. The enthusiasm of the spectators was a fine sight: some threw their caps in the air and shouted for joy, while others wrung M. Alphonse's hands, calling him the honor of the country. If he had repulsed an invasion I doubt if he would have received warmer or sincerer congratulations. The vexation of the vanquished added to the splendor of the victory.

"We will play other games, my good fellow," he said to the Aragonese in a tone of superiority, "but I will give you points."

I should have wished M. Alphonse to be more modest, and I was almost pained by his rival's humiliation.

The Spanish giant felt the insult deeply. I saw him pale beneath his tan. He looked sullenly at his racquet and clinched his teeth, then in a smothered voice me muttered:

"Me lo pagarás."

M. de Peyrehorade's voice interrupted his son's triumph. Astonished at not finding him presiding over the preparation of the new carriage, my host was even more surprised on seeing him racquet in hand and bathed in perspiration. M. Alphonse hurried to the house, washed his hands and face, put on again his new coat and patent-leather shoes, and in five minutes we were galloping on the road to Puygarrig. All the racquet players of the town and a crowd of spectators followed us with shouts of joy. The strong horses which drew us could hardly keep ahead of the intrepid Catalans.

We were at Puygarrig, and the procession was about to set out for the town-hall, when M. Alphonse, striking his forehead whispered to me:

"What a mess! I have forgotten the ring! It is on the finger of the Venus; may the devil carry her off! Do not tell my mother at any rate. Perhaps she will not notice it."

"You can send some one for it," I replied.

"My servant remained at Ille. I do not trust these here. Twelve hundred francs' worth of diamonds might well tempt almost any one. Moreover, what would they think of my forgetfulness. They would laugh at me. They would call me the husband of the statue. If it only is not stolen! Fortunately the rascals are afraid of the idol. They do not dare approach it by an arm's length. After all, it does not matter; I have another ring."

The two ceremonies, civil and religious, were accomplished with suitable pomp, and Mademoiselle de Puygarrig received the ring of a Parisian milliner without suspecting that her betrothed was making her the sacrifice of a love-token. Then we seated ourselves at table, where we ate, drank, and even sang, all at great length. I suffered for the bride at the coarse merriment which exploded around her; still, she faced it better than I would have expected, and her embarrassment was neither awkward nor affected.

Perhaps courage comes with difficult situations.

The breakfast ended when heaven pleased. It was four o'clock. The men went to walk in the park, which was magnificent, or watched the peasants, in their holiday attire, dance on the lawn of the château. In this way we passed several hours. Meanwhile, the women were eagerly attentive to the bride, who showed them her presents. Then she changed her dress, and I noticed that she had covered her beautiful hair with a befeathered bonnet; for women are in no greater hurry than to assume, as soon as possible, the attire which custom forbids their wearing while they are still young girls.

It was nearly eight o'clock when preparations were made to start for Ille. But first a pathetic scene took place.

Mlle. de Puygarrig's aunt, a very old and pious woman, who stood to her mother's place, was not to go with us. Before the departure she gave her niece a touching sermon on her wifely duties, from which sermon resulted a flood of tears and endless embraces.

M. de Peyrehorade compared this separation to the Rape of the Sabines.

At last, however, we got off, and, on the way, every one exerted himself to amuse the bride and make her laugh; but all in vain.

At Ille supper awaited us, and what a supper! If the coarse jokes of the morning had shocked me, I was now much more so by the equivocations and pleasantries of which the bride and groom were the principal objects. The bridegroom, who had disappeared for a moment before seating himself at the table, was pale, cold, and grave.

He drank incessantly some old Collioure wine almost as strong as brandy. I sat next to him, and thought to myself obliged to warn him. "Be careful! they say that wine"—I hardly know what stupid nonsense I said to be in harmony with the other guests.

He touched my knee, and whispered:

"When we have left the table . . . let me have two words with you."

His solemn tone surprised me. I looked more closely at him, and noticed a strange alteration in his features.

"Do you feel ill?" I asked.

"No."

And he began to drink again.

Meanwhile, amidst much shouting and clapping of hands, a child of twelve, who had slipped under the table, held up to the company a pretty pink and white ribbon which he had untied from the bride's ankle. It was called her garter, and at once cut into pieces and distributed among the young men, who, following an old custom still preserved in some patriarchal families, ornamented their button-holes with it. This was the time for the bride to flush up to the whites of her eyes. But her confusion was at its height when M. de Peyrehorade, having called for silence, sang several verses in Catalan, which he said were impromptu. Here is the meaning, if I understood it correctly:

"What is this, my friends? Has the wine I have drunk made me see double? There are two Venuses here . . ."

The bridegroom turned his head suddenly with a frightened look, which made every one laugh.

"Yes," continued M. de Peyrehorade, "there are two Venuses under my roof. The one, I found in the ground like a truffle; the other, descended from heaven, has just divided among us her belt."

He meant her garter.

"My son, choose between the Roman Venus and the Catalan the one you prefer. The rascal takes the Catalan, and his choice is the best. The Roman is black, the Catalan is white. The Roman is cold, the Catalan inflames all who approach her."

This equivocal allusion excited such a shout, such noisy applause, and sonorous laughter, that I thought the ceiling would fall on our heads. Around the table there were but three serious faces, those of the newly married couple and mine. I had a terrible headache; and besides, I do not know why, a wedding always saddens me. This one, moreover, even disgusted me a little.

The final verses having been sung, and very lively they were, I must say, every one adjourned to the drawing-room to enjoy the withdrawal of the bride, who, as it was nearly midnight, was soon to be conducted to her room.

M. Alphonse drew me into the embrasure of a window, and, turning away his eyes, said:

"You will laugh at me—but I don't know what is the matter with me. . . . I am bewitched!"

My first thought was that he fancied himself threatened with one of those misfortunes of which Montaigne and Madame de Sévigné speak:

"All the world of love is full of tragic histories," etc.

"I thought only clever people were subject to this sort of accident," I said to myself.

To him I said: "You drank too much Collioure wine, my dear Monsieur Alphonse; I warned you against it."

"Yes, perhaps. But something much more terrible than that has happened."

His voice was broken. I though him completely inebriated.

"You know about my ring?" he continued, after a pause.

"Well, has it been stolen?"

"No."

"Then you have it?"

"No—I—I cannot get if off the finger of that infernal Venus."

"You did not pull hard enough."

"Yes, indeed I did. But the Venus—she has bent her finger."

He stared at me wildly, and leaned against the window-sash to prevent himself from falling.

"What nonsense!" I said. "You pushed the ring on too far. You can get it off tomorrow with pincers. But be careful not to damage the statue."

"No, I tell you. The Venus' finger is crooked, bent under; she clinches her hand, do you hear me? . . . She is my wife apparently, since I have given her my ring. . . . She will not return it."

I shivered, and, for a moment, I was all goose-flesh. Then a great sigh from him brought me to a whiff of wine, and all my emotions disappeared.

The wretch, I though, is dead drunk.

"You are an antiquarian, sir," added the bridegroom in a mournful tone; "you understand statues; there is, perhaps, some hidden spring, some deviltry which I do not know about. Will you go and see?"

"Certainly," I replied. "Come with me."

"No, I would prefer to have you go alone."

I left the drawing room.

The weather had changed during supper, and a heavy rain had begun to fall. I was about to ask for an umbrella, when a sudden thought stopped me. I should be a great fool, I reflected, to go and verify what had been told me by a drunken man! Besides, he may have wished to play some silly trick on me to give cause for laughter to the honest country people; and the least that can happen to me from it is drenched to the bone and catch a bad cold.

From the door I cast a glance at the statue running with water, and I went up to my room without returning to the drawing room. I went to bed; but sleep was long in coming. All the scenes of the day passed through my mind. I thought of the young girl, so pure and lovely, abandoned to a drunken brute. What an odious thing a marriage of convenience is! A mayor dons a tricolored scarf, a priest a stole, and then the most virtuous girl in the world is delivered over to the Minotaur! What can two people who do not love each other find to say at a moment, which two lovers would buy at the price of their lives? Can a woman ever love a man whom she has once seen coarse? First impressions are never effaced, and I am sure M. Alphonse will deserve to be hated.

During my monologue, which I abridge very much, I heard a great deal of coming and going in the house. Doors opened and shut, and carriages drove away. Then I seemed to hear on the stairs the light steps of a number of women going towards the end of the hall opposite my room. It was probably the bride's train of attendants leading her to bed. After that they went down stairs again. Madame de Peyrehorade's door closed. How troubled and ill at ease that poor girl must be, I thought. I tossed about my bed with bad temper. A bachelor plays a stupid part in a house where a marriage is accomplished.

Silence had reigned for some time when it was disturbed by a heavy tread mounting the stairs. The wooden steps creaked loudly.

"What a clown!" I cried to myself. "I wager that he will fall on the stairs." All was quiet again. I took up a book to change the current of my thoughts. It was the country statistics, supplemented with an address by M. de Peyrehorade on the Druidical remains of the district of Prades. I grew drowsy at the third page. I slept badly, and awoke repeatedly. It might have been five o'clock in the morning, and I had been awake more than twenty minutes, when the cock crew. Day was about to dawn. Then I heard distinctly the same heavy footsteps, the same creaking of the stairs which I had heard before I fell asleep. I thought it strange. Yawning, I tried to guess why M. Alphonse got up so early. I could imagine no reason. I was about to close my eyes again, when my attention was freshly excited by a singular trampling of feet, which soon intermingled with the ringing of bells and the sound of doors opened noisily; then I distinguished confused cries.

"My drunkard has set something on fire," I thought jumping out of bed. I dressed quickly and went into the hall. From the opposite end came cries and lamentations, and a heartrending voice dominated all others: "My son! my son!" It was evident that an accident had happened to M. Alphonse. I ran to the bridal apartment: it was full of people. The first sight which struck my gaze was the young man partly dressed and stretched across the bed, the wood-work of which was broken. He was livid and motionless. His mother sobbed and wept beside him. M. de Peyrehorade moved about frantically; he rubbed his son's temples with cologne water, or held salts to his nose. Alas! his son had long been dead. On a sofa at the other side of the room lay the bride, a prey to dreadful convulsions. She was making inarticulate cries, and two robust maid-servants had all the trouble in the world to hold her down. "Good heavens!" I exclaimed, "what has happened?"

I approached the bed and raised the body of the unfortunate young man: it was already stiff and cold. His clinched teeth and black face expressed the most fearful anguish. It was evident enough that his death had been violent and his agony terrible.

Nevertheless, no sign of blood was on his clothes. I opened his shirt, and on his chest I found a livid mark which extended around the ribs to the back. One would have said he had been squeezed in an iron ring. My foot touched something hard on the carpet; I stooped and saw it was the diamond ring. I dragged M. de Peyrehorade and his wife into their room, and had the bride carried there.

"You still have a daughter," I said to them. "You owe her your care." Then I left them alone.

To me it did not seem to admit of a doubt that M. Alphonse had been the victim of murder whose authors had discovered a way to introduce themselves into the bride's room during the night. The bruises on the chest and their circular direction, however, perplexed me, for they could not have been made either by a club or an iron bar. Suddenly I remembered having heard that at Valencia *bravi* used long leather bags filled with sand to stun people whom they had been paid to kill. Immediately I thought of the Aragonese muleteer and his threat. Yet I hardly dared suppose he would have taken such a terrible revenge for a trifling jest.

I went through the house seeking everywhere for traces of house-breaking, but could find none. I descended to the garden to see if the assassins could have made their entrance from there; but there were no conclusive signs of it. In any case, the evening's rain had so softened the ground that it could not have retained any very clear impress. Nevertheless, I noticed some deeply marked footprints; they ran in two contrary directions, but on the same path. They started from the corner of the hedge next the racquet-court and ended at the door of the house. They might have been made by M. Alphonse when he went to get his ring from the finger of the statue. Then again, the hedge at this spot was narrower than elsewhere, and it must have been here that the murders got over it. Passing and repassing before the statue, I stopped a moment and considered it. This time, I must confess, I could not contemplate its expression of vicious irony without fear; and, my mind being filled with the horrible scene I had just witnessed, I seemed to see in it a demoniacal goddess applauding the sorrow fallen on the house.

I returned to my room and stayed there till noon. Then I left it to ask news of my hosts. They were a little calmer. Mlle. de Puygarrig, or I should say the widow of M. Alphonse, had regained consciousness. She had even spoken to the procureur du roi from Perpignan, then in circuit at Ille, and this magistrate had received her depositions. He asked for mine. I told him what I knew, and did not hide from him my suspicions about the Aragonese muleteer. He ordered him to be arrested on the spot.

"Have you learned anything from Mme. Alphonse?" I asked the procureur du roi when my deposition was written and signed.

"That unfortunate young woman has gone crazy," he said, smiling sadly. "Crazy, quite crazy. That is what she says:

"She had been in bed for several minutes with the curtains drawn, when the door of her room opened and some one entered. Mme. Alphonse was on the inside of the bed with her face turned to the wall. Assured that is was her husband she did not move. Presently the bed creaked as if laden with a tremendous weight. She was terribly frightened, but dared not turn her head. Five minutes, or ten minutes perhaps—she has no idea of the time—passed in this way. Then she made an involuntary movement, or else it was the other person who made one, and she felt contact of something as cold as ice, that is her expression. She buried herself against the wall trembling in all her limbs.

"Shortly afterwards, the door opened a second time, and some one came in who said, 'Good evening, my little wife.' Then the curtains were drawn back. She heard a stifled cry. The person who was in the bed beside her sat up apparently with extended arms. Then she turned her head and saw her husband, kneeling by the bed with his head on a level with the pillow, held close in the arms of a sort of greenish-colored giant. She says, and she repeated it to me twenty times, poor woman!—she says that she recognized—do you guess whom?—the bronze Venus, M. de Peyrehorade's statue. Since it has been here every one dreams about it. But to continue the poor lunatic's story. At this sight she lost consciousness, and probably she had already lost her mind. She cannot tell how long she remained in this condition. Returned to her sense she saw the phantom, or the statue as she insists on calling it, lying immovable, the legs and lower part of the body on the bed, the bust and arms extended forward, and between the arms her husband, quite motionless. A cock crew. Then the statue left the bed, let fall the body, and went out. Mme. Alphonse rushed to the bell, and you know the rest."

The Spaniard was brought in; he was calm, and defended himself with much coolness and presence of mind.

He did not deny the remark which I had overhead, but he explained it, pretending that he did not mean anything except that the next day, when rested, he would beat his victor at a game of racquets. I remember that he added:

"An Aragonese when insulted does not wait till the next day to revenge himself. If I had believed that M. Alphonse wished to insult me I would have ripped him up with my knife on the spot."

His shoes were compared with the footprints in the garden; the shoes were much larger.

Finally, the innkeeper with whom the man lodged asserted that he had spent the entire night rubbing and dosing one of his mules which was sick. And, moreover, the Aragonese was a man of good reputation, well known in the neighborhood, where he came from every year on business.

So he was released with many apologies.

I have forgotten to mention the statement of a servant who was the last person to see M. Alphonse alive. It was just as he was about to join his wife, and calling to this man he asked him in an anxious way if he know where I was. The servant answered that he had not seen me. M. Alphonse sighed, and stood a minute without speaking, then he said: "Well! the devil must have carried him off also!"

I asked the man if M. Alphonse had on his diamond ring. The servant hesitated; at last he said he thought not; but for that he matter he had not noticed.

"If the ring had been on M. Alphonse's finger," he added, recovering himself, "I should probably have noticed, for I thought he had given it to Mme. Alphonse."

When questioning the man I felt a little superstitious terror which Mme. Alphonse's statement had spread through the house. The procureur du roi smiled at me, and I was careful not to insist further.

A few hours after the funeral of M. Alphonse I prepared to leave Ille. M. de Peyrehorade's carriage was to
take me as far as the garden gate. We crossed the garden in
silence, he creeping along supported by my arm. As we
were about to part I threw a last glance at the Venus. I
foresaw that my host, though he did not share the fear and
hatred which it inspired in his family, would wish to rid
himself of an object which must ceaselessly recall to him
a dreadful misfortune. My intention was to induce him to
place it in a museum. As I hesitated to open the subject,
M. de Peyrehorade turned his head mechanically in the
direction he saw I was looking so fixedly. He perceived
the statue, and immediately melted into tears. I embraced
him, and got into the carriage without daring to say a
word.

Since my departure I have not learned that any new
light has been thrown on this mysterious catastrophe.

M. de Peyrehorade died several months after his son.
In his will he left me his manuscripts which I may publish
someday. I did not find among them the article relative to
the inscriptions on the Venus.

P.S.—My friend M. de P. has just written to me from Perpignan that the statue no longer exists. After her husband's death Madame de Peyrehorade's first care was to
have it cast into a bell, and in this new shape it does duty
in the church of Ille. "But," adds M. de P., "it seems as if
bad luck pursues those who own the bronze. Since the bell
rings at Ille the vines have twice been frozen."

# The Prophetic Pictures

NATHANIEL HAWTHORNE

1837

"But this painter!" cried Walter Ludlow, with animation. "He not only excels in his peculiar art, but possesses vast acquirements in all other learning and science. He talks Hebrew with Doctor Mather, and gives lectures in anatomy to Doctor Boylston. In a word, he will meet the best instructed man among us, on his own ground. Moreover, he is a polished gentleman—a citizen of the world—yes, a true cosmopolite; for he will speak like a native of each clime and country on the globe, except our own forests, whither he is now going. Nor is all this what I most admire in him."

"Indeed!" said Elinor, who had listened with a woman's interest to the description of such a man. "Yet this is admirable enough."

"Surely it is," replied her lover, "but far less so than his natural gift of adapting himself to every variety of character, insomuch that all men—and women too, Elinor—shall find a mirror of themselves in this wonderful painter. But the greatest wonder is yet to be told."

"Nay, if he have more wonderful attributes than these," said Elinor, laughing, "Boston is a perilous abode for the poor gentleman. Are you telling me of a painter, or a wizard?"

"In truth," answered he, "that question might be asked much more seriously than you suppose. They say that he paints not merely a man's features, but his mind and heart. He catches the secret sentiments and passions, and throws them upon the canvas, like sunshine—or perhaps, in the portraits of dark-souled men, like a gleam of infernal fire. It is an awful gift," added Walter, lowering his voice from its tone of enthusiasm. "I shall be almost afraid to sit to him."

"Walter, are you in earnest?" exclaimed Elinor.

"For Heaven's sake, dearest Elinor, do not let him paint the look which you now wear," said her lover, smiling, though rather perplexed. "There: it is passing away now, but when you spoke, you seemed frightened to death, and very sad besides. What were you thinking of?"

"Nothing, nothing," answered Elinor, hastily. "You paint my face with your own fantasies. Well, come for me tomorrow, and we will visit this wonderful artist."

But when the young man had departed, it cannot be denied that a remarkable expression was again visible on the fair and youthful face of his mistress. It was a sad and anxious look, little in accordance with what should have been the feelings of a maiden on the eve of wedlock. Yet Walter Ludlow was the chosen of her heart.

"A look!" said Elinor to herself. "No wonder that it startled him, if it expressed what I sometimes feel. I know, by my own experience, how frightful a look may be. But it was all fancy, I thought nothing of it at the time—I have seen nothing of it since—I did but dream it."

And she busied herself about the embroidery of a ruff, in which she meant that her portrait should be taken.

The painter, of whom they had been speaking, was not one of those native artists, who at a later period than this, borrowed their colors from the Indians, and manufactured their pencils of the furs of wild beasts. Perhaps, if he could have revoked his life and pre-arranged his destiny, he might have chosen to belong to that school without a master, in the hope of being at least original, since there were no works of art to imitate, nor rules to follow. But he had been born and educated in Europe. People said that he had studied the grandeur or beauty of conception, and every touch of the master-hand, in all the most famous pictures, in cabinets and galleries, and on the walls of churches, till there was nothing more for his powerful mind to learn. Art could add nothing to its lessons, but Nature might. He had therefore visited a world whither none of his professional brethren had preceded him, to feast his eyes on visible images, that were noble and picturesque, yet had never been transferred to canvas. America was too poor to afford other temptations to an artist of eminence, though many of the colonial gentry, on the painter's arrival, had expressed a wish to transmit their lineaments to posterity, by means of his skill. Whenever such proposals were made, he fixed his piercing eyes on the applicant, and seemed to look him through and through. If he beheld a sleek and comfortable visage, though there were a gold-laced coat to adorn the picture, and golden guineas to pay for it, he civilly rejected the task and the reward. But if the face were the index of anything uncommon, in thought, sentiment, or experience; or if he met a beggar in the street, with a white beard and a furrowed brow; or if, sometimes a child happened to look up and smile, he would exhaust all the art on them that he denied to wealth.

Pictorial skill being so rare in the colonies, the painter became an object of general curiosity. If few or none could appreciate the technical merit of his productions, yet there were points, in regard to which the opinion of the crowd was as valuable as the refined judgment of the amateur. He watched the effect that each picture produced on such untutored beholders, and derived profit from their remarks, while they would as soon have thought of instructing Nature herself, as him who seemed to rival her. Their admiration, it must be owned, was tinctured with the prejudices of the age and country. Some deemed it an offence against the Mosaic law, and even a presumptuous mockery of the Creator, to bring into existence such lively images of his creatures. Others, frightened at the art which could raise phantoms at will, and keep the form of the dead among the living, were inclined to consider the painter as a magician, or perhaps the famous Black Man of old witch-times, plotting mischief in a new guise. These foolish fancies were more than half believed, among the mob. Even in superior circles, his character was invested with a vague awe, partly rising like smoke-wreaths from the popular superstitions, but chiefly caused by the varied knowledge and talents which he made subservient to his profession.

Being on the eve of marriage, Walter Ludlow and Elinor were eager to obtain their portraits, as the first of what, they doubtless hoped, would be a long series of family pictures. The day after the conversation above recorded, they visited the painter's rooms. A servant ushered them into an apartment, where, though the artist himself was not visible, there were personages, whom they could hardly forbear greeting with reverence. They knew, indeed, that the whole assembly were but pictures, yet felt it impossible to separate the idea of life and intellect from such striking counterfeits. Several of the portraits were known to them, either as distinguished characters of the day, or their private acquaintances. There was Governor Burnett, looking as if he had just received an undutiful communication from the House of Representatives, and were inditing a most sharp response. Mr. Cooke hung beside the ruler whom he opposed, sturdy, and somewhat puritanical, as befitted a popular leader. The ancient lady of Sir William Phipps eyed them from the wall, in ruff and farthingale,—

an imperious old dame, not unsuspected of witchcraft. John Winslow, then a very young man, wore the expression of warlike enterprise, which long afterwards made him a distinguished general. Their personal friends were recognized at a glance. In most of the pictures, the whole mind and character were brought out on the countenance, and concentrated into a single look, so that, to speak paradoxically, the originals hardly resembled themselves so strikingly as the portraits did.

Among these modern worthies, there were two old bearded Saints, who had almost vanished into the darkening canvas. There was also a pale, but unfaded Madonna, who had perhaps been worshiped in Rome, and now regarded the lovers with such a mild and holy look, that they longed to worship too.

"How singular a thought," observed Walter Ludlow, "that this beautiful face has been beautiful for above two hundred years! Oh, if all beauty would endure so well! Do you not envy her, Elinor?"

"If earth were heaven, I might," she replied. "But where all things fade, how miserable to be the one that could not fade!"

"This dark old St. Peter has a fierce and ugly scowl, saint though he be," continued Walter. "He troubles me. But the Virgin looks kindly at us."

"Yes; but very sorrowfully, methinks," said Elinor.

The easel stood beneath these three old pictures, sustaining one that had been recently commenced. After a little inspection, they began to recognize the features of their own minister, the Rev. Dr. Colman, growing into shape and life, as it were, out of a cloud.

"Kind old man!" exclaimed Elinor. "He gazes at me, as if he were about to utter a word of paternal advice."

"And at me," said Walter, "as if he were about to shake his head and rebuke me, for some suspected iniquity. But so does the original. I shall never feel quite comfortable under his eye, till we stand before him to be married."

They now heard a footstep on the floor, and turning, beheld the painter, who had been some moments in the room, and had listened to a few of their remarks. He was a middle-aged man, with a countenance well worthy of his own pencil. Indeed, by the picturesque, though careless arrangement of his rich dress, and, perhaps, because his soul dwelt always among painted shapes, he looked somewhat like a portrait himself. His visitors were sensible of a kindred between the artist and his works, and felt as if one of the pictures had stepped from the canvas to salute them.

Walter Ludlow, who was slightly known to the painter, explained the object of their visit. While he spoke, a sunbeam was falling athwart his figure and Elinor's, with so happy an effect, that they also seemed living pictures of youth and beauty, gladdened by bright fortune. The artist was evidently struck.

"My easel is occupied for several ensuing days, and my stay in Boston must be brief," said he, thoughtfully; then after an observant glance, he added: "but your wishes shall be gratified, though I disappoint the chief Justice and Madame Oliver. I must not lose this opportunity, for the sake of painting a few ells of broadcloth and brocade."

The painter expressed a desire to introduce both their portraits into one picture, and represent them engaged in some appropriate action. This plan would have delighted the lovers, but was necessarily rejected, because so large a space of canvas would have been unfit for the room which it was intended to decorate. Two half-length portraits were therefore fixed upon. After they had taken leave, Walter Ludlow asked Elinor, with a smile, whether she knew what an influence over their fates the painter was about to acquire.

"The old women of Boston affirm," continued he, "that after he has once got possession of a person's face and figure, he may paint him in any act or situation whatever—and the picture will be prophetic. Do you believe it?"

"Not quite," said Elinor, smiling. "Yet if he has such magic, there is something so gentle in his manner, that I am sure he will use it well."

It was the painter's choice to proceed with both the portraits at the same time, assigning as a reason, in the mystical language which he sometimes used, that the faces threw light upon each other. Accordingly, he gave now a touch to Walter, and now to Elinor, and the features of one and the other began to start forth so vividly, that it appeared as if his triumphant art would actually disengage them from the canvas. Amid the rich light and deep shade, they beheld their phantom selves. But, though the likeness promised to be perfect, they were not quite satisfied with the expression; it seemed more vague than in most of the painter's works. He, however, was satisfied with the prospect of success, and being much interested in the lovers, employed his leisure moments, unknown to them, in making a crayon sketch of their two figures. During their sittings, he engaged them in conversation, and kindled up their faces with characteristic traits, which, though continually varying, it was his purpose to combine and fix. At length he announced, that at their next visit, both the portraits would be ready for delivery.

"If my pencil will but be true to my conception, in the few last touches which I meditate," observed he, "these two pictures will be my very best performances. Seldom, indeed, has an artist such subjects."

While speaking, he still bent his penetrative eye upon them, nor withdrew it till they had reached the bottom of the stairs.

Nothing, in the whole circle of human vanities, takes stronger hold of the imagination, than this affair of having a portrait painted. Yet why should it be so? The looking-glass, the polished globes of the andirons, the mirror-like water, and all other reflecting surfaces, continually present us with portraits, or rather ghosts of ourselves, which we glance at, and straightway forget them. But we forget them, only because they vanish. It is the idea of duration—of earthly immortality—that gives such a mysterious interest to our own portraits. Walter and Elinor were not insensible to this feeling, and hastened to the painter's rooms, punctually at the appointed hour, to meet those pictured shapes, which were to be their representatives with posterity. The sunshine flashed after them into the apartment, but left it somewhat gloomy, as they closed the door.

Their eyes were immediately attracted to their portraits, which rested against the farthest wall of the room. At the first glance, through the dim light and the distance, seeing themselves in precisely their natural attitudes, and with all the air that they recognized so well, they uttered a simultaneous exclamation of delight.

"There we stand," cried Walter, enthusiastically, "fixed in sunshine forever! No dark passions can gather on our faces!"

"No," said Elinor, more calmly; "no dreary change can sadden us."

This was said while they were approaching, and had yet gained only an imperfect view of the pictures. The painter, after saluting them, busied himself at a table in completing a crayon sketch, leaving his visitors to form their own judgment as to his perfected labors. At intervals, he sent a glance from beneath his deep eyebrows, watching their countenances in profile, with his pencil suspended over the sketch. They had now stood some moments, each in front of the other's picture, contemplating it with entranced attention, but without uttering a word. At length, Walter stepped forward—then back—viewing Elinor's portrait in various lights, and finally spoke.

"Is there not a change?" said he, in a doubtful and meditative tone. "Yes; the perception of it grows more vivid, the longer I look. It is certainly the same picture that I saw yesterday; the dress—the features—all are the same; and yet something is altered."

"Is then the picture less like than it was yesterday?" inquired the painter, now drawing near, with irrepressible interest.

"The features are perfect Elinor," answered Walter; "and, at the first glance, the expression seemed also hers. But, I could fancy that the portrait has changed countenance, while I have been looking at it. The eyes are fixed on mine with a strangely sad and anxious expression. Nay, it is grief and terror! Is this like Elinor?"

"Compare the living face with the pictured one," said the painter.

Walter glanced sidelong at his mistress, and started. Motionless and absorbed—fascinated, as it were—in contemplation of Walter's portrait, Elinor's face had assumed precisely the expression of which he had just been complaining. Had she practiced for whole hours before a mirror, she could not have caught the look so successfully. Had the picture itself been a mirror, it could not have thrown back her present aspect, with stronger and more melancholy truth. She appeared quite unconscious of the dialogue between the artist and her lover.

"Elinor," exclaimed Walter, in amazement, "what change has come over you?"

She did not hear him, nor desist from her fixed gaze, till he seized her hand, and thus attracted her notice; then, with a sudden tremor, she looked from the picture to the face of the original.

"Do you see no change in your portrait?" asked she.

"In mine?—None!" replied Walter, examining it. "But let me see! Yes; there is a slight change—an improvement, I think, in the picture, though none in the likeness. It has a livelier expression than yesterday, as if some bright thought were flashing from the eyes, and about to be uttered from the lips. Now that I have caught the look, it becomes very decided."

While he was intent on these observations, Elinor turned to the painter. She regarded him with grief and awe, and felt that he repaid her with sympathy and commiseration, though wherefore, she could but vaguely guess.

"That look!" whispered she, and shuddered. "How came it there?"

"Madam," said the painter, sadly, taking her hand, and leading her apart, "in both these pictures, I have painted what I saw. The artist—the true artist—must look beneath the exterior. It is his gift—his proudest, but often a melancholy one—to see the inmost soul, and, by a power indefinable even to himself, to make it glow or darken upon the canvas, in glances that express the thought and sentiment of years. Would that I might convince myself of error in the present instance!"

They had now approached the table, on which were heads in chalk, hands almost as expressive as ordinary faces, ivied church-towers, thatched cottages, old thunder-stricken trees, oriental and antique costume, and all such picturesque vagaries of an artist's idle moments. Turning them over, with seeming carelessness, a crayon sketch of two figures was disclosed.

"If I have failed," continued he—"if your heart does not see itself reflected in your own portrait—if you have no secret cause to trust my delineation of the other—it is not yet too late to alter them. I might change the action of these figures too. But would it influence the event?"

He directed her notice to the sketch. A thrill ran through Elinor's frame; a shriek was upon her lips; but she stifled it, with the self-command that becomes habitual to all, who hide thoughts of fear and anguish within their bosoms. Turning from the table, she perceived that Walter had advanced near enough to have seen the sketch, though she could not determine whether it had caught his eye.

"We will not have the pictures altered," said she, hastily. "If mine is sad, I shall but look the gayer for the contrast."

"Be it so," answered the painter, bowing. "May your griefs be such fanciful ones, that only your picture may mourn for them! For your joys—may they be true and deep, and paint themselves upon this lovely face, till it quite belie my art!"

After the marriage of Walter and Elinor, the pictures formed the two most splendid ornaments of their abode. They hung side by side, separated by a narrow panel, appearing to eye each other constantly, yet always returning the gaze of the spectator. Travelled gentlemen, who professed a knowledge of such subjects, reckoned these among the most admirable specimens of modern portraiture; while common observers compared them with the originals, feature by feature, and were rapturous in praise of the likeness. But, it was on a third class,—neither travelled connoisseurs nor common observers, but people of natural sensibility—that the pictures wrought their strongest effect. Such persons might gaze carelessly at first, but, becoming interested, would return day after day, and study these painted faces like the pages of a mystic volume. Walter Ludlow's portrait attracted their earliest notice. In the absence of himself and his bride, they sometimes disputed as to the expression which the painter had intended to throw upon the features; all agreeing that there was a look of earnest import, though no two explained it alike.

There was less diversity of opinion in regard to Elinor's picture. They differed, indeed, in their attempts to estimate the nature and depth of the gloom that dwelt upon her face, but agreed that it was gloom, and alien from the natural temperament of their youthful friend. A certain fanciful person announced, as the result of much scrutiny, that both these pictures were parts of one design, and that the melancholy strength of feeling, in Elinor's countenance, bore reference to the more vivid emotion, or, as he termed it, the wild passion, in that of Walter. Though unskilled in the art, he even began a sketch, in which the action of the two figures was to correspond with their mutual expression.

It was whispered among friends, that, day by day, Elinor's face was assuming a deeper shade of pensiveness, which threatened soon to render her too true a counterpart of her melancholy picture. Walter, on the other hand, instead of acquiring the vivid look which the painter had given him on the canvas, became reserved and downcast, with no outward flashes of emotion, however it might be smoldering within. In course of time, Elinor hung a gorgeous curtain of purple silk, wrought with flowers, and fringed with heavy golden tassels, before the pictures, under pretense that the dust would tarnish their hues, or the light dim them. It was enough. Her visitors felt, that the massive folds of the silk must never be withdrawn, nor the portraits mentioned in her presence.

Time wore on; and the painter came again. He had been far enough to the north to see the silver cascade of the Crystal Hills, and to look over the vast round of cloud and forest, from the summit of New England's loftiest mountain. But he did not profane that scene by the mockery of his art. He had also lain in a canoe on the bosom of Lake George, making his soul the mirror of its loveliness and grandeur, till not a picture in the Vatican was more vivid than his recollection. He had gone with the Indian hunters to Niagara, and there, again, had flung his hopeless pencil down the precipice, feeling that he could as soon paint the roar, as aught else that goes to make up the wondrous cataract. In truth, it was seldom his impulse to copy natural scenery, except as a frame-work for the delineations of the human form and face, instinct with thought, passion, or suffering. With store of such, his adventurous ramble had enriched him; the stern dignity of Indian chiefs; the dusky loveliness of Indian girls; the domestic life of wigwams; the stealthy march; the battle beneath gloomy pine-trees; the frontier fortress with its garrison; the anomaly of the old French partisan, bred in courts, but grown gray in shaggy deserts; such were the scenes and portraits that he had sketched. The glow of perilous moments; flashes of wild feeling; struggles of fierce power—love, hate, grief, frenzy—in a word, all the worn-out heart of the old earth, had been revealed to him under a new form. His portfolio was filled with graphic illustrations of the volume of his memory, which genius would transmute into its own substance, and imbue with immortality. He felt that the deep wisdom in his art, which he had sought so far, was found.

But, amid stern or lovely nature, in the perils of the forest, or its overwhelming peacefulness, still there had been two phantoms, the companions of his way. Like all other men around whom an engrossing purpose wreathes itself, he was insulated from the mass of human kind. He had no aim—no pleasure—no sympathies—but what were ultimately connected with his art. Though gentle in manner, and upright in intent and action, he did not possess kindly feelings; his heart was cold; no living creature could be brought near enough to keep him warm. For these two beings, however, he had felt, in its greatest intensity, the sort of interest which always allied him to the subjects of his pencil. He had pried into their souls with his keenest insight, and pictured the result upon their features, with his utmost skill, so as barely to fail short of that standard which no genius ever reached, his own severe conception. He had caught from the duskiness of the future—at least, so he fancied—a fearful secret, and had obscurely revealed it on the portraits. So much of himself—of his imagination and all other powers—had been lavished on the study of Walter and Elinor, that he almost regarded them as creations of his own, like the thousands with which he had peopled the realms of Picture. Therefore did they flit through the twilight of the woods, hover on the mist of waterfalls, look forth from the mirror of the lake, nor melt away in the noontide sun. They haunted his pictorial fancy, not as mockeries of life, nor pale goblins of the dead, but in the guise of portraits, each with the unalterable expression which his magic had evoked from the caverns of the soul. He could not recross the Atlantic, till he had again beheld the originals of those airy pictures.

"Oh, glorious Art!" thus mused the enthusiastic painter, as he trod the street. "Thou art the image of the Creator's own. The innumerable forms, that wander in nothingness, start into being at thy beck. The dead live again. Thou recallest them to their old scenes, and givest their gray shadows the lustre of a better life, at once earthly and immortal. Thou snatchest back the fleeting moments of History. With thee, there is no Past; for, at thy touch, all that is great becomes for ever present; and illustrious men live through long ages, in the visible performance of the very deeds, which made them what they are. Oh, potent Art! as thou bringest the faintly revealed Past to stand in that narrow strip of sunlight, which we call Now, canst thou summon the shrouded Future to meet her there? Have I not achieved it! Am I not thy Prophet?"

Thus, with a proud, yet melancholy fervor, did he almost cry aloud, as he passed through the toilsome street, among people that knew not of his reveries, nor could understand nor care for them. It is not good for man to cherish a solitary ambition. Unless there be those around him, by whose example he may regulate himself, his thoughts, desires, and hopes will become extravagant, and he the semblance, perhaps the reality, of a madman. Reading other bosoms, with an acuteness almost preternatural, the painter failed to see the disorder of his own.

"And this should be the house," said he, looking up and down the front, before he knocked. "Heaven help my brains! That picture! Methinks it will never vanish. Whether I look at the windows or the door, there it is framed within them, painted strongly, and glowing in the richest tints—the faces of the portraits—the figures and action of the sketch!"

He knocked.

"The Portraits! Are they within?" inquired he, of the domestic; then recollecting himself—"your master and mistress! Are they at home?"

"They are, sir," said the servant, adding, as he noticed that picturesque aspect of which the painter could never divest himself,—"and the Portraits too!"

The guest was admitted into a parlor, communicating by a central door, with an interior room of the same size. As the first apartment was empty, he passed to the entrance of the second, within which, his eyes were greeted by those living personages, as well as their pictured representatives, who had long been the objects of so singular an interest. He involuntarily paused on the threshold.

They had not perceived his approach. Walter and Elinor were standing before the portraits, whence the former had just flung back the rich and voluminous folds of the silken curtain, holding its golden tassel with one hand, while the other grasped that of his bride. The pictures, concealed for months, gleamed forth again in undiminished splendor, appearing to throw a sombre light across the room, rather than to be disclosed by a borrowed radiance. That of Elinor had been almost prophetic. A pensiveness, and next a gentle sorrow, had successively dwelt upon her countenance, deepening, with the lapse of time, into a quiet anguish. A mixture of affright would now have made it the very expression of the portrait. Walter's face was moody and dull, or animated only by fitful flashes, which left a heavier darkness for their momentary illumination. He looked from Elinor to her portrait, and thence to his own, in the contemplation of which he finally stood absorbed.

The painter seemed to hear the step of Destiny approaching behind him, on its progress towards its victims. A strange thought darted into his mind. Was not his own the form in which that Destiny had embodied itself, and he a chief agent of the coming evil which he had foreshadowed?

Still, Walter remained silent before the picture, communing with it, as with his own heart, and abandoning himself to the spell of evil influence, that the painter had cast upon the features. Gradually his eyes kindled; while as Elinor watched the increasing wildness of his face, her own assumed a look of terror; and when at last, he turned upon her, the resemblance of both to their portraits was complete.

"Our fate is upon us!" howled Walter. "Die!"

Drawing a knife, he sustained her, as she was sinking to the ground, and aimed it at her bosom. In the action, and in the look and attitude of each, the painter beheld the figures of his sketch. The picture, with all its tremendous coloring, was finished.

"Hold, madman!" cried he sternly.

He had advanced from the door, and interposed himself between the wretched beings, with the same sense of power to regulate their destiny, as to alter a scene upon the canvas. He stood like a magician, controlling the phantoms which he had evoked.

"What!" muttered Walter Ludlow, as he relapsed from fierce excitement into sullen gloom. "Does Fate impede its own decree?"

"Wretched lady!" said the painter. "Did I not warn you?"

"You did," replied Elinor calmly, as her terror gave place to the quiet grief which it had disturbed. "But—I loved him!"

Is there not a deep moral in the tale? Could the result of one, or all our deeds, be shadowed forth and set before us—some would call it Fate, and hurry onward—others be swept along by their passionate desires—and none be turned aside by the Prophetic Pictures.

# Schalken the Painter

JOSEPH SHERIDAN LE FANU

1839

*"For he is not a man as I am that we should come together; neither is there any that might lay his hand upon us both. Let him, therefore, take his rod away from me, and let not his fear terrify me."*

There exists, at this moment, in good preservation a remarkable work of Schalken's. The curious management of its lights constitutes, as usual in his pieces, the chief apparent merit of the picture. I say *apparent,* for in its subject, and not in its handling, however exquisite, consists its real value. The picture represents the interior of what might be a chamber in some antique religious building; and its foreground is occupied by a female figure, in a species of white robe, part of which is arranged so as to form a veil. The dress, however, is not that of any religious order. In her hand the figure bears a lamp, by which alone her figure and face are illuminated; and her features wear such an arch smile, as well becomes a pretty woman when practicing some prankish roguery; in the background, and, excepting where the dim red light of an expiring fire serves to define the form, in total shadow, stands the figure of a man dressed in the old Flemish fashion, in an attitude of alarm, his hand being placed upon the hilt of his sword, which he appears to be in the act of drawing.

There are some pictures, which impress one, I know not how, with a conviction that they represent not the mere ideal shapes and combinations which have floated through the imagination of the artist, but scenes, faces, and situations which have actually existed. There is in that strange picture, something that stamps it as the representation of a reality.

And such in truth it is, for it faithfully records a remarkable and mysterious occurrence, and perpetuates, in the face of the female figure, which occupies the most prominent place in the design, an accurate portrait of Rose Velderkaust, the niece of Gerard Douw, the first, and, I believe, the only love of Godfrey Schalken. My great grandfather knew the painter well; and from Schalken himself he learned the fearful story of the painting, and from him too he ultimately received the picture itself as a bequest. The story and the picture have become heir-looms in my family, and having described the latter, I shall, if you please, attempt to relate the tradition which has descended with the canvas.

There are few forms on which the mantle of romance hangs more ungracefully than upon that of the uncouth Schalken—the boorish but most cunning worker in oils, whose pieces delight the critics of our day almost as much as his manners disgusted the refined of his own; and yet this man, so rude, so dogged, so slovenly, in the midst of his celebrity, had in his obscure, but happier days, played the hero in a wild romance of mystery and passion.

When Schalken studied under the immortal Gerard Douw, he was a very young man; and in spite of his phlegmatic temperament, he at once fell over head and ears in love with the beautiful niece of his wealthy master. Rose Velderkaust was still younger than he, having not yet attained her seventeenth year, and, if tradition speaks truth, possessed all the soft and dimpling charms of the fair, light-haired Flemish maidens. The young painter loved honestly and fervently. His frank adoration was rewarded. He declared his love, and extracted a faltering confession in return. He was the happiest and proudest painter in all Christendom. But there was somewhat to dash his elation; he was poor and undistinguished. He dared not ask old Gerard for the hand of his sweet ward. He must first win a reputation and a competence.

There were, therefore, many dread uncertainties and cold days before him; he had to fight his way against sore odds. But he had won the heart of dear Rose Velderkaust, and that was half the battle. It is needless to say his exertions were redoubled, and his lasting celebrity proves that his industry was not unrewarded by success.

These ardent labours, and worse still, the hopes that elevated and beguiled them, were however, destined to experience a sudden interruption—of a character so strange and mysterious as to baffle all inquiry and to throw over the events themselves a shadow of preternatural horror.

Schalken had one evening outstayed all his fellow-pupils, and still pursued his work in the deserted room. As the daylight was fast falling, he laid aside his colours, and applied himself to the completion of a sketch on which he had expressed extraordinary pains. It was a religious composition, and represented the temptations of a pot-bellied Saint Anthony. The young artist, however destitute of elevation, had, nevertheless, discernment enough to be dissatisfied with his own work, and many were the patient erasures and improvements which saint and devil underwent, yet all in vain. The large, old-fashioned room was silent, and, with the exception of himself, quite emptied of its usual inmates. An hour had thus passed away, nearly two, without any improved result. Daylight had already

declined, and twilight was deepening into the darkness of
night. The patience of the young painter was exhausted,
and he stood before his unfinished production, angry and
mortified, one hand buried in the folds of his long hair,
and the other holding the piece of charcoal which had so
ill-performed its office, and which he now rubbed, without much regard to the sable streaks it produced, with
irritable pressure upon his ample Flemish inexpressibles.

"Curse the subject!" said the young man aloud; "curse
the picture, the devils, the saint—"

At this moment a short, sudden sniff uttered close beside him made the artist turn sharply round, and he now,
for the first time, became aware that his labours had been
overlooked by a stranger. Within about a yard and half,
and rather behind him, there stood the figure of an elderly
man in a cloak and broad-brimmed, conical hat; in his
hand, which was protected with a heavy gauntlet-shaped
glove, he carried a long ebony walking-stick, surmounted
with what appeared, as it glittered dimly in the twilight,
to be a massive head of gold, and upon his breast, through
the folds of the cloak, there shone the links of a rich chain
of the same metal. The room was so obscure that nothing
further of the appearance of the figure could be ascertained, and his hat threw his features into profound shadow. It would not have been easy to conjecture the age of
the intruder; but a quantity of dark hair escaping from
beneath this sombre hat, as well as his firm and upright
carriage served to indicate that his years could not yet
exceed threescore, or thereabouts. There was an air of
gravity and importance about the garb of the person, and
something indescribably odd, I might say awful, in the
perfect, stone-like stillness of the figure, that effectually
checked the testy comment which had at once risen to the
lips of the irritated artist. He, therefore, as soon as he
had sufficiently recovered his surprise, asked the stranger,

civilly, to be seated, and desired to know if he had any
message to leave for his master.

"Tell Gerard Douw," said the unknown, without alter-
ing his attitude in the smallest degree, "that Minheer Vanderhausen, of Rotterdam, desires to speak with him on
tomorrow evening at this hour, and if he please, in this
room, upon matters of weight; that is all."

The stranger, having finished this message, turned
abruptly, and, with a quick, but silent step quitted the
room, before Schalken had time to say a word in reply.
The young man felt a curiosity to see in what direction
the burgher of Rotterdam would turn, on quitting the studio, and for that purpose he went directly to the window
which commanded the door. A lobby of considerable extent intervened between the inner door of the painter's
room and the street entrance, so that Schalken occupied
the post of observation before the old man could possibly have reached the street. He watched in vain, however.
There was no other mode of exit. Had the queer old man
vanished, or was he lurking about the recesses of the lobby
for some sinister purpose? This last suggestion filled the
mind of Schalken with a vague uneasiness, which was so
unaccountably intense as to make him alike afraid to remain in the room alone, and reluctant to pass through the
lobby. However, with an effort which appeared very dis-
proportioned to the occasion, he summoned resolution to
leave the room, and, having locked the door and thrust the
key in his pocket, without looking to the right or left, he
traversed the passage which had so recently, perhaps still,
contained the person of his mysterious visitant, scarcely
venturing to breathe till he had arrived in the open street.

"Minheer Vanderhausen!" said Gerard Douw within himself, as the appointed hour approached, "Minheer
Vanderhausen, of Rotterdam! I never heard of the man till
yesterday. What can he want of me? A portrait, perhaps,

to be painted; or a poor relation to be apprenticed; or a collection to be valued; or—pshaw! there's no one in Rotterdam to leave me a legacy. Well, whatever the business may be, we shall soon know it all."

It was now the close of day, and again every easel, except that of Schalken, was deserted. Gerard Douw was pacing the apartment with the restless step of impatient expectation, sometimes pausing to glance over the work of one of his absent pupils, but more frequently placing himself at the window, from whence he might observe the passengers who threaded the obscure by-street in which his studio was placed.

"Said you not, Godfrey," exclaimed Douw, after a long and fruitful gaze from his post of observation, and turning to Schalken, "that the hour he appointed was about seven by the clock of the Stadhouse?"

"It had just told seven when I first saw him, sir," answered the student.

"The hour is close at hand, then," said the master, consulting a horologe as large and as round as an orange. "Minheer Vanderhausen from Rotterdam—is it not so?"

"Such was the name."

"And an elderly man, richly clad?" pursued Douw, musingly.

"As well as I might see," replied his pupil; "he could not be young, nor yet very old, neither; and his dress was rich and grave, as might become a citizen of wealth and consideration."

At this moment the sonorous boom of the Stadhouse clock told, stroke after stroke, the hour of seven; the eyes of both master and student were directed to the door; and it was not until the last peal of the bell had ceased to vibrate, that Douw exclaimed—

"So, so; we shall have his worship presently, that is, if he means to keep his hour; if not, you may wait for him,

Godfrey, if you court his acquaintance. But what, after all, if it should prove but a mummery got up by Vankarp, or some such wag? I wish you had run all risks, and cudgeled the old burgomaster soundly. I'd wager a dozen of Rhenish, his worship would have unmasked, and pleaded old acquaintance in a trice."

"Here he comes, sir," said Schalken, in a low monitory tone; and instantly, upon turning towards the door, Gerard Douw observed the same figure which had, on the day before, so unexpectedly greeted his pupil Schalken.

There was something in the air of the figure which at once satisfied the painter that there was no masquerading in the case, and that he really stood in the presence of a man of worship; and so, without hesitation, he doffed his cap, and courteously saluting the stranger, requested him to be seated. The visitor waved his hand slightly, as if in acknowledgment of the courtesy, but remained standing.

"I have the honour to see Minheer Vanderhausen of Rotterdam?" said Gerard Douw.

"The same," was the laconic reply of his visitor.

"I understand your worship desires to speak with me," continued Douw, "and I am here by appointment to wait your commands."

"Is that a man of trust?" said Vanderhausen, turning towards Schalken, who stood at a little distance behind his master.

"Certainly," replied Gerard.

"Then let him take this box, and get the nearest jeweler or goldsmith to value its contents, and let him return hither with a certificate of the valuation."

At the same time, he placed a small case about nine inches square in the hands of Gerard Douw, who was as much amazed at its weight as at the strange abruptness with which it was handed to him. In accordance with the wishes of the stranger, he delivered it into the hands of

Schalken, and repeating his direction, despatched him upon the mission.

Schalken disposed his precious charge securely beneath the folds of his cloak, and rapidly traversing two or three narrow streets, he stopped at a corner house, the lower part of which was then occupied by the shop of a Jewish goldsmith. He entered the shop, and calling the little Hebrew into the obscurity of its back recesses, he proceeded to lay before him Vanderhausen's casket. On being examined by the light of a lamp, it appeared entirely cased with lead, the outer surface of which was much scraped and soiled, and nearly white with age. This having been partially removed, there appeared beneath a box of some hard wood; which also they forced open and after the removal of two or three folds of linen, they discovered its contents to be a mass of golden ingots, closely packed, and, as the Jew declared, of the most perfect quality. Every ingot underwent the scrutiny of the little Jew, who seemed to feel an epicurean delight in touching and testing these morsels of the glorious metal; and each one of them was replaced in its berth with the exclamation: *"Mein Gott,* how very perfect! not one grain of alloy—beautiful, beautiful!" The task was at length finished, and the Jew certified under his hand the value of the ingots submitted to his examination, to amount to many thousand rix-dollars. With the desired document in his pocket, and the rich box of gold carefully pressed under his arm, and concealed by his cloak, he retraced his way, and entering the studio, found his master and the stranger in close conference. Schalken had no sooner left the room, in order to execute the commission he had taken in charge, than Vanderhausen addressed Gerard Douw in the following terms:—

"I cannot tarry with you to-night more than a few minutes, and so I shall shortly tell you the matter upon which I come. You visited the town of Rotterdam some

four months ago, and then I saw in the church of St. Law-
rence your niece, Rose Velderkaust. I desire to marry her;
and if I satisfy you that I am wealthier than any husband
you can dream of for her, I expect that you will forward
my suit with your authority. If you approve my proposal,
you must close with it here and now, for I cannot wait for
calculations and delays."

Gerard Douw was hugely astonished by the nature of
Minheer Vanderhausen's communication, but he did not
venture to express surprise; for besides the motives supplied by prudence and politeness, the painter experienced
a kind of chill and oppression like that which is said to
intervene when one is placed in unconscious proximity
with the object of a natural antipathy—an undefined but
overpowering sensation, while standing in the presence of
the eccentric stranger, which made him very unwilling to
say anything which might reasonably offend him.

"I have no doubt," said Gerard, after two or three pref-
atory hems, "that the alliance which you propose would
prove alike advantageous and honourable to my niece; but
you must be aware that she has a will of her own, and may
not acquiesce in what *we* may design for her advantage."

"Do not seek to deceive me, sir painter," said Vanderhausen; "you are her guardian—she is your ward—she is
mine if *you* like to make her so."

The man of Rotterdam moved forward a little as he
spoke, and Gerard Douw, he scarce knew why, inwardly
prayed for the speedy return of Schalken.

"I desire," said the mysterious gentleman, "to place in
your hands at once an evidence of my wealth, and a security for my liberal dealing with your niece. The lad will
return in a minute or two with a sum in value five times
the fortune which she has a right to expect from her husband. This shall lie in your hands, together with her dowry,
and you may apply the united sum as suits her interest

best; it shall be all exclusively hers while she lives: is that liberal?"

Douw assented, and inwardly acknowledged that fortune had been extraordinarily kind to his niece; the stranger, he thought, must be both wealthy and generous, and such an offer was not to be despised, though made by a humourist, and one of no very prepossessing presence. Rose had no very high pretensions for she had but a modest dowry, which she owed entirely to the generosity of her uncle; neither had she any right to raise exceptions on the score of birth, for her own origin was far from splendid, and as the other objections, Gerald resolved, and indeed, by the usages of the time, was warranted in resolving, not to listen to them for a moment.

"Sir," said he, addressing the stranger, "your offer is liberal, and whatever hesitation I may feel in closing with it immediately, arises solely from my not having the honour of knowing anything of your family or station. Upon these points you can, of course, satisfy me without difficulty?'

"As to my respectability," said the stranger, drily, "you must take that for granted at present; pester me with no inquiries; you can discover nothing more about me than I choose to make known. You shall have sufficient security for my respectability—my word, if you are honourable: if you are sordid, my gold."

"A testy old gentleman," thought Douw, "he must have his own way; but, all things considered, I am not justified to declining his offer. I will not pledge myself unnecessarily, however."

"You will not pledge yourself unnecessarily," said Vanderhausen, strangely uttering the very words which had just floated through the mind of his companion; "but you will do so if it is necessary, I presume; and I will show you that I consider it indispensable. If the gold I mean to leave in your hands satisfy you, and if you don't wish my proposal to be at once withdrawn, you must, before I leave this room, write your name to this engagement."

Having thus spoken, he placed a paper in the hands of the master, the contents of which expressed an engagement entered into by Gerard Douw, to give to Wilken Vanderhausen of Rotterdam, in marriage, Rose Velderkaust, and so forth, within one week of the date thereof. While the painter was employed in reading this covenant, by the light of a twinkling oil lamp in the far wall of the room, Schalken, as we have stated, entered the studio, and having delivered the box and the valuation of the Jew, into the hands of the stranger, he was about to retire, when Vanderhausen called to him to wait; and, presenting the case and the certificate to Gerard Douw, he paused in silence until he had satisfied himself, by an inspection of both, respecting the value of the pledge left in his hands. At length he said—

"Are you content?"

The painter said he would fain have another day to consider.

"Not an hour," said the suitor, apathetically.

"Well then," said Douw, with a sore effort, "I am content, it is a bargain."

"Then sign at once," said Vanderhausen, "for I am weary."

At the same time he produced a small case of writing materials, and Gerard signed the important document.

"Let this youth witness the covenant," said the old man; and Godfrey Schalken unconsciously attested the instrument which for ever bereft him of his dear Rose Velderkaust.

The compact being thus completed, the strange visitor folded up the paper, and stowed it safely in an inner pocket.

"I will visit you to-morrow night at nine o'clock, at your own house, Gerard Douw, and will see the object of

our contract;" and so saying Wilken Vanderhausen moved
stiffly, but rapidly, out of the room.

Schalken, eager to resolve his doubts, had placed himself by the window, in order to watch the street entrance;
but the experiment served only to support his suspicions, for the old man did not issue from the door. This
was *very* strange—odd, nay fearful. He and his master returned together, and talked but little on the way, for each
had his own subjects of reflection, of anxiety, and of hope.
Schalken, however, did not know the ruin which menaced
his dearest projects.

Gerard Douw knew nothing of the attachment which
had sprung up between his pupil and his niece; and even
if he had, it is doubtful whether he would have regarded
its existence as any serious obstruction to the wishes of
Minheer Vanderhausen. Marriages were then and there
matters of traffic and calculation; and it would have
appeared as absurd in the eyes of the guardian to make a
mutual attachment an essential element in a contract of
the sort, as it would have been to draw up his bonds and
receipts in the language of romance.

The painter, however, did not communicate to his niece
the important step which he had taken in her behalf, a for-
bearance caused not by any anticipated opposition on her
part, but solely by a ludicrous consciousness that if she
were to ask him for a description of her destined bridegroom, he would be forced to confess that he had not once
seen his face, and if called upon, would find it absolutely
impossible to identify him. Upon the next day, Gerard
Douw, after dinner, called his niece to him and having
scanned her person with an air of satisfaction, he took her
hand, and looking upon her pretty innocent face with a
smile of kindness, he said:—

"Rose, my girl, that face of yours will make your
fortune." Rose blushed and smiled. "Such faces and such

tempers seldom go together, and when they do, the com-
pound is a love charm, few heads or hearts can resist; trust
me, you will soon be a bride, girl. But this is trifling, and
I am pressed for time, so make ready the large room by
eight o'clock to-night, and give directions for supper at
nine. I expect a friend; and observe me, child, do you trick
yourself out handsomely. I will not have him think us poor
or sluttish."

With these words he left her, and took his way to the
room in which his pupils worked.

When the evening closed in, Gerard called Schalken,
who was about to take his departure to his own obscure
and comfortless lodgings, and asked him to come home
and sup with Rose and Vanderhausen. The invitation was,
of course, accepted and Gerard Douw and his pupil soon
found themselves in the handsome and, even then, antique
chamber, which had been prepared for the reception of the
stranger. A cheerful wood fire blazed in the hearth, a little
at one side of which an old-fashioned table, which shone
in the fire-light like burnished gold, was awaiting the
supper, for which preparations were going forward; and
ranged with exact regularity, stood the tall-backed chairs,
whose ungracefulness was more than compensated by their
comfort. The little party, consisting of Rose, her uncle,
and the artist, awaited the arrival of the expected visitor
with considerable impatience. Nine o'clock at length came,
and with it a summons at the street door, which being
speedily answered, was followed by a slow and emphatic
tread upon the staircase; the steps moved heavily across
the lobby, the door of the room in which the party we have
described were assembled slowly opened, and there entered
a figure which startled, almost appalled, the phlegmatic
Dutchmen, and nearly made Rose scream with terror. It
was the form, and arrayed in the garb of Minheer Vanderhausen; the air, the gait, the height were the same, but the

features had never been seen by any of the party before. The stranger stopped at the door of the room, and displayed his form and face completely. He wore a dark-coloured cloth cloak, which was short and full, not falling quite to his knees; his legs were cased in dark purple silk stockings, and his shoes were adorned with roses of the same colour. The opening of the cloak in front showed the under-suit to consist of some very dark, perhaps sable material, and his hands were enclosed in a pair of heavy leather gloves, which ran up considerably above the wrist, in the manner of a gauntlet. In one hand he carried his walking-stick and his hat, which he had removed, and the other hung heavily by his side. A quantity of grizzled hair descended in long tresses from his head, and rested upon the plaits of a stiff ruff, which effectually concealed his neck. So far all was well; but the face!—all the flesh of the face was coloured with the bluish leaden hue, which is sometimes produced by metallic medicines, administered in excessive quantities; the eyes showed an undue proportion of muddy white, and had a certain indefinable character of insanity; the hue of the lips bearing the usual relation to that of the face, was, consequently, nearly black; and the entire character of the face was sensual, malignant, and even satanic. It was remarkable that the worshipful stranger suffered as little as possible of his flesh to appear, and that during his visit he did not once remove his gloves. Having stood for some moments at the door, Gerard Douw at length found breath and collectedness to bid him welcome, and with a mute inclination of the head, the stranger stepped forward into the room. There was something indescribably odd, even horrible, about all his motions, something undefinable, that was unnatural, unhuman; it was as if the limbs were guided and directed by a spirit unused to the management of bodily machinery. The stranger spoke hardly at all during his visit, which did not exceed half an hour;

and the host himself could scarcely muster courage enough to utter the few necessary salutations and courtesies; and, indeed, such was the nervous terror which the presence of Vanderhausen inspired, that very little would have made all his entertainers fly in downright panic from the room. They had not so far lost all self-possession, however, as to fail to observe two strange peculiarities of their visitor. During his stay his eyelids did not once close, or, indeed, move in the slightest degree; and farther, there was a deathlike stillness in his whole person, owing to the absence of the heaving motion of the chest, caused by the process of respiration. These two peculiarities, though when told they may appear trifling, produced a very striking and unpleasant effect when seen and observed. Vanderhausen at length relieved the painter of Leyden of his inauspicious presence; and with no trifling sense of relief the little party heard the street door close after him.

"Dear uncle," said Rose, "what a frightful man! I would not see him again for the wealth of the States."

"Tush, foolish girl," said Douw, whose sensations were anything but comfortable. "A man may be as ugly as the devil, and yet, if his heart and actions are good, he is worth all the pretty-faced perfumed puppies that walk the Mall. Rose, my girl, it is very true he has not thy pretty face, but I know him to be wealthy and liberal; and were he ten times more ugly, these two virtues would be enough to counter balance all his deformity, and if not sufficient actually to alter the shape and hue of his features, at least enough to prevent one thinking them so much amiss."

"Do you know, uncle," said Rose, "when I saw him standing at the door, I could not get it out of my head that I saw the old painted wooden figure that used to frighten me so much in the Church of St. Laurence at Rotterdam."

Gerard laughed, though he could not help inwardly acknowledging the justness of the comparison. He was resolved, however, as far as he could, to check his niece's disposition to dilate upon the ugliness of her intended bridegroom, although he was not a little pleased, as well as puzzled, to observe that she appeared totally exempt from that mysterious dread of the stranger which, he could not disguise it from himself, considerably affected him, as also his pupil Godfrey Schalken.

Early on the next day there arrived, from various quarters of the town, rich presents of silks, velvets, jewelry, and so forth, for Rose; and also a packet directed to Gerard Douw, which on being opened, was found to contain a contract of marriage, formally drawn up, between Wilken Vanderhausen of the Boom-quay, in Rotterdam, and Rose Velderkaust of Leyden, niece to Gerard Douw, master in the art of painting, also of the same city; and containing engagements on the part of Vanderhausen to make settlements upon his bride, far more splendid than he had before led her guardian to believe likely, and which were to be secured to her use in the most unexceptionable manner possible—the money being placed in the hand of Gerard Douw himself.

I have no sentimental scenes to describe, no cruelty of guardians, no magnanimity of wards, no agonies, or transport of lovers. The record I have to make is one of sordidness, levity, and heartlessness. In less than a week after the first interview which we have just described, the contract of marriage was fulfilled, and Schalken saw the prize which he would have risked existence to secure, carried off in solemn pomp by his repulsive rival. For two or three days he absented himself from the school; he then returned and worked, if with less cheerfulness, with far more dogged resolution than before; the stimulus of love had given place to that of ambition. Months passed away, and, contrary to his expectation, and, indeed, to the direct promise of the parties, Gerard Douw heard nothing of his niece or her worshipful spouse. The interest of the money, which was to have been demanded in quarterly sums, lay unclaimed in his hands.

He began to grow extremely uneasy. Minheer Vanderhausen's direction in Rotterdam he was fully possessed of; after some irresolution he finally determined to journey thither—a trifling undertaking, and easily accomplished—and thus to satisfy himself of the safety and comfort of his ward, for whom he entertained an honest and strong affection. His search was in vain, however; no one in Rotterdam had ever heard of Minheer Vanderhausen. Gerard Douw left not a house in the Boom-quay untried, but all in vain. No one could give him any information whatever touching the object of his inquiry, and he was obliged to return to Leyden nothing wiser and far more anxious, than when he had left it.

On his arrival he hastened to the establishment from which Vanderhausen had hired the lumbering, though, considering the times, most luxurious vehicle, which the bridal party had employed to convey them to Rotterdam. From the driver of this machine he learned, that having proceeded by slow stages, they had late in the evening approached Rotterdam; but that before they entered the city, and while yet nearly a mile from it, a small party of men, soberly clad, and after the old fashion, with peaked beards and moustaches, standing in the centre of the road, obstructed the further progress of the carriage. The driver reined in his horses, much fearing, from the obscurity of the hour, and the loneliness, of the road, that some mischief was intended. His fears were, however, somewhat allayed by his observing that these strange men carried a large litter, of an antique shape, and which they immediately set down upon the pavement, whereupon the bridegroom, having opened the coach-door from within, descended, and having assisted his bride to do likewise,

led her, weeping bitterly, and wringing her hands, to the
litter, which they both entered. It was then raised by the
men who surrounded it, and speedily carried towards the
city, and before it had proceeded very far, the darkness
concealed it from the view of the Dutch coachman. In
the inside of the vehicle he found a purse, whose contents
more than thrice paid the hire of the carriage and man. He
saw and could tell nothing more of Minheer Vanderhausen
and his beautiful lady.

This mystery was a source of profound anxiety and even
grief to Gerard Douw. There was evidently fraud in the
dealing of Vanderhausen with him, though for what purpose committed he could not imagine. He greatly doubted
how far it was possible for a man possessing such a countenance to be anything but a villain, and every day that
passed without his hearing from or of his niece, instead of
inducing him to forget his fears, on the contrary tended
more and more to aggravate them. The loss of her cheerful
society tended also to depress his spirits; and in order to
dispel the gloom, which often crept upon his mind after
his daily occupations were over, he was wont frequently
to ask Schalken to accompany him home, and share his
otherwise solitary supper.

One evening, the painter and his pupil were sitting
by the fire, having accomplished a comfortable meal, and
had yielded to the silent and delicious melancholy of
digestion, when their ruminations were disturbed by a loud
sound at the street door, as if occasioned by some person
rushing and scrambling vehemently against it. A domestic
had run without delay to ascertain the cause of the dis-
turbance, and they heard him twice or thrice interrogate
the applicant for admission, but without eliciting any
other answer but a sustained reiteration of the sounds.
They heard him then open the hall-door, and immediately

there followed a light and rapid tread on the staircase.
Schalken advanced towards the door. It opened before he
reached it, and Rose rushed into the room. She looked
wild, fierce and haggard with terror and exhaustion, but
her dress surprised them as much as even her unexpected
appearance. It consisted of a kind of white woolen wrap-
per, made close about the neck, and descending to the
very ground. It was much deranged and travel-soiled. The
poor creature had hardly entered the chamber when she
fell senseless on the floor. With some difficulty they succeeded in reviving her, and on recovering her senses, she
instantly exclaimed, in a tone of terror rather than mere
impatience:—

"Wine! wine! quickly, or I'm lost!"

Astonished and almost scared at the strange agitation
in which the call was made, they at once administered
to her wishes, and she drank some wine with a haste and
eagerness which surprised them. She had hardly swallowed
it, when she exclaimed, with the same urgency:

"Food, for God's sake, food, at once, or I perish."

A considerable fragment of a roast joint was upon the
table, and Schalken immediately began to cut some, but
he was anticipated, for no sooner did she see it than she
caught it, a more than mortal image of famine, and with
her hands, and even with her teeth, she tore off the flesh,
and swallowed it. When the paroxysm of hunger had been
a little appeased, she appeared on a sudden overcome with
shame, or it may have been that other more agitating
thoughts overpowered and scared her, for she began to
weep bitterly and to wring her hands.

"Oh, send for a minister of God," said she; "I am not
safe till he comes; send for him speedily."

Gerard Douw despatched a messenger instantly, and
prevailed on his niece to allow him to surrender his bed

chamber to her use. He also persuaded her to retire to it at once to rest; her consent was extorted upon the condition that they would not leave her for a moment.

"Oh that the holy man were here," she said; "he can deliver me: the dead and the living can never be one: God has forbidden it."

With these mysterious words she surrendered herself to their guidance, and they proceeded to the chamber which Gerard Douw had assigned to her use.

"Do not, do not leave me for a moment," said she; "I am lost for ever if you do."

Gerard Douw's chamber was approached through a spacious apartment, which they were now about to enter. He and Schalken each carried a candle, so that a sufficiency of light was cast upon all surrounding objects. They were now entering the large chamber, which as I have said, communicated with Douw's apartment, when Rose suddenly stopped, and, in a whisper which thrilled them both with horror, she said—

"Oh, God! he is here! he is here! See, see! there he goes!"

She pointed towards the door of the inner room, and Schalken thought he saw a shadowy and ill-defined form gliding into that apartment. He drew his sword, and, raising the candle so as to throw its light with increased distinctness upon the objects in the room, he entered the chamber into which the shadow had glided. No figure was there—nothing but the furniture which belonged to the room, and yet he could not be deceived as to the fact that something had moved before them into the chamber. A sickening dread came upon him, and the cold perspiration broke out in heavy drops upon his forehead; nor was he more composed, when he heard the increased urgency and agony of entreaty, with which Rose implored them not to leave her for a moment.

"I saw him," said she; "he's here. I cannot be deceived; I know him; he's by me; he is with me; he's in the room. Then, for God's sake, as you would save me, do not stir from beside me."

They at length prevailed upon her to lie down upon the bed, where she continued to urge them to stay by her. She frequently uttered incoherent sentences, repeating, again and again, "the dead and the living cannot be one: God has forbidden it." And then again, "Rest to the wakeful—sleep to the sleep-walkers." These and such mysterious and broken sentences, she continued to utter until the clergyman arrived. Gerard Douw began to fear, naturally enough, that terror or ill-treatment, had unsettled the poor girl's intellect, and he half suspected, by the suddenness of her appearance, the unseasonableness of the hour, and above all, from the wildness and terror of her manner, that she had made her escape from some place of confinement for lunatics, and was in imminent fear of pursuit. He resolved to summon medical advice as soon as the mind of his niece had been in some measure set at rest by the offices of the clergyman whose attendance she had so earnestly desired; and until this object had been attained, he did not venture to put any questions to her, which might possibly, by reviving painful or horrible recollections, increase her agitation. The clergyman soon arrived—a man of ascetic countenance and venerable age—one whom Gerard Douw respected very much, forasmuch as he was a veteran polemic, though one perhaps more dreaded as a combatant than beloved as a Christian—of pure morality, subtle brain, and frozen heart. He entered the chamber which communicated with that in which Rose reclined and immediately on his arrival, she requested him to pray for her, as for one who lay in the hands of Satan, and who could hope for deliverance only from heaven.

That you may distinctly understand all the circumstances of the event which I am going to describe, it is
necessary to state the relative position of the parties who
were engaged in it. The old clergyman and Schalken were
in the anteroom of which I have already spoken; Rose lay
in the inner chamber, the door of which was open; and by
the side of the bed, at her urgent desire, stood her guardian; a candle burned in the bedchamber, and three were
lighted in the outer apartment. The old man now cleared
his voice as if about to commence, but before he had time
to begin, a sudden gust of air blew out the candle which
served to illuminate the room in which the poor girl lay,
and she, with hurried alarm, exclaimed:—

"Godfrey, bring in another candle; the darkness is un-
safe."

Gerard Douw forgetting for the moment her repeated
injunctions, in the immediate impulse, stepped from the
bedchamber into the other, in order to supply what she
desired.

"Oh God! do not go, dear uncle," shrieked the unhappy
girl—and at the same time she sprung from the bed, and
darted after him, in order, by her grasp, to detain him.
But the warning came too late, for scarcely had he passed
the threshold, and hardly had his niece had time to utter
the startling exclamation, when the door which divided
the two rooms closed violently after him, as if swung by
a strong blast of wind. Schalken and he both rushed to
the door, but their united and desperate efforts could not
avail so much as to shake it. Shriek after shriek burst from
the inner chamber, with all the piercing loudness of despairing terror. Schalken and Douw applied every nerve to
force open the door; but all in vain. There was no sound of
struggling from within, but the screams seemed to increase
in loudness, and at the same time they heard the bolts
of the latticed window withdrawn, and the window itself

grated upon the sill as if thrown open. One last shriek, so long and piercing and agonized as to be scarcely human, swelled from the room, and suddenly there followed a death-like silence. A light step was heard crossing the floor, as if from the bed to the window; and almost at the same instant the door gave way, and, yielding to the pressure of the external applicants, nearly precipitated them into the room. It was empty. The window was open, and Schalken sprung to a chair and gazed out upon the street and canal below. He saw no form, but he saw, or thought he saw, the waters of the broad canal beneath settling ring after ring in heavy circles, as if a moment before disturbed by the submission of some ponderous body.

No trace of Rose was ever after found, nor was anything certain respecting her mysterious wooer discovered or even suspected—no clue whereby to trace the intricacies of the labyrinth and to arrive at its solution, presented itself. But an incident occurred, which, though it will not be received by our rational readers in lieu of evidence, produced nevertheless a strong and a lasting impression upon the mind of Schalken. Many years after the events which we have detailed, Schalken, then residing far away received an intimation of his father's death, and of his intended burial upon a fixed day in the church of Rotterdam. It was necessary that a very considerable journey should be performed by the funeral procession, which as it will be readily believed, was not very numerously attended. Schalken with difficulty arrived in Rotterdam late in the day upon which the funeral was appointed to take place. It had not then arrived. Evening closed in, and still it did not appear.

Schalken strolled down to the church; he found it open; notice of the arrival of the funeral had been given, and the vault in which the body was to be laid had been opened. The sexton, on seeing a well-dressed gentleman, whose object was to attend the expected obsequies, pacing the aisle of the church, hospitably invited him to share with him the comforts of a blazing fire, which, as was his custom in winter time upon such occasions, he had kindled in the hearth of a chamber in which he was accustomed to await the arrival of such grisly guests and which communicated, by a flight of steps, with the vault below. In this chamber, Schalken and his entertainer seated themselves; and the sexton, after some fruitless attempts to engage his guest in conversation, was obliged to apply himself to his tobacco-pipe and can, to solace his solitude. In spite of his grief and cares, the fatigues of a rapid journey of nearly forty hours gradually overcame the mind and body of Godfrey Schalken, and he sank into a deep sleep, from which he awakened by someone's shaking him gently by the shoulder. He first thought that the old sexton had called him, but he was no longer in the room. He roused himself, and as soon as he could clearly see what was around him, he perceived a female form, clothed in a kind of light robe of white, part of which was so disposed as to form a veil, and in her hand she carried a lamp. She was moving rather away from him, in the direction of the flight of steps which conducted towards the vaults. Schalken felt a vague alarm at the sight of this figure and at the same time an irresistible impulse to follow its guidance. He followed it towards the vaults, but when it reached the head of the stairs, he paused; the figure paused also, and, turning gently round, displayed, by the light of the lamp it carried, the face and features of his first love, Rose Velderkaust. There was nothing horrible, or even sad, in the countenance. On the contrary, it wore the same arch smile which used to enchant the artist long before in his happy days. A feeling of awe and interest, too intense to be resisted, prompted him to follow the spectre, if spectre it were. She descended the stairs—he followed—and turning to the left, through a narrow passage, she led him, to his infinite surprise, into what appeared to be an old-fashioned Dutch apartment, such as the pictures of Gerard Douw have served to immortalize. Abundance of costly antique furniture was disposed about the room, and in one corner stood a four-post bed, with heavy black cloth curtains around it; the figure frequently turned towards him with the same arch smile; and when she came to the side of the bed, she drew the curtains, and, by the light of the lamp, which she held towards its contents, she disclosed to the horror-stricken painter, sitting bolt upright in the bed, the livid and demoniac form of Vanderhausen. Schalken had hardly seen him, when he fell senseless upon the floor, where he lay until discovered, on the next morning, by persons employed in closing the passages into the vaults. He was lying in a cell of considerable size, which had not been disturbed for a long time, and he had fallen beside a large coffin, which was supported upon small pillars, a security against the attacks of vermin.

To his dying day Schalken was satisfied of the reality of the vision which he had witnessed, and he has left behind him a curious evidence of the impression which it wrought upon his fancy, in a painting executed shortly after the event I have narrated, and which is valuable as exhibiting not only the peculiarities which have made Schalken's pictures sought after, but even more so as presenting a portrait of his early love, Rose Velderkaust, whose mysterious fate must always remain matter of speculation.

# Edward Randolph's Portrait

### NATHANIEL HAWTHORNE

### 1842

The old legendary guest of the Province House abode in my remembrance from midsummer till January. One idle evening, last winter, confident that he would be found in the snuggest corner of the bar-room, I resolved to pay him another visit, hoping to deserve well of my country by snatching from oblivion some else unheard of fact of history. The night was chill and raw, and rendered boisterous by almost a gale of wind, which whistled along Washington street, causing the gas-lights to flare and flicker within the lamps. As I hurried onward, my fancy was busy with a comparison between the present aspect of the street, and that which it probably wore when the British Governors inhabited the mansion whither I was now going. Brick edifices in those times were few, till a succession of destructive fires had swept, and swept again, the wooden dwellings and warehouses from the most populous quarters of the town. The buildings stood insulated and independent, not, as now, merging their separate existences into connected ranges, with a front of tiresome identity,— but each possessing features of its own, as if the owner's individual taste had shaped it,—and the whole presenting a picturesque irregularity, the absence of which is hardly compensated by any beauties of our modern architecture. Such a scene, dimly vanishing from the eye by the ray of here and there a tallow candle, glimmering through the small panes of scattered windows, would form a sombre contrast to the street, as I beheld it, with the gas-lights blazing from corner to corner, flaming within the shops, and throwing a noonday brightness through the huge plates of glass.

But the black, lowering sky, as I turned my eyes upward, wore, doubtless, the same visage as when it frowned upon the ante-revolutionary New Englanders. The wintry blast had the same shriek that was familiar to their ears. The Old South church, too, still pointed its antique spire into the darkness, and was lost between earth and heaven; and as I passed, its clock, which had warned so many generations how transitory was their lifetime, spoke heavily and slow the same unregarded moral to myself. "Only seven o'clock," thought I. "My old friend's legends will scarcely kill the hours 'twixt this and bedtime."

Passing through the narrow arch, I crossed the courtyard, the confined precincts of which were made visible by a lantern over the portal of the Province House. On entering the bar-room, I found, as I expected, the old tradition-monger seated by a special good fire of anthracite, compelling clouds of smoke from a corpulent cigar. He recognized me with evident pleasure; for my rare properties as a patient listener invariably make me a favorite with elderly gentlemen and ladies of narrative propensities. Drawing a chair to the fire, I desired mine host to favor us with a glass a-piece of whisky punch, which was speedily prepared, steaming hot, with a slice of lemon at the bottom, a dark-red stratum of port wine upon the surface, and a sprinkling of nutmeg strewn over all. As we touched our glasses together, my legendary friend made himself known to me as Mr. Bela Tiffany; and I rejoiced at the oddity of the name, because it gave his image and character a sort of individuality in my conception. The old gentleman's draught acted as a solvent upon his memory, so that it overflowed with tales, traditions, anecdotes of famous dead people, and traits of ancient manners, some of which were childish as a nurse's lullaby, while others might have been worth the notice of the grave historian. Nothing impressed me more than a story of a black, mysterious picture, which used to hang in one the chambers of the Province House, directly above the room where we were now sitting. The following is as correct a version of the fact as the reader would be likely to obtain from any other source, although, assuredly, it has a tinge of romance approaching to the marvelous.

In one of the apartments of the Province House there was long preserved an ancient picture, the frame of which was as black as ebony, and the canvas itself so dark with age, damp, and smoke, that not a touch of the painter's art could be discerned. Time had thrown an impenetrable veil over it, and left to tradition, and fable, and conjecture, to say what had once been there portrayed. During the rule of many successive governors, it had hung, by prescriptive and undisputed right, over the mantelpiece of the same chamber; and it still kept its place when Lieutenant Governor Hutchinson assumed the administration of the province, on the departure of Sir Francis Bernard.

The Lieutenant Governor sat, one afternoon, resting his head against the carved back of his stately arm chair, and gazing up thoughtfully at the void blackness of the picture. It was scarcely a time for such inactive musing, when affairs of the deepest moment required the ruler's decision; for, within that very hour Hutchinson had received intelligence of the arrival of a British fleet, bringing three regiments from Halifax to overawe the insubordination of the people. These troops awaited his permission to occupy the fortress of Castle William, and the town itself.

Yet, instead of affixing his signature to an official order, there sat the Lieutenant Governor, so carefully scrutinizing the black waste of canvas, that his demeanor attracted the notice of two young persons who attended him. One, wearing a military dress of buff, was his kinsman, Francis Lincoln, the Provincial Captain of Castle William; the other, who sat on a low stool beside his chair, was Alice Vane, his favorite niece.

She was clad entirely in white, a pale, ethereal creature, who, though a native of New England, had been educated abroad, and seemed not merely a stranger from another clime, but almost a being from another world. For several years, until left an orphan, she had dwelt with her father in sunny Italy, and there had acquired a taste and enthusiasm for sculpture and painting, which she found few opportunities of gratifying in the undecorated dwellings of the colonial gentry. It was said that the early productions of her own pencil exhibited no inferior genius, though, perhaps, the rude atmosphere of New England had cramped her hand, and dimmed the glowing colors of her fancy. But observing her uncle's steadfast gaze, which appeared to search through the mist of years to discover the subject of the picture, her curiosity was excited.

"Is it known, my dear uncle," inquired she, "what this old picture once represented? Possibly, could it be made visible, it might prove a masterpiece of some great artist— else why has it so long held such a conspicuous place?"

As her uncle, contrary to his usual custom, (for he was as attentive to all the humors and caprices of Alice as if she had been his own best beloved child,) did not immediately reply, the young Captain of Castle William took that office upon himself.

"This dark old square of canvas, my fair cousin," said he, "has been an heirloom in the Province House from time immemorial. As to the painter, I can tell you nothing;

but, if half the stories told of it be true, not one of the great Italian masters has ever produced so marvelous a piece of work, as that before you."

Captain Lincoln proceeded to relate some of the strange fables and fantasies, which, as it was impossible to refute them by ocular demonstration, had grown to be articles of popular belief, in reference to this old picture. One of the wildest, and at the same time the best accredited accounts, stated it to be an original and authentic portrait of the Evil One, taken at a witch meeting near Salem; and that its strong and terrible resemblance has been confirmed by several of the confessing wizards and witches, at their trial, in open court. It was likewise affirmed that a familiar spirit, or demon, abode behind the blackness of the picture, and had shown himself, at seasons of public calamity, to more than one of the royal governors. Shirley, for instance, had beheld this ominous apparition, on the eve of General Abercrombie's shameful and bloody defeat under the walls of Ticonderoga. Many of the servants of the Province House had caught glimpses of a visage frowning down upon them, at morning or evening twilight,— or in the depths of night, while raking up the fire that glimmered on the hearth beneath; although, if any were bold enough to hold a torch before the picture, it would appear as black and undistinguishable as ever. The oldest inhabitant of Boston recollected that his father, in whose days the portrait had not wholly faded out of sight, had once looked upon, it, but would never suffer himself to be questioned as to the face which was there represented. In connection with such stories, it was remarkable that over the top of the frame there were some ragged remnants of black silk, indicating that a veil had formerly hung down before the picture, until the duskiness of time had so effectually concealed it. But, after all, it was the most singular part of the affair, that so many of the pompous governors of Massachusetts had allowed the obliterated picture to remain in the state-chamber of the Province House.

"Some of these fables are really awful," observed Alice Vane, who had occasionally shuddered, as well as smiled, while her cousin spoke. "It would be almost worth while to wipe away the black surface of the canvas, since the original picture can hardly be so formidable as those which fancy paints instead of it."

"But would it be possible," inquired her cousin, "to restore this dark picture to its pristine hues?"

"Such arts are known in Italy," said Alice.

The Lieutenant Governor had roused himself from his abstracted mood, and listened with a smile to the conversation of his young relatives. Yet his voice had something peculiar in its tones, when he undertook the explanation of the mystery.

"I am sorry, Alice, to destroy your faith in the legends of which you are so fond," remarked he; "but my antiquarian researches have long since made me acquainted with the subject of this picture—if picture it can be called—which is no more visible, nor ever will be, than the face of the long buried man whom it once represented. It was the portrait of Edward Randolph, the founder of this house, a person famous in the history of New England."

"Of that Edward Randolph," exclaimed Captain Lincoln, "who obtained the repeal of the first provincial charter, under which our forefathers had enjoyed almost democratic privileges! He that was styled the arch-enemy of New England, and whose memory is still held in detestation, as the destroyer of our liberties!"

"It was the same Randolph," answered Hutchinson, moving uneasily in his chair. "It was his lot to taste the bitterness of popular odium."

"Our annals tell us," continued the Captain of Castle William, "that the curse of the people followed this Randolph where he went, and wrought evil in all the subsequent events of his life, and that its effect was seen likewise in the manner of his death. They say, too, that the inward misery of that curse worked itself outward, and was visible on the wretched man's countenance, making it too horrible to be looked upon. If so, and if this picture truly represented his aspect, it was in mercy that the cloud of blackness has gathered over it."

"These traditions are folly, to one who has proved, as I have, how little of historic truth lies at the bottom," said the Lieutenant Governor. "As regards the life and character of Edward Randolph, too implicit credence has been given to Dr. Cotton Mather, who—I must say it, though some of his blood runs in my veins—has filled our early history with old women's tales, as fanciful and extravagant as those of Greece or Rome."

"And yet," whispered Alice Vane, "may not such fables have a moral? And, methinks, if the visage of this portrait be so dreadful, it is not without a cause that it has hung so long in a chamber of the Province House. When the rulers feel themselves irresponsible, it were well that they should be reminded of the awful weight of a people's curse."

The Lieutenant Governor started, and gazed for a moment at his niece, as if her girlish fantasies had struck upon some feeling in his own breast, which all his policy or principles could not entirely subdue. He knew, indeed, that Alice, in spite of her foreign education, retained the native sympathies of a New England girl.

"Peace, silly child," cried he, at last, more harshly than he had ever before addressed the gentle Alice. "The rebuke of a king is more to be dreaded than the clamor of a wild, misguided multitude. Captain Lincoln, it is decided. The fortress of Castle William must be occupied by the Royal troops. The two remaining regiments shall be billeted in the town, or encamped upon the Common. It is time, after years of tumult, and almost rebellion, that his majesty's government should have a wall of strength about it."

"Trust, sir—trust yet awhile to the loyalty of the people," said Captain Lincoln; "nor teach them that they can ever be on other terms with British soldiers than those of brotherhood, as when they fought side by side through the French war. Do not convert the streets of your native town into a camp. Think twice before you give up old Castle William, the key of the province, into other keeping than that of true-born New Englanders."

"Young man, it is decided," repeated Hutchinson, rising from his chair. "A British officer will be in attendance this evening, to receive the necessary instructions for the disposal of the troops. Your presence also will be required. Till then, farewell."

With these words the Lieutenant Governor hastily left the room, while Alice and her cousin more slowly followed, whispering together, and once pausing to glance back at the mysterious picture. The captain of Castle William fancied that the girl's air and mien were such as might have belonged to one of those spirits of fable—fairies, or creatures of a more antique mythology,—who sometimes mingled their agency with mortal affairs, half in caprice, yet with a sensibility to human weal or woe. As he held the door for her to pass, Alice beckoned to the picture and smiled.

"Come forth, dark and evil Shape!" cried she. "It is thine hour!"

In the evening, Lieutenant Governor Hutchinson sat in the same chamber where the foregoing scene had occurred, surrounded by several persons whose various interests had summoned them together. There were the Selectmen of

Boston, plain, patriarchal fathers of the people, excellent
representatives of the old puritanical founders, whose
sombre strength had stamped so deep an impress upon the
New England character. Contrasting with these were one
or two members of Council, richly dressed in the white
wigs, the embroidered waistcoats and other magnificence
of the time, and making a somewhat ostentatious display
of courtier-like ceremonial. In attendance, likewise, was a
major of the British army, awaiting the Lieutenant Governor's orders for the landing of the troops, which still
remained on board the transports. The Captain of Castle
William stood beside Hutchinson's chair, with folded
arms, glancing rather haughtily at the British officer, by
whom he was soon to be superseded in his command. On a
table, in the centre of the chamber, stood a branched silver
candlestick, throwing down the glow of half a dozen wax
lights upon a paper apparently ready for the Lieutenant
Governor's signature.

Partly shrouded in the voluminous folds of one of the
window curtains, which fell from the ceiling to the floor,
was seen the white drapery of a lady's robe. It may appear
strange that Alice Vane should have been there, at such a
time; but there was something so childlike, so wayward,
in her singular character, so apart from ordinary rules,
that her presence did not surprise the few who noticed
it. Meantime, the chairman of the Selectmen was addressing to the Lieutenant Governor a long and solemn protest
against the reception of the British troops into the town.

"And if your Honor," concluded this excellent, but
somewhat prosy old gentleman, "shall see fit to persist in
bringing these mercenary sworders and musketeers into
our quiet streets, not on our heads be the responsibility.
Think, sir, while there is yet time, that if one drop of
blood be shed, that blood shall be an eternal stain upon
your Honor's memory. You, sir, have written, with an able

pen, the deeds of our forefathers. The more to be desired is it, therefore, that yourself should deserve honorable mention, as a true patriot and upright ruler, when your own doings shall be written down in history."

"I am not insensible, my good sir, to the natural desire to stand well in the annals of my country," replied Hutchinson, controlling his impatience into courtesy, "nor know I any better method of attaining that end than by withstanding the merely temporary spirit of mischief, which, with your pardon, seems to have infected elder men than myself. Would you have me wait till the mob shall sack the Province House, as they did my private mansion? Trust me, sir, the time may come when you will be glad to flee for protection to the King's banner, the raising of which is now so distasteful to you."

"Yes," said the British major, who was impatiently expecting the Lieutenant Governor's orders. "The demagogues of this Province have raised the devil, and cannot lay him again. We will exorcise him, in God's name and the King's."

"If you meddle with the devil, take care of his claws!" answered the Captain of Castle William, stirred by the taunt against his countrymen.

"Craving your pardon, young sir," said the venerable Selectman, "let not an evil spirit enter into your words. We will strive against the oppressor with prayer and fasting, as our forefathers would have done. Like them, moreover, we will submit to whatever lot a wise Providence may send us,—always, after our own best exertions to amend it."

"And there peep forth the devil's claws!" muttered Hutchinson, who well understood the nature of Puritan submission. "This matter shall be expedited forthwith. When there shall be a sentinel at every corner, and a court of guard before the town-house, a loyal gentleman may venture to walk abroad. What to me is the outcry of a mob, in this remote province of the realm? The King is my master, and England is my country! Upheld by their armed strength, I set my foot upon the rabble, and defy them!"

He snatched a pen, and was about to affix his signature to the paper that lay on the table, when the Captain of Castle William placed his hand upon his shoulder. The freedom of the action, so contrary to the ceremonious respect which was then considered due to rank and dignity, awakened general surprise, and in none more than in the Lieutenant Governor himself. Looking angrily up, he perceived that his young relative was pointing his finger to the opposite wall. Hutchinson's eye followed the signal; and he saw, what had hitherto been unobserved, that a black silk curtain was suspended before the mysterious picture, so as completely to conceal it. His thoughts immediately recurred to the scene of the preceding afternoon; and, in his surprise, confused by indistinct emotions, yet sensible that his niece must have had an agency in this phenomenon, he called loudly upon her.

"Alice!—Come hither, Alice!"

No sooner had he spoken than Alice Vane glided from her station, and pressing one hand across her eyes, with the other snatched away the sable curtain that concealed the portrait. An exclamation of surprise burst from every beholder; but the Lieutenant Governor's voice had a tone of horror.

"By heaven," said he, in a low, inward murmur, speaking rather to himself than to those around him, "if the spirit of Edward Randolph were to appear among us from the place of torment, he could not wear more of the terrors of hell upon his face!"

"For some wise end," said the aged Selectman, solemnly, "hath Providence scattered away the mist of years that had so long hid this dreadful effigy. Until this hour no living man hath seen what we behold!"

Within the antique frame, which so recently had enclosed a sable waste of canvas, now appeared a visible picture, still dark, indeed, in its hues and shadings, but thrown forward in strong relief. It was a half-length figure of a gentleman in a rich, but very old-fashioned dress of embroidered velvet, with a broad ruff and a beard, and wearing a hat, the brim of which overshadowed his forehead. Beneath this cloud the eyes had a peculiar glare, which was almost lifelike. The whole portrait started so distinctly out of the background, that it had the effect of a person looking down from the wall at the astonished and awe-stricken spectators. The expression of the face, if any words can convey an idea of it, was that of a wretch detected in some hideous guilt, and exposed to the bitter hatred, and laughter, and withering scorn, of a vast surrounding multitude. There was the struggle of defiance, beaten down and overwhelmed by the crushing weight of ignominy. The torture of the soul had come forth upon the countenance. It seemed as if the picture, while hidden behind the cloud of immemorial years, had been all the time acquiring an intenser depth and darkness of expression, till now it gloomed forth again, and threw its evil omen over the present hour. Such, if the wild legend may be credited, was the portrait of Edward Randolph, as he appeared when a people's curse had wrought its influence upon his nature.

"'T would drive me mad—that awful face!" said Hutchinson, who seemed fascinated by the contemplation of it.

"Be warned, then!" whispered Alice. "He trampled on a people's rights. Behold his punishment—and avoid a crime like his!"

The Lieutenant Governor actually trembled for an instant; but, exerting his energy—which was not, however, his most characteristic feature—he strove to shake off the spell of Randolph's countenance.

"Girl!" cried he, laughing bitterly, as he turned to Alice, "have you brought hither your painter's art—your Italian spirit of intrigue—your tricks of stage-effect—and think to influence the councils of rulers and the affairs of nations, by such shallow contrivances? See here!"

"Stay yet awhile," said the Selectman, as Hutchinson again snatched the pen; "for if ever mortal man received a warning from a tormented soul, your Honor is that man!"

"Away!" answered Hutchinson fiercely. "Though yonder senseless picture cried 'Forbear!'—it should not move me!"

Casting a scowl of defiance at the pictured face, (which seemed, at that moment, to intensify the horror of its miserable and wicked look,) he scrawled on the paper, in characters that betokened it a deed of desperation, the name of Thomas Hutchinson. Then, it is said, he shuddered, as if that signature had granted away his salvation.

"It is done," said he; and placed his hand upon his brow.

"May Heaven forgive the deed," said the soft, sad accents of Alice Vane, like the voice of a good spirit flitting away.

When morning came there was a stifled whisper through the household, and spreading thence about the town, that the dark, mysterious picture had started from the wall, and spoken face to face with Lieutenant Governor Hutchinson. If such a miracle had been wrought, however, no traces of it remained behind; for within the antique frame, nothing could be discerned, save the impenetrable cloud, which had covered the canvas since the memory of man. If the figure had, indeed, stepped forth, it had fled back, spirit-like, at the day-dawn, and hidden itself behind a century's obscurity. The truth probably was, that Alice Vane's secret for restoring the hues of the picture had merely effected a temporary renovation. But those who, in that brief interval, had beheld the awful visage of Edward Randolph, desired no second glance, and ever afterwards trembled at the recollection of the scene, as if an evil spirit had appeared visibly among them. And as for Hutchinson, when, far over the ocean, his dying hour drew on, he gasped for breath, and complained that he was choking with the blood of the Boston Massacre; and Francis Lincoln, the former Captain of Castle William, who was standing at his bedside, perceived a likeness in his frenzied look to that of Edward Randolph. Did his broken spirit feel, at that dread hour, the tremendous burden of a People's curse?

At the conclusion of this miraculous legend, I inquired of mine host whether the picture still remained in the chamber over our heads; but Mr. Tiffany informed me that it had long since been removed, and was supposed to be hidden in some out-of-the-way corner of the New England Museum. Perchance some curious antiquary may light upon it there, and, with the assistance of Mr. Howorth, the picture cleaner, may supply a not unnecessary proof of the authenticity of the facts here set down. During the progress of the story a storm had been gathering abroad, and raging and rattling so loudly in the upper regions of the Province House, that it seemed as if all the old Governors and great men were running riot above stairs, while Mr. Bela Tiffany babbled of them below. In the course of generations, when many people have lived and died in an ancient house, the whistling of the wind through its crannies, and the creaking of its beams and rafters, become strangely like the tones of the human voice, or thundering laughter, or heavy footsteps treading the deserted chambers. It is as if the echoes of half a century were revived. Such were the ghostly sounds that roared and murmured in our ears, when I took leave of the circle round the fireside of the Province House, and plunging down the door-steps, fought my way homeward against a drifting snow-storm.

# The Oval Portrait

EDGAR ALLAN POE

1842

The château into which my valet had ventured to make forcible entrance, rather than permit me, in my desperately wounded condition, to pass a night in the open air, was one of those piles of commingled gloom and grandeur which have so long frowned among the Apennines, not less in fact than in the fancy of Mrs. Radcliffe. To all appearance it had been temporarily and very lately abandoned. We established ourselves in one of the smallest and least sumptuously furnished apartments. It lay in a remote turret of the building. Its decorations were rich, yet tattered and antique. Its walls were hung with tapestry and bedecked with manifold and multiform armorial trophies, together with an unusually great number of very spirited modern paintings in frames of rich golden arabesque. In these paintings, which depended from the walls not only in their main surfaces, but in very many nooks which the bizarre architecture of the château rendered necessary—in these paintings my incipient delirium, perhaps, had caused me to take deep interest; so that I bade Pedro to close the heavy shutters of the room—since it was already night— to light the tongues of a tall candelabrum which stood by the head of my bed—and to throw open far and wide the fringed curtains of black velvet which enveloped the bed itself. I wished all this done that I might resign myself, if not to sleep, at least alternately to the contemplation of these pictures, and the perusal of a small volume which had been found upon the pillow, and which purported to criticize and describe them.

Long—long I read—and devoutly, devotedly I gazed. Rapidly and gloriously the hours flew by and the deep midnight came. The position of the candelabrum displeased me, and outreaching my hand with difficulty, rather than disturb my slumbering valet, I placed it so as to throw its rays more fully upon the book.

But the action produced an effect altogether unanticipated. The rays of the numerous candles (for there were many) now fell within a niche of the room which had hitherto been thrown into deep shade by one of the bed-posts. I thus saw in vivid light a picture all unnoticed before. It was the portrait of a young girl just ripening into womanhood. I glanced at the painting hurriedly, and then closed my eyes. Why I did this was not at first apparent even to my own perception. But while my lids remained thus shut, I ran over in my mind my reason for so shutting them. It was an impulsive movement to gain time for thought—to make sure that my vision had not deceived me—to calm and subdue my fancy for a more sober and more certain gaze. In a very few moments I again looked fixedly at the painting.

That I now saw aright I could not and would not doubt; for the first flashing of the candles upon that canvas had seemed to dissipate the dreamy stupor which was stealing over my senses, and to startle me at once into waking life.

The portrait, I have already said, was that of a young girl. It was a mere head and shoulders, done in what is technically termed a *vignette* manner; much in the style of the favorite heads of Sully. The arms, the bosom, and even the ends of the radiant hair melted imperceptibly into the vague yet deep shadow which formed the back-ground of the whole. The frame was oval, richly gilded and filigreed in *Moresque*. As a thing of art nothing could be more admirable than the painting itself. But it could have been neither the execution of the work, nor the immortal beauty of the countenance, which had so suddenly and so vehemently moved me. Least of all, could it have been that my fancy, shaken from its half slumber, had mistaken the head for that of a living person. I saw at once that the peculiarities of the design, of the *vignetting*, and of the frame, must have instantly dispelled such idea—must have prevented even its momentary entertainment. Thinking earnestly upon these points, I remained, for an hour perhaps, half sitting, half reclining, with my vision riveted upon the portrait. At length, satisfied with the true secret of its effect, I fell back within the bed. I had found the spell of the picture in an absolute *life-likeliness* of expression, which, at first startling, finally confounded, subdued, and appalled me. With deep and reverent awe I replaced the candelabrum in its former position. The cause of my deep agitation being thus shut from view, I sought eagerly the volume which discussed the paintings and their histories. Turning to the number which designated the oval portrait, I there read the vague and quaint words which follow:

"She was a maiden of rarest beauty, and not more lovely than full of glee. And evil was the hour when she saw, and loved, and wedded the painter. He, passionate, studious, austere, and having already a bride in his Art; she a maiden of rarest beauty, and not more lovely than full of glee; all light and smiles, and frolicsome as the young fawn; loving and cherishing all things; hating only the Art which was her rival; dreading only the pallet and brushes and other untoward instruments which deprived her of the countenance of her lover. It was thus a terrible thing for this lady to hear the painter speak of his desire to portray even his young bride. But she was humble and obedient, and sat meekly for many weeks in the dark, high turret-chamber where the light dripped upon the pale canvas only from overhead. But he, the painter, took glory in his work, which went on from hour to hour, and from day to day. And he was a passionate, and wild, and moody man, who became lost in reveries; so that he *would* not see that the light which fell so ghastly in that lone turret withered the health and the spirits of his bride, who pined visibly to all but him. Yet she smiled on and still on, uncomplainingly, because she saw that the painter (who had high renown) took a fervid and burning pleasure in his task, and wrought day and night to depict her who so loved him, yet who grew daily more dispirited and weak. And in sooth some who beheld the portrait spoke of its resemblance in low words, as of a mighty marvel, and a proof not less of the power of the painter than of his deep love for her whom he depicted so surpassingly well. But at length, as the labor drew nearer to its conclusion, there were admitted none into the turret; for the painter had grown wild with the ardor of his work, and turned his eyes from canvas merely, even to regard the countenance of his wife. And he *would* not see that the tints which he spread upon the canvas were drawn from the cheeks of her who sat beside him. And when many weeks had passed, and but little remained to do, save one brush upon the mouth and one tint upon the eye, the spirit of the lady again flickered up as the flame within the socket of the lamp. And then the brush was given, and then the tint was placed; and, for one moment, the painter stood entranced before the work which he had wrought; but in the next, while he yet gazed, he grew tremulous and very pallid, and aghast, and crying with a loud voice, 'This is indeed *Life* itself!' turned suddenly to regard his beloved:—*She was dead!*"

# Man-size in Marble
## Edith Nesbit
### 1887

Although every word of this story is as true as despair, I do not expect people to believe it. Nowadays a "rational explanation" is required before belief is possible. Let me then, at once, offer the "rational explanation" which finds most favour among those who have heard the tale of my life's tragedy. It is held that we were "under a delusion," Laura and I, on that 31st of October; and that this supposition places the whole matter on a satisfactory and believable basis. The reader can judge, when he, too, has heard my story, how far this is an "explanation," and in what sense it is "rational." There were three who took part in this: Laura and I and another man. The other man still lives, and can speak to the truth of the least credible part of my story.

I never in my life knew what it was to have as much money as I required to supply the most ordinary needs—good colours, books, and cab-fares—and when we were married we knew quite well that we should only be able to live at all by "strict punctuality and attention to business." I used to paint in those days, and Laura used to write, and we felt sure we could keep the pot at least simmering. Living in town was out of the question, so we went to look for a cottage in the country, which should be at once sanitary and picturesque. So rarely do these two qualities meet in one cottage that our search was for some time quite fruitless. We tried advertisements, but most of the desirable rural residences which we did look at proved to be lacking in both essentials, and when a cottage chanced to have drains it always had stucco as well and was shaped like a tea-caddy. And if we found a vine or rose-covered porch, corruption invariably lurked within. Our minds got so befogged by the eloquence of house-agents and the rival disadvantages of the fever-traps and outrages to beauty which we had seen and scorned, that I very much doubt whether either of us, on our wedding morning, knew the difference between a house and a haystack. But when we got away from friends and house-agents, on our honeymoon, our wits grew clear again, and we knew a pretty cottage when at last we saw one. It was at Brenzett—a little village set on a hill over against the southern marshes. We had gone there, from the seaside village where we were staying, to see the church, and two fields from the church we found this cottage. It stood quite by itself, about two miles from the village. It was a long, low building, with rooms sticking out in unexpected places. There was a bit of stone-work—ivy-covered and moss-grown, just two old rooms, all that was left of a big house that had once stood there—and round this stone-work the house had grown up. Stripped of its roses and jasmine it would have been hideous. As it stood it was charming, and after a brief examination we took it. It was absurdly cheap. The rest of our honeymoon we spent in grubbing about in second-hand shops in the county town, picking up bits of old oak and Chippendale chairs for our furnishing. We wound up with a run up to town and a visit to Liberty's, and soon the low oak-beamed lattice-windowed rooms began to be home. There was a jolly old-fashioned garden, with grass paths, and no end of hollyhocks and sunflowers, and big lilies. From the window you could see the marsh-pastures, and beyond them the blue, thin line of the sea. We were as happy as the summer was glorious, and settled down into work sooner than we ourselves expected. I was never tired of sketching the view and the wonderful cloud effects from the open lattice, and Laura would sit at the table and write verses about them, in which I mostly played the part of foreground.

We got a tall old peasant woman to do for us. Her face and figure were good, though her cooking was of the homeliest; but she understood all about gardening, and told us all the old names of the coppices and cornfields, and the stories of the smugglers and highwaymen, and, better still, of the "things that walked," and of the "sights" which met one in lonely glens of a starlight night. She was a great comfort to us, because Laura hated housekeeping as much as I loved folklore, and we soon came to leave all the domestic business to Mrs. Dorman, and to use her legends in little magazine stories which brought in the jingling guinea.

We had three months of married happiness, and did not have a single quarrel. One October evening I had been down to smoke a pipe with the doctor—our only neighbour—a pleasant young Irishman. Laura had stayed at home to finish a comic sketch of a village episode for the *Monthly Marplot*. I left her laughing over her own jokes, and came in to find her a crumpled heap of pale muslin weeping on the window seat.

"Good heavens, my darling, what's the matter?" I cried, taking her in my arms. She leaned her little dark head against my shoulder and went on crying. I had never seen her cry before—we had always been so happy, you see— and I felt sure some frightful misfortune had happened.

"What *is* the matter? Do speak."

"It's Mrs. Dorman," she sobbed.

"What has she done?" I inquired, immensely relieved.

"She says she must go before the end of the month, and she says her niece is ill; she's gone down to see her now, but I don't believe that's the reason, because her niece is always ill. I believe someone has been setting her against us. Her manner was so queer—"

"Never mind, Pussy," I said; "whatever you do, don't cry, or I shall have to cry too, to keep you in countenance, and then you'll never respect your man again!"

She dried her eyes obediently on my handkerchief, and even smiled faintly.

"But you see," she went on, "it is really serious, because these village people are so sheepy, and if one won't do a thing you may be quite sure none of the others will. And I shall have to cook the dinners, and wash up the hateful greasy plates; and you'll have to carry cans of water about, and clean the boots and knives—and we shall never have any time for work, or earn any money, or anything. We shall have to work all day, and only be able to rest when we are waiting for the kettle to boil!"

I represented to her that even if we had to perform these duties, the day would still present some margin for other toils and recreations. But she refused to see the matter in any but the greyest light. She was very unreasonable, my Laura, but I could not have loved her any more if she had been as reasonable as Whately.

"I'll speak to Mrs. Dorman when she comes back, and see if I can't come to terms with her," I said. "Perhaps she wants a rise in her screw. It will be all right. Let's walk up to the church."

The church was a large and lonely one, and we loved to go there, especially upon bright nights. The path skirted a wood, cut through it once, and ran along the crest of the hill through two meadows, and round the churchyard wall, over which the old yews loomed in black masses of shadow. This path, which was partly paved, was called "the bier-balk," for it had long been the way by which the corpses had been carried to burial. The churchyard was richly treed, and was shaded by great elms which stood just outside and stretched their majestic arms in benediction over the happy dead. A large, low porch let one into the building by a Norman doorway and a heavy oak door studded with iron. Inside, the arches rose into darkness, and between them the reticulated windows, which stood out white in the moonlight. In the chancel, the windows were of rich glass, which showed in faint light their noble colouring, and made the black oak of the choir pews hardly more solid than the shadows. But on each side of the altar lay a grey marble figure of a knight in full plate armour lying upon a low slab, with hands held up in everlasting prayer, and these figures, oddly enough, were always to be seen if there was any glimmer of light in the church. Their names were lost, but the peasants told of them that they had been fierce and wicked men, marauders by land and sea, who had been the scourge of their time, and had been guilty of deeds so foul that the house they had lived in—the big house, by the way, that had stood on the site of our cottage—had been stricken by lightning and the vengeance of Heaven. But for all that, the gold of their heirs had bought them a place in the church. Looking at the bad hard faces reproduced in the marble, this story was easily believed.

The church looked at its best and weirdest on that night, for the shadows of the yew trees fell through the windows upon the floor of the nave and touched the pillars with tattered shade. We sat down together without speaking, and watched the solemn beauty of the old church, with some of that awe which inspired its early builders. We walked to the chancel and looked at the sleeping warriors. Then we rested some time on the stone seat in the porch, looking out over the stretch of quiet moonlit meadows, feeling in every fibre of our being the peace of the night and of our happy love; and came away at last with a sense that even scrubbing and blackleading were but small troubles at their worst.

Mrs. Dorman had come back from the village, and I at once invited her to a *tête-à-tête*.

"Now, Mrs. Dorman," I said, when I had got her into my painting room, "what's all this about your not staying with us?"

"I should be glad to get away, sir, before the end of the month," she answered, with her usual placid dignity.

"Have you any fault to find, Mrs. Dorman?"

"None at all, sir; you and your lady have always been most kind, I'm sure—"

"Well, what is it? Are your wages not high enough?"

"No, sir, I gets quite enough."

"Then why not stay?"

"I'd rather not"—with some hesitation—"my niece is ill."

"But your niece has been ill ever since we came."

No answer. There was a long and awkward silence. I broke it.

"Can't you stay for another month?" I asked.

"No, sir. I'm bound to go by Thursday."

And this was Monday!

"Well, I must say, I think you might have let us know before. There's no time now to get any one else, and your mistress is not fit to do heavy housework. Can't you stay till next week?"

"I might be able to come back next week."

I was now convinced that all she wanted was a brief holiday, which we should have been willing enough to let her have, as soon as we could get a substitute.

"But why must you go this week?" I persisted. "Come, out with it."

Mrs. Dorman drew the little shawl, which she always wore, tightly across her bosom, as though she were cold. Then she said, with a sort of effort—

"They say, sir, as this was a big house in Catholic times, and there was a many deeds done here."

The nature of the "deeds" might be vaguely inferred from the inflection of Mrs. Dorman's voice—which was enough to make one's blood run cold. I was glad that Laura was not in the room. She was always nervous, as highly -strung natures are, and I felt that these tales about our house, told by this old peasant woman, with her impressive manner and contagious credulity, might have made our home less dear to my wife.

"Tell me all about it, Mrs. Dorman," I said; "you needn't mind about telling me. I'm not like the young people who make fun of such things."

Which was partly true.

"Well, sir"—she sank her voice—"you may have seen in the church, beside the altar, two shapes."

"You mean the effigies of the knights in armour," I said cheerfully.

"I mean them two bodies, drawed out man-size in marble," she returned, and I had to admit that her description was a thousand times more graphic than mine, to say nothing of a certain weird force and uncanniness about the phrase "drawed out man-size in marble."

"They do say, as on All Saints' Eve them two bodies sits up on their slabs, and gets off of them, and then walks down the aisle, *in their marble*"—(another good phrase, Mrs. Dorman)—"and as the church clock strikes eleven they walks out of the church door, and over the graves, and along the bier-balk, and if it's a wet night there's the marks of their feet in the morning."

"And where do they go?" I asked, rather fascinated.

"They comes back here to their home, sir, and if any one meets them—"

"Well, what then?" I asked.

But no—not another word could I get from her, save that her niece was ill and she must go. After what I had heard I scorned to discuss the niece, and tried to get from Mrs. Dorman more details of the legend. I could get nothing but warnings.

"Whatever you do, sir, lock the door early on All Saints' Eve, and make the cross-sign over the doorstep and on the windows."

"But has any one ever seen these things?" I persisted.

"That's not for me to say. I know what I know, sir."

"Well, who was here last year?"

"No one, sir; the lady as owned the house only stayed here in summer, and she always went to London a full month afore the night. And I'm sorry to inconvenience you and your lady, but my niece is ill and I must go on Thursday."

I could have shaken her for her absurd reiteration of that obvious fiction, after she had told me her real reasons.

She was determined to go, nor could our united entreaties move her in the least.

I did not tell Laura the legend of the shapes that "walked in their marble," partly because a legend concerning our house might perhaps trouble my wife, and partly, I think, from some more occult reason. This was not quite the same to me as any other story, and I did not want to talk about it till the day was over. I had very soon ceased to think of the legend, however. I was painting a portrait of Laura, against the lattice window, and I could not think of much else. I had got a splendid background of yellow and grey sunset, and was working away with enthusiasm at her lace. On Thursday Mrs. Dorman went. She relented, at parting, so far as to say—

"Don't you put yourself about too much, ma'am, and if there's any little thing I can do next week, I'm sure I shan't mind."

From which I inferred that she wished to come back to us after Hallowe'en. Up to the last she adhered to the fiction of the niece with touching fidelity.

Thursday passed off pretty well. Laura showed marked ability in the matter of steak and potatoes, and I confess that my knives, and the plates, which I insisted upon washing, were better done than I had dared to expect.

Friday came. It is about what happened on that Friday that this is written. I wonder if I should have believed it, if anyone had told it to me. I will write the story of it as quickly and plainly as I can. Everything that happened on that day is burnt into my brain. I shall not forget anything, nor leave anything out.

I got up early, I remember, and lighted the kitchen fire, and had just achieved a smoky success, when my little wife came running down, as sunny and sweet as the clear October morning itself. We prepared breakfast together, and found it very good fun. The housework was soon done, and when brushes and brooms and pails were quiet again, the house was still indeed. It is wonderful what a difference one makes in a house. We really missed Mrs. Dorman, quite apart from considerations concerning pots and pans. We spent the day in dusting our books and putting them straight, and dined gaily on cold steak and coffee. Laura was, if possible, brighter and gayer and sweeter than usual, and I began to think that a little domestic toil was really good for her. We had never been so merry since we were married, and the walk we had that afternoon was, I think, the happiest time of all my life. When we had watched the deep scarlet clouds slowly pale into leaden grey against a pale-green sky, and saw the white mists curl up along the hedgerows in the distant marsh, we came back to the house, silently, hand in hand.

"You are sad, my darling," I said, half-jestingly, as we sat down together in our little parlour. I expected a disclaimer, for my own silence had been the silence of complete happiness. To my surprise she said—

"Yes. I think I am sad, or rather I am uneasy. I don't think I'm very well. I have shivered three or four times since we came in, and it is not cold, is it?"

"No," I said, and hoped it was not a chill caught from the treacherous mists that roll up from the marshes in the dying light. No—she said, she did not think so. Then, after a silence, she spoke suddenly—

"Do you ever have presentiments of evil?"

"No," I said, smiling, "and I shouldn't believe in them if I had."

"I do," she went on; "the night my father died I knew it, though he was right away in the north of Scotland."

I did not answer in words.

She sat looking at the fire for some time in silence, gently stroking my hand. At last she sprang up, came behind me, and, drawing my head back, kissed me.

"There, it's over now," she said. "What a baby I am! Come, light the candles, and we'll have some of these new Rubinstein duets."

And we spent a happy hour or two at the piano.

At about half-past ten I began to long for the good-night pipe, but Laura looked so white that I felt it would be brutal of me to fill our sitting-room with the fumes of strong cavendish.

"I'll take my pipe outside," I said.

"Let me come, too."

"No, sweetheart, not to-night; you're much too tired. I shan't be long. Get to bed, or I shall have an invalid to nurse to-morrow as well as the boots to clean."

I kissed her and was turning to go, when she flung her arms round my neck, and held me as if she would never let me go again. I stroked her hair.

"Come, Pussy, you're over-tired. The housework has been too much for you."

She loosened her clasp a little and drew a deep breath.

"No. We've been very happy to-day, Jack, haven't we? Don't stay out too long."

"I won't, my dearie."

I strolled out of the front door, leaving it unlatched. What a night it was! The jagged masses of heavy dark cloud were rolling at intervals from horizon to horizon, and thin white wreaths covered the stars. Through all the rush of the cloud river, the moon swam, breasting the waves and disappearing again in the darkness. When now and again her light reached the woodlands they seemed to be slowly and noiselessly waving in time to the swing of the clouds above them. There was a strange grey light over all the earth; the fields had that shadowy bloom over them which only comes from the marriage of dew and moonshine, or frost and starlight.

I walked up and down, drinking in the beauty of the quiet earth and the changing sky. The night was absolutely silent. Nothing seemed to be abroad. There was no scurrying of rabbits, or twitter of the half-asleep birds. And though the clouds went sailing across the sky, the wind that drove them never came low enough to rustle the dead leaves in the woodland paths. Across the meadows I could see the church tower standing out black and grey against the sky. I walked there thinking over our three months of happiness—and of my wife, her dear eyes, her loving ways. Oh, my little girl! my own little girl; what a vision came then of a long, glad life for you and me together!

I heard a bell-beat from the church. Eleven already! I turned to go in, but the night held me. I could not go back into our little warm rooms yet. I would go up to the church. I felt vaguely that it would be good to carry my love and thankfulness to the sanctuary whither so many loads of sorrow and gladness had been borne by the men and women of the dead years.

I looked in at the low window as I went by. Laura was half lying on her chair in front of the fire. I could not see her face, only her little head showed dark against the pale blue wall. She was quite still. Asleep, no doubt. My heart reached out to her, as I went on. There must be a God, I thought, and a God who was good. How otherwise could anything so sweet and dear as she have ever been imagined?

I walked slowly along the edge of the wood. A sound broke the stillness of the night, it was a rustling in the wood. I stopped and listened. The sound stopped too. I went on, and now distinctly heard another step than mine answer mine like an echo. It was a poacher or a wood-stealer, most likely, for these were not unknown in our Arcadian neighbourhood. But whoever it was, he was a fool not to step more lightly. I turned into the wood, and now the footstep seemed to come from the path I had just left. It must be an echo, I thought. The wood looked perfect in the moonlight. The large dying ferns and the brushwood showed where through thinning foliage the pale light came down. The tree trunks stood up like Gothic columns all around me. They reminded me of the church, and I turned into the bier-balk, and passed through the corpse-gate between the graves to the low porch. I paused for a moment on the stone seat where Laura and I had watched the fading landscape. Then I noticed that the door of the church was open, and I blamed myself for having left it unlatched the other night. We were the only people who ever cared to come to the church except on Sundays, and I was vexed to think that through our carelessness the damp autumn airs had had a chance of getting in and injuring the old fabric. I went in. It will seem strange, perhaps, that I should have gone half-way up the aisle before I remembered—with a sudden chill, followed by as sudden a rush of self-contempt—that this was the very day and hour when, according to tradition, the "shapes drawn out man-size in marble" began to walk.

Having thus remembered the legend, and remembered it with a shiver, of which I was ashamed, I could not do otherwise than walk up towards the altar, just to look at the figures—as I said to myself; really what I wanted was to assure myself, first, that I did not believe the legend, and, secondly, that it was not true. I was rather glad that I had come. I thought now I could tell Mrs. Dorman how vain her fancies were, and how peacefully the marble figures slept on through the ghastly hour. With my hands in my pockets I passed up the aisle. In the grey dim light the eastern end of the church looked larger than usual, and the arches above the two tombs looked larger too. The moon came out and showed me the reason. I stopped short, my heart gave a leap that nearly choked me, and then sank sickeningly.

The "bodies drawn out man-size" *were gone,* and their marble slabs lay wide and bare in the vague moonlight that slanted through the east window.

Were they really gone? or was I mad? Clenching my nerves, I stooped and passed my hand over the smooth slabs, and felt their flat unbroken surface. Had some one taken the things away? Was it some vile practical joke? I would make sure, anyway. In an instant I had made a torch of a newspaper, which happened to be in my pocket, and lighting it held it high above my head. Its yellow glare illumined the dark arches and those slabs. The figures *were* gone. And I was alone in the church; or was I alone?

And then a horror seized me, a horror indefinable and indescribable—an overwhelming certainty of supreme and accomplished calamity. I flung down the torch and tore along the aisle and out through the porch, biting my lips as I ran to keep myself from shrieking aloud. Oh, was I mad—or what was this that possessed me? I leaped the churchyard wall and took the straight cut across the fields, led by the light from our windows. Just as I got over the first stile, a dark figure seemed to spring out of the ground. Mad still with that certainty of misfortune, I made for the thing that stood in my path, shouting, "Get out of the way, can't you!"

But my push met with a more vigorous resistance than I had expected. My arms were caught just above the elbow and held as in a vice, and the raw-boned Irish doctor actually shook me.

"Would ye?" he cried, in his own unmistakable accents—"would ye, then?"

"Let me go, you fool," I gasped. "The marble figures have gone from the church; I tell you they've gone."

He broke into a ringing laugh. "I'll have to give ye a draught to-morrow, I see. Ye've bin smoking too much and listening to old wives' tales."

"I tell you, I've seen the bare slabs."

"Well, come back with me. I'm going up to old Palmer's—his daughter's ill; we'll look in at the church and let me see the bare slabs."

"You go, if you like," I said, a little less frantic for his laughter; "I'm going home to my wife."

"Rubbish, man," said he; "d'ye think I'll permit of that? Are ye to go saying all yer life that ye've seen solid marble endowed with vitality, and me to go all me life saying ye were a coward? No, sir—ye shan't do it."

The night air—a human voice—and I think also the physical contact with this six feet of solid common sense, brought me back a little to my ordinary self, and the word "coward" was a mental shower-bath.

"Come on, then," I said sullenly; "perhaps you're right."

He still held my arm tightly. We got over the stile and back to the church. All was still as death. The place smelt very damp and earthy. We walked up the aisle. I am not ashamed to confess that I shut my eyes: I knew the figures would not be there. I heard Kelly strike a match.

"Here they are, ye see, right enough; ye've been dreaming or drinking, asking yer pardon for the imputation."

I opened my eyes. By Kelly's expiring vesta I saw two shapes lying "in their marble" on their slabs. I drew a deep breath, and caught his hand.

"I'm awfully indebted to you," I said. "It must have been some trick of light, or I have been working rather hard, perhaps that's it. Do you know, I was quite convinced they were gone."

"I'm aware of that," he answered rather grimly; "ye'll have to be careful of that brain of yours, my friend, I assure ye."

He was leaning over and looking at the right-hand figure, whose stony face was the most villainous and deadly in expression.

"By Jove," he said, "something has been afoot here—this hand is broken."

And so it was. I was certain that it had been perfect the last time Laura and I had been there.

"Perhaps some one has *tried* to remove them," said the young doctor.

"That won't account for my impression," I objected.

"Too much painting and tobacco will account for that, well enough."

"Come along," I said, "or my wife will be getting anxious. You'll come in and have a drop of whisky and drink confusion to ghosts and better sense to me."

"I ought to go up to Palmer's, but it's so late now I'd best leave it till the morning," he replied. "I was kept late at the Union, and I've had to see a lot of people since. All right, I'll come back with ye."

I think he fancied I needed him more than did Palmer's girl, so, discussing how such an illusion could have been possible, and deducing from this experience large generalities concerning ghostly apparitions, we walked up to our cottage. We saw, as we walked up the garden-path, that bright light streamed out of the front door, and presently saw that the parlour door was open too. Had she gone out?

"Come in," I said, and Dr. Kelly followed me into the parlour. It was all ablaze with candles, not only the wax ones, but at least a dozen guttering, glaring tallow dips, stuck in vases and ornaments in unlikely places. Light, I knew, was Laura's remedy for nervousness. Poor child! Why had I left her? Brute that I was.

We glanced round the room, and at first we did not see her. The window was open, and the draught set all the candles flaring one way. Her chair was empty and her handkerchief and book lay on the floor. I turned to the window. There, in the recess of the window, I saw her. Oh, my child, my love, had she gone to that window to watch for me? And what had come into the room behind her? To what had she turned with that look of frantic fear and horror? Oh, my little one, had she thought that it was I whose step she heard, and turned to meet—what?

She had fallen back across a table in the window, and her body lay half on it and half on the window-seat, and her head hung down over the table, the brown hair loosened and fallen to the carpet. Her lips were drawn back, and her eyes wide, wide open. They saw nothing now. What had they seen last?

The doctor moved towards her, but I pushed him aside and sprang to her; caught her in my arms and cried—

"It's all right, Laura! I've got you safe, wifie."

She fell into my arms in a heap. I clasped her and kissed her, and called her by all her pet names, but I think I knew all the time that she was dead. Her hands were tightly clenched. In one of them she held something fast. When I was quite sure that she was dead, and that nothing mattered at all any more, I let him open her hand to see what she held.

It was a grey marble finger.

# The Ebony Frame
### Edith Nesbit
### 1891

To be rich is a luxurious sensation—the more so when you have plumbed the depths of hard-up-ness as a Fleet Street hack, a picker-up of unconsidered pars, a reporter, an un-appreciated journalist—all callings utterly inconsistent with one's family feeling and one's direct descent from the Dukes of Picardy.

When my Aunt Dorcas died and left me seven hundred a year and a furnished house in Chelsea, I felt that life had nothing left to offer except immediate possession of the legacy. Even Mildred Mayhew, whom I had hitherto regarded as my life's light, became less luminous. I was not engaged to Mildred, but I lodged with her mother, and I sang duets with Mildred, and gave her gloves when it would run to it, which was seldom. She was a dear good girl, and I meant to marry her some day. It is very nice to feel that a good little woman is thinking of you—it helps you in your work—and it is pleasant to know she will say "Yes" when you say "Will you?"

But, as I say, my legacy almost put Mildred out of my head, especially as she was staying with friends in the country just then.

Before the first gloss was off my new mourning I was seated in my aunt's own armchair in front of the fire in the dining-room of my own house. My own house! It was grand, but rather lonely. I *did* think of Mildred just then.

The room was comfortably furnished with oak and leather. On the walls hung a few fairly good oil-paintings, but the space above the mantelpiece was disfigured by an exceedingly bad print, *The Trial of Lord William Russell*, framed in a dark frame. I got up to look at it. I had visited my aunt with dutiful regularity, but I never remembered seeing this frame before. It was not intended for a print, but for an oil-painting. It was of fine ebony, beautifully and curiously carved.

I looked at it with growing interest, and when my aunt's housemaid—I had retained her modest staff of servants—came in with the lamp, I asked her how long the print had been there.

"Mistress only bought it two days afore she was took ill," she said; "but the frame—she didn't want to buy a new one—so she got this out of the attic. There's lots of curious old things there, sir."

"Had my aunt had this frame long?"

"Oh yes, sir. It come long afore I did, and I've been here seven years come Christmas. There was a picture in it—that's upstairs too—but it's that black and ugly it might as well be a chimley-back."

I felt a desire to see this picture. What if it were some priceless old master in which my aunt's eyes had only seen rubbish?

Directly after breakfast next morning I paid a visit to the lumber-room.

It was crammed with old furniture enough to stock a curiosity shop. All the house was furnished solidly in the early Victorian style, and in this room everything not in keeping with the 'drawing-room suite' ideal was stowed away. Tables of papier-mâché and mother-of-pearl, straight-backed chairs with twisted feet and faded needlework cushions, firescreens of old-world design, oak bureaux with brass handles, a little work-table with its faded moth-eaten silk flutings hanging in disconsolate shreds: on these and the dust that covered them blazed the full daylight as I drew up the blinds. I promised myself a good time in re-enshrining these household gods in my parlour, and promoting the Victorian suite to the attic. But at present my business was to find the picture as 'black as the chimley-back;' and presently, behind a heap of hideous still-life studies, I found it.

Jane the housemaid identified it at once. I took it downstairs carefully and examined it. No subject, no colour were distinguishable. There was a splodge of a darker tint in the middle, but whether it was figure or tree or house no man could have told. It seemed to be painted on a very thick panel bound with leather. I decided to send it to one of those persons who pour on rotting family portraits the water of eternal youth—mere soap and water Mr. Besant tells us it is; but even as I did so the thought occurred to me to try my own restorative hand at a corner of it.

My bath-sponge, soap, and nailbrush vigorously applied for a few seconds showed me that there was no picture to clean! Bare oak presented itself to my persevering brush. I tried the other side, Jane watching me with indulgent interest. The same result. Then the truth dawned on me. Why was the panel so thick? I tore off the leather binding, and the panel divided and fell to the ground in a cloud of dust. There were two pictures—they had been nailed face to face. I leaned them against the wall, and the next moment I was leaning against it myself.

For one of the pictures was myself—a perfect portrait—no shade of expression or turn of feature wanting. Myself—in a cavalier dress, 'love-locks and all!' When had this been done? And how, without my knowledge? Was this some whim of my aunt's?

"Lor', sir!" the shrill surprise of Jane at my elbow; "what a lovely photo it is! Was it a fancy ball, sir?"

"Yes," I stammered. "I—I don't think I want anything more now. You can go."

She went; and I turned, still with my heart beating violently, to the other picture. This was a woman of the type of beauty beloved of Burne Jones and Rossetti—straight nose, low brows, full lips, thin hands, large deep luminous eyes. She wore a black velvet gown. It was a full-length portrait. Her arms rested on a table beside her, and her head on her hands; but her face was turned full forward, and her eyes met those of the spectator bewilderingly. On the table by her were compasses and instruments whose uses I did not know, books, a goblet, and a miscellaneous heap of papers and pens. I saw all this afterwards. I believe it was a quarter of an hour before I could turn my eyes away from hers. I have never seen any other eyes like hers. They appealed, as a child's or a dog's do; they commanded, as might those of an empress.

"Shall I sweep up the dust, sir?" Curiosity had brought Jane back. I acceded. I turned from her my portrait. I kept between her and the woman in the black velvet. When I was alone again I tore down *The Trial of Lord William Russell,* and I put the picture of the woman in its strong ebony frame.

Then I wrote to a frame-maker for a frame for my portrait. It had so long lived face to face with this beautiful witch that I had not the heart to banish it from her presence; from which, it will be perceived that I am by nature a somewhat sentimental person.

The new frame came home, and I hung it opposite the fireplace. An exhaustive search among my aunt's papers showed no explanation of the portrait of myself, no history of the portrait of the woman with the wonderful eyes. I only learned that all the old furniture together had come to my aunt at the death of my great-uncle, the head of the family; and I should have concluded that the resemblance was only a family one, if every one who came in had not exclaimed at the 'speaking likeness.' I adopted Jane's 'fancy ball' explanation.

And there, one might suppose, the matter of the portraits ended. One might suppose it, that is, if there were not evidently a good deal more written here about it. However, to me, then, the matter seemed ended.

I went to see Mildred; invited her and her mother to come and stay with me. I rather avoided glancing at the picture in the ebony frame. I could not forget, nor remember without singular emotion, the look in the eyes of that woman when mine first met them. I shrank from meeting that look again.

I reorganized the house somewhat, preparing for Mildred's visit. I turned the dining-room into a drawing-room. I brought down much of the old-fashioned furniture, and, after a long day of arranging and re-arranging, I sat down before the fire, and, lying back in a pleasant languor, I idly raised my eyes to the picture. I met her dark, deep hazel eyes, and once more my gaze was held fixed as by a strong magic—the kind of fascination that keeps one sometimes staring for whole minutes into one's own eyes in the glass. I gazed into her eyes, and felt my own dilate, pricked with a smart like the smart of tears.

"I wish," I said, "oh, how I wish you were a woman, and not a picture! Come down! Ah, come down!"

I laughed at myself as I spoke; but even as I laughed I held out my arms.

I was not sleepy; I was not drunk. I was as wide awake and as sober as ever was a man in this world. And yet, as I held out my arms, I saw the eyes of the picture dilate, her lips tremble—if I were to be hanged for saying it, it is true. Her hands moved slightly, and a sort of flicker of a smile passed over her face.

I sprang to my feet. "This won't do," I said, still aloud. "Firelight does play strange tricks. I'll have the lamp."

I pulled myself together and made for the bell. My hand was on it, when I heard a sound behind me, and turned—the bell still unrung. The fire had burned low, and the corners of the room were deeply shadowed; but, surely, there—behind the tall worked chair—was something darker than a shadow.

"I must face this out," I said, "or I shall never be able to face myself again." I left the bell, I seized the poker, and battered the dull coals to a blaze. Then I stepped back resolutely, and looked up at the picture. The ebony frame was empty! From the shadow of the worked chair came a silken rustle, and out of the shadow the woman of the picture was coming—coming towards me.

I hope I shall never again know a moment of terror so blank and absolute. I could not have moved or spoken to save my life. Either all the known laws of nature were nothing, or I was mad. I stood trembling, but, I am thankful to remember, I stood still, while the black velvet gown swept across the hearthrug towards me.

Next moment a hand touched me—a hand soft, warm, and human—and a low voice said, "You called me. I am here."

At that touch and that voice the world seemed to give a sort of bewildering half-turn. I hardly know how to express it, but at once it seemed not awful—not even unusual—for portraits to become flesh—only most natural, most right, most unspeakably fortunate.

I laid my hand on hers. I looked from her to my portrait. I could not see it in the firelight.

"We are not strangers," I said.

"Oh no, not strangers." Those luminous eyes were looking up into mine—those red lips were near me. With a passionate cry—a sense of having suddenly recovered life's one great good, that had seemed wholly lost—I clasped her in my arms. She was no ghost—she was a woman—the only woman in the world.

"How long," I said, "O love—how long since I lost you?"

She leaned back, hanging her full weight on the hands that were clasped behind my head.

"How can I tell how long? There is no time in hell," she answered.

It was not a dream. Ah, no—there are no such dreams. I wish to God there could be. When in dreams do I see her eyes, hear her voice, feel her lips against my cheek, hold her hands to my lips, as I did that night—the supreme night of my life? At first we hardly spoke. It seemed enough,

> *after long grief and pain,*
> *To feel the arms of my true love*
> *Round me once again.*

It is very difficult to tell this story. There are no words to express the sense of glad reunion, the complete realization of every hope and dream of a life, that came upon me as I sat with my hand in hers and looked into her eyes.

How could it have been a dream, when I left her sitting in the straight-backed chair, and went down to the kitchen to tell the maids I should want nothing more—that I was busy, and did not wish to be disturbed; when I fetched wood for the fire with my own hands, and, bringing it in, found her still sitting there—saw the little brown head turn as I entered, saw the love in her dear eyes; when I threw myself at her feet and blessed the day I was born, since life had given me this?

Not a thought of Mildred: all the other things in my life were a dream—this, its one splendid reality.

"I am wondering," she said after a while, when we had made such cheer each of the other as true lovers may after long parting—"I am wondering how much you remember of our past."

"I remember nothing," I said. "Oh, my dear lady, my dear sweetheart—I remember nothing but that I love you—that I have loved you all my life."

"You remember nothing—really nothing?"

"Only that I am yours; that we have both suffered; that— Tell me, my mistress dear, all that you remember. Explain it all to me. Make me understand. And yet— No, I don't want to understand. It is enough that we are together."

If it was a dream, why have I never dreamed it again?

She leaned down towards me, her arm lay on my neck, and drew my head till it rested on her shoulder. "I am a ghost, I suppose," she said, laughing softly; and her laughter stirred memories which I just grasped at, and just missed. "But you and I know better, don't we? I will tell you everything you have forgotten. We loved each other —ah! no, you have not forgotten that—and when you came back from the war we were to be married. Our pictures were painted before you went away. You know I was more learned than women of that day. Dear one, when you were gone they said I was a witch. They tried me. They said I should be burned. Just because I had looked at the stars and had gained more knowledge than they, they must needs bind me to a stake and let me be eaten by the fire. And you far away!"

Her whole body trembled and shrank. O love, what dream would have told me that my kisses would soothe even that memory?

"The night before," she went on, "the devil did come to me. I was innocent before—you know it, don't you? And even then my sin was for you—for you—because of the exceeding love I bore you. The devil came, and I sold my soul to eternal flame. But I got a good price. I got the right to come back, through my picture (if any one looking at it wished for me), as long as my picture stayed in its ebony frame. That frame was not carved by man's hand. I got the right to come back to you. Oh, my heart's heart, and another thing I won, which you shall hear anon. They burned me for a witch, they made me suffer hell on earth. Those faces, all crowding round, the crackling wood and the smell of the smoke—"

"O love! no more—no more."

"When my mother sat that night before my picture she wept, and cried, 'Come back, my poor lost child!' And I went to her, with glad leaps of heart. Dear, she shrank from me, she fled, she shrieked and moaned of ghosts. She had our pictures covered from sight and put again in the ebony frame. She had promised me my picture should stay always there. Ah, through all these years your face was against mine."

She paused.

"But the man you loved?"

"You came home. My picture was gone. They lied to you, and you married another woman; but some day I knew you would walk the world again and that I should find you."

"The other gain?" I asked.

"The other gain," she said slowly, "I gave my soul for. It is this. If you also will give up your hopes of heaven I can remain a woman, I can move in your world—I can be your wife. Oh, my dear, after all these years, at last—at last."

"If I sacrifice my soul," I said slowly, with no thought of the imbecility of such talk in our 'so-called nineteenth century'—"if I sacrifice my soul, I win you? Why, love, it's a contradiction in terms. You *are* my soul."

Her eyes looked straight into mine. Whatever might happen, whatever did happen, whatever may happen, our two souls in that moment met, and became one.

"Then you choose—you deliberately choose—to give up your hopes of heaven for me, as I gave up mine for you?"

"I decline," I said, "to give up my hope of heaven on any terms. Tell me what I must do, that you and I may make our heaven here—as now, my dear love."

"I will tell you to-morrow," she said. "Be alone here to-morrow night—twelve is ghost's time, isn't it?—and then I will come out of the picture and never go back to it. I shall live with you, and die, and be buried, and there will be an end of me. But we shall live first, my heart's heart."

I laid my head on her knee. A strange drowsiness overcame me. Holding her hand against my cheek, I lost consciousness. When I awoke the grey November dawn was glimmering, ghost-like, through the uncurtained window. My head was pillowed on my arm, which rested—I raised my head quickly—ah! not on my lady's knee, but on the needle-worked cushion of the straight-backed chair. I sprang to my feet. I was stiff with cold, and dazed with dreams, but I turned my eyes on the picture. There she sat, my lady, my dear love. I held out my arms, but the passionate cry I would have uttered died on my lips. She had said twelve o'clock. Her lightest word was my law. So I only stood in front of the picture and gazed into those grey-green eyes till tears of passionate happiness filled my own.

"Oh, my dear, my dear, how shall I pass the hours till I hold you again?"

No thought, then, of my whole life's completion and consummation being a dream.

I staggered up to my room, fell across my bed, and slept heavily and dreamlessly. When I awoke it was high noon. Mildred and her mother were coming to lunch.

I remembered, at one shock, Mildred's coming and her existence.

Now, indeed, the dream began.

With a penetrating sense of the futility of any action apart from *her,* I gave the necessary orders for the reception of my guests. When Mildred and her mother came I received them with cordiality; but my genial phrases all seemed to be some one else's. My voice sounded like an echo; my heart was other where.

Still, the situation was not intolerable until the hour when afternoon tea was served in the drawing-room. Mildred and her mother kept the conversational pot boiling with a profusion of genteel commonplaces, and I bore it, as one can bear mild purgatories when one is in sight of heaven. I looked up at my sweetheart in the ebony frame, and I felt that anything that might happen, any irresponsible imbecility, any bathos of boredom, was nothing, if, after it all, she came to me again.

And yet, when Mildred, too, looked at the portrait, and said, "What a fine lady! One of your flames, Mr. Devigne?" I had a sickening sense of impotent irritation, which became absolute torture when Mildred—how could I ever have admired that chocolate-box barmaid style of prettiness?—threw herself into the high-backed chair, covering the needlework with her ridiculous flounces, and added, "Silence gives consent! Who is it, Mr. Devigne? Tell us all about her: I am sure she has a story."

Poor little Mildred, sitting there smiling, serene in her confidence that her every word charmed me—sitting there with her rather pinched waist, her rather tight boots, her rather vulgar voice—sitting in the chair where my dear lady had sat when she told me her story! I could not bear it.

"Don't sit there," I said; "it's not comfortable!"

But the girl would not be warned. With a laugh that set every nerve in my body vibrating with annoyance, she said, "Oh, dear! mustn't I even sit in the same chair as your black-velvet woman?"

I looked at the chair in the picture. It was the same; and in her chair Mildred was sitting. Then a horrible sense of the reality of Mildred came upon me. Was all this a reality after all? But for fortunate chance might Mildred have occupied, not only her chair, but her place in my life? I rose.

"I hope you won't think me very rude," I said; "but I am obliged to go out."

I forget what appointment I alleged. The lie came readily enough.

I faced Mildred's pouts with the hope that she and her mother would not wait dinner for me. I fled. In another minute I was safe, alone, under the chill, cloudy autumn sky—free to think, think, think of my dear lady.

I walked for hours along streets and squares; I lived over again and again every look, word, and hand-touch—every kiss; I was completely, unspeakably happy.

Mildred was utterly forgotten: my lady of the ebony frame filled my heart and soul and spirit.

As I heard eleven boom through the fog, I turned, and went home.

When I got to my street, I found a crowd surging through it, a strong red light filling the air.

A house was on fire. Mine.

I elbowed my way through the crowd.

The picture of my lady—that, at least, I could save!

As I sprang up the steps, I saw, as in a dream—yes, all this was *really* dream-like—I saw Mildred leaning out of the first-floor window, wringing her hands.

"Come back, sir," cried a fireman; "we'll get the young lady out right enough."

But *my* lady? I went on up the stairs, cracking, smoking, and as hot as hell, to the room where her picture was. Strange to say, I only felt that the picture was a thing we should like to look on through the long glad wedded life that was to be ours. I never thought of it as being one with her.

As I reached the first floor I felt arms round my neck. The smoke was too thick for me to distinguish features.

"Save me!" a voice whispered. I clasped a figure in my arms, and, with a strange dis-ease, bore it down the shaking stairs and out into safety. It was Mildred. I knew that directly I clasped her.

"Stand back," cried the crowd.

"Every one's safe," cried a fireman.

The flames leaped from every window. The sky grew redder and redder. I sprang from the hands that would have held me. I leaped up the steps. I crawled up the stairs. Suddenly the whole horror of the situation came on me. *"As long as my picture remains in the ebony frame."* What if picture and frame perished together?

I fought with the fire, and with my own choking inability to fight with it. I pushed on. I must save my picture. I reached the drawing-room.

As I sprang in I saw my lady—I swear it—through the smoke and the flames, hold out her arms to me—to me—who came too late to save her, and to save my own life's joy. I never saw her again.

Before I could reach her, or cry out to her, I felt the floor yield beneath my feet, and I fell into the fiery hell below.

How did they save me? What does that matter? They saved me somehow—curse them. Every stick of my aunt's furniture was destroyed. My friends pointed out that, as the furniture was heavily insured, the carelessness of a nightly-studious housemaid had done me no harm.

No harm!

That was how I won and lost my only love.

I deny, with all my soul in the denial, that it was a dream. There are no such dreams. Dreams of longing and pain there are in plenty, but dreams of complete, of unspeakable happiness—ah, no—it is the rest of life that is the dream.

But if I think that, why have I married Mildred, and grown stout and dull and prosperous?

I tell you it is all *this* that is the dream; my dear lady only is the reality. And what does it matter what one does in a dream?

# The Phantom Model

## Hume Nisbet

### 1894

### I

### THE STUDIO

"Rhoda is a very nice girl in her way, Algy, my boy, and poses wonderfully, considering the hundreds of times she has had to do it; but she isn't the model for that Beatrice of yours, and if you want to make a hit of it, you must go further afield, and hook a face not quite so familiar to the British Public."

It was a large apartment, one of a set of studios in that artistic barrack off the Fulham Road, which the landlord, himself a theatrical Bohemian of the first class, has rushed up for the accommodation of youthful luminaries who are yet in the nebulous stage of their Art-course. Each of these hazy specks hopes to shine out a full-lustred star in good time; they have all a proper contempt also for those servile daubsters who consent to the indignity of having R.A. added to their own proper, or assumed, names. Most of them belong to the advanced school of Impressionists, and allow, with reservations, that Jimmy Whitetuft has genius, as they know that he is the most generous, as well as the most epigrammatical, of painters, while Rhoda, the model, also knows that he is the kindest and most chivalrous of patrons, who stands more of her caprices than most of her other masters do, allows her more frequent as well as longer rests in the two hours' sitting, and can always be depended upon for a half-crown on an emergency; good-natured, sardonic Jimmy Whitetuft, who can well appreciate the caprices of any woman, or butterfly of the hour, seeing that he has so many of them himself.

Rhoda Prettyman is occupied at the present moment in what she likes best, warming her young, lithe, Greek-like figure at the stove, while she puffs out vigorous wreaths of smoke from the cigarette she has picked up at the table, in the passing from the dais to the stove. She is perfect in face, hair, figure and colour, not yet sixteen, and greatly in demand by artists and sculptors; a good girl and a merry one, who prefers bitter beer to champagne, a night in the pit to the ceremony of a private box, with a dozen or so of oysters afterwards at a little shop, rather than run her entertainer into the awful expense of a supper at the Criterion or Gatti's. Her father and mother having served as models before her, she has been accustomed to the disporting of her charms *à la vue* on raised daïses from her tenderest years, and to the *patois* of the studios since she could lisp, so that she is as unconscious as a Solomon Island young lady in the bosom of her own family, and can patter "Art" as fluently as any picture dealer in the land.

They are all smoking hard, while they criticize the unfinished Exhibition picture of their host, Algar Gray, during this rest time of the model; Rhoda has not been posing for that picture now, for at the present time the studio is devoted to a life-club, and Rhoda has been hired for this purpose by those hard-working students, who form the young school. Jimmy Whitetuft is the visitor who drops in to cut them up; a marvelous eye for colour and effect Jimmy has, and they are happy in his friendly censorship.

All round the room the easels are set up, with their canvases, in a half-moon range, and on these canvases Rhoda can see herself as in half-a-dozen mirrors, reflected in the same number of different styles as well as postures, for these students aim at originality. But the picture which now occupies their attention is a bishop, half-length, in the second working upon which the well-known features and figure of Rhoda are depicted in thirteenth-century costume as the Beatrice of Dante, and while the young painter looks at his stale design with discontented eyes, his friends act the part of Job's comforters.

"There isn't a professional model in London who can stand for Beatrice, if you want to make her live. They have all been in too many characters already. You must have something fresh."

"Yes, I know," muttered Algar Gray. "But where the deuce shall I find her?"

"Go to the country. You may see something there," suggested Jack Brunton, the landscapist. "I always manage to pick up something fresh in the country."

"The country be blowed for character," growled Will Murray. "Go to the East End of London, if you want a proper Beatrice; to the half-starved crew, with their big eyes and thin cheeks. That's the sort of thing to produce the spiritual longing, wistful look you want. I saw one the other day, near the Thames Tunnel, while I was on the prowl, who would have done exactly."

"What was she?" asked Algar eagerly.

"A Ratcliff Highway stroller, I should say. At any rate, I met her in one of the lowest pubs, pouring down Irish whiskey by the tumbler, with never a wink, and using the homespun in a most delectable fashion. Her mate might have served for Semiramis, and she took four ale from the quart pot, but the other, the Beatrice, swallowed her dose neat, and as if it had been cold water from one of the springs of Paradise, where, in olden times, she was wont to gather flowers."

"Good Heavens! Will, you are atrocious. The sentiment of Dante would be killed by such a woman."

"Realistic, dear boy, that's all. You will find very exquisite flowers sometimes even on a dust-heap, as well as where humanity grows thickest and rankest. We have all to go through the different stages of earthly experience, according to Blavatsky. This Beatrice may have been the original of Dante in the thirteenth century, now going through her Wapping experience. It seems nasty, yet it may be necessary."

"What like was she?"

"What sort of an ideal had you when you first dreamt of that picture, Algy?"

"A tall, slender woman, of about twenty or twenty-two, graceful and refined, with pale face blue-veined and clear, with dark hair and eyes indifferent as to shade, yet out-looking—a soulful gaze from a classical, passive and passionless face."

"That is exactly the Beatrice of the East End shanty and the Irish whisky, the sort of holy after-death calm pervading her, the alabaster-lamp-like complexion lit up by pure spirits undiluted, the general dreamy, indifferent pose—it was all there when I first saw her, only a battle royal afterwards occurred between her and the Amazon over a sailor, during which the alabaster lamp flamed up and Semiramis came off second best; for commend me to your spiritual demons when claws and teeth are wanted. No matter, I have found your model for you; take a turn with me this evening and I'll perhaps be able to point her out to you, the after negotiations I leave in your own romantic hands."

## II

### Dante in the Inferno

It is a considerable distance from the Fulham Road to Wapping even going by 'bus, but as the two artist friends went, it was still farther and decidedly more picturesque.

They were both young men under thirty. Art is not so precocious as literature, and does not send quite so many early potatoes into the market, so that the age of thirty is considered young enough for a painter to have learnt his business sufficiently to be marketable from the picture-dealing point of view.

Will Murray was the younger of the two by a couple of years, but as he had been sent early to fish in the troubled waters of illustration, and forced to provide for himself while studying, he looked much the elder; of a more realistic and energetic turn, he did not indulge in dreams of painting any single *magnum opus,* with which he would burst upon an astonished and enthusiastic world, he could not afford to dream, for he had to work hard or go fasting, and so the height of his aspirations was to paint well enough to win a note of approval from his own particular school, and keep the pot boiling with black and white work.

Algar Gray was a dreamer on five hundred per year, the income beneficent Fortune had endowed him with by reason of his lucky birth; he did not require to work for his daily bread, and as he had about as much prospect of selling his paint-creations, or imitations, as the other members of this new school, he spent the time he was not painting in dreaming about a possible future.

It wasn't a higher ideal, this brooding over fame, than the circumscribed ideal of Will Murray; each member of that young school was too staunch to his principles, and idealized his art as represented by canvas and paints too highly to care one jot about the pecuniary side of it; they painted their pictures as the true poet writes his poems, because it was right in their eyes; they held exhibitions, and preached their canons to a blinded public; the blinded public did not purchase, or even admire; but all that did not matter to the exhibitors so long as they had enough left to pay for more canvases and frames.

Will Murray was keen sighted and blue-eyed, robust in body and for ever on the alert for fresh material to fill his sketch book. Algar Gray was dark to swarthiness, with long, thin face, rich-toned, melancholy eyes, and slender figure; he did not jot down trifles as did his friend, he absorbed the general effect and seldom produced his sketching-block.

Having time on their hands and a glorious October evening before them, they walked to Fulham Wharf and, hiring a wherry there, resolved to go by the old water way to the Tower, and after that begin their search for the Spiritual, through the Inferno of the East.

There is no river in the world to be compared for majesty and the witchery of association, to the Thames; it impresses even the unreading and unimaginative watcher with a solemnity which he cannot account for, as it rolls under his feet and swirls past the buttresses of its many bridges; he may think, as he experiences the unusual effect, that it is the multiplicity of buildings which line its banks, or the crowd of sea-craft which floats upon its surface, or its own extensive spread. In reality he feels, although he cannot explain it, the countless memories which hang for ever like a spiritual fog over its rushing current.

This unseen fog closes in upon the two friends as they take up their oars and pull out into mid-stream; it is a human fog which depresses and prepares them for the scenes into which they must shortly add their humanity; there is no breaking away from it, for it reaches up to Oxford and down to Sheppey, the voiceless thrilling of past voices, the haunting chill of dead tragedies, the momentous hush of acted history.

It wafts towards them on the brown sails of the gliding barges where the solitary figures stand upright at the stern like so many Charons steering their hopeless freights; it

shapes the fantastic clouds of dying day overhead, from
the fumes of countless fires, and the breaths from countless lips, it is the overpowering absorption of a single soul
composed of many parts; the soul of a great city, past
and present, of a mighty nation with its crowded events,
crushing down upon the heart of a responsive stream, and
this is the mystic power of the pulsating, eternal Thames.

They bear down upon Westminster, the ghost-con-
secrated Abbey, and the history-crammed Hall, through
the arches of the bridge with a rush as the tide swelters
round them; the city is buried in a dusky gloom save where
the lights begin to gleam and trail with lurid reflections
past black, velvety-looking hulls—a dusky city of golden
gleams. St. Paul's looms up like an immense bowl reversed,
squat, un-English, and undignified in spite of its great
size; they dart within the sombre shadows of the Bridge
of Sighs, and pass the Tower of London, with the rising
moon making the sky behind it luminous, and the crowd
of shipping in front appear like a dense forest of withered
pines, and then mooring their boat at the steps beyond,
with a shuddering farewell look at the eel-like shadows
and the glittering lights of that writhing river, with its
burthen seen and invisible, they plunge into the purlieus
of Wapping.

Through silent alleys where dark shadows fleeted past
them like forest beasts on the prowl; through bustling
market-places where bloaters predominated, into crammed
gin-palaces where the gas flashed over faces whereon was
stamped the indelible impression of a protest against
creation; brushing tatters which were in gruesome harmony with the haggard or bloated features.

Will Murray was used to this medley and pushed on
with a definite purpose, treating as burlesque what made
the dreamer groan with impotent fury that so dire a poverty,
so unspeakable a degradation, could laugh and seem hilarious

even under the fugitive influence of Old Tom. They were not human beings these breathing and roaring masses, they were an appalling army of spectres grinning at an abashed Maker.

"Here we are at last, Algy," observed Will, cheerily, as the pair pushed through the swinging doors of a crammed bar and approached the counter, "and there is your Beatrice."

III

THE PICTURE

The impressionists of Fulham Road knew Algy Gray no more, after that first glimpse which he had of Beatrice. His studio was once again to let, for he had removed his baggage and tent eastward, so as to be near the woman who would not and could not come West.

His first impressions of her might have cured many a man less refined or sensitive;—a tall young woman with pallid face leaning against the bar and standing treat to some others of her kind; drinking furiously, while from her lips flowed a husky torrent of foulness, unrepeatable; she was in luck when he met her, and enjoying a holiday with some of her own sex, and therefore wanted no male interference for that night, so she repulsed his advances with frank brutality, and forced him to retire from her side baffled.

Yet, if she offended his refined ears, there was nothing about her to offend his artistic eyes; she had no ostrich feathers in her hat, and no discordancy about the colours of her shabby costume; it was plain and easy-fitting, showing the grace of her willowy shape; her features were statuesque, and as Will had said, alabaster-like in their pure pallor.

That night Algar Gray followed her about, from place to place, watching her beauty hungrily, even while he wondered at the unholy thirst that possessed her, and which seemed to be sateless, a quenchless desire which gave her no rest, but drove her from bar to bar, while her money lasted; she appeared to him like a soulless being, on whom neither fatigue nor debauchery could take effect.

At length, as midnight neared, she turned to him with a half smile and beckoned him towards her; she had ignored him hitherto, although she knew he was hunting her down.

"I say, matey, I'm stumped up, so you can stand me some drink if you like."

She laughed scornfully when she saw him take soda water for his share, it was a weakness which she could neither understand nor appreciate.

"You ain't Jacky the Terror, are you?" she enquired carelessly as she asked him for another drink.

"Certainly not, why do you ask?"

"'Cos you stick so close to me. I thought perhaps you had spotted me out for the next one, not that I care much whether you are or not, now that my money is done."

His heart thrilled at the passivity of her loneliness as he looked at her; she had accepted his companionship with indifference, unconscious of her own perfection, utterly apathetic to everything; she a woman that nothing could warm up.

She led him to the home which she rented, a single attic devoid of furniture, with the exception of a broken chair and dilapidated table, and a mattress which was spread out in the corner, a wretched nest for such a matchless Beatrice.

And as she reclined on the mattress and drank herself to sleep from the bottle which she had made him buy for her, he sat at the table, and while the tallow candle lasted, he watched her, and sketched her in his pocket-book, after which, when the candle had dropped to the bottom of the bottle which served for a candlestick, and the white moonlight fell through the broken window upon that pure white slumbering face, so still-and death-like, he crept softly down the stairs, thralled with but one idea.

Next day when he came again she greeted him almost affectionately, for she remembered his lavishness the night before and was grateful for the refreshment which he sent out for her. Yes, she had no objections to let him paint her if he paid well for it, and came to her, but she wasn't going out of her beat for any man; so finding that there was another attic in the same house to let, he hired it, got the window altered to suit him and set to work on his picture.

The model, although untrained, was a patient enough sitter to Algar Gray when the mood took her, but she was very variable in her moods, and uncertain in her temper, as spirit-drunkards mostly are. Sometimes she was reticent and sullen, and would not be coaxed or bribed into obedience to his wishes, at other times she was lazy and would not stir from her own mattress, where she lay like a lovely savage, letting him admire her transparent skin, with the blue veins intersecting it, and a luminous glow pervading it, until his spirit melted within him, and he grew almost as purposeless as she was.

Under these conditions the picture did not advance very fast, for now November was upon them with its fogs. Very often on the days when she felt amiable enough to sit, he had no light to take advantage of her mood, while at other times she was either away drinking with her own kind or else sulking in her bleak den.

If he wondered at first how she could keep the purity of her complexion with the life she led or how she never appeared overcome with the quantity of spirits she consumed, he no longer did so since she had given him her confidence.

She was a child of the slums in spite of her refinement of face, figure and neatness of attire; who, six years before had been given up by the doctors for consumption, and informed that she had not four months of life left. Previous to this medical verdict she had worked at a match factory, and been fairly well conducted, but with the recklessness of her kind, who resemble sailors closely, she had pitched aside caution, resolved to make the most of her four months left, and so abandoned herself to the life she was still leading.

She had existed almost entirely upon raw spirits for the past six years, surprised herself that she had lived so long past her time, yet expecting death constantly; she was as one set apart by Death, and no power could reclaim her from that doom, a reckless, condemned prisoner, living under a very uncertain reprieve, and without an emotion or a desire left except the vain craving to deaden thought, and be able to die *game,* a craving which would not be satisfied.

Algar Gray, for the sake of an ideal, had linked himself to a soul already damned, which still held on to its fragile casement, a soul which was dragging him down to her own hell; her very cold indifference to him drew him after her, and enslaved him, her unholy transparent loveliness bewitched him, and the foulness of her lips and language no longer caused him a shudder, since it could not alter her exquisite lines or those pearly tints which defied his palette; and yet he did not love the woman; his whole desire was to transfer her perfection to his canvas before grim Death came to snatch her clay from the vileness of its surroundings.

## IV

### A Lost Soul

December and January had passed with clear, frosty skies, and the picture of Beatrice was at length ready for the Exhibition.

When a man devotes himself body and spirit to a single object, if he has training and aptitude, no matter how mediocre he may be in ordinary affairs, he will produce something so nearly akin to a work of genius as to deceive half the judges who think themselves competent to decide between genius and talent.

Algar Gray had studied drawing at a good training-school, and was acknowledged by competent critics to be a true colourist, and for the last three months he had lived for the picture which he had just completed, therefore the result was satisfactory even to him. Beatrice, the ideal love of Dante, looked out from his canvas in the one attic of this Wapping slum, while Beatrice, the model, lay dead on her old mattress in the other.

He had attempted to make her home more home-like and comfortable for her, but without success; what he ordered from the upholsterer she disposed of promptly to the brokers, laughing scornfully at his efforts to redeem her, and mocking coarsely at his remonstrances, as she always had done at his temperate habits. He was not of her kind, and she had no sympathy with him, or in any of his ways; she had tolerated him only for the money he was able to give her, and so had burnt herself out of life without a kindly word or thought about him.

She had died as she wished to do, that is, she had passed away silently and in the darkness, leaving him to discover what was left of her, in the chill of a winter morning, a corpse not whiter or less luminous than she had been in life, with the transparent neck and delicate arms, blue-veined and beautiful, and the face composed with the immortal air of quiet which it had always possessed.

She had lasted just long enough to enable him to put the finishing touches upon her replica, and now that the undertakers had taken away the matchless original, he thought that he might return to his own people, and take with him the object which he had coveted and won. The woman herself seemed nothing to him while she lay waiting upon her last removal in the room next to his, but now that it was empty, and only her image remained before him, he was strangely dissatisfied and restless.

He had caught the false appearance of purity which was about her, but all unaware to himself, this constant communication of the more natural part had been absorbed into his being, until now the picture looked like a body waiting for the return of its own mocking spirit, and for the first time, regretful wishes began to tug at his heart-strings; it was no longer the Beatrice of Dante that he wanted, but the Beatrice who had mockingly enslaved him with her vileness, and whom he had permitted to escape from him for an ideal, she who had never tempted him in life, was now tormenting him past endurance with hopeless longings.

He had gone out that afternoon with the intention of returning to his studio in the West End, and making arrangements for bringing his picture there, but after wandering aimlessly about the evil haunts where he had so often followed his late model, he found that he could not tear himself from that dismal round. A shadowy form seemed to glide before him from one gin-palace to another as she had done in life; the places where she had leaned against the bars seemed still to be occupied by her cold and mocking presence, no longer passive, but repulsing him as she had done in the early part of the first night, while he grew hungry and eager for her friendship.

She was before him on the pavement as he turned towards his attic; her husky, oath-clogged voice sounded in his ears as he passed an alley, and when he rushed forward to seize her, two other women fled from him out of the gloom with shrieks of fear. All the voices of these unfortunates are alike, and he had made a mistake.

The ice had given way on the morning of her death, and the streets were now slushy and wet, with a drizzling fog obscuring objects, so that only an instinct led him

back to his temporary studio; he would draw down his
blind and light his lamp, and spend the last evening of the
slums in looking at his work.

It appeared almost a perfect piece of painting, and likely to attract much notice when it was exhibited. The dress
which Beatrice had worn still lay over the back of the chair
near the door, where she had carelessly flung it when last
she took it off. He turned his back to the dress-covered
chair and looked at the picture. Yes, it was the Beatrice
whom Dante yearned over all his life—as she appeared to
him at the bridge, with the same pure face and pathetic
eyes, but not the Beatrice whom he, Algar Gray, passed
over while she lived, and now longed for with such unutterable longing when it was too late.

He flung himself down before his *magnum opus,* and
buried his face in his hands with passionate and hopeless
regret.

Was that a husky laugh down in the court below, on the
stairs, or in the room beside him?—her devil's laugh when
she would go her own way in spite of his remonstrances.

He raised his head and looked behind him to where the
dress had been lying crumpled and away from his picture.
God of Heaven! his dead model had returned and now
stood at the open door beckoning upon him to come to
her, with her lovely transparent arm bare to the elbow, and
once more dressed in the costume which she had cast aside.

He looked no more at his replica, but followed the
mocking spirit down the stairs, into the fog-wrapped alley,
and onwards where she led him.

Down towards Wapping Old Stairs, where the shapeless hulks of the ships and barges loomed out from the
swirling, rushing black river like ghosts, as she was, who
floated towards them, luring him downwards, amongst
the slime, to the abyss from which her lost soul had been
recalled by his evil longings.

# Huguenin's Wife

M. P. SHIEL

1895

Huguenin, my friend—the man of Art and thrills and impulses,—the finished *boulevardier,* the *persifleur*—must, I concluded with certainty, be frenzied. So, at least, I reasoned when, after long years of silence, I received from him this letter:—

"'*Sdili,*' my friend; that is the name by which they now call this ancient Delos. Wherefore has it been written, 'so passeth the glory of the world.'

"Ah! but to me it is—as to her it was—still Delos, the Sacred Island, the birthplace of Apollo, son of Leto! On the summit of Cynthus I look from my dwelling, and within the wide reach of the Cyclades perceive even yet the fruity offerings arriving from Syria, from Sicily, from Egypt; I see the barks that bring the sacred envoys of Pan-Ionium to festival—I note the flutter of their hallowed garments— on the breeze once more floats to me their 'Songs of Deliverance.'

"The island now belongs almost entirely to me. I am, too, almost its sole inhabitant. It is, you know, only four miles long, and half as broad, and I have purchased every available foot of its surface. On the flat top of the granite Cynthus I live, and here, my friend, shall I die. Chains more inexorable and horrible than any which the limbs of Prometheus ever knew bind me to this crag.

"A friend! a friend! That is the thing after which my sick spirit pants. A *living man:* of the dead I have enough; of living monsters, ah, too much! An aged servant or two, who seem persistently to shun me—this is all I possess of human fellowship. Would that I dared to ask you, an old companion, to come to the solace of a sinking man in this place of desolation!"

The letter continued long in this strain of mingled rhapsody and despair, containing, moreover, a lengthy disquisition on the Pythagorean doctrine of the metempsychosis of the soul. Three times did the words "living monsters" occur. Such a communication, coming from *him,* did not fail to excite my utmost curiosity and pity.

From London to Delos is no inconsiderable journey; yet, conquered during the course of a long vacation by an irresistible impulse, and the fond memories of other days, I actually found myself, on a starry night, disembarking on the sands that bound the once famous harbour of the tiny Greek island. My arrival may be dated by the fact that it fell out just two months before the very extraordinary natural phenomena of which Delos was the scene during the night of August 13th, 1880. I crossed the ring of flat land which nearly encircles the islet, and began the ascent of the central mountain. The slumberous air languished with the wild breath of rose and jessamine and almond; the pipe of the cicala and the gleam of the firefly were not wanting to add to the narcotic charms of this land of dreams. In less than an hour I walked into a tangled garden, and placed my hand on the shoulder of a tall, stooping man, dressed in Attic attire, who walked solitary under the trees.

With a fearful start he turned and faced me.

"Oh," he said, panting, and placing both his hands upon his chest, "I was greatly surprised! My heart—"

He could utter no more. It was Huguenin, and yet not he. The heavy beard rolling down his white woolen garments was, I could see, still black as ever; but the masses of unkempt hair which floated with every zephyr about his face and neck were bleached to the whiteness of snow. He stared at me through the dull and cavernous eyes of a man long dead.

We walked into the house together. The mere sight of the building was enough to convince me that in some mysterious way, to some morbid degree, the Past had fettered and darkened the intellect of my friend. The mansion was of the purely Hellenic type, but nothing less than inconceivable in extent—a wilderness rather than a habitation. I found myself in an ancient Greek house—only, a Greek house multiplied many times over into an endless, continuous congeries of Greek houses. It consisted of a single story, though here and there on the vast flat roof there rose a second layer of apartments. These latter were reached by ladders. We walked through a door—opening inwards—into a passage, which in turn led us to an oblong marble court-yard; this was the *aule,* surrounded by Corinthian pillars, and having in the centre an altar of stone to *Zeus Herkeios.* Around this court on every hand was ranged a series of halls, chambers, *thalamoi,* hung with rich velvets; and the whole mighty house—made up of a hundred and a hundred reproductions of such court-yards with their surrounding chambers—formed a trackless desert of rooms, through whose uniform labyrinths the most cunning would assuredly fail to find his way.

"This building," said Huguenin to me, some days after my arrival, "this building—every stone, plank, drapery of it—was the creation of my wife's wild and restless fancy."

I stared at him.

"You doubt that I have, or had, a wife? Come, then, with me; you shall—you shall—see her face."

He led the way through the dark and windowless house, lighted throughout the day and night by the dim purple radiance shed from many small, open lamps of earthenware filled with the fragrant *nardinum,* an oil pressed from the flower of the Arabian grass *nardus.*

I followed the emaciated figure of Huguenin through a great number of the gloomy chambers. As he moved slowly forward, visibly panting, I noticed that he kept his form bent downward, seeming to seek for something; and this something I soon found to be a scarlet thread, laid down to afford guidance for the feet through the mazes of the house, and running along the black floor. Suddenly he stopped before the door of one of the apartments called *amphithalamoi,* and, himself remaining without, motioned to me to enter.

I am not a man of what might be called "a tremulous diathesis," yet not without a tremor did I glance round the room. For a time I could discern nothing under the sombre glimmer radiated from a single *lampas* pendent from wrought brazen chains. But at length a great painting in oils, unframed, occupying nearly one whole side of the chamber, grew upon my sight. It was the picture of a woman. My heart throbbed with a most strange, deep excitement as I gazed upon her lineaments.

She stood erect, robed in a flowing, crimson, embroidered peplos, with head slightly thrown back, and one hand and arm pointing stiffly outward and upward. The countenance was not merely Grecian—ancient Grecian, as distinct from modern—but it was so in a highly exaggerated and unlifelike degree. Was the woman, I asked myself, more lovely than ever mortal was before—or more hideous? She was the one or the other, or both; but the riddle baffled me. The Lamia of Keats arose before me—

that "shape of gorgeous hue, vermilion-spotted, golden, green and blue." A hardly-breathing surprise of eyes held me fixed as the image slowly took possession of my vision. Here, then, I muttered, was the Gorgon's head, whose hair was serpents and her eye a basilisk's; and as I so thought, I reflected, too, on the myth of how from the dripping blood of Medusa's head strange creatures sprang to life; and then, with a shuddering abhorrence, I remembered Huguenin's childish ravings about "monsters." I drew nearer, in order to analyze the impression almost of dread wrought upon me, and I quickly found—or thought I found—the key. It lay, surely, in the woman's eyes. They were the very eyes of the tiger: circular, green, large, with glittering yellow radii. I hurried from the room.

"You have seen her?" asked Huguenin, with a cunning, eager distortion of his ashen face.

"Yes, Huguenin, I have seen her. She is very beautiful."

"She painted it herself," he said in a whisper.

"Really!"

"She considered herself—she was—the greatest painter who has lived since Apelles."

"But now—where is she now?"

He brought his lips quite close to my ear.

"She is dead. You, at any rate, would call her so."

This ambiguity appeared to me only the more singular when I discovered that it was his habit, at stated intervals, to make regular and stealthy visits to distant parts of the dwelling. Our bed-chambers being contiguous, I could not fail, as time passed, to notice that he would rise in the dead of night, when he supposed me asleep, and gathering together the fragments of our last meal, depart rapidly and silently with them through the dim and vast house, led always in one particular direction by the scarlet thread of silk which ran along the floor.

I now set myself strenuously to the study of Huguenin.
The nature of his physical malady, at least, was clear. He
laboured under the singular affection to which physicians
have given the name of Cheyne Stoke's Respiration, the
disease manifesting itself at intervals by compelling him
to lie back in a perfect agony of inhalation, and groan for
air; the bones of his cheeks seemed on the point of appearing through their sere wrapping of mummy-skin; the *alœ*
of his nose never rested from an extravagance of expansion and retraction. But even this ruin of a body might,
I considered, be made partially whole, were it not that
to lull the rage and fever of such a *mind* the world contained no anodyne. For one thing, a most curious belief
in some unnamed fate hanging over the island on which
he lived haunted him. Again and again he recalled to me
all that in the long past had been written about Delos:
the strange notion contained both in the Homeric and the
Alexandrian hymns to the Delian Apollo that the island
was *floating;* or that it was merely secured by chains; or
that it had only been thrown up from the deeps as a temporary resting-place for Ortygia in her travail; or that it
might *sink* before the spurning foot of the new-born god.
He was never tired, through long hours, of pursuing, as
if in soliloquy, a kind of somnolent, mystical exegesis of
such passages as we read together. "Do you know," he said,
"that the ancients really supposed the streams of Delos to
rise and fall with the rise and fall of the Nile? Could anything point more clearly to a belief in the extraordinary
nature of the island, its far-reaching volcanic affinities,
occult geologic eccentricities?" Often would he repeat
the punning hexameter line of the very ancient Sibylline
prophecy—

ἔσται καὶ Σάμος ἄμμος ἐσεῖται Δῆλος ἄδηλος;
(And Samos shall be sand, and Delos (the far-seen) sink from sight.)

often, too, having repeated it, he would strike from the
repining chords of an Æolian lyre the air of a threnody
which, as he told me, his wife had composed to suit the
verse; and when to the funeral wail of this dirge—so wild,
so mournful, that I could never hear it without a shudder—Huguenin added the melancholy note of his now hollow and plaintive voice, the intensity of effect produced
on me reached the intolerable degree, and I was glad of the
dubious and pallid and purple gloaming of the mansion,
which partially hid my face from him.

"Observe, however," he added one day, "the meaning
of the implied epithet 'far-seen' as applied to Delos: it
means 'glorious,' 'illustrious'—far-seen to the spiritual
rather than to the bodily eye, for the island is not very
mountainous. The words 'sink from sight' must therefore
be supposed to have the corresponding significance of an
extinction of this glory. And now judge whether or no this
prophecy has not been already fulfilled, when I tell you
that this sacrosanct land, which no dog's foot was once
allowed to touch, on which no man was permitted to be
born or to die, bears at this moment on its bosom a monster fouler than the brain of demon ever conceived. A fearful literal and physical fulfilment of the prophecy cannot,
I consider, be far distant."

That all this esotericism was not native to Huguenin I
was certain. His mind, I was convinced, had been ploughed
into by some tremendous energy, before ever this rank
growth had choked it. I drew him on, little by little, to
speak of his wife.

She was, he told me, of a very antique Athenian family, which by constant effort had conserved its purity of
blood. It was while passing southward through Greece in
a world-weary mood, some years before my visit, that he
came one night to the village of Castri; and there, on
the site of the ancient Delphi, in the centre of an angry

crowd of Greeks and Turks, who threatened to rend her to pieces, he first saw Andromeda, his wife. "This incredible courage," he said, "this vast originality was hers, to take upon herself the part of a modern Hypatia—to venture on the task of the bringing back of the gods, in the midst of a fanatical people, at the latter end of a century like the present. The furious mob from which I rescued her was standing around her in front of the vestibule of a just completed temple to Apollo, whose worship she was then and there attempting to restore."

The love of the woman fastened on her preserver with passionate intensity. Huguenin felt himself constrained by the impulse of an irresistible Will. They were united, and came at her bidding to live in the grey abode of her creation at Delos. In this solitude, under this shadow, the man and the woman faced each other. As the months passed the husband found that he had married a seer of visions and a dreamer of dreams. And visions of what hue! and dreams of what madness! He confessed to me that he was greatly awed by her, and with this awe was blended a feeling which, if it was not fear, was akin to fear. That he loved her not at all he now knew, while the excess of her passion for him he grew to regard with the hate which men feel for the distilled elixir of the hemlock. Yet his mind inevitably took on the lurid hue of hers. He drank in unfailingly all her creeds. He followed her in the same way that a satellite follows a world. When for days together she hid herself from him and disappeared, he would wander desolate and full of search over the pathless house. Finding that she habitually yielded her body to the lotus delights of certain opiate seeds produced on the island, he found the courage to frown and warn, and ended by himself becoming a bond-slave to the drowsy ganja of India. So too with the most strange fascination she exercised over the animal world: he disliked it—he dreaded it; regarded

it as excessive and unnatural; but he looked on only with
the furtive, pale eye of suspicion, and said nothing. When
she walked she was accompanied by a long magnetized
queue of living things, felines in particular, and birds of
large size. Dogs, on the contrary, shunned her, bristling.
She had brought with her from the mainland a collection of these followers, of which Huguenin had never seen
the half; they were imprisoned in unknown nooks of the
building; ever and anon she would vanish from the house,
to reappear with new companions. Her kindness to these
dumb creatures should, I presume, have been amply sufficient to account for her power over them; but Huguenin's
mind, already grown morbid, probed darkly after some
other explanation. The primary *motif* of this unquietness
doubtless lay in his wife's fanaticism on the subject of the
Pythagorean theory of the transmigration of souls. On this
theme Andromeda, it was clear, was violently deranged.
She would stand, he declared, with outstretched arm, with
eye wild-staring, with rigid body, and in a rapid, guttural
recitative—like a rapt, delirious Pythoness—would proph-
esy of the eternal mutations prepared for the spirit of man.
She would dwell, above all, with a kind of contempt, on
the limitations of animal forms in the actual world, and
would indignantly insist that the spirit of an extraordinary
and original man, disembodied, *should and must* re-em-
body itself in a correspondingly extraordinary and original
form. "And," she would often add, "such forms do really
exist on the earth, but the God, willing to save the race
from frenzy, hides them from the eyes of common men."

It was long, however, before I could induce Huguenin
to speak of the final catastrophe of his singular wedded
life. He related it in these words:—

"You now know that Andromeda was among the great
painters of the world—you have seen her picture of
herself. One day, after dilating, as was her wont, on the

narrow limitation of forms, she said suddenly, 'But you, too, shall be of the initiated: come, come, you shall see *something.*' She went swiftly forward, beckoning, looking back repeatedly to smile on me a loving patronage, with the condescension of a priestess to a neophyte; I followed, till before a lately finished painting she stopped, pointing. I will not attempt—the attempt would be folly—to tell you what thing of horror and madness I saw before me on the canvas; nor can I explain in words the tempest of anger, of loathing and disgust, that stirred within me at the sight. Kindled by the blasphemy of her fancy, I raised my hand to strike her head; and to this hour I know not if I struck her. My hand, it is true, felt the sensation of contact with something soft and yielding; but the blow, if blow there were, was surely too slight to harm the frame of a creature far feebler than the human. Yet she fell; the film of coming death grew over her dull, upbraiding eyes; one last word only she spoke, pointing to the Uncleanness: 'In the flesh you may yet behold it!' and so, still pointing, pointing, she passed away.

"I bore her body, embalmed in the Greek manner by an expert of Corinth, to one of the smaller apartments on the roof of the house. I saw, as I turned to leave her in the gloom of the strait and lonely chamber, the mortal smile on her waxen face within the open coffin. Two weeks later I went again to visit her. My friend, she had vanished utterly—save that the bones remained; and from the vacant coffin, above the now fleshless skull, two eyes—living— the very eyes of Andromeda's soul, but full of a new-born, intenser light—the eyes, too, of the pictured horror whose whole form I now discerned in the darkness—gleamed out upon me. I slammed to the door, and fainted on the floor."

"The suggestion," I said, "which you seem to wish to convey is that of a transition of forms from the human to the animal; but, surely, the explanation that the monster, brought secretly by your wife into the house, imprisoned unawares by you with the dead, and maddened by hunger, fed on the uncovered body, is, if not less horrible, at least less improbable."

He looked doubtingly at me for a moment, and then replied: "There was no monster imprisoned with the dead. Be not rash with 'explanations.' You do not require me to tell you, what you must know, that there are many more things in earth—to say nothing of heaven—than were ever dreamt of in your philosophy."

But at least, I urged, he would see the necessity of flying from that place. He answered with the extraordinary avowal that it was no longer doubtful to him, from the effect which any neglect to minister to the creature's wants produced on his own bodily health, that his life was intimately bound up with the life of the being he stayed to maintain; that with the *second* murder of which he should be guilty—nay, with the very attempt to commit it, as, for example, by flight from the house—his own life would inevitably be forfeited.

I accordingly formed the resolution to work the deliverance of my friend in spite of himself. Two months had now passed; the end of my visit was drawing near; yet his maladies of brain and body were not alleviated. It tortured me to think of leaving him once more alone, a prey to the manias which distracted him.

That very day, while he slept his damp, unquiet, opiate slumbers, I started out on the track indicated by the scarlet thread. So far it led—and the rooms through which it passed were of such uniformity, and the path so serpentine, and the sameness of construction on every hand so unbroken—that I could not doubt but that, the clue once snapped at any point, the journey to the desired end could be accomplished only by the most improbable good fortune. I followed the thread to its termination: it stopped at the foot of a ladder-like stair, which I ascended. At the top of the stair, and close to it, I was faced by a narrow wall, in which was a closed wooden door; in the door a hole large enough to admit the hand. As I placed my foot on the topmost step, a long, low, plaintive whine, with a sickening likeness to a human wail, broke upon my ear.

I hurriedly descended the steps. Some little distance from them I broke the silken thread, and, gathering it up in my hand as I went, again broke it near the region of the house which we occupied.

"Hereby," I said, as I held the gathered portion to the flame of a lamp, "shall a soul be saved alive."

I watched him later on through half-closed lids, as he departed, haggard and shivering, on his nightly errand. My heart throbbed under an agony of disquiet while I awaited his long-delayed return.

He came swiftly and softly into my room, and shook me by the shoulder. On his face was a look of unusual calmness, of dignity and mystery.

"Wake up," he said. "I wish you—I am a sorry host, am I not?—I wish you to leave me to-night, at once; to leave the island—*now.*"

"But tell me—" I gasped.

"Nay, nay; I will take no refusal. Trust me this once, and go. There is a danger here. Destiny is against me—an impudent destiny, careless even to conceal its hand. Go. One or two of the fisher-folk of the harbour will convey you over to Rhenea before the morning light, and you will be saved."

"But saved from what?"

"From what? I cannot tell you: from the destiny, whatever it be, which awaits me. Do you know—can you dream—that the thread on which my life depends is *snapped?*"

"But suppose I tell you—"

"You can tell me nothing. Ah . . . you hear that?"

He held up his hand and listened. It was a sudden shriek of the wind around the house.

"It is but the rising wind," I muttered, starting up.

"Ah, but that—that which followed. Did you not *feel* it?"

"Huguenin, I felt nothing."

He had clasped with both arms a marble pillar, against which his forehead rested, while with one foot he gently and mechanically patted the floor. In this posture, now utterly demoralized and craven, he remained for some minutes. The wail of the wind was heard at intervals. Suddenly he turned towards me, with a ghastly face and the scream of a frightened woman.

"Now—now at least—*you feel it!*"

I could no longer deny. It was as if the whole island had gently rocked to and fro on a pivot.

Thoroughly unnerved myself, trembling more with awe than with terror, I seized Huguenin's arm, and sought to draw him from the pillar, which, muttering low, he still embraced. He sullenly refused to stir; and I, resolved in any event to stay by him, sat near. The seismic agitation increased. But he seemed to take no further note of anything,—only, with the regularity of a clock's oscillations, the tripudiary automatic motion of his foot persisted. In this way an hour, two hours, passed. At the end of that time the rocking movement of the earth had become intense, rapid and continuous.

There came a moment when, overwhelmed by a new panic, I sprang to my feet and shook him.

"Headstrong man!" I cried, "have you then parted with every sense? Do you not smell—can you not feel—that the house is in flames?"

His eyes, which had grown dark and dull, blazed up instantly with a new madness.

"Then," he shouted, with the roar of a clarion,—"then she shall—I say she *shall* be saved! The cheetah—*the feathered cheetah!*"

Before I could lay hold of the now foaming maniac, he had dashed past me into a corridor. I followed behind in hottest pursuit. The carpets and hangings, as yet but dully glowing, filled the passages with the smoke of Tophet. I hoped that Huguenin, weak of lung, would fall choked and exhausted. Some power seemed to lend him strength— he rushed onward like the wind; some sure, mysterious instinct seemed to guide him—not once did he falter or hesitate.

The long chase through the cracking house, burning now on every side, was over. The just intuitions of insanity had not failed the madman—he reached the goal for which he panted. I saw him hasten up the half-consumed ladder, whose foot was already in a lake of flame. He rushed to the smouldering wooden door of the tomb of Andromeda, and tore it wide open. And now from out the vault there burst—above the roaring of the fire, and the whistle of the tempest, and the thousandfold rattle of the earthquake—a shrill and raucous shriek, which turned my blood to ice; and I saw proceeding from the darkness a creature whose native loathsomeness human language has no vocabulary to describe. For if I say that it was a cheetah—of very large size—its eyes a yellow liquid conflagration—its fat and boneless body swathed in a thick panoply of dark grey feathers, vermilion-tipped—with a similitude of miniature wings on its back—with a wide, vast, downward-sweeping tail like the tail of a bird of paradise,—how by such words can I image forth all the retching nausea, all the bottomless hate and fear, with which I looked? The fire, it was evident, had already reached the body of the beast; already it flamed. I saw it fly, rather than spring, at Huguenin's head; the burial of its fangs in his flesh, the meeting of its teeth about his windpipe, I saw. He tottered—gurgling—tearing at the feathery horror—backward over the spot where a moment before the stair had stood; together they fell into the sea of flame beneath.

I ran in headlong haste from the house, discovering by good chance an egress. The night was clear, yet all the winds seemed to tumble in disenchained ecstasy about the islet. As I descended I noted the scathed and scorched aspect of the trees and of certain of the rocks; at one spot a multitude of deep, smooth, conical openings, edged with grey, glowing scoriae, riveted my attention. Still lower, I stood on a bluff promontory and looked sheer into the sea. The sight was sublime and appalling. The deep—without billow or foam or ripple—luminous far down with phosphorescences—rushed, like some lambent lamina yoked to the fiery steeds of Diomedes, with a steady, intense, almost dazzling impetuosity towards the island. Delos, indeed, seemed to float—to swim, painfully struggling, like a little doomed bird, against the all-engulfing element. I passed with the earliest light from this mystic shrine of ancient piety. Among the last sights that greeted my gaze was the still ascending reek of the blighted and accursed dwelling of Huguenin.

# The Old Portrait
## Hume Nisbet
### 1900

Old-fashioned frames are a hobby of mine. I am always on the prowl amongst the framers and dealers in curiosities for something quaint and unique in picture frames. I don't care much for what is inside them, for being a painter it is my fancy to get the frames first and then paint a picture which I think suits their probable history and design. In this way I get some curious and I think also some original ideas.

One day in December, about a week before Christmas, I picked up a fine but dilapidated specimen of wood-carving in a shop near Soho. The gilding had been worn nearly away, and three of the corners broken off; yet as there was one of the corners still left, I hoped to be able to repair the others from it. As for the canvas inside this frame, it was so smothered with dirt and time stains that I could only distinguish it had been a very badly painted likeness of some sort, of some commonplace person, daubed in by a poor pot-boiling painter to fill the secondhand frame which his patron may have picked up cheaply as I had done after him; but as the frame was alright I took the spoiled canvas along with it, thinking it might come in handy.

For the next few days my hands were full of work of one kind and another, so that it was only on Christmas

Eve that I found myself at liberty to examine my purchase which had been lying with its face to the wall since I had brought it to my studio.

Having nothing to do on this night, and not in the mood to go out, I got my picture and frame from the corner, and laying them upon the table, with a sponge, basin of water, and some soap, I began to wash so that I might see them the better. They were in a terrible mess, and I think I used the best part of a packet of soap-powder and had to change the water about a dozen times before the pattern began to show up on the frame, and the portrait within it asserted its awful crudeness, vile drawing, and intense vulgarity. It was the bloated, piggish visage of a publican clearly, with a plentiful supply of jewelry displayed, as is usual with such masterpieces, where the features are not considered of so much importance as a strict fidelity in the depicting of such articles as watch-guard and seals, finger rings, and breast pins; these were all there, as natural and hard as reality.

The frame delighted me, and the picture satisfied me that I had not cheated the dealer with my price, and I was looking at the monstrosity as the gaslight beat full upon it, and wondering how the owner could be pleased with himself as thus depicted, when something about the background attracted my attention—a slight marking underneath the thin coating as if the portrait had been painted over some other subject.

It was not much certainly, yet enough to make me rush over to my cupboard, where I kept my spirits of wine and turpentine, with which, and a plentiful supply of rags, I began to demolish the publican ruthlessly in the vague hope that I might find something worth looking at underneath.

A slow process that was, as well as a delicate one, so that it was close upon midnight before the gold cable rings and vermilion visage disappeared and another picture loomed up before me; then giving it the final wash over, I wiped it dry, and set it in a good light on my easel, while I filled and lit my pipe, and then sat down to look at it.

What had I liberated from that vile prison of crude paint? For I did not require to set it up to know that this bungler of the brush had covered and defiled a work as far beyond his comprehension as the clouds are from the caterpillar.

The bust and head of a young woman of uncertain age, merged within a gloom of rich accessories painted as only a master hand can paint who is above asserting his knowledge, and who has learnt to cover his technique. It was as perfect and natural in its sombre yet quiet dignity as if it had come from the brush of Moroni.

A face and neck perfectly colourless in their pallid whiteness, with the shadows so artfully managed that they could not be seen, and for this quality would have delighted the strong-minded Queen Bess.

At first as I looked I saw in the centre of a vague darkness a dim patch of grey gloom that drifted into the shadow. Then the greyness appeared to grow lighter as I sat from it, and leaned back in my chair until the features stole out softly, and became clear and definite, while the figure stood out from the background as if tangible, although, having washed it, I knew that it had been smoothly painted.

An intent face, with delicate nose, well-shaped, although bloodless, lips, and eyes like dark caverns without a spark of light in them. The hair loosely about the head and oval cheeks, massive, silky-textured, jet black, and lustreless, which hid the upper portion of her brow, with the ears, and fell in straight indefinite waves over the left breast, leaving the right portion of the transparent neck exposed.

The dress and background were symphonies of ebony, yet full of subtle colouring and masterly feeling; a dress of rich brocaded velvet with a background that represented vast receding space, wondrously suggestive and awe-inspiring.

I noticed that the pallid lips were parted slightly, and showed a glimpse of the upper front teeth, which added to the intent expression of the face. A short upper lip, which curled upward, with the underlip full and sensuous, or rather, if colour had been in it, would have been so.

It was an eerie-looking face that I had resurrected on this midnight hour of Christmas Eve; in its passive pallidity it looked as if the blood had been drained from the body, and that I was gazing upon an open-eyed corpse.

The frame, also, I noticed for the first time, in its details appeared to have been designed with the intention of carrying out the idea of life in death; what had before looked like scroll-work of flowers and fruit were loathsome snake-like worms twined amongst charnel-house bones which they half covered in a decorative fashion; a hideous design in spite of its exquisite workmanship, that made me shudder and wish that I had left the cleaning to be done by daylight.

I am not at all of a nervous temperament, and would have laughed had anyone told me that I was afraid, and yet, as I sat here alone, with that portrait opposite to me in this solitary studio, away from all human contact—for none of the other studios were tenanted on this night, and the janitor had gone on his holiday—I wished that I had spent my evening in a more congenial manner, for in spite of a good fire in the stove and the brilliant gas, that intent face and those haunting eyes were exercising a strange influence upon me.

I heard the clocks from the different steeples chime out the last hour of the day, one after the other, like echoes taking up the refrain and dying away in the distance, and still I sat spellbound, looking at that weird picture, with my neglected pipe in my hand, and a strange lassitude creeping over me.

It was the eyes which fixed me now with the unfathomable depths and absorbing intensity. They gave out no light, but seemed to draw my soul into them, and with it my life and strength as I lay inert before them, until overpowered I lost consciousness and dreamt.

I thought that the frame was still on the easel with the canvas, but the woman had stepped from them and was approaching me with a floating motion, leaving behind her a vault filled with coffins, some of them shut down whilst others lay or stood upright and open, showing the grizzly contents in their decaying and stained cerements.

I could only see her head and shoulders with the sombre drapery of the upper portion and the inky wealth of hair hanging round.

She was with me now, that pallid face touching my face and those cold bloodless lips glued to mine with a close lingering kiss, while the soft black hair covered me like a cloud and thrilled me through and through with a delicious thrill that, whilst it made me grow faint, intoxicated me with delight.

As I breathed she seemed to absorb it quickly into herself, giving me back nothing, getting stronger as I was becoming weaker, while the warmth of my contact passed into her and made her palpitate with vitality.

And all at once the horror of approaching death seized upon me, and with a frantic effort I flung her from me and started up from my chair dazed for a moment and uncertain where I was, then consciousness returned and I looked round wildly.

The gas was still blazing brightly, while the fire burned ruddy in the stove. By the timepiece on the mantel I could see that it was half-past twelve.

The picture and frame were still on the easel, only as I looked at them the portrait had changed, a hectic flush was on the cheeks while the eyes glittered with life and the sensuous lips were red and ripe-looking with a drop of blood still upon the nether one. In a frenzy of horror I seized my scraping knife and slashed out the vampire picture, then tearing the mutilated fragments out I crammed them into my stove and watched them frizzle with savage delight.

I have that frame still, but I have not yet had courage to paint a suitable subject for it.

## The Mezzotint
### M. R. JAMES
### 1904

Some time ago I believe I had the pleasure of telling you the story of an adventure which happened to a friend of mine by the name of Dennistoun, during his pursuit of objects of art for the museum at Cambridge.

He did not publish his experiences very widely upon his return to England; but they could not fail to become known to a good many of his friends, and among others to the gentleman who at that time presided over an art museum at another University. It was to be expected that the story should make a considerable impression on the mind of a man whose vocation lay in lines similar to Dennistoun's, and that he should be eager to catch at any explanation of the matter which tended to make it seem improbable that he should ever be called upon to deal with so agitating an emergency. It was, indeed, somewhat consoling to him to reflect that he was not expected to acquire ancient MSS. for his institution; that was the business of the Shelburnian Library. The authorities of that institution might, if they pleased, ransack obscure corners of the Continent for such matters. He was glad to be obliged at the moment to confine his attention to enlarging the already unsurpassed collection of English topographical drawings and engravings possessed by his museum. Yet, as it turned out, even a department so homely and familiar

**173**

as this may have its dark corners, and to one of these Mr. Williams was unexpectedly introduced.

Those who have taken even the most limited interest in the acquisition of topographical pictures are aware that there is one London dealer whose aid is indispensable to their researches. Mr. J. W. Britnell publishes at short intervals very admirable catalogues of a large and constantly changing stock of engravings, plans, and old sketches of mansions, churches, and towns in England and Wales. These catalogues were, of course, the ABC of his subject to Mr. Williams: but as his museum already contained an enormous accumulation of topographical pictures, he was a regular, rather than a copious, buyer; and he rather looked to Mr. Britnell to fill up gaps in the rank and file of his collection than to supply him with rarities.

Now, in February of last year there appeared upon Mr. Williams's desk at the museum a catalogue from Mr. Britnell's emporium, and accompanying it was a typewritten communication from the dealer himself. This latter ran as follows:

> Dear Sir,
> We beg to call your attention to No. 978 in our accompanying catalogue, which we shall be glad to send on approval.
> Yours faithfully,
>
> J. W. Britnell.

To turn to No. 978 in the accompanying catalogue was with Mr. Williams (as he observed to himself) the work of a moment, and in the place indicated he found the following entry:

> 978.—*Unknown.* Interesting mezzotint: View of a manor-house, early part of the century. 15 by 10 inches; black frame. £2 2s.

It was not specially exciting, and the price seemed high. However, as Mr. Britnell, who knew his business and his customer, seemed to set store by it, Mr. Williams wrote a postcard asking for the article to be sent on approval, along with some other engravings and sketches which appeared in the same catalogue. And so he passed without much excitement of anticipation to the ordinary labours of the day.

A parcel of any kind always arrives a day later than you expect it, and that of Mr. Britnell proved, as I believe the right phrase goes, no exception to the rule. It was delivered at the museum by the afternoon post of Saturday, after Mr. Williams had left his work, and it was accordingly brought round to his rooms in college by the attendant, in order that he might not have to wait over Sunday before looking through it and returning such of the contents as he did not propose to keep. And here he found it when he came in to tea, with a friend.

The only item with which I am concerned was the rather large, black-framed mezzotint of which I have already quoted the short description given in Mr. Britnell's catalogue. Some more details of it will have to be given, though I cannot hope to put before you the look of the picture as clearly as it is present to my own eye. Very nearly the exact duplicate of it may be seen in a good many old inn parlours, or in the passages of undisturbed country mansions at the present moment. It was a rather indifferent mezzotint, and an indifferent mezzotint is, perhaps, the worst form of engraving known. It presented a full-face view of a not very large manor-house of the last century, with three rows of plain sashed windows with rusticated masonry about them, a parapet with balls or vases at the angles, and a small portico in the centre. On either side were trees, and in front a considerable expanse of lawn. The legend *A. W. F. sculpsit* was engraved on the narrow margin; and there was no further inscription. The whole thing gave the impression that it was the work of an amateur. What in the world Mr. Britnell could mean by affixing the price of £2 2s. to such an object was more than Mr. Williams could imagine. He turned it over with a good deal of contempt; upon the back was a paper label, the left-hand half of which had been torn off. All that remained were the ends of two lines of writing; the first had the letters—*ngley Hall*; the second,—*ssex*.

It would, perhaps, be just worth while to identify the place represented, which he could easily do with the help of a gazetteer, and then he would send it back to Mr. Britnell, with some remarks reflecting upon the judgement of that gentleman.

He lighted the candles, for it was now dark, made the tea, and supplied the friend with whom he had been playing golf (for I believe the authorities of the University I write of indulge in that pursuit by way of relaxation); and tea was taken to the accompaniment of a discussion which golfing persons can imagine for themselves, but which the conscientious writer has no right to inflict upon any non-golfing persons.

The conclusion arrived at was that certain strokes might have been better, and that in certain emergencies neither player had experienced that amount of luck which a human being has a right to expect. It was now that the friend—let us call him Professor Binks—took up the framed engraving and said:

"What's this place, Williams?"

"Just what I am going to try to find out," said Williams, going to the shelf for a gazetteer. "Look at the back. Something*ley Hall*, either in Sussex or Essex. Half the name's gone, you see. You don't happen to know it, I suppose?"

"It's from that man Britnell, I suppose, isn't it?" said Binks. "Is it for the museum?"

"Well, I think I should buy it if the price was five shillings," said Williams; "but for some unearthly reason he wants two guineas for it. I can't conceive why. It's a wretched engraving, and there aren't even any figures to give it life."

"It's not worth two guineas, I should think," said Binks; "but I don't think it's so badly done. The moonlight seems rather good to me; and I should have thought there *were* figures, or at least a figure, just on the edge in front."

"Let's look," said Williams. "Well, it's true the light is rather cleverly given. Where's your figure? Oh, yes! Just the head, in the very front of the picture."

And indeed there was—hardly more than a black blot on the extreme edge of the engraving—the head of a man or woman, a good deal muffled up, the back turned to the spectator, and looking towards the house.

Williams had not noticed it before.

"Still," he said, "though it's a cleverer thing than I thought, I can't spend two guineas of museum money on a picture of a place I don't know."

Professor Binks had his work to do, and soon went; and very nearly up to Hall time Williams was engaged in a vain attempt to identify the subject of his picture. "If the vowel before the *ng* had only been left, it would have been easy enough," he thought; "but as it is, the name may be anything from Guestingley to Langley, and there are many more names ending like this than I thought; and this rotten book has no index of terminations."

Hall in Mr. Williams's college was at seven. It need not be dwelt upon; the less so as he met there colleagues who had been playing golf during the afternoon, and words with which we have no concern were freely bandied across the table—merely golfing words, I would hasten to explain.

I suppose an hour or more to have been spent in what is called common-room after dinner. Later in the evening some few retired to Williams's rooms, and I have little doubt that whist was played and tobacco smoked. During a lull in these operations Williams picked up the mezzotint from the table without looking at it, and handed it to a person mildly interested in art, telling him where it had come from, and the other particulars which we already know.

The gentleman took it carelessly, looked at it, then said, in a tone of some interest:

"It's really a very good piece of work, Williams; it has quite a feeling of the romantic period. The light is admirably managed, it seems to me, and the figure, though it's rather too grotesque, is somehow very impressive."

"Yes, isn't it?" said Williams, who was just then busy giving whisky and soda to others of the company, and was unable to come across the room to look at the view again.

It was by this time rather late in the evening, and the visitors were on the move. After they went Williams was obliged to write a letter or two and clear up some odd bits of work. At last, some time past midnight, he was disposed to turn in, and he put out his lamp after lighting his bedroom candle. The picture lay face upwards on the table where the last man who looked at it had put it, and it caught his eye as he turned the lamp down. What he saw made him very nearly drop the candle on the floor, and he declares now if he had been left in the dark at that moment he would have had a fit. But, as that did not happen, he was able to put down the light on the table and take a good look at the picture. It was indubitable—rankly impossible, no doubt, but absolutely certain. In the middle of the lawn in front of the unknown house there was a figure where no figure had been at five o'clock that afternoon. It was crawling on all fours towards the house, and it was muffled in a strange black garment with a white cross on the back.

I do not know what is the ideal course to pursue in a situation of this kind, I can only tell you what Mr. Williams did. He took the picture by one corner and carried it across the passage to a second set of rooms which he possessed. There he locked it up in a drawer, sported the doors of both sets of rooms, and retired to bed; but first he wrote out and signed an account of the extraordinary change which the picture had undergone since it had come into his possession.

Sleep visited him rather late; but it was consoling to reflect that the behaviour of the picture did not depend upon his own unsupported testimony. Evidently the man who had looked at it the night before had seen something of the same kind as he had, otherwise he might have been tempted to think that something gravely wrong was happening either to his eyes or his mind. This possibility being fortunately precluded, two matters awaited him on the morrow. He must take stock of the picture very carefully, and call in a witness for the purpose, and he must make a determined effort to ascertain what house it was that was represented. He would therefore ask his neighbour Nisbet to breakfast with him, and he would subsequently spend a morning over the gazetteer.

Nisbet was disengaged, and arrived about 9.20. His host was not quite dressed, I am sorry to say, even at this late hour. During breakfast nothing was said about the mezzotint by Williams, save that he had a picture on which he wished for Nisbet's opinion. But those who are familiar with University life can picture for themselves the wide and delightful range of subjects over which the conversation of two Fellows of Canterbury College is likely to extend during a Sunday morning breakfast. Hardly a topic was left unchallenged, from golf to lawn-tennis. Yet I am bound to say that Williams was rather distraught; for his interest naturally centred in that very strange picture which was now reposing, face downwards, in the drawer in the room opposite.

The morning pipe was at last lighted, and the moment had arrived for which he looked. With very considerable—almost tremulous—excitement he ran across, unlocked the drawer, and, extracting the picture—still face downwards—ran back, and put it into Nisbet's hands.

"Now," he said, "Nisbet, I want you to tell me exactly what you see in that picture. Describe it, if you don't mind, rather minutely. I'll tell you why afterwards."

"Well," said Nisbet, "I have here a view of a country-house—English, I presume—by moonlight."

"Moonlight? You're sure of that?"

"Certainly. The moon appears to be on the wane, if you wish for details, and there are clouds in the sky."

"All right. Go on. I'll swear," added Williams in an aside, "there was no moon when I saw it first."

"Well, there's not much more to be said," Nisbet continued. "The house has one—two—three rows of windows, five in each row, except at the bottom, where there's a porch instead of the middle one, and—"

"But what about figures?" said Williams, with marked interest.

"There aren't any," said Nisbet; "but—"

"What! No figure on the grass in front?"

"Not a thing."

"You'll swear to that?"

"Certainly I will. But there's just one other thing."

"What?"

"Why, one of the windows on the ground-floor—left of the door—is open."

"Is it really so? My goodness! he must have got in," said Williams, with great excitement; and he hurried to the back of the sofa on which Nisbet was sitting, and, catching the picture from him, verified the matter for himself.

It was quite true. There was no figure, and there was the open window. Williams, after a moment of speechless surprise, went to the writing-table and scribbled for a short time. Then he brought two papers to Nisbet, and asked him first to sign one—it was his own description of the picture, which you have just heard—and then to read the other which was Williams's statement written the night before.

"What can it all mean?" said Nisbet.

"Exactly," said Williams. "Well, one thing I must do—or three things, now I think of it. I must find out from Garwood"—this was his last night's visitor—"what he saw, and then I must get the thing photographed before it goes further, and then I must find out what the place is."

"I can do the photographing myself," said Nisbet, "and I will. But, you know, it looks very much as if we were assisting at the working out of a tragedy somewhere. The question is, has it happened already, or is it going to come off? You must find out what the place is. Yes," he said, looking at the picture again, "I expect you're right: he has got in. And if I don't mistake, there'll be the devil to pay in one of the rooms upstairs."

"I'll tell you what," said Williams: "I'll take the picture across to old Green" (this was the senior Fellow of the College, who had been Bursar for many years). "It's quite likely he'll know it. We have property in Essex and Sussex, and he must have been over the two counties a lot in his time."

"Quite likely he will," said Nisbet; "but just let me take my photograph first. But look here, I rather think Green isn't up today. He wasn't in Hall last night, and I think I heard him say he was going down for the Sunday."

"That's true, too," said Williams; "I know he's gone to Brighton. Well, if you'll photograph it now, I'll go across to Garwood and get his statement, and you keep an eye on it while I'm gone. I'm beginning to think two guineas is not a very exorbitant price for it now."

In a short time he had returned, and brought Mr. Garwood with him. Garwood's statement was to the effect that the figure, when he had seen it, was clear of the edge of the picture, but had not got far across the lawn. He remembered a white mark on the back of its drapery, but could not have been sure it was a cross. A document to this effect was then drawn up and signed, and Nisbet proceeded to photograph the picture.

"Now what do you mean to do?" he said. "Are you going to sit and watch it all day?"

"Well, no, I think not," said Williams. "I rather imagine we're meant to see the whole thing. You see, between the time I saw it last night and this morning there was time for lots of things to happen, but the creature only got into the house. It could easily have got through its business in the time and gone to its own place again; but the fact of the window being open, I think, must mean that it's in there now. So I feel quite easy about leaving it. And besides, I have a kind of idea that it wouldn't change much, if at all, in the daytime. We might go out for a walk this afternoon, and come in to tea, or whenever it gets dark. I shall leave it out on the table here, and sport the door. My skip can get in, but no one else."

The three agreed that this would be a good plan; and, further, that if they spent the afternoon together they would be less likely to talk about the business to other people; for any rumour of such a transaction as was going on would bring the whole of the Phasmatological Society about their ears.

We may give them a respite until five o'clock.

At or near that hour the three were entering Williams's staircase. They were at first slightly annoyed to see that the door of his rooms was unsported; but in a moment it was remembered that on Sunday the skips came for orders an hour or so earlier than on weekdays. However, a surprise was awaiting them. The first thing they saw was the picture leaning up against a pile of books on the table, as it had been left, and the next thing was Williams's skip, seated on a chair opposite, gazing at it with undisguised horror. How was this? Mr. Filcher (the name is not my own invention) was a servant of considerable standing, and set the standard of etiquette to all his own college and to several neighbouring ones, and nothing could be more alien to his practice than to be found sitting on his master's chair, or appearing to take any particular notice of his master's furniture or pictures. Indeed, he seemed to feel this himself. He started violently when the three men were in the room, and got up with a marked effort. Then he said:

"I ask your pardon, sir, for taking such a freedom as to set down."

"Not at all, Robert," interposed Mr. Williams. "I was meaning to ask you some time what you thought of that picture."

"Well, sir, of course I don't set up my opinion against yours, but it ain't the pictur I should 'ang where my little girl could see it, sir."

"Wouldn't you, Robert? Why not?"

"No, sir. Why, the pore child, I recollect once she see a Door Bible, with pictures not 'alf what that is, and we 'ad to set up with her three or four nights afterwards, if you'll believe me; and if she was to ketch a sight of this skelinton here, or whatever it is, carrying off the pore baby, she would be in a taking. You know 'ow it is with children; 'ow nervish they git with a little thing and all. But what I should say, it don't seem a right pictur to be laying about, sir, not where anyone that's liable to be startled could come on it. Should you be wanting anything this evening, sir? Thank you, sir."

With these words the excellent man went to continue the round of his masters, and you may be sure the gentlemen whom he left lost no time in gathering round the engraving. There was the house, as before under the waning moon and the drifting clouds. The window that had been open was shut, and the figure was once more on the lawn: but not this time crawling cautiously on hands and knees. Now it was erect and stepping swiftly, with long strides, towards the front of the picture. The moon was behind it, and the black drapery hung down over its face so that only hints of that could be seen, and what was visible made the spectators profoundly thankful that they could see no more than a white dome-like forehead and a few straggling hairs. The head was bent down, and the arms were tightly clasped over an object which could be dimly seen and identified as a child, whether dead or living it was not possible to say. The legs of the appearance alone could be plainly discerned, and they were horribly thin.

From five to seven the three companions sat and watched the picture by turns. But it never changed. They agreed at last that it would be safe to leave it, and that they would return after Hall and await further developments.

When they assembled again, at the earliest possible moment, the engraving was there, but the figure was gone, and the house was quiet under the moonbeams. There was nothing for it but to spend the evening over gazetteers and guide-books. Williams was the lucky one at last, and perhaps he deserved it. At 11.30 p.m. he read from Murray's *Guide to Essex* the following lines:

> 16-1/2 miles, *Anningley*. The church has been
> an interesting building of Norman date, but
> was extensively classicized in the last century.

It contains the tomb of the family of Francis, whose mansion, Anningley Hall, a solid Queen Anne house, stands immediately beyond the churchyard in a park of about 80 acres. The family is now extinct, the last heir having disappeared mysteriously in infancy in the year 1802. The father, Mr. Arthur Francis, was locally known as a talented amateur engraver in mezzotint. After his son's disappearance he lived in complete retirement at the Hall, and was found dead in his studio on the third anniversary of the disaster, having just completed an engraving of the house, impressions of which are of considerable rarity.

This looked like business, and, indeed, Mr. Green on his return at once identified the house as Anningley Hall.

"Is there any kind of explanation of the figure, Green?" was the question which Williams naturally asked.

"I don't know, I'm sure, Williams. What used to be said in the place when I first knew it, which was before I came up here, was just this: old Francis was always very much down on these poaching fellows, and whenever he got a chance he used to get a man whom he suspected of it turned off the estate, and by degrees he got rid of them all but one. Squires could do a lot of things then that they daren't think of now. Well, this man that was left was what you find pretty often in that country—the last remains of a very old family. I believe they were Lords of the Manor at one time. I recollect just the same thing in my own parish."

"What, like the man in *Tess o' the Durbervilles*?" Williams put in.

"Yes, I dare say; it's not a book I could ever read myself. But this fellow could show a row of tombs in the church there that belonged to his ancestors, and all that went to sour him a bit; but Francis, they said, could never get at him—he always kept just on the right side of the law—until one night the keepers found him at it in a wood right at the end of the estate. I could show you the place now; it marches with some land that used to belong to an uncle of mine. And you can imagine there was a row; and this man Gawdy (that was the name, to be sure—Gawdy; I thought I should get it—Gawdy), he was unlucky enough, poor chap! to shoot a keeper. Well, that was what Francis wanted, and grand juries—you know what they would have been then—and poor Gawdy was strung up in double-quick time; and I've been shown the place he was buried in, on the north side of the church—you know the way in that part of the world: anyone that's been hanged or made away with themselves, they bury them that side. And the idea was that some friend of Gawdy's—not a relation, because he had none, poor devil! he was the last of his line: kind of *spes ultima gentis*—must have planned to get hold of Francis's boy and put an end to *his* line, too. I don't know—it's rather an out-of-the-way thing for an Essex poacher to think of—but, you know, I should say now it looks more as if old Gawdy had managed the job himself. Booh! I hate to think of it! have some whisky, Williams!"

The facts were communicated by Williams to Dennistoun, and by him to a mixed company, of which I was one, and the Sadducean Professor of Ophiology another. I am sorry to say that the latter when asked what he thought of it, only remarked: "Oh, those Bridgeford people will say anything"—a sentiment which met with the reception it deserved.

I have only to add that the picture is now in the Ashleian Museum; that it has been treated with a view to discovering whether sympathetic ink has been used in it, but without effect; that Mr. Britnell knew nothing of it save that he was sure it was uncommon; and that, though carefully watched, it has never been known to change again.

# The Man with the Roller

### E. G. SWAIN

### 1912

On the edge of that vast tract of East Anglia, which retains its ancient name of the Fens, there may be found, by those who know where to seek it, a certain village called Stoneground. It was once a picturesque village. To-day it is not to be called either a village, or picturesque. Man dwells not in one "house of clay," but in two, and the material of the second is drawn from the earth upon which this and the neighbouring villages stood. The unlovely signs of the industry have changed the place alike in aspect and in population. Many who have seen the fossil skeletons of great saurians brought out of the clay in which they have lain from pre-historic times, have thought that the inhabitants of the place have not since changed for the better. The chief habitations, however, have their foundations not upon clay, but upon a bed of gravel which anciently gave to the place its name, and upon the highest part of this gravel stands, and has stood for many centuries, the Parish Church, dominating the landscape for miles around.

Stoneground, however, is no longer the inaccessible village, which in the middle ages stood out above a waste of waters. Occasional floods serve to indicate what was once its ordinary outlook, but in more recent times the construction of roads and railways, and the drainage of the Fens, have given it freedom of communication with the world from which it was formerly isolated.

The Vicarage of Stoneground stands hard by the Church, and is renowned for its spacious garden, part of which, and that (as might be expected) the part nearest the house, is of ancient date. To the original plot successive Vicars have added adjacent lands, so that the garden has gradually acquired the state in which it now appears.

The Vicars have been many in member. Since Henry de Greville was instituted in the year 1140 there have been 30, all of whom have lived, and most of whom have died, in successive vicarage houses upon the present site.

The present incumbent, Mr. Batchel, is a solitary man of somewhat studious habits, but is not too much enamoured of his solitude to receive visits, from time to time, from schoolboys and such. In the summer of the year 1906 he entertained two, who are the occasion of this narrative, though still unconscious of their part in it, for one of the two, celebrating his 15th birthday during his visit to Stoneground, was presented by Mr. Batchel with a new camera, with which he proceeded to photograph, with considerable skill, the surroundings of the house.

One of these photographs Mr. Batchel thought particularly pleasing. It was a view of the house with the lawn in the foreground. A few small copies, such as the boy's camera was capable of producing, were sent to him by his young friend, some weeks after the visit, and again Mr. Batchel was so much pleased with the picture, that he begged for the negative, with the intention of having the view enlarged.

The boy met the request with what seemed a needlessly modest plea. There were two negatives, he replied, but each of them had, in the same part of the picture, a small blur for which there was no accounting otherwise than by carelessness. His desire, therefore, was to discard these films, and to produce something more worthy of enlargement, upon a subsequent visit.

Mr. Batchel, however, persisted in his request, and upon receipt of the negative, examined it with a lens. He was just able to detect the blur alluded to; an examination under a powerful glass, in fact revealed something more than he had at first detected. The blur was like the nucleus of a comet as one sees it represented in pictures, and seemed to be connected with a faint streak which extended across the negative. It was, however, so inconsiderable a defect that Mr. Batchel resolved to disregard it. He had a neighbour whose favourite pastime was photography, one who was notably skilled in everything that pertained to the art, and to him he sent the negative, with the request for an enlargement, reminding him of a longstanding promise to do any such service, when as had now happened, his friend might see fit to ask it.

This neighbour who had acquired such skill in photography, was one Mr. Groves, a young clergyman, residing in the Precincts of the Minster near at hand, which was visible from Mr. Batchel's garden. He lodged with a Mrs. Rumney, a superannuated servant of the Palace, and a strong-minded vigorous woman still, exactly such a one as Mr. Groves needed to have about him. For he was a constant trial to Mrs. Rumney, and but for the wholesome fear she begot in him, would have converted his rooms into a mere den. Her carpets and tablecloths were continually bespattered with chemicals; her chimney-piece ornaments had been unceremoniously stowed away and replaced by labelled bottles; even the bed of Mr. Groves was, by day, strewn with drying film and mounts, and her old and favourite cat had a bald patch on his flank, the result of a mishap with the pyrogallic acid.

Mrs. Rumney's lodger, however, was a great favourite with her, as such helpless men are apt to be with motherly women, and she took no small pride in his work. A life-size portrait of herself, originally a, peace-offering, hung in her parlour, and had long excited the envy of every friend who took tea with her.

"Mr. Groves," she was wont to say, "is a nice gentleman, *and* a gentleman; and chemical though he may be, I'd rather wait on him for nothing than what I would on anyone else for twice the money."

Every new piece of photographic work was of interest to Mrs. Rumney, and she expected to be allowed both to admire and to criticism. The view of Stoneground Vicarage, therefore, was shown to her upon its arrival. "Well may it want enlarging," she remarked, "and it no bigger than a postage stamp; it looks more like a doll's house than a vicarage," and with this she went about her work, whilst Mr. Groves retired to his dark room with the film, to see what he could make of the task assigned to him.

Two days later, after repeated visits to his dark room, he had made something considerable; and when Mrs. Rumney brought him his chop for luncheon, she was lost in admiration. A large but unfinished print stood upon his easel, and such a picture of Stoneground Vicarage was in the making as was calculated to delight both the young photographer and the Vicar.

Mr. Groves spent only his mornings, as a rule, in photography. His afternoons he gave to pastoral work, and the work upon this enlargement was over for the day. It required little more than "touching up," but it was this "touching up" which made the difference between the enlargements of Mr. Groves and those of other men. The print, therefore, was to be left upon the easel until the morrow, when it was to be finished. Mrs. Rumney and he, together, gave it an admiring inspection as she was carrying away the tray, and what they agreed in admiring most particularly was the smooth and open stretch of lawn, which made so excellent a foreground for the picture. "It looks," said Mrs. Rumney, who had once been young, "as if it was waiting for someone to come and dance on it."

Mr. Groves left his lodgings—we must now be particular about the hours—at half-past two, with the intention of returning, as usual, at five. "As reg'lar as a clock," Mrs. Rumney was wont to say, "and a sight more reg'lar than some clocks I knows of."

Upon this day he was, nevertheless, somewhat late, some visit had detained him unexpectedly, and it was a quarter-past five when he inserted his latch-key in Mrs. Rumney's door.

Hardly had he entered, when his landlady, obviously awaiting him, appeared in the passage: her face, usually florid, was of the colour of parchment, and, breathing hurriedly and shortly, she pointed at the door of Mr. Groves' room.

In some alarm at her condition, Mr. Groves hastily questioned her; all she could say was: "The photograph! the photograph!" Mr. Groves could only suppose that his enlargement had met with some mishap for which Mrs. Rumney was responsible. Perhaps she had allowed it to flutter into the fire. He turned towards his room in order to discover the worst, but at this Mrs. Rumney laid a trembling hand upon his arm, and held him back. "Don't go in," she said, "have your tea in the parlour."

"Nonsense," said Mr. Groves, "if that is gone we can easily do another."

"Gone," said his landlady, "I wish to Heaven it was."

The ensuing conversation shall not detain us. It will suffice to say that after a considerable time Mr. Groves succeeded in quieting his landlady, so much so that she consented, still trembling violently, to enter the room with him. To speak truth, she was as much concerned for him as for herself, and she was not by nature a timid woman.

The room, so far from disclosing to Mr. Groves any cause for excitement, appeared wholly unchanged. In its usual place stood every article of his stained and ill-used furniture, on the easel stood the photograph, precisely where he had left it; and except that his tea was not upon the table, everything was in its usual state and place.

But Mrs. Rumney again became excited and tremulous, "It's there," she cried. "Look at the lawn."

Mr. Groves stopped quickly forward and looked at the photograph. Then he turned as pale as Mrs. Rumney herself.

There was a man, a man with an indescribably horrible suffering face, rolling the lawn with a large roller.

Mr. Groves retreated in amazement to where Mrs. Rumney had remained standing. "Has anyone been in here?" he asked.

"Not a soul," was the reply, "I came in to make up the fire, and turned to have another look at the picture, when I saw that dead-alive face at the edge. It gave me the creeps," she said, "particularly from not having noticed it before. If that's anyone in Stoneground, I said to myself, I wonder the Vicar has him in the garden with that awful face. It took that hold of me I thought I must come and look at it again, and at five o'clock I brought your tea in. And then I saw him moved along right in front, with a roller dragging behind him, like you see."

Mr. Groves was greatly puzzled. Mrs. Rumney's story, of course, was incredible, but this strange evil-faced man had appeared in the photograph somehow. That he had not been there when the print was made was quite certain.

The problem soon ceased to alarm Mr. Groves; in his mind it was investing itself with a scientific interest. He began to think of suspended chemical action, and other possible avenues of investigation. At Mrs. Rumney's urgent entreaty, however, he turned the photograph upon the easel, and with only its white back presented to the room, he sat down and ordered tea to be brought in.

He did not look again at the picture. The face of the man had about it something unnaturally painful: he could remember, and still see, as it were, the drawn features, and the look of the man had unaccountably distressed him.

He finished his slight meal, and having lit a pipe, began to brood over the scientific possibilities of the problem. Had any other photograph upon the original film become involved in the one he had enlarged? Had the image of any other face, distorted by the enlarging lens, become a part of this picture? For the space of two hours he debated this possibility, and that, only to reject them all. His optical knowledge told him that no conceivable accident could have brought into his picture a man with a roller. No negative of his had ever contained such a man; if it had, no natural causes would suffice to leave him, as it were, hovering about the apparatus.

His repugnance to the actual thing had by this time lost its freshness, and he determined to end his scientific musings with another inspection of the object. So he approached the easel and turned the photograph round again. His horror returned, and with good cause. The man with the roller had now advanced to the middle of the lawn. The face was stricken still with the same indescribable look of suffering. The man seemed to be appealing to the spectator for some kind of help. Almost, he spoke.

Mr. Groves was naturally reduced to a condition of extreme nervous excitement. Although not by nature what is called a nervous man, he trembled from head to foot. With a sudden effort, he turned away his head, took hold of the picture with his outstretched hand, and opening a drawer in his sideboard thrust the thing underneath a folded tablecloth which was lying there. Then he closed the drawer and took up an entertaining book to distract his thoughts from the whole matter.

In this he succeeded very ill. Yet somehow the rest of the evening passed, and as it wore away, be lost something of his alarm. At ten o'clock, Mrs. Rumney, knocking and receiving answer twice, lest by any chance she should find herself alone in the room, brought in the cocoa usually taken by her lodger at that hour. A hasty glance at the easel showed her that it stood empty, and her face betrayed her relief. She made no comment, and Mr. Groves invited none.

The latter, however, could not make up his mind to go to bed. The face he had seen was taking firm hold upon his imagination, and seemed to fascinate him and repel him at the same time. Before long, he found himself wholly unable to resist the impulse to look at it once more. He took it again, with some indecision, from the drawer and laid it under the lamp.

The man with the roller had now passed completely over the lawn, and was near the left of the picture.

The shock to Mr. Groves was again considerable. He stood facing the fire, trembling with excitement which refused to be suppressed. In this state his eye lighted upon the calendar hanging before him, and it furnished him with some distraction. The next day was his mother's birthday. Never did he omit to write a letter which should lie upon her breakfast-table, and the pre-occupation of this evening had made him wholly forgetful of the matter. There was a collection of letters, however, from the pillar-box near at hand, at a quarter before midnight, so he turned to his desk, wrote a letter which would at least serve to convey his affectionate greetings, and having written it, went out into the night and posted it.

The clocks were striking midnight as he returned to his room. We may be sure that he did not resist the desire to glance at the photograph he had left on his table. But the results of that glance, he, at any rate, had not anticipated. The man with the roller had disappeared. The lawn lay as smooth and clear as at first, "looking," as Mrs. Rumney had said, "as if it was waiting for someone to come and dance on it."

The photograph, after this, remained a photograph and nothing more. Mr. Groves would have liked to persuade himself that it had never undergone these changes which he had witnessed, and which we have endeavoured to describe, but his sense of their reality was too insistent. He kept the print lying for a week upon his easel. Mrs. Rumney, although she had ceased to dread it, was obviously relieved at its disappearance, when it was carried to Stoneground to be delivered to Mr. Batchel. Mr. Groves said nothing of the man with the roller, but gave the enlargement, without comment, into his friend's hands. The work of enlargement had been skilfully done, and was deservedly praised.

Mr. Groves, making some modest disclaimer, observed that the view, with its spacious foreground of lawn, was such as could not have failed to enlarge well. And this lawn, he added, as they sat looking out of the Vicar's study, looks as well from within your house as from without. It must give you a sense of responsibility, he added, reflectively, to be sitting where your predecessors have sat for so many centuries and to be continuing their peaceful work. The mere presence before your window, of the turf upon which good men have walked, is an inspiration.

The Vicar made no reply to these somewhat sententious remarks. For a moment he seemed as if he would speak some words of conventional assent. Then he abruptly left the room, to return in a few minutes with a parchment book.

"Your remark, Groves," he said as he seated himself again, "recalled to me a curious bit of history: I went up to the old library to get the book. This is the journal of William Longue who was Vicar here up to the year 1602. What you said about the lawn will give you an interest in a certain portion of the journal. I will read it."

> Aug. 1, 1600.—I am now returned in haste from a journey to Brightelmstone whither I had gone with full intention to remain about the space of two months. Master Josiah Wilburton, of my dear College of Emmanuel, having consented to assume the charge of my parish of Stoneground in the meantime. But I had intelligence, after 12 days' absence, by a messenger from the Churchwardens, that Master Wilburton had disappeared last Monday sennight, and had been no more seen. So here I am again in my study to the entire frustration of my plans, and can do nothing in my perplexity but sit and look out from my window, before which Andrew Birch rolleth the grass with much persistence. Andrew passeth so many times over the same place with his roller that I have just now stepped without to demand why he so wasteth his labour, and upon this he hath pointed out a place which is not levelled, and hath continued his rolling.
>
> Aug. 2.—There is a change in Andrew Birch since my absence, who hath indeed the aspect of one in great depression, which is noteworthy of so chearful a man. He haply shares our

common trouble in respect of Master Wilburton, of whom we remain without tidings. Having made part of a sermon upon the seventh
Chapter of the former Epistle of St. Paul to
the Corinthians and the 27th verse, I found
Andrew again at his task, and bade him desist
and saddle my horse, being minded to ride
forth and take counsel with my good friend
John Palmer at the Deanery, who bore Master
Wilburton great affection.

Aug. 2 continued.—Dire news awaiteth me
upon my return. The Sheriff's men have dis-
interred the body of poor Master W. from beneath the grass Andrew was rolling, and have
arrested him on the charge of being his cause
of death.

Aug. 10.—Alas! Andrew Birch hath been
hanged, the Justice having mercifully ordered
that he should hang by the neck until he
should be dead, and not sooner molested. May
the Lord have mercy on his soul. He made full
confession before me, that he had slain Master Wilburton in heat upon his threatening to
make me privy to certain peculation of which
I should not have suspected so old a servant.
The poor man bemoaned his evil temper in
great contrition, and beat his breast, saying
that he knew himself doomed for ever to roll
the grass in the place where he had tried to
conceal his wicked fact.

"Thank you," said Mr. Groves. "Has that little negative got the date upon it?" Yes, replied Mr. Batchel, as he

examined it with his glass. The boy has marked it August 10. The Vicar seemed not to remark the coincidence with the date of Birch's execution. Needless to say that it did not escape Mr. Groves. But he kept silence about the man with the roller, who has been no more seen to this day.

Doubtless there is more in our photography than we yet know of. The camera sees more than the eye, and chemicals in a freshly prepared and active state, have a power which they afterwards lose. Our units of time, adopted for the convenience of persons dealing with the ordinary movements of material objects, are of course conventional. Those who turn the instruments of science upon nature will always be in danger of seeing more than they looked for. There is such a disaster as that of knowing too much, and at some time or another it may overtake each of us. May we then be as wise as Mr. Groves in our reticence, if our turn should come.

# The Room in the Tower
### E. F. BENSON
### 1912


It is probable that everybody who is at all a constant dreamer has had at least one experience of an event or a sequence of circumstances which have come to his mind in sleep being subsequently realized in the material world. But, in my opinion, so far from this being a strange thing, it would be far odder if this fulfilment did not occasionally happen, since our dreams are, as a rule, concerned with people whom we know and places with which we are familiar, such as might very naturally occur in the awake and daylit world. True, these dreams are often broken into by some absurd and fantastic incident, which puts them out of court in regard to their subsequent fulfilment, but on the mere calculation of chances, it does not appear in the least unlikely that a dream imagined by anyone who dreams constantly should occasionally come true. Not long ago, for instance, I experienced such a fulfilment of a dream which seems to me in no way remarkable and to have no kind of psychical significance. The manner of it was as follows.

A certain friend of mine, living abroad, is amiable enough to write to me about once in a fortnight. Thus, when fourteen days or thereabouts have elapsed since I last heard from him, my mind, probably, either consciously or subconsciously, is expectant of a letter from him. One night last week I dreamed that as I was going upstairs to dress for dinner I heard, as I often heard, the sound of the postman's knock on my front door, and diverted my direction downstairs instead. There, among other correspondence, was a letter from him. Thereafter the fantastic entered, for on opening it I found inside the ace of diamonds, and scribbled across it in his well-known handwriting, "I am sending you this for safe custody, as you know it is running an unreasonable risk to keep aces in Italy." The next evening I was just preparing to go upstairs to dress when I heard the postman's knock, and did precisely as I had done in my dream. There, among other letters, was one from my friend. Only it did not contain the ace of diamonds. Had it done so, I should have attached more weight to the matter, which, as it stands, seems to me a perfectly ordinary coincidence. No doubt I consciously or subconsciously expected a letter from him, and this suggested to me my dream. Similarly, the fact that my friend had not written to me for a fortnight suggested to him that he should do so. But occasionally it is not so easy to find such an explanation, and for the following story I can find no explanation at all. It came out of the dark, and into the dark it has gone again.

All my life I have been a habitual dreamer: the nights are few, that is to say, when I do not find on awaking in the morning that some mental experience has been mine, and sometimes, all night long, apparently, a series of the most dazzling adventures befall me. Almost without exception these adventures are pleasant, though often merely trivial. It is of an exception that I am going to speak.

It was when I was about sixteen that a certain dream first came to me, and this is how it befell. It opened with my being set down at the door of a big red-brick house, where, I understood, I was going to stay. The servant who opened the door told me that tea was being served in the garden, and led me through a low dark-paneled hall, with a large open fireplace, on to a cheerful green lawn set round with flower beds. There were grouped about the tea-table a small party of people, but they were all strangers to me except one, who was a schoolfellow called Jack Stone, clearly the son of the house, and he introduced me to his mother and father and a couple of sisters. I was, I remember, somewhat astonished to find myself here, for the boy in question was scarcely known to me, and I rather disliked what I knew of him; moreover, he had left school nearly a year before. The afternoon was very hot, and an intolerable oppression reigned. On the far side of the lawn ran a red-brick wall, with an iron gate in its center, outside which stood a walnut tree. We sat in the shadow of the house opposite a row of long windows, inside which I could see a table with cloth laid, glimmering with glass and silver. This garden front of the house was very long, and at one end of it stood a tower of three stories, which looked to me much older than the rest of the building.

Before long, Mrs. Stone, who, like the rest of the party, had sat in absolute silence, said to me, "Jack will show you your room: I have given you the room in the tower."

Quite inexplicably my heart sank at her words. I felt as if I had known that I should have the room in the tower, and that it contained something dreadful and significant. Jack instantly got up, and I understood that I had to follow him. In silence we passed through the hall, and mounted a great oak staircase with many corners, and arrived at a small landing with two doors set in it. He pushed one of these open for me to enter, and without coming in himself, closed it after me. Then I knew that my conjecture had been right: there was something awful in the room, and with the terror of nightmare growing swiftly and enveloping me, I awoke in a spasm of terror.

Now that dream or variations on it occurred to me intermittently for fifteen years. Most often it came in exactly this form, the arrival, the tea laid out on the lawn, the deadly silence succeeded by that one deadly sentence, the mounting with Jack Stone up to the room in the tower where horror dwelt, and it always came to a close in the nightmare of terror at that which was in the room, though I never saw what it was. At other times I experienced variations on this same theme. Occasionally, for instance, we would be sitting at dinner in the dining-room, into the windows of which I had looked on the first night when the dream of this house visited me, but wherever we were, there was the same silence, the same sense of dreadful oppression and foreboding. And the silence I knew would always be broken by Mrs. Stone saying to me, "Jack will show you your room: I have given you the room in the tower." Upon which (this was invariable) I had to follow him up the oak staircase with many corners, and enter the place that I dreaded more and more each time that I visited it in sleep. Or, again, I would find myself playing cards still in silence in a drawing-room lit with immense chandeliers, that gave a blinding illumination. What the game was I have no idea; what I remember, with a sense of miserable anticipation, was that soon Mrs. Stone would get up and say to me, "Jack will show you your room: I have given you the room in the tower." This drawing-room where we played cards was next to the dining-room, and, as I have said, was always brilliantly illuminated, whereas the rest of the house was full of dusk and shadows. And yet, how often, in spite of those bouquets of lights, have I not pored over the cards that were dealt me, scarcely able for some reason to see them. Their designs, too, were strange: there were no red suits, but all were black, and among them there were certain cards which were black all over. I hated and dreaded those.

As this dream continued to recur, I got to know the greater part of the house. There was a smoking-room beyond the drawing-room, at the end of a passage with a green baize door. It was always very dark there, and as often as I went there I passed somebody whom I could not see in the doorway coming out. Curious developments, too, took place in the characters that peopled the dream as might happen to living persons. Mrs. Stone, for instance, who, when I first saw her, had been black-haired, became gray, and instead of rising briskly, as she had done at first when she said, "Jack will show you your room: I have given you the room in the tower," got up very feebly, as if the strength was leaving her limbs. Jack also grew up, and became a rather ill-looking young man, with a brown moustache, while one of the sisters ceased to appear, and I understood she was married.

Then it so happened that I was not visited by this dream for six months or more, and I began to hope, in such inexplicable dread did I hold it, that it had passed away for good. But one night after this interval I again found myself being shown out onto the lawn for tea, and Mrs. Stone was not there, while the others were all dressed in black. At once I guessed the reason, and my heart leaped at the thought that perhaps this time I should not have to sleep in the room in the tower, and though we usually all sat in silence, on this occasion the sense of relief made me talk and laugh as I had never yet done. But even then matters were not altogether comfortable, for no one else spoke, but they all looked secretly at each other. And soon the foolish stream of my talk ran dry, and gradually an apprehension worse than anything I had previously known gained on me as the light slowly faded.

Suddenly a voice which I knew well broke the stillness, the voice of Mrs. Stone, saying, "Jack will show you your room: I have given you the room in the tower." It seemed to come from near the gate in the red-brick wall that bounded the lawn, and looking up, I saw that the grass outside was sown thick with gravestones. A curious greyish light shone from them, and I could read the lettering on the grave nearest me, and it was, "In evil memory of Julia Stone." And as usual Jack got up, and again I followed him through the hall and up the staircase with many corners. On this occasion it was darker than usual, and when I passed into the room in the tower I could only just see the furniture, the position of which was already familiar to me. Also there was a dreadful odor of decay in the room, and I woke screaming.

The dream, with such variations and developments as I have mentioned, went on at intervals for fifteen years. Sometimes I would dream it two or three nights in succession; once, as I have said, there was an intermission of six months, but taking a reasonable average, I should say that I dreamed it quite as often as once in a month. It had, as is plain, something of nightmare about it, since it always ended in the same appalling terror, which so far from getting less, seemed to me to gather fresh fear every time that I experienced it. There was, too, a strange and dreadful consistency about it. The characters in it, as I have mentioned, got regularly older, death and marriage visited this silent family, and I never in the dream, after Mrs. Stone had died, set eyes on her again. But it was always her voice that told me that the room in the tower was prepared for me, and whether we had tea out on the lawn, or the scene was laid in one of the rooms overlooking it, I could always see her gravestone standing just outside the iron gate. It was the same, too, with the married daughter; usually she was not present, but once or twice she returned again, in company with a man, whom I took to be her husband. He, too, like the rest of them, was always silent. But, owing to the constant repetition of the dream, I had ceased to

attach, in my waking hours, any significance to it. I never
met Jack Stone again during all those years, nor did I ever
see a house that resembled this dark house of my dream.
And then something happened.

I had been in London in this year, up till the end of
the July, and during the first week in August went down to
stay with a friend in a house he had taken for the summer
months, in the Ashdown Forest district of Sussex. I left
London early, for John Clinton was to meet me at Forest
Row Station, and we were going to spend the day golfing,
and go to his house in the evening. He had his motor with
him, and we set off, about five of the afternoon, after
a thoroughly delightful day, for the drive, the distance
being some ten miles. As it was still so early we did not
have tea at the club house, but waited till we should get
home. As we drove, the weather, which up till then had
been, though hot, deliciously fresh, seemed to me to alter in quality, and become very stagnant and oppressive,
and I felt that indefinable sense of ominous apprehension
that I am accustomed to before thunder. John, however,
did not share my views, attributing my loss of lightness to
the fact that I had lost both my matches. Events proved,
however, that I was right, though I do not think that the
thunderstorm that broke that night was the sole cause of
my depression.

Our way lay through deep high-banked lanes, and before we had gone very far I fell asleep, and was only awakened by the stopping of the motor. And with a sudden
thrill, partly of fear but chiefly of curiosity, I found myself standing in the doorway of my house of dream. We
went, I half wondering whether or not I was dreaming
still, through a low oak-paneled hall, and out onto the
lawn, where tea was laid in the shadow of the house. It
was set in flower beds, a red-brick wall, with a gate in
it, bounded one side, and out beyond that was a space of

rough grass with a walnut tree. The facade of the house was very long, and at one end stood a three-storied tower, markedly older than the rest.

Here for the moment all resemblance to the repeated dream ceased. There was no silent and somehow terrible family, but a large assembly of exceedingly cheerful persons, all of whom were known to me. And in spite of the horror with which the dream itself had always filled me, I felt nothing of it now that the scene of it was thus reproduced before me. But I felt intensest curiosity as to what was going to happen.

Tea pursued its cheerful course, and before long Mrs. Clinton got up. And at that moment I think I knew what she was going to say. She spoke to me, and what she said was:

"Jack will show you your room: I have given you the room in the tower."

At that, for half a second, the horror of the dream took hold of me again. But it quickly passed, and again I felt nothing more than the most intense curiosity. It was not very long before it was amply satisfied.

John turned to me.

"Right up at the top of the house," he said, "but I think you'll be comfortable. We're absolutely full up. Would you like to go and see it now? By Jove, I believe that you are right, and that we are going to have a thunderstorm. How dark it has become."

I got up and followed him. We passed through the hall, and up the perfectly familiar staircase. Then he opened the door, and I went in. And at that moment sheer unreasoning terror again possessed me. I did not know what I feared: I simply feared. Then like a sudden recollection, when one remembers a name which has long escaped the memory, I knew what I feared. I feared Mrs. Stone, whose grave with the sinister inscription, "In evil memory," I had so often seen in my dream, just beyond the lawn which lay below my window. And then once more the fear passed so completely that I wondered what there was to fear, and I found myself, sober and quiet and sane, in the room in the tower, the name of which I had so often heard in my dream, and the scene of which was so familiar.

I looked around it with a certain sense of proprietorship, and found that nothing had been changed from the dreaming nights in which I knew it so well. Just to the left of the door was the bed, lengthways along the wall, with the head of it in the angle. In a line with it was the fireplace and a small bookcase; opposite the door the outer wall was pierced by two lattice-paned windows, between which stood the dressing-table, while ranged along the fourth wall was the washing-stand and a big cupboard. My luggage had already been unpacked, for the furniture of dressing and undressing lay orderly on the wash-stand and toilet-table, while my dinner clothes were spread out on the coverlet of the bed. And then, with a sudden start of unexplained dismay, I saw that there were two rather conspicuous objects which I had not seen before in my dreams: one a life-sized oil painting of Mrs. Stone, the other a black-and-white sketch of Jack Stone, representing him as he had appeared to me only a week before in the last of the series of these repeated dreams, a rather secret and evil-looking man of about thirty. His picture hung between the windows, looking straight across the room to the other portrait, which hung at the side of the bed. At that I looked next, and as I looked I felt once more the horror of nightmare seize me.

It represented Mrs. Stone as I had seen her last in my dreams: old and withered and white-haired. But in spite of the evident feebleness of body, a dreadful exuberance and vitality shone through the envelope of flesh, an exuberance wholly malign, a vitality that foamed and frothed with unimaginable evil. Evil beamed from the narrow, leering eyes; it laughed in the demon-like mouth. The whole face was instinct with some secret and appalling mirth; the hands, clasped together on the knee, seemed shaking with suppressed and nameless glee. Then I saw also that it was signed in the left-hand bottom corner, and wondering who the artist could be, I looked more closely, and read the inscription, "Julia Stone by Julia Stone."

There came a tap at the door, and John Clinton entered.

"Got everything you want?" he asked.

"Rather more than I want," said I, pointing to the picture.

He laughed.

"Hard-featured old lady," he said. "By herself, too, I remember. Anyhow she can't have flattered herself much."

"But don't you see?" said I. "It's scarcely a human face at all. It's the face of some witch, of some devil."

He looked at it more closely.

"Yes; it isn't very pleasant," he said. "Scarcely a bedside manner, eh? Yes; I can imagine getting the nightmare if I went to sleep with that close by my bed. I'll have it taken down if you like."

"I really wish you would," I said. He rang the bell, and with the help of a servant we detached the picture and carried it out onto the landing, and put it with its face to the wall.

"By Jove, the old lady is a weight," said John, mopping his forehead. "I wonder if she had something on her mind."

The extraordinary weight of the picture had struck me too. I was about to reply, when I caught sight of my own hand. There was blood on it, in considerable quantities, covering the whole palm.

"I've cut myself somehow," said I.

John gave a little startled exclamation.

"Why, I have too," he said.

Simultaneously the footman took out his handkerchief and wiped his hand with it. I saw that there was blood also on his handkerchief.

John and I went back into the tower room and washed the blood off; but neither on his hand nor on mine was there the slightest trace of a scratch or cut. It seemed to me that, having ascertained this, we both, by a sort of tacit consent, did not allude to it again. Something in my case had dimly occurred to me that I did not wish to think about. It was but a conjecture, but I fancied that I knew the same thing had occurred to him.

The heat and oppression of the air, for the storm we had expected was still undischarged, increased very much after dinner, and for some time most of the party, among whom were John Clinton and myself, sat outside on the path bounding the lawn, where we had had tea. The night was absolutely dark, and no twinkle of star or moon ray could penetrate the pall of cloud that overset the sky. By degrees our assembly thinned, the women went up to bed, men dispersed to the smoking or billiard room, and by eleven o'clock my host and I were the only two left. All the evening I thought that he had something on his mind, and as soon as we were alone he spoke.

"The man who helped us with the picture had blood on his hand, too, did you notice?" he said.

"I asked him just now if he had cut himself, and he said he supposed he had, but that he could find no mark of it. Now where did that blood come from?"

By dint of telling myself that I was not going to think about it, I had succeeded in not doing so, and I did not want, especially just at bedtime, to be reminded of it.

"I don't know," said I, "and I don't really care so long as the picture of Mrs. Stone is not by my bed."

He got up.

"But it's odd," he said. "Ha! Now you'll see another odd thing."

A dog of his, an Irish terrier by breed, had come out of the house as we talked. The door behind us into the hall was open, and a bright oblong of light shone across the lawn to the iron gate which led on to the rough grass outside, where the walnut tree stood. I saw that the dog had all his hackles up, bristling with rage and fright; his lips were curled back from his teeth, as if he was ready to spring at something, and he was growling to himself. He took not the slightest notice of his master or me, but stiffly and tensely walked across the grass to the iron gate. There he stood for a moment, looking through the bars and still growling. Then of a sudden his courage seemed to desert him: he gave one long howl, and scuttled back to the house with a curious crouching sort of movement.

"He does that half-a-dozen times a day." said John. "He sees something which he both hates and fears."

I walked to the gate and looked over it. Something was moving on the grass outside, and soon a sound which I could not instantly identify came to my ears. Then I remembered what it was: it was the purring of a cat. I lit a match, and saw the purrer, a big blue Persian, walking round and round in a little circle just outside the gate, stepping high and ecstatically, with tail carried aloft like a banner. Its eyes were bright and shining, and every now and then it put its head down and sniffed at the grass.

I laughed.

"The end of that mystery, I am afraid." I said. "Here's a large cat having Walpurgis night all alone."

"Yes, that's Darius," said John. "He spends half the day and all night there. But that's not the end of the dog mystery, for Toby and he are the best of friends, but the beginning of the cat mystery. What's the cat doing there? And why is Darius pleased, while Toby is terror-stricken?"

At that moment I remembered the rather horrible detail of my dreams when I saw through the gate, just where the cat was now, the white tombstone with the sinister inscription. But before I could answer the rain began, as suddenly and heavily as if a tap had been turned on, and simultaneously the big cat squeezed through the bars of the gate, and came leaping across the lawn to the house for shelter. Then it sat in the doorway, looking out eagerly into the dark. It spat and struck at John with its paw, as he pushed it in, in order to close the door.

Somehow, with the portrait of Julia Stone in the passage outside, the room in the tower had absolutely no alarm for me, and as I went to bed, feeling very sleepy and heavy, I had nothing more than interest for the curious incident about our bleeding hands, and the conduct of the cat and dog. The last thing I looked at before I put out my light was the square empty space by my bed where the portrait had been. Here the paper was of its original full tint of dark red: over the rest of the walls it had faded. Then I blew out my candle and instantly fell asleep.

My awaking was equally instantaneous, and I sat bolt upright in bed under the impression that some bright light had been flashed in my face, though it was now absolutely pitch dark. I knew exactly where I was, in the room which I had dreaded in dreams, but no horror that I ever felt when asleep approached the fear that now invaded and froze my brain. Immediately after a peal of thunder crackled just above the house, but the probability that it was only a flash of lightning which awoke me gave no reassurance to my galloping heart. Something I knew was in the room with me, and instinctively I put out my right hand, which was nearest the wall, to keep it away. And my hand touched the edge of a picture-frame hanging close to me.

I sprang out of bed, upsetting the small table that stood by it, and I heard my watch, candle, and matches clatter onto the floor. But for the moment there was no need of light, for a blinding flash leaped out of the clouds, and showed me that by my bed again hung the picture of Mrs. Stone. And instantly the room went into blackness again. But in that flash I saw another thing also, namely a figure that leaned over the end of my bed, watching me. It was dressed in some close-clinging white garment, spotted and stained with mold, and the face was that of the portrait.

Overhead the thunder cracked and roared, and when it ceased and the deathly stillness succeeded, I heard the rustle of movement coming nearer me, and, more horrible yet, perceived an odor of corruption and decay. And then a hand was laid on the side of my neck, and close beside my ear I heard quick-taken, eager breathing. Yet I knew that this thing, though it could be perceived by touch, by smell, by eye and by ear, was still not of this earth, but something that had passed out of the body and had power to make itself manifest. Then a voice, already familiar to me, spoke.

"I knew you would come to the room in the tower," it said. "I have been long waiting for you. At last you have come. Tonight I shall feast; before long we will feast together."

And the quick breathing came closer to me; I could feel it on my neck.

At that the terror, which I think had paralyzed me for the moment, gave way to the wild instinct of self-preservation. I hit wildly with both arms, kicking out at the same moment, and heard a little animal-squeal, and something soft dropped with a thud beside me. I took a couple of steps forward, nearly tripping up over whatever it was that lay there, and by the merest good-luck found the handle of the door. In another second I ran out on the landing, and had banged the door behind me. Almost at the same moment I heard a door open somewhere below, and John Clinton, candle in hand, came running upstairs.

"What is it?" he said. "I sleep just below you, and heard a noise as if—Good heavens, there's blood on your shoulder."

I stood there, so he told me afterwards, swaying from side to side, white as a sheet, with the mark on my shoulder as if a hand covered with blood had been laid there.

"It's in there," I said, pointing. "She, you know. The portrait is in there, too, hanging up on the place we took it from."

At that he laughed.

"My dear fellow, this is mere nightmare," he said.

He pushed by me, and opened the door, I standing there simply inert with terror, unable to stop him, unable to move.

"Phew! What an awful smell," he said.

Then there was silence; he had passed out of my sight behind the open door. Next moment he came out again, as white as myself, and instantly shut it.

"Yes, the portrait's there," he said, "and on the floor is a thing—a thing spotted with earth, like what they bury people in. Come away, quick, come away."

How I got downstairs I hardly know. An awful shuddering and nausea of the spirit rather than of the flesh had seized me, and more than once he had to place my feet upon the steps, while every now and then he cast glances of terror and apprehension up the stairs. But in time we came to his dressing-room on the floor below, and there I told him what I have here described.

The sequel can be made short; indeed, some of my readers have perhaps already guessed what it was, if they remember that inexplicable affair of the churchyard at West Fawley, some eight years ago, where an attempt was made three times to bury the body of a certain woman who had committed suicide. On each occasion the coffin was found in the course of a few days again protruding from the ground. After the third attempt, in order that the thing should not be talked about, the body was buried elsewhere in unconsecrated ground. Where it was buried was just outside the iron gate of the garden belonging to the house where this woman had lived. She had committed suicide in a room at the top of the tower in that house. Her name was Julia Stone.

Subsequently the body was again secretly dug up, and the coffin was found to be full of blood.

# The Picture in the House
## H. P. Lovecraft
### 1921

Searchers after horror haunt strange, far places. For them
are the catacombs of Ptolemais, and the carven mausolea
of the nightmare countries. They climb to the moonlit
towers of ruined Rhine castles, and falter down black cob-
webbed steps beneath the scattered stones of forgotten
cities in Asia. The haunted wood and the desolate mountain are their shrines, and they linger around the sinister
monoliths on uninhabited islands. But the true epicure in
the terrible, to whom a new thrill of unutterable ghastliness is the chief end and justification of existence, esteems
most of all the ancient, lonely farmhouses of backwoods
New England; for there the dark elements of strength,
solitude, grotesqueness, and ignorance combine to form
the perfection of the hideous.

Most horrible of all sights are the little unpainted
wooden houses remote from travelled ways, usually squatted upon some damp, grassy slope or leaning against some
gigantic outcropping of rock. Two hundred years and more
they have leaned or squatted there, while the vines have
crawled and the trees have swelled and spread. They are
almost hidden now in lawless luxuriances of green and
guardian shrouds of shadow; but the small-paned windows
still stare shockingly, as if blinking through a lethal stupor

which wards off madness by dulling the memory of unutterable things.

In such houses have dwelt generations of strange people, whose like the world has never seen. Seized with a gloomy and fanatical belief which exiled them from their kind, their ancestors sought the wilderness for freedom. There the scions of a conquering race indeed flourished free from the restrictions of their fellows, but cowered in an appalling slavery to the dismal phantasms of their own minds. Divorced from the enlightenment of civilization, the strength of these Puritans turned into singular channels; and in their isolation, morbid self-repression, and struggle for life with relentless Nature, there came to them dark furtive traits from the prehistoric depths of their cold Northern heritage. By necessity practical and by philosophy stern, these folk were not beautiful in their sins. Erring as all mortals must, they were forced by their rigid code to seek concealment above all else; so that they came to use less and less taste in what they concealed. Only the silent, sleepy, staring houses in the backwoods can tell all that has lain hidden since the early days; and they are not communicative, being loath to shake off the drowsiness which helps them forget. Sometimes one feels that it would be merciful to tear down these houses, for they must often dream.

It was to a time-battered edifice of this description that I was driven one afternoon in November, 1896, by a rain of such chilling copiousness that any shelter was preferable to exposure. I had been travelling for some time amongst the people of the Miskatonic Valley in quest of certain genealogical data; and from the remote, devious, and problematical nature of my course, had deemed it convenient to employ a bicycle despite the lateness of the season. Now I found myself upon an apparently abandoned road which I had chosen as the shortest cut to Arkham; overtaken by

the storm at a point far from any town, and confronted
with no refuge save the antique and repellent wooden
building which blinked with bleared windows from between two huge leafless elms near the foot of a rocky
hill. Distant though it was from the remnant of a road,
the house nonetheless impressed me unfavorably the very
moment I espied it. Honest, wholesome structures do
not stare at travelers so slyly and hauntingly, and in my
genealogical researches I had encountered legends of a
century before which biased me against places of this
kind. Yet the force of the elements was such as to overcome
my scruples, and I did not hesitate to wheel my machine
up the weedy rise to the closed door which seemed at once
so suggestive and secretive.

I had somehow taken it for granted that the house was
abandoned, yet as I approached it I was not so sure; for
though the walks were indeed overgrown with weeds, they
seemed to retain their nature a little too well to argue
complete desertion. Therefore instead of trying the door I
knocked, feeling as I did so a trepidation I could scarcely
explain. As I waited on the rough, mossy rock which
served as a doorstep, I glanced at the neighboring windows
and the panes of the transom above me, and noticed that
although old, rattling, and almost opaque with dirt, they
were not broken. The building, then, must still be inhabited, despite its isolation and general neglect. However,
my rapping evoked no response, so after repeating the
summons I tried the rusty latch and found the door unfas-
tened. Inside was a little vestibule with walls from which
the plaster was falling, and through the doorway came a
faint but peculiarly hateful odor. I entered, carrying my
bicycle, and closed the door behind me. Ahead rose a narrow staircase, flanked by a small door probably leading to
the cellar, while to the left and right were closed doors
leading to rooms on the ground floor.

Leaning my cycle against the wall I opened the door at the left, and crossed into a small low-ceiled chamber but dimly lighted by its two dusty windows and furnished in the barest and most primitive possible way. It appeared to be a kind of sitting-room, for it had a table and several chairs, and an immense fireplace above which ticked an antique clock on a mantel. Books and papers were very few, and in the prevailing gloom I could not readily discern the titles. What interested me was the uniform air of archaism as displayed in every visible detail. Most of the houses in this region I had found rich in relics of the past, but here the antiquity was curiously complete; for in all the room I could not discover a single article of definitely post-revolutionary date. Had the furnishings been less humble, the place would have been a collector's paradise.

As I surveyed this quaint apartment, I felt an increase in that aversion first excited by the bleak exterior of the house. Just what it was that I feared or loathed, I could by no means define; but something in the whole atmosphere seemed redolent of unhallowed age, of unpleasant crudeness, and of secrets which should be forgotten. I felt disinclined to sit down, and wandered about examining the various articles which I had noticed. The first object of my curiosity was a book of medium size lying upon the table and presenting such an antediluvian aspect that I marveled at beholding it outside a museum or library. It was bound in leather with metal fittings, and was in an excellent state of preservation; being altogether an unusual sort of volume to encounter in an abode so lowly. When I opened it to the title page my wonder grew even greater, for it proved to be nothing less rare than Pigafetta's account of the Congo region, written in Latin from the notes of the sailor Lopez and printed at Frankfort in 1598. I had often heard of this work, with its curious illustrations by the brothers De Bry, hence for a moment forgot my uneasiness in my desire to turn the pages before me. The engravings were indeed interesting, drawn wholly from imagination and careless descriptions, and represented negroes with white skins and Caucasian features; nor would I soon have closed the book had not an exceedingly trivial circumstance upset my tired nerves and revived my sensation of disquiet. What annoyed me was merely the persistent way in which the volume tended to fall open of itself at Plate XII, which represented in gruesome detail a butcher's shop of the cannibal Anziques. I experienced some shame at my susceptibility to so slight a thing, but the drawing nevertheless disturbed me, especially in connection with some adjacent passages descriptive of Anzique gastronomy.

I had turned to a neighboring shelf and was examining its meagre literary contents—an eighteenth-century Bible, a *Pilgrim's Progress* of like period, illustrated with grotesque woodcuts and printed by the almanack-maker Isaiah Thomas, the rotting bulk of Cotton Mather's *Magnalia Christi Americana,* and a few other books of evidently equal age—when my attention was aroused by the unmistakable sound of walking in the room overhead. At first astonished and startled, considering the lack of response to my recent knocking at the door, I immediately afterward concluded that the walker had just awakened from a sound sleep; and listened with less surprise as the footsteps sounded on the creaking stairs. The tread was heavy, yet seemed to contain a curious quality of cautiousness; a quality which I disliked the more because the tread was heavy. When I had entered the room I had shut the door behind me. Now, after a moment of silence during which the walker may have been inspecting my bicycle in the hall, I heard a fumbling at the latch and saw the paneled portal swing open again.

In the doorway stood a person of such singular appearance that I should have exclaimed aloud but for the restraints of good breeding. Old, white-bearded, and ragged, my host possessed a countenance and physique which inspired equal wonder and respect. His height could not have been less than six feet, and despite a general air of age and poverty he was stout and powerful in proportion. His face, almost hidden by a long beard which grew high on the cheeks, seemed abnormally ruddy and less wrinkled than one might expect; while over a high forehead fell a shock of white hair little thinned by the years. His blue eyes, though a trifle bloodshot, seemed inexplicably keen and burning. But for his horrible unkemptness the man would have been as distinguished-looking as he was impressive. This unkemptness, however, made him offensive despite his face and figure. Of what his clothing consisted I could hardly tell, for it seemed to me no more than a mass of tatters surmounting a pair of high, heavy boots; and his lack of cleanliness surpassed description.

The appearance of this man, and the instinctive fear he inspired, prepared me for something like enmity; so that I almost shuddered through surprise and a sense of uncanny incongruity when he motioned me to a chair and addressed me in a thin, weak voice full of fawning respect and ingratiating hospitality. His speech was very curious, an extreme form of Yankee dialect I had thought long extinct; and I studied it closely as he sat down opposite me for conversation.

"Ketched in the rain, be ye?" he greeted. "Glad ye was nigh the haouse en' hed the sense ta come right in. I calc'late I was asleep, else I'd a heerd ye—I ain't as young as I uster be, an' I need a paowerful sight o' naps naowadays. Trav'lin' fur? I hain't seed many folks 'long this rud sence they tuk off the Arkham stage."

I replied that I was going to Arkham, and apologized for my rude entry into his domicile, whereupon he continued.

"Glad ta see ye, young Sir—new faces is scurce arount here, an' I hain't got much ta cheer me up these days. Guess yew hail from Bosting, don't ye? I never ben thar, but I kin tell a taown man when I see 'im—we hed one fer deestrick schoolmaster in 'eighty-four, but he quit suddent an' no one never heerd on 'im sence—" Here the old man lapsed into a kind of chuckle, and made no explanation when I questioned him. He seemed to be in an aboundingly good humor, yet to possess those eccentricities which one might guess from his grooming. For some time he rambled on with an almost feverish geniality, when it struck me to ask him how he came by so rare a book as Pigafetta's *Regnum Congo*. The effect of this volume had not left me, and I felt a certain hesitancy in speaking of it; but curiosity overmastered all the vague fears which had steadily accumulated since my first glimpse of the house. To my relief, the question did not seem an awkward one; for the old man answered freely and volubly.

"Oh, thet Afriky book? Cap'n Ebenezer Holt traded me thet in 'sixty-eight—him as was kilt in the war." Something about the name of Ebenezer Holt caused me to look up sharply. I had encountered it in my genealogical work, but not in any record since the Revolution. I wondered if my host could help me in the task at which I was laboring, and resolved to ask him about it later on. He continued.

"Ebenezer was on a Salem merchantman for years, an' picked up a sight o' queer stuff in every port. He got this in London, I guess—he uster like ter buy things at the shops. I was up ta his haouse onct, on the hill, tradin' hosses, when I see this book. I relished the picters, so he give it in on a swap. 'Tis a queer book—here, leave me git on my spectacles—" The old man fumbled among his rags, producing a pair of dirty and amazingly antique glasses with small octagonal lenses and steel bows. Donning these, he reached for the volume on the table and turned the pages lovingly.

"Ebenezer cud read a leetle o' this—'tis Latin—but I can't. I hed two er three schoolmasters read me a bit, and Passon Clark, him they say got draownded in the pond— kin yew make anything outen it?" I told him that I could, and translated for his benefit a paragraph near the beginning. If I erred, he was not scholar enough to correct me; for he seemed childishly pleased at my English version. His proximity was becoming rather obnoxious, yet I saw no way to escape without offending him. I was amused at the childish fondness of this ignorant old man for the pictures in a book he could not read, and wondered how much better he could read the few books in English which adorned the room. This revelation of simplicity removed much of the ill-defined apprehension I had felt, and I smiled as my host rambled on:

"Queer haow picters kin set a body thinkin'. Take this un here near the front. Hev yew ever seed trees like thet, with big leaves a-floppin' over an' daown? And them men— them can't be niggers—they dew beat all. Kinder like Injuns, I guess, even ef they be in Afriky. Some o' these here critters looks like monkeys, or half monkeys an' half men, but I never heerd o' nothing like this un." Here he pointed to a fabulous creature of the artist, which one might describe as a sort of dragon with the head of an alligator.

"But naow I'll shew ye the best un—over here nigh the middle—" The old man's speech grew a trifle thicker and his eyes assumed a brighter glow; but his fumbling hands, though seemingly clumsier than before, were entirely adequate to their mission. The book fell open, almost of its own accord and as if from frequent consultation at this place, to the repellent twelfth plate shewing a butcher's shop amongst the Anzique cannibals. My sense of restlessness returned, though I did not exhibit it. The especially bizarre thing was that the artist had made his Africans look like white men—the limbs and quarters hanging about the walls of the shop were ghastly, while the butcher with his axe was hideously incongruous. But my host seemed to relish the view as much as I disliked it.

"What d'ye think o' this—ain't never see the like hereabouts, eh? When I see this I telled Eb Holt, 'That's suthin' ta stir ye up an' make yer blood tickle!' When I read in Scripter about slayin'—like them Midianites was slew—I kinder think things, but I ain't got no picter of it. Here a body kin see all they is to it—I s'pose 'tis sinful, but ain't we all born an' livin' in sin?—Thet feller bein' chopped up gives me a tickle every time I look at 'im—I hev ta keep lookin' at 'im—see whar the butcher cut off his feet? Thar's his head on thet bench, with one arm side of it, an' t'other arm's on the graound side o' the meat block."

As the man mumbled on in his shocking ecstasy the expression on his hairy, spectacled face became indescribable, but his voice sank rather than mounted. My own sensations can scarcely be recorded. All the terror I had dimly felt before rushed upon me actively and vividly, and I knew that I loathed the ancient and abhorrent creature so near me with an infinite intensity. His madness, or at least his partial perversion, seemed beyond dispute. He was almost whispering now, with a huskiness more terrible than a scream, and I trembled as I listened.

"As I says, 'tis queer haow picters sets ye thinkin'. D'ye know, young Sir, I'm right sot on this un here. Arter I got the book off Eb I uster look at it a lot, especial when I'd heerd Passon Clark rant o' Sundays in his big wig. Onct I tried suthin' funny—here, young Sir, don't git skeert—all

I done was ter look at the picter afore I kilt the sheep for market—killin' sheep was kinder more fun arter lookin' at it—" The tone of the old man now sank very low, sometimes becoming so faint that his words were hardly audible. I listened to the rain, and to the rattling of the bleared, small-paned windows, and marked a rumbling of approaching thunder quite unusual for the season. Once a terrific flash and peal shook the frail house to its foundations, but the whisperer seemed not to notice it.

"Killin' sheep was kinder more fun—but d'ye know, 'twan't quite satisfyin'. Queer haow a cravin' gits a holt on ye— As ye love the Almighty, young man, don't tell nobody, but I swar ter Gawd thet picter begun ta make me hungry fer victuals I couldn't raise nor buy—here, set still, what's ailin' ye?—I didn't do nothin', only I wondered haow 'twud be ef I did— They say meat makes blood an' flesh, an' gives ye new life, so I wondered ef 'twudn't make a man live longer an' longer ef 'twas more the same—" But the whisperer never continued. The interruption was not produced by my fright, nor by the rapidly increasing storm amidst whose fury I was presently to open my eyes on a smoky solitude of blackened ruins. It was produced by a very simple though somewhat unusual happening.

The open book lay flat between us, with the picture staring repulsively upward. As the old man whispered the words "more the same" a tiny spattering impact was heard, and something shewed on the yellowed paper of the upturned volume. I thought of the rain and of a leaky roof, but rain is not red. On the butcher's shop of the Anzique cannibals a small red spattering glistened picturesquely, lending vividness to the horror of the engraving. The old man saw it, and stopped whispering even before my expression of horror made it necessary; saw it and glanced quickly toward the floor of the room he had left an hour before. I followed his glance, and beheld just above us

on the loose plaster of the ancient ceiling a large irreg-
ular spot of wet crimson which seemed to spread even
as I viewed it. I did not shriek or move, but merely shut
my eyes. A moment later came the titanic thunderbolt of
thunderbolts; blasting that accursed house of unutterable
secrets and bringing the oblivion which alone saved my
mind.

# A Square of Canvas
## ANTHONY M. RUD
### 1923


"No, Madame, I am *not* insane! I see you hide a smile. Never mind attempting to mask the expression. You are a newcomer here and have learned nothing of my story. I do not blame any visitor—the burden of proof rests upon us, *n'est-ce-pas?*

"In this same ward you have met several peculiar characters, have you not? We have a motley assemblage of conquerors, diplomats, courtesans and divinities—if you'll take their words for it There is Alexander the Great, Richelieu, Julius Caesar, Spartacus, Cleopatra—but no matter. *I* have no delusion. I am Hal Pemberton.

"You start? You believe *this* my delusion? Look closely at me! I have aged, it is true, yet if you have glimpsed the Metropolitan gallery portrait that Paul Gauguin did of me when I visited Tahiti. . . .?"

I gasped, and fell back a pace. This silver-haired, kindly old soul the mad genius, Pemberton? The temptation was strong to flee when I realized that he told the truth! I knew the portrait, indeed, and for an art student like myself there could be no mistaking the resemblance. I stopped, half-turned. After all, they allowed him freedom of the grounds. He could be no worse surely, than the malignant Cleopatra whom I just had left playing with her "asp"—a five-inch garter snake she had found crossing the gravel path.

"I—I believe you," came my stammered reply

What I meant, of course, was that no doubt could exist that he was, certainly, Hal Pemberton. His seamed face lighted up; it was plain *he* believed that establishment of identity made the matter of his detention absurd.

"They have me registered as Chase—John Chase," he confided. "Come! Would a true story of an artist's persecution interest you? It is a recital of misunderstanding, bigotry. . . ."

He left the sentence incomplete, and beckoned with a curl of his tapered, spatulate index finger toward a bench set fair in the sunshine just beyond range of blowing mists from the fountain.

I was tempted. A guard was stationed less than two hundred feet distant. Notwithstanding the horrid and distorted legends which shrouded our memories of this man— supposed to have died in far-off Polynesia—he could not harm me easily before assistance was available. Beside, I am an active, bony woman of the grenadier type. I waited until he sat down, then placed myself gingerly upon the opposite end of the bench.

"You are the first person who has not laughed in my face when learning my true identity," he continued then, making no attempt to close the six-foot gap between us— much to my comfort. "*Ignorance* placed me here. Ignorance keeps me. I shall give you every detail, Madame. Then you may inform others and procure my release. The *cognoscenti* will demand it, once they know of the cruel intolerance which has stolen nine years from my career and from my life. You know—" and here Pemberton glanced guardedly about before he added in a whisper, "*they won't let me paint!*

"My youth and training are known in part. Alden Sef-
ferich's brochure dealt with the externals, at least. You
have read it? Ah, yes! Dear Alden knew nothing, really.
When I look at his etchings of buildings—at his word
sketch of myself—I see behind the lines and letters to a
great void.

"At best, he was an admirable camera equipped with
focal-plane shutter and finest anastigmatic lenses depicting three dimensions faithfully in two, yet ignoring the
most important fourth dimension of temperament and
soul as though it were as mythical as that fourth dimension played with by mathematicians.

"It is not. Artistic inspiration—what the underworld
calls *yen*—has been my whole life. Beyond the technique
and inspiration furnished by Guarneresi, one might scrap
the whole of tutelage and still have left—myself, and the
divine spark!

"I was one of the Long Island Pembertons. Two sisters
still are living. They are staid, respectable ladies who married well. To hell with them! They *really* believed that Hal
Pemberton disgraced them, the nauseating prigs!

"Our mother was Sheila Varro, the singer. Father was
an unimaginative sort, president of the Everest Life and
Casualty Company for many years. I mention these facts
merely to show you there was no hereditary taint, no con-
nate reason for warped mentality such as they attribute
to me. That I inherited the whole of my poor mother's
artistic predilection there is possibility for doubt, for she
was brilliant always. I was a dullard in my youth. It was
only with education and inspiration that even a spark of
her divine creative fury came to me—but the story of that
I shall reach later."

"As a boy, I hated school. Before the age of ten I had
been expelled from three academies, always on account

of the way I treated my associates. I was cruel to other boys, because lessons did not capture my attention. Nothing quiet, static, like the pursuit of facts, *ever* has done so.

"When I tired of sticking pins into younger lads, or pulling their hair, I sought out one or another of my own size and fought with him. Often—usually—I was trounced, but this never bothered. Hurt, blood and heat of combat always were curiosities to me—impersonal, somehow. As long as I could stand on my feet I would punch for the nose or eyes of my antagonist, for nothing delighted me like seeing the involuntary pain flood his countenance, and red blood stream from his mashed nostrils.

"Father sent me to the New York public schools, but there I lasted only six or seven weeks. I was not popular either with my playmates or with the teachers, who complained of what they took to be abnormality. I had done nothing except arrange a pin taken from the hat of one of the women teachers where I thought it would do the most good. This was in the sleeve of the principal's greatcoat

When he slid in his right hand the long pin pierced his palm, causing him to cry out loudly with pain. I did not see him at the moment, but I was waiting outside his office at the time, and I gloated in my mind at the picture of his stabbed hand, ebbing drops of blood where the blue steel entered.

"I longed to rush in and view my work, but did not dare. Later, when by some shrewd deduction they fastened the blame on me, Mr. Mortenson had his right hand bandaged.

"Father gave up the idea of public school after this, and procured me a tutor. He thought me a trifle deficient, and I suppose my attitude lent color to such a theory. I tormented the three men who took me in hand, one after the other, until each one resigned. I malingered. I shirked. I prepared 'accidents' in which all were injured.

"It was not that I could not learn—I realized all along that simple tasks assigned me by these men could be accomplished without great effort—but that I had no desire to study algebra, geography and language, or other dull things of the kind. Only zoology tempted in the least, and none of the men I had before Jackson came was competent to do much of anything with this absorbing subject.

"Jackson was the fourth, and last. He proved himself an earnest soul, and something of a scientist. He tried patiently for a fortnight to teach me all that Dad desired, but found his pupil responsive only when he gave me animals to study. These, while alive, interested me.

"One day, after a discouraging session with my other studies, he left me with some small beetles which he intended to classify on his return. It was a hot day, and the little sheath-winged insects were stimulated out of dormance to lively movement. I had them under a glass cover to prevent their escape.

"Just to see how they acted, I took them out, one by one, and performed slight operations upon parts of their anatomy with the point of my penknife. One I deprived of wings, another lost two legs of many, a third was deprived of antennae, and so on. Then I squatted close with a hand-lens and eyed their desperate struggles.

"Here was *life, pain, struggle*—death close by, leering at the tiny creatures. It fascinated me. I watched eagerly, and then, when one of the beetles grew slower in moving, I stimulated it with the heated point of a pin.

"At the time—I was then only sixteen years of age—I had no analytical explanation of interest, but now I know that the artist in me was swept through a haze of adolescence by sight of that most sincere of all the struggles of life, the struggle against *death!*

"A fever raced in my blood. I knew the beetles could not last. An instinct made me wish to preserve some form

of record of their supreme moment. I seized my pencil. I
wrote a paragraph, telling how I would feel in case some
huge, omnipotent force should put me under glass, remove
my legs, stab me with the point of a great knife, a red-hot
dagger, and watch my writhings.

"The description was pale, colorless, of course. It did
not satisfy, even while I scribbled. As you may readily
understand. I possessed no power of literary expression;
crude sentences selected at random only emphasized the
need of expression of a better sort. Without reasoning—
indeed, many a person would have considered me quite
mad at the time—I tore a clean sheet of paper from a thick
tablet and fell to *sketching* rapidly, furiously!

"As with writing, I knew nothing of technique—I never
had drawn a line before—but the impelling force was great.
Before my eyes I saw the picture I wished to portray—the
play of protest against death. I drew the death struggle. . . .

"By the time Jackson returned the fire had died out of me.

"The horrid sketch was finished, and all but one of the
beetles lay, legs upturned, under the glass. That one had
managed to escape somehow, and was dragging itself hope-
lessly across the table, leaving a wet streak of colorless
blood to mark its passing. Exhausted in body and mind. I
had collapsed in the nearest chair, not caring whether I,
myself, lived or died.

"Poor Jackson was horrified when he saw what I had
done to the *Coleoptera,* and he began reproaching me for
my needless cruelty. Just as he was waxing eloquent, however, his eye caught sight of my crude sketch. He stopped
speaking.

"I saw him tremble, adjust his pince-nez and stare long
at the poor picture I had made, and then at the dead beetles.
Finally, seeming in a torment of anger, he read the paragraph of description, turning to examine me with horror
and amazement in his glance.

"Then, suddenly, he sprang to his feet, gripping the two sheets of paper in his hands, swung about, and made off before I could rouse from my lassitude sufficiently to question him. I never saw Jackson again. The poor fool.

"An hour later father sent for me. I knew that the tutor had been to see him, and I expected another of the terrible lectures I had been in habit of receiving each time a new lack or iniquity made itself apparent to others. On several occasions in the past father had flogged me, and driven himself close to the verge of apoplexy because of his extreme anger at what he deemed deliberate obstinacy. I feared whippings: they sickened me. My knees were quaking as I went to his study.

"This time, however, it was plain that father had given up. He was pale, weighed down with what must have been the great disappointment of his life; but he neither stormed nor offered to chastise me. Instead he told me quietly that Jackson had resigned, finding me impossible to instruct.

"In a few sentences father reviewed the efforts he had made for my education, then stated that all the tutors had been convinced that my lack of progress had been due more to a chronic disinclination for work rather than to any innate defect of body or mind.

"'So far,' he told me, 'you have refused steadfastly to accept opportunity. Now we come to the end. Mr. Jackson has showed me a sketch made by you in which he professes to see real talent. He advises that you be sent abroad to study drawing or painting. Would you care for this last chance? Otherwise I must place you in an institution of some kind, where you no longer can bring disgrace and pain upon me—a reform school, in short. I tell you frankly, Hal. that I am ready to wash my hands of you.'

"What could I do? I chose, of course, to go to Paris. Father made the necessary arrangements for me to enter

Guarneresi's big studios as a beginner, paying for a year in advance, and making me a liberal allowance in addition.

"'I shall not attempt to conceal from you, Hal,' he told me at parting, 'that I do not wish you to return. Your allowance will continue just as long as you remain abroad. If, in time, a moderate success in some line of endeavor comes to you I shall be glad to see you again, but not before. The Pembertons never were failures or parasites.'

"Thus I left him. He died while I was in my third year at the studio, and by his express wish I was not notified until after the funeral was over. I wept over the letter that came, but only because of the knowledge that now I never could make up in any way for the great sorrow I had caused my father. Had he lived only ten years longer—and this would not have been extraordinary, as he died at the age of fifty-two—I could have restored some of that lost pride to him.

"Is it necessary to tell of my years with Guarneresi? No; you confessed slight knowledge of me. Very well, I shall pass over them lightly. Suffice it to say that here at last I found my forte. I could paint. The *maestro* never valued my efforts very highly, but he taught with conscientious diligence nevertheless. In the use of sweeping line and chiaroscuro I excelled the majority of his pupils, but in color I exhibited no talent—in *his* estimation, at least.

"It was strange, too, for through my mind at odd intervals swept riots of crimson, orange and purple, which never could be mixed satisfactorily upon my palette for any given picture. I told myself that the fault lay as much in the subjects of my pictures as in myself—the excuse of a liar, of course.

"There *was* some excuse there, however. For instance, when we painted nudes Guarneresi would assemble a half-dozen old hags with yellowed skin, bony torsos and shriveled breasts, asking us to portray youth and beauty.

Instead of attempting to pin a fabric of imagination upon such skeletons, I used to search out the more beautiful of the cocottes of the night cafes, and bring with me to the studio the next day memories and hurried sketches of poses in which I had seen them. This was more interesting, but unsatisfactory withal.

"I had been five years in the studio, and had traveled three winters to Sicily, Sardinia and Italy, before the first hint of a resolution of my problem came to me. It was in month of July when north-loving students take their vacations.

"I was alone in the vast studio one afternoon. Guarneresi himself was absent, which accounted for the holiday taken by the faithful who remained during the hot days. On one side of the room were the cages where the *maestro* kept small live animals, used for models with beginners. There were a few rabbits, a dozen white mice and a red fox.

"Wandering about, near to my wits' end for inspiration to further work, I chanced to see one of the rabbits looking in my direction. Rays of sunlight, falling through the open skylight, caught the beast's eyes in such a manner that they showed to me as round discs of *glowing scarlet*.

"Never had I witnessed this phenomenon before, which I since have learned is common. It had an extraordinary effect upon me. In that second I thought of my delinquent boyhood, of dozens of cruel impulses since practically forgotten—of the mutilated, dying beetles which had been instrumental in embarking me upon an art career.

"Blood rose in torrents to my own temples. A fever consumed me. There was life and *there could be death*. I could renew the inspiration of those tortured beetles.

"With agitated stealth, I glanced out into the empty hallway, locked the door of the studio, drew four shades over windows through which I might be seen, and crept to the rabbit cage.

"Opening it, I seized by the long ears the white-furred animal which had stared at me The warm softness of its palpitating body raised my artistic desire to a frenzy. I pulled a table from the wall, and holding down the animal upon it I drew my knife. Overcoming the mad, futile struggles of the rabbit, I slit long incisions in the white back and belly. The blood welled out. . . .

"Perfect fury of delight sent me to my canvas. My finger trembled as I mixed the colors, but there was no indecision now, and no hint of muddiness in the result. I painted. . . .

"You perhaps have seen a reproduction of that picture? It was called *The Lusts of the Magi,* and now hangs in one of the Paris galleries. Some day it will grace the Louvre. And all because our white rabbit had sacrificed its heart's blood.

"At eleven next morning Guarneresi himself, coming to the studio, found me exhausted and asleep upon the floor. When he demanded explanations, I pointed in silence to the finished picture upon my easel.

"I thought the man would go frantic. He regarded it for an instant, with intolerance fading from his bearded face. Then his mouth gaped open, and a succession of low exclamations in his native tongue came forth. His raised hands opened and shut in the gesture I knew to mean unrestrained delight.

"Suddenly he dashed to the easel, and, before I could offer resistance, he snatched down my picture and ran with it out of the studio and down the stairs into the narrow street. I followed, but I was not swift enough. He had disappeared.

"In half an hour he returned with four brother artists who had studios nearby. The others were more than lavish in their praise, terming my picture the greater masterpiece turned out in the Quarter for years. Guarneresi himself was less demonstrative now, but I detected tears in his eyes when he turned to me.

"'The pupil has become the master,' he said simply. 'Go! I did not teach you this, and I cannot teach you more. Always I shall boast, however, that Signor Pemberton painted his first great picture in my studio.'

"The next day I rented a studio of my own and moved out my effects immediately. I started to paint in earnest. There is little to relate of the next few months. A wraith of the inspiration which had given birth to my great picture still lingered, but I was no better than mediocre in my work. True the experience and accomplishment had improved me somewhat in use of color, but I learned the galling truth soon enough that never could I attain that same fervor of artistry again—unless . . .

"After four months of ineffectual striving—during which time I completed two unsatisfactory canvases—I yielded, and bought myself a second white rabbit. What was my horror now to discover, when I treated the beast as I had treated its predecessor, that no wild thrill of inspiration assaulted me.

"I could mix and apply colors a trifle more gaudily, yet the suffering and blood of this animal had lost its potent effect upon me. After a day or two the solution occurred. Lusts of The Magi had exhausted the stimulus which rabbits could furnish.

"Disconsolate now. I allowed my work to flag. Though I knew in my heart that the one picture I had done was splendid in its way, I hated to believe that in it I had reached the peak of artistic production. Yet I could arouse in myself no more than the puerile enthusiasm for methodical slapping on of oils I so ridiculed in other mediocre painters. Finally I stopped altogether, and gave myself over to a fit of depression, absinthe and cigarettes.

"Guarneresi visited me one day, and finding me so badly in the dumps prescribed fresh air and sunshine. As I refused flatly to travel, knowing my ailment to be of the subjective sort, not cured by glimpses of pastures new, he lent me his saddle mare, a fine black animal with white fetlocks and a star upon her forehead. I agreed listlessly to ride her each day.

"Three weeks slipped by. I had kept my promise—actually enjoying the exercise—but without any of the beneficent results appearing. I was in fair physical health—only a trifle listless—it is true, yet whenever I set myself to paint a greater inhibition of spiritual and mental weariness seemed to hold me back. Little by little, the ghastly conviction forced itself upon me that as an artist I had shot my bolt.

"One day, when I was riding a league or two beyond Passy, I had occasion to dismount and slake my thirst at a spring on which it was necessary to break a thin crust of ice. Drinking my fill I led the mare to the spot, and she drank also. In raising her head, however, a sharp edge of ice cut her tender skin the distance of a quarter inch. There, as I watched, *I saw red drops of blood gather on her cheek.*

"I cannot describe adequately the sensations that gripped me! In that second I remembered the beetles and the rabbit; and I *knew* that this splendid animal had been given to me for no purpose other than to renew the wasted inspiration within me. It was the hand of Providence."

"Preparations soon were made. I obtained the use of a spacious well-lighted barn in the vicinity, and put the mare therein while I returned to Paris for canvases and materials. Then, when I was all ready for work, I hobbled the mare with strong ropes, and tied her so she could not budge. Then I treated her as I had treated the rabbit.

"Deep down I hated to inflict this pain, for I had grown to care for that mare almost as one cares for a dear friend; but the fury of artistic desire would not be denied.

"Next day, when all was over, I took the canvas in to Paris and showed it to Guarneresi. He went into ecstasies, proclaiming that I had reawakened, indeed. Yet when I told him of the mare and offered to pay his own price, he became very white of countenance and drew himself up, shuddering.

"'Any but as great a man as yourself, Signor,' he shrilled, his cracked old voice breaking with emotion, 'I should kill for that. Yourself are without the law which would damn another, but *not* outside the sphere of undying hatred. You are great, but awful. *Go!*'

"I found, then, that no one wished to look at my picture. Guarneresi had told the story to sympathetic friends, and it had spread like a fire in spruce throughout the Quarter. I was ostracized, deserted by all who had called me their friend.

"A month later, nearly broken in spirit, I came to New York. I was done with Paris. Here in America none knew the story of my last painting, and when it was put on exhibition the critics heralded it as greater far than the finest production of any previous or contemporary American artist. I sold it for twenty thousand dollars, which was a good price in those days.

"I was swept up on a tide of popularity. As you know, in this country even the poorest works of a popular man are snatched up avidly. Criticism seems to die when once a reputation is attained. I got rid of all the canvases I had painted in Paris, and was besieged for portrait sittings by society women of the city.

"Because I had no particular idea in mind for my next painting I did allow myself to drift into this work. It was easy and paid immensely well. Also I was called upon to exercise no ingenuity or imagination. All I did was paint them as they came, two a week, and get rich, wasting five years in the process.

"Then I fell in love. Beatrice was much younger than myself, just turned nineteen at the time. I was first attracted to her because my eye always seeks out the beautiful in face and form as if I were choosing models among all the women I meet.

"She was slim of waist and of ankle, though with the soft curve of neck and shoulder which intrigues an artist instantly. She was more mature in some ways than one might have expected of her years—but the more delightful for that reason.

"Her eyes were dark pools rippled by the breeze of each passing fancy. The moment I looked into them I knew that wrench of the heart which bespeaks the advent of the one great emotion. Many times before I had thought myself in love, yet in company of Beatrice I wondered at my self-deception. In the evening, as she sat beside me in a nook of Sebastian's Spice Gardens—you know, the great indoor reproduction of the famous gardens of Kandy, Ceylon—I gloried in her beauty, and in the way soft silk clung to her person. The desire for possession was intolerable within me. Before parting I asked her, and for answer she lifted her soft, white arms to my neck and met my lips with a caress in which I felt the whole fervor of love. That was the sweetest and happiest moment of my life.

"We married, and built ourselves a home upon Long Island. After three months of honeymoon we settled there, more than ever in love with each other if that were possible.

"A year sped by. Ten months of this I spent without lifting a brush to canvas. It was idyllic, yet toward the last a sense of shame began to pervade my mind. Was I of such weak fibre that the love of one woman must stamp out all ambition, all desire for accomplishment?

"At the end of the year I was painting again, making portraits. The long rest and happiness had made me impatient with such piffle, however. I had all the money that either of us could need in our lifetime, so I could not take the portraiture seriously. I dabbled with it another full year, without once endeavoring to start a serious piece of work.

"Then, after Beatrice bore me a daughter, I began to lay plans for continuing serious endeavor. It is useless to repeat the story of those struggles. It was the same experience I had had after that first successful picture.

"My technique now was as near perfection as I could hope to attain, and the mere matter of color mixing I had learned from those two wild flights of frenzy. I found myself, however, psychologically unable to attack a subject smacking in the least of the gruesome—and that, of course, always had been my talent and interest.

"I rebelled against the instinct which urged me to try the experiment of the mare again. In cold blood I hated the thought of it, and also I feared, with a great sinking of the heart, that I should find no more inspiration there even if I did repeat.

"I turned to landscape painting, choosing sordid, dirty or powerful scenes. I painted the fish-and-milk carts on Hester Street, showing the hordes of dirty urchins in the background playing on the pavement. Somehow, the picture fell short of being really good, although I had no difficulty in selling it.

"I portrayed, then, a street in the Ghetto on a rainy night, with greasy mud shining on the cobblestones and the shapeless figure of a man slouched in a doorway. This was called powerful—the 'awakening of an American Franz Hals' one critic termed it—but I knew better. Beside the work I *could* do under powerful stimulus and inspiration, this was slush, slime. I *hated* it!

"Even waterscapes did not satisfy. I painted half of one picture depicting two sooty, straining tugs bringing a great leviathan of a steamer into harbor, but this I never finished. I felt as if I drooled at the mouth while I was working.

"Thus two more years went by, happy enough when I was with Beatrice, but sad and savage when I was by myself in the studio. My wife had blossomed early into the full beauty of womanhood, and yet she retained enough of modesty and reticence of self that I never wearied of her. Because up to this time, when I turned thirty-three years of age, the powers of both of us, physical and mental, had been on the increase, we still were exploring the delight of love and true affection.

"There was an impelling force within me, however, which would not be denied. I had been born to accomplish great things. Weak compromise, or weaker yielding to delights of the mind and body, could but heap fresh fuel on the flame which consumed me when I got off by myself. I fought against it months longer, but in the end I had to yield. With fear and trepidation struggling with ambition and lust within me, I took a trip to a distant town of New York State, procured a fine, blooded mare and repeated the experiment which had lost me the friendship of Guarneresi and my Parisian contemporaries.

"All in vain. Out of the hideous slaughter of the animal I obtained only a single grim picture—a canvas which I painted weeks later, when the shudder of revulsion in my frame had died down somewhat. I called the picture *Cannibalism*, for it showed African savages gorging themselves on human flesh. It never sold, for the instant I placed it on exhibition the art censors of New York threw it under ban—and, I believe, no one really wanted the thing in his house.

"I did not like it myself, and finally, after much urging by my wife, I burned it. This sacrifice, however, merely accentuated the fury in my heart. I *must* do better than that!

"Since I have told you of my other periods of frenzy and self-hatred, I may pass over the ensuing month. One day the inspiration for my last great picture came, and as with the second, through pure accident. Beatrice was cutting weeds in the garden with a sickle, while I sat cross-legged beside her, watching. I always could find surcease from discontent in being near her, and watching the fine play of animal forces in her supple body.

"The sickle slipped. Beatrice cried out, and I jumped to place a handkerchief over the wound that lay open on her wrist, but not before my eyes had caught the sight of the red blood bubbling out upon her satiny skin.

"A madness leaped into my soul. My fingers trembled and a throbbing made itself felt in my temples as I laved on antiseptic and bound a bandage over the wound. This was the logical, the inevitable conclusion! She was my mate; she was duty bound to furnish inspiration for the picture I must paint, my *masterpiece*.

"I of course, told Beatrice nothing of what was passing in my mind, but went immediately about my preparations.

"I placed a cot in the studio, fastening strong straps to it. Then I made ready a gag, and sharpened a keen Weiss knife I possessed until its edge would cut a hair at a touch. Last I made ready my canvas.

"She came at my call. At first, when I seized her and tore off her clothing she thought me joking, and protested, laughing. When I came to placing the gag, and bound her arms and legs with strong straps, however, the terror of death began to steal into her dark eyes.

"To show her that I loved her still, no matter what duty impelled me to do, I kissed her hair, her eyes, her breast. Then I set to work. . . .

"In a few minutes I was away and painting as I never had painted before. A red stream dripped from the steel cot, down to the floor, and ran slowly toward where I stood. It elated me. I felt the fire of a fervor of inspiration greater than ever had beset me. I painted. *I painted!* This was my masterpiece.

"Drunk with the fury of creation, I threw myself on the floor in the midst of the red puddle time and time again. I even dipped my brushes in it. Mad with the delight of unstinted accomplishment, I kept on and on, until late in the evening I heard my little daughter crying in her room for the dinner she had not received. Then I went downstairs, laughing at the horror I saw in the faces of the servants.

"They found Beatrice, of course. The servants 'phoned immediately for the police. I fooled them all, however. I knew that they might do something to me, such is the lack of understanding against which true artists always must labor, so I took the canvas of my masterpiece and hid it in a secret cupboard in the wall known only to myself. I did not care what they did to me, but this picture, for which Beatrice had offered up her love and life, was sacred.

"They came and took me away. Then ensued a terrible scandal, and some foolish examinations of me in which I took not the slightest interest. And then they put me here.

"I have not been in duress all the time, though. Oh, no! Three years later some of my old friends contrived at escape, and secreted me away to the South Seas. There they gave me a studio, meaning to allow me to paint. I was guarded, though. They would not allow me full freedom.

"I painted, but I have not the slightest idea what was done with those canvases. I had no interest in them personally. All I could think of now was the one great masterpiece hidden in the cupboard of my old studio. I wanted to see it, to glory in the flame of color and in the tremendous conception itself.

"At last I gave my guards the slip, and after long wandering about in native proas, made my way to this country again, to New York. I found the canvas, and, rolling it, secreted it upon my person. Then I went out and gave myself up to them. I was brought here again.

"Imprisonment was not important to me any more. I was getting old. Though I would like to be released now it is a matter of less urgency than before, because I have with me always my masterpiece. *See!*"

The old man tugged at something inside his blouse, and brought forth a dirtied roll which he unsnapped with fingers that trembled in eagerness.

"See, Madame!" he repeated triumphantly.

And, before my horrified eyes, he unrolled *a blank square of white canvas!*

# Pickman's Model

## H. P. LOVECRAFT
### 1927

You needn't think I'm crazy, Eliot—plenty of others have queerer prejudices than this. Why don't you laugh at Oliver's grandfather, who won't ride in a motor? If I don't like that damned subway, it's my own business; and we got here more quickly anyhow in the taxi. We'd have had to walk up the hill from Park Street if we'd taken the car.

I know I'm more nervous than I was when you saw me last year, but you don't need to hold a clinic over it. There's plenty of reason, God knows, and I fancy I'm lucky to be sane at all. Why the third degree? You didn't use to be so inquisitive.

Well, if you must hear it, I don't know why you shouldn't. Maybe you ought to, anyhow, for you kept writing me like a grieved parent when you heard I'd begun to cut the Art Club and keep away from Pickman. Now that he's disappeared I go around to the club once in a while, but my nerves aren't what they were.

No, I don't know what's become of Pickman, and I don't like to guess. You might have surmised I had some inside information when I dropped him—and that's why I don't want to think where he's gone. Let the police find what they can—it won't be much, judging from the fact that they don't know yet of the old North End place he hired under the name of Peters. I'm not sure that I could find it again myself—not that I'd ever try, even in broad daylight! Yes, I do know, or am afraid I know, why he maintained it. I'm coming to that. And I think you'll understand before I'm through why I don't tell the police. They would ask me to guide them, but I couldn't go back there even if I knew the way. There was something there—and now I can't use the subway or (and you may as well have your laugh at this, too) go down into cellars any more.

I should think you'd have known I didn't drop Pickman for the same silly reasons that fussy old women like Dr. Reid or Joe Minot or Bosworth did. Morbid art doesn't shock me, and when a man has the genius Pickman had I feel it an honor to know him, no matter what direction his work takes. Boston never had a greater painter than Richard Upton Pickman. I said it at first and I say it still, and I never swerved an inch, either, when he showed that *Ghoul Feeding*. That, you remember, was when Minot cut him.

You know, it takes profound art and profound insight into Nature to turn out stuff like Pickman's. Any magazine-cover hack can splash paint around wildly and call it a nightmare or a Witches' Sabbath or a portrait of the devil, but only a great painter can make such a thing really scare or ring true. That's because only a real artist knows the actual anatomy of the terrible or the physiology of fear—the exact sort of lines and proportions that connect up with latent instincts or hereditary memories of fright, and the proper color contrasts and lighting effects to stir the dormant sense of strangeness. I don't have to tell you why a Fuseli really brings a shiver while a cheap ghost-story frontispiece merely makes us laugh. There's something those fellows catch—beyond life—that they're able to make us catch for a second. Doré had it. Sime has it. Angarola of Chicago has it. And Pickman had it as no man ever had it before or—I hope to heaven—ever will again.

Don't ask me what it is they see. You know, in ordinary art, there's all the difference in the world between the vital, breathing things drawn from Nature or models and the artificial truck that commercial small fry reel off in a bare studio by rule. Well, I should say that the really weird artist has a kind of vision which makes models, or summons up what amounts to actual scenes from the spectral world he lives in. Anyhow, he manages to turn out results that differ from the pretender's mince-pie dreams in just about the same way that the life painter's results differ from the concoctions of a correspondence-school cartoonist. If I had ever seen what Pickman saw—but no! Here, let's have a drink before we get any deeper. Gad, I wouldn't be alive if I'd ever seen what that man—if he was a man—saw!

You recall that Pickman's forte was faces. I don't believe anybody since Goya could put so much of sheer hell into a set of features or a twist of expression. And before Goya you have to go back to the mediaeval chaps who did the gargoyles and chimaeras on Notre Dame and Mont Saint-Michel. They believed all sorts of things—and maybe they saw all sorts of things, too, for the Middle Ages had some curious phases. I remember your asking Pickman yourself once, the year before you went away, wherever in thunder he got such ideas and visions. Wasn't that a nasty laugh he gave you? It was partly because of that laugh that Reid dropped him. Reid, you know, had just taken up comparative pathology, and was full of pompous "inside stuff" about the biological or evolutionary significance of this or that mental or physical symptom. He said Pickman repelled him more and more every day, and almost frightened him toward the last—that the fellow's features and expression were slowly developing in a way he didn't like; in a way that wasn't human. He had a lot of talk about diet, and said Pickman must be abnormal and eccentric to the last degree. I suppose you told Reid, if you and he had any correspondence over it, that he'd let Pickman's paintings get on his nerves or harrow up his imagination. I know I told him that myself—then.

But keep in mind that I didn't drop Pickman for anything like this. On the contrary, my admiration for him kept growing; for that *Ghoul Feeding* was a tremendous achievement. As you know, the club wouldn't exhibit it, and the Museum of Fine Arts wouldn't accept it as a gift; and I can add that nobody would buy it, so Pickman had it right in his house till he went. Now his father has it in Salem—you know Pickman comes of old Salem stock, and had a witch ancestor hanged in 1692.

I got into the habit of calling on Pickman quite often, especially after I began making notes for a monograph on weird art. Probably it was his work which put the idea into my head, and anyhow, I found him a mine of data and suggestions when I came to develop it. He showed me all the paintings and drawings he had about; including some pen-and-ink sketches that would, I verily believe, have got him kicked out of the club if many of the members had seen them. Before long I was pretty nearly a devotee, and would listen for hours like a schoolboy to art theories and philosophic speculations wild enough to qualify him for the Danvers asylum. My hero-worship, coupled with the fact that people generally were commencing to have less and less to do with him, made him get very confidential with me; and one evening he hinted that if I were fairly close-mouthed and none too squeamish, he might show me something rather unusual—something a bit stronger than anything he had in the house.

"You know," he said, "there are things that won't do for Newbury Street—things that are out of place here, and that can't be conceived here, anyhow. It's my business to catch the overtones of the soul, and you won't find those in a parvenu set of artificial streets on made land. Back Bay isn't Boston—it isn't anything yet, because it's had no time to pick up memories and attract local spirits. If there are any ghosts here, they're the tame ghosts of a salt marsh and a shallow cove; and I want human ghosts—the ghosts of beings highly organized enough to have looked on hell and known the meaning of what they saw.

"The place for an artist to live is the North End. If any aesthete were sincere, he'd put up with the slums for the sake of the massed traditions. God, man! Don't you realize that places like that weren't merely *made,* but actually *grew?* Generation after generation lived and felt and died there, and in days when people weren't afraid to live and feel and die. Don't you know there was a mill on Copp's Hill in 1632, and that half the present streets were laid out by 1650? I can show you houses that have stood two centuries and a half and more; houses that have witnessed what would make a modern house crumble into powder. What do moderns know of life and the forces behind it? You call the Salem witchcraft a delusion, but I'll wage my four-times-great-grandmother could have told you things. They hanged her on Gallows Hill, with Cotton Mather looking sanctimoniously on. Mather, damn him, was afraid somebody might succeed in kicking free of this accursed cage of monotony—I wish someone had laid a spell on him or sucked his blood in the night!

"I can show you a house he lived in, and I can show you another one he was afraid to enter in spite of all his fine bold talk. He knew things he didn't dare put into that stupid *Magnalia* or that puerile *Wonders of the Invisible World.* Look here, do you know the whole North End once had a set of tunnels that kept certain people in touch with each other's houses, and the burying-ground, and the sea?

Let them prosecute and persecute above ground—things went on every day that they couldn't reach, and voices laughed at night that they couldn't place!

"Why, man, out of ten surviving houses built before 1700 and not moved since I'll wager that in eight I can show you something queer in the cellar. There's hardly a month that you don't read of workmen finding bricked-up arches and wells leading nowhere in this or that old place as it comes down—you could see one near Henchman Street from the elevated last year. There were witches and what their spells summoned; pirates and what they brought in from the sea; smugglers; privateers—and I tell you, people knew how to live, and how to enlarge the bounds of life, in the old times! This wasn't the only world a bold and wise man could know—faugh! And to think of today in contrast, with such pale-pink brains that even a club of supposed artists gets shudders and convulsions if a picture goes beyond the feelings of a Beacon Street tea-table!

"The only saving grace of the present is that it's too damned stupid to question the past very closely. What do maps and records and guide-books really tell of the North End? Bah! At a guess I'll guarantee to lead you to thirty or forty alleys and networks of alleys north of Prince Street that aren't suspected by ten living beings outside of the foreigners that swarm them. And what do those Dagoes know of their meaning? No, Thurber, these ancient places are dreaming gorgeously and overflowing with wonder and terror and escapes from the commonplace, and yet there's not a living soul to understand or profit by them. Or rather, there's only one living soul—for I haven't been digging around in the past for nothing!

"See here, you're interested in this sort of thing. What if I told you that I've got another studio up there, where I can catch the night-spirit of antique horror and paint things that I couldn't even think of in Newbury Street?

Naturally I don't tell those cursed old maids at the club—
with Reid, damn him, whispering even as it is that I'm
a sort of monster bound down the toboggan of reverse
evolution. Yes, Thurber, I decided long ago that one must
paint terror as well as beauty from life, so I did some
exploring in places where I had reason to know terror lives.

"I've got a place that I don't believe three living Nor-
dic men besides myself have ever seen. It isn't so very far
from the elevated as distance goes, but it's centuries away
as the soul goes. I took it because of the queer old brick
well in the cellar—one of the sort I told you about. The
shack's almost tumbling down, so that nobody else would
live there, and I'd hate to tell you how little I pay for it.
The windows are boarded up, but I like that all the better, since I don't want daylight for what I do. I paint in
the cellar, where the inspiration is thickest, but I've other
rooms furnished on the ground floor. A Sicilian owns it,
and I've hired it under the name of Peters.

"Now if you're game, I'll take you there tonight. I think
you'd enjoy the pictures, for as I said, I've let myself go
a bit there. It's no vast tour—I sometimes do it on foot,
for I don't want to attract attention with a taxi in such
a place. We can take the shuttle at the South Station for
Battery Street, and after that the walk isn't much."

Well, Eliot, there wasn't much for me to do after that
harangue but to keep myself from running instead of walking for the first vacant cab we could sight. We changed
to the elevated at the South Station, and at about twelve
o'clock had climbed down the steps at Battery Street and
struck along the old waterfront past Constitution Wharf.
I didn't keep track of the cross streets, and can't tell you
yet which it was we turned up, but I know it wasn't Gree-
nough Lane.

When we did turn, it was to climb through the deserted length of the oldest and dirtiest alley I ever saw in my

life, with crumbling-looking gables, broken small-paned windows, and archaic chimneys that stood out half-disintegrated against the moonlit sky. I don't believe there were three houses in sight that hadn't been standing in Cotton Mather's time—certainly I glimpsed at least two with an overhang, and once I thought I saw a peaked roof-line of the almost forgotten pre-gambrel type, though antiquarians tell us there are none left in Boston.

From that alley, which had a dim light, we turned to the left into an equally silent and still narrower alley with no light at all; and in a minute made what I think was an obtuse-angled bend toward the right in the dark. Not long after this Pickman produced a flashlight and revealed an antediluvian ten-paneled door that looked damnably worm-eaten. Unlocking it, he ushered me into a barren hallway with what was once splendid dark-oak paneling—simple, of course, but thrillingly suggestive of the times of Andros and Phipps and the Witchcraft. Then he took me through a door on the left, lighted an oil lamp, and told me to make myself at home.

Now, Eliot, I'm what the man in the street would call fairly "hard-boiled", but I'll confess that what I saw on the walls of that room gave me a bad turn. They were his pictures, you know—the ones he couldn't paint or even show in Newbury Street—and he was right when he said he had "let himself go." Here—have another drink—I need one anyhow!

There's no use in my trying to tell you what they were like, because the awful, the blasphemous horror, and the unbelievable loathsomeness and moral fetor came from simple touches quite beyond the power of words to classify. There was none of the exotic technique you see in Sidney Sime, none of the trans-Saturnian landscapes and lunar fungi that Clark Ashton Smith uses to freeze the blood. The backgrounds were mostly old churchyards,

deep woods, cliffs by the sea, brick tunnels, ancient paneled rooms, or simple vaults of masonry. Copp's Hill Burying Ground, which could not be many blocks away from
this very house, was a favorite scene.

The madness and monstrosity lay in the figures in the
foreground—for Pickman's morbid art was preeminently
one of demoniac portraiture. These figures were seldom
completely human, but often approached humanity in
varying degree. Most of the bodies, while roughly bipedal,
had a forward slumping, and a vaguely canine cast. The
texture of the majority was a kind of unpleasant rubberi-
ness. Ugh! I can see them now! Their occupations—well,
don't ask me to be too precise. They were usually feeding—I won't say on what. They were sometimes shown in
groups in cemeteries or underground passages, and often
appeared to be in battle over their prey—or rather, their
treasure-trove. And what damnable expressiveness Pickman
sometimes gave the sightless faces of this charnel booty!
Occasionally the things were shown leaping through open
windows at night, or squatting on the chests of sleepers,
worrying at their throats. One canvas showed a ring of
them baying about a hanged witch on Gallows Hill, whose
dead face held a close kinship to theirs.

But don't get the idea that it was all this hideous business of theme and setting which struck me faint. I'm not
a three-year-old kid, and I'd seen much like this before. It
was the *faces,* Eliot, those accursed *faces,* that leered and
slavered out of the canvas with the very breath of life! By
God, man, I verily believe they were alive! That nauseous
wizard had waked the fires of hell in pigment, and his
brush had been a nightmare-spawning wand. Give me that
decanter, Eliot!

There was one thing called *The Lesson*—heaven pity
me, that I ever saw it! Listen—can you fancy a squatting
circle of nameless dog-like things in a churchyard teaching

a small child how to feed like themselves? The price of a
changeling, I suppose—you know the old myth about how
the weird people leave their spawn in cradles in exchange
for the human babes they steal. Pickman was showing what
happens to those stolen babes—how they grow up—and
then I began to see a hideous relationship in the faces of
the human and non-human figures. He was, in all his gra-
dations of morbidity between the frankly non-human and
the degradedly human, establishing a sardonic linkage and
evolution. The dog-things were developed from mortals!

And no sooner had I wondered what he made of their
own young as left with mankind in the form of change-
lings, than my eye caught a picture embodying that very
thought. It was that of an ancient Puritan interior—a
heavily beamed room with lattice windows, a settle, and
clumsy seventeenth-century furniture, with the family sitting about while the father read from the Scriptures. Every
face but one showed nobility and reverence, but that one
reflected the mockery of the pit. It was that of a young
man in years, and no doubt belonged to a supposed son
of that pious father, but in essence it was the kin of the
unclean things. It was their changeling—and in a spirit of
supreme irony Pickman had given the features a very per-
ceptible resemblance to his own.

By this time Pickman had lighted a lamp in an adjoining room and was politely holding open the door for me;
asking me if I would care to see his "modern studies." I
hadn't been able to give him much of my opinions—I was
too speechless with fright and loathing—but I think he
fully understood and felt highly complimented. And now
I want to assure you again, Eliot, that I'm no mollycod-
dle to scream at anything which shows a bit of departure
from the usual. I'm middle-aged and decently sophisticat-
ed, and I guess you saw enough of me in France to know
I'm not easily knocked out. Remember, too, that I'd just

about recovered my wind and gotten used to those frightful pictures which turned colonial New England into a
kind of annex of hell. Well, in spite of all this, that next
room forced a real scream out of me, and I had to clutch at
the doorway to keep from keeling over. The other chamber
had shown a pack of ghouls and witches overrunning the
world of our forefathers, but this one brought the horror
right into our own daily life!

Gad, how that man could paint! There was a study
called *Subway Accident,* in which a flock of the vile
things were clambering up from some unknown catacomb
through a crack in the floor of the Boylston Street subway
and attacking a crowd of people on the platform. Another
showed a dance on Copp's Hill among the tombs with
the background of today. Then there were any number of
cellar views, with monsters creeping in through holes and
rifts in the masonry and grinning as they squatted behind
barrels or furnaces and waited for their first victim to
descend the stairs.

One disgusting canvas seemed to depict a vast cross-
section of Beacon Hill, with ant-like armies of the mephit-
ic monsters squeezing themselves through burrows that
honeycombed the ground. Dances in the modern cemeteries were freely pictured, and another conception somehow
shocked me more than all the rest—a scene in an unknown
vault, where scores of the beasts crowded about one who
held a well-known Boston guide-book and was evidently
reading aloud. All were pointing to a certain passage, and
every face seemed so distorted with epileptic and rever-
berant laughter that I almost thought I heard the fiendish
echoes. The title of the picture was, *Holmes, Lowell, and
Longfellow Lie Buried in Mount Auburn.*

As I gradually steadied myself and got readjusted to
this second room of deviltry and morbidity, I began to
analyze some of the points in my sickening loathing. In the

first place, I said to myself, these things repelled because of the utter inhumanity and callous cruelty they showed in Pickman. The fellow must be a relentless enemy of all mankind to take such glee in the torture of brain and flesh and the degradation of the mortal tenement. In the second place, they terrified because of their very greatness. Their art was the art that convinced—when we saw the pictures we saw the daemons themselves and were afraid of them. And the queer part was, that Pickman got none of his power from the use of selectiveness or bizarrerie. Nothing was blurred, distorted, or conventionalized; outlines were sharp and life-like, and details were almost painfully defined. And the faces!

It was not any mere artist's interpretation that we saw; it was pandemonium itself, crystal clear in stark objectivity. That was it, by heaven! The man was not a fantaisiste or romanticist at all—he did not even try to give us the churning, prismatic ephemera of dreams, but coldly and sardonically reflected some stable, mechanistic, and well-established horror-world which he saw fully, brilliantly, squarely, and unfalteringly. God knows what that world can have been, or where he ever glimpsed the blasphemous shapes that loped and trotted and crawled through it; but whatever the baffling source of his images, one thing was plain. Pickman was in every sense—in conception and in execution—a thorough, painstaking, and almost scientific *realist*.

My host was now leading the way down cellar to his actual studio, and I braced myself for some hellish effects among the unfinished canvases. As we reached the bottom of the damp stairs he turned his flashlight to a corner of the large open space at hand, revealing the circular brick curb of what was evidently a great well in the earthen floor. We walked nearer, and I saw that it must be five feet across, with walls a good foot thick and some six inches above the ground level—solid work of the seventeenth century, or I was much mistaken. That, Pickman said, was the kind of thing he had been talking about—an aperture of the network of tunnels that used to undermine the hill. I noticed idly that it did not seem to be bricked up, and that a heavy disc of wood formed the apparent cover. Thinking of the things this well must have been connected with if Pickman's wild hints had not been mere rhetoric, I shivered slightly; then turned to follow him up a step and through a narrow door into a room of fair size, provided with a wooden floor and furnished as a studio. An acetylene gas outfit gave the light necessary for work.

The unfinished pictures on easels or propped against the walls were as ghastly as the finished ones upstairs, and showed the painstaking methods of the artist. Scenes were blocked out with extreme care, and penciled guide lines told of the minute exactitude which Pickman used in getting the right perspective and proportions. The man was great—I say it even now, knowing as much as I do. A large camera on a table excited my notice, and Pickman told me that he used it in taking scenes for backgrounds, so that he might paint them from photographs in the studio instead of carting his outfit around the town for this or that view. He thought a photograph quite as good as an actual scene or model for sustained work, and declared he employed them regularly.

There was something very disturbing about the nauseous sketches and half-finished monstrosities that leered around from every side of the room, and when Pickman suddenly unveiled a huge canvas on the side away from the light I could not for my life keep back a loud scream—the second I had emitted that night. It echoed and echoed through the dim vaultings of that ancient and nitrous cellar, and I had to choke back a flood of reaction that threatened to burst out as hysterical laughter. Merciful

Creator! Eliot, but I don't know how much was real and how much was feverish fancy. It doesn't seem to me that earth can hold a dream like that!

It was a colossal and nameless blasphemy with glaring red eyes, and it held in bony claws a thing that had been a man, gnawing at the head as a child nibbles at a stick of candy. Its position was a kind of crouch, and as one looked one felt that at any moment it might drop its present prey and seek a juicier morsel. But damn it all, it wasn't even the fiendish subject that made it such an immortal fountain-head of all panic—not that, nor the dog face with its pointed ears, bloodshot eyes, flat nose, and drooling lips. It wasn't the scaly claws nor the mold-caked body nor the half-hooved feet—none of these, though any one of them might well have driven an excitable man to madness.

It was the technique, Eliot—the cursed, the impious, the unnatural technique! As I am a living being, I never elsewhere saw the actual breath of life so fused into a canvas. The monster was there—it glared and gnawed and gnawed and glared—and I knew that only a suspension of Nature's laws could ever let a man paint a thing like that without a model—without some glimpse of the nether world which no mortal unsold to the Fiend has ever had.

Pinned with a thumb-tack to a vacant part of the canvas was a piece of paper now badly curled up—probably, I thought, a photograph from which Pickman meant to paint a background as hideous as the nightmare it was to enhance. I reached out to uncurl and look at it, when suddenly I saw Pickman start as if shot. He had been listening with peculiar intensity ever since my shocked scream had waked unaccustomed echoes in the dark cellar, and now he seemed struck with a fright which, though not comparable to my own, had in it more of the physical than of the spiritual. He drew a revolver and motioned me to silence, then stepped out into the main cellar and closed the door behind him.

I think I was paralyzed for an instant. Imitating Pickman's listening, I fancied I heard a faint scurrying sound somewhere, and a series of squeals or bleats in a direction I couldn't determine. I thought of huge rats and shuddered. Then there came a subdued sort of clatter which somehow set me all in gooseflesh—a furtive, groping kind of clatter, though I can't attempt to convey what I mean in words. It was like heavy wood falling on stone or brick—wood on brick—what did that make me think of?

It came again, and louder. There was a vibration as if the wood had fallen farther than it had fallen before. After that followed a sharp grating noise, a shouted gibberish from Pickman, and the deafening discharge of all six chambers of a revolver, fired spectacularly as a lion-tamer might fire in the air for effect. A muffled squeal or squawk, and a thud. Then more wood and brick grating, a pause, and the opening of the door—at which I'll confess I started violently. Pickman reappeared with his smoking weapon, cursing the bloated rats that infested the ancient well.

"The deuce knows what they eat, Thurber," he grinned, "for those archaic tunnels touched graveyard and witch-den and sea-coast. But whatever it is, they must have run short, for they were devilish anxious to get out. Your yelling stirred them up, I fancy. Better be cautious in these old places—our rodent friends are the one drawback, though I sometimes think they're a positive asset by way of atmosphere and color."

Well, Eliot, that was the end of the night's adventure. Pickman had promised to show me the place, and heaven knows he had done it. He led me out of that tangle of alleys in another direction, it seems, for when we sighted

a lamp post we were in a half-familiar street with monotonous rows of mingled tenement blocks and old houses.
Charter Street, it turned out to be, but I was too flus-
tered to notice just where we hit it. We were too late for
the elevated, and walked back downtown through Hanover
Street. I remember that walk. We switched from Trem-
ont up Beacon, and Pickman left me at the corner of Joy,
where I turned off. I never spoke to him again.

Why did I drop him? Don't be impatient. Wait till I
ring for coffee. We've had enough of the other stuff, but
I for one need something. No—it wasn't the paintings I
saw in that place; though I'll swear they were enough to
get him ostracized in nine-tenths of the homes and clubs
of Boston, and I guess you won't wonder now why I have
to steer clear of subways and cellars. It was—something I
found in my coat the next morning. You know, the curled-
up paper tacked to that frightful canvas in the cellar; the
thing I thought was a photograph of some scene he meant
to use as a background for that monster. That last scare
had come while I was reaching to uncurl it, and it seems
I had vacantly crumpled it into my pocket. But here's the
coffee—take it black, Eliot, if you're wise.

Yes, that paper was the reason I dropped Pickman;
Richard Upton Pickman, the greatest artist I have ever
known—and the foulest being that ever leaped the bounds
of life into the pits of myth and madness. Eliot—old Reid
was right. He wasn't strictly human. Either he was born in
strange shadow, or he'd found a way to unlock the forbidden gate. It's all the same now, for he's gone—back into
the fabulous darkness he loved to haunt. Here, let's have
the chandelier going.

Don't ask me to explain or even conjecture about what
I burned. Don't ask me, either, what lay behind that
mole-like scrambling Pickman was so keen to pass off as
rats. There are secrets, you know, which might have come

down from old Salem times, and Cotton Mather tells even stranger things. You know how damned life-like Pickman's paintings were—how we all wondered where he got those faces.

Well—that paper wasn't a photograph of any background, after all. What it showed was simply the monstrous being he was painting on that awful canvas. It was the model he was using—and its background was merely the wall of the cellar studio in minute detail. But by God, Eliot, *it was a photograph from life.*

# Nude with a Dagger

JOHN FLANDERS

1934


Old Gryde was a money-lender, and a hard one. In the course of his career, five thousand clients owed him money, he was the occasion of one hundred and twelve suicides, of nine sensational murders, of assignments, bankruptcies and financial disasters without number.

A hundred thousand maledictions were called down on his head, and he laughed at all of them. But the hundred thousand and first malediction killed him, in the strangest and most frightful fashion.

I owed him two hundred pounds, he ground out of me the most abominable interest payments every month, and yet he had made me his intimate friend. As a matter of fact, this was only a way he had of torturing me, for I was forced to submit to every sort of cruelty and malice at his hands, to echo his boisterous laughter as his victims begged, entreated, and even died at his hands.

He scrupulously recorded all this suffering and blood in his day-book and his ledger, as his ill-gotten fortune grew day after day.

But today I do not regret the pain he caused me, because I was allowed at last to witness his death-agony. And I wish all his dear colleagues a like fate.

One morning I found him in his office engaged in an argument with a client, a very pale and very handsome young man. The young man was speaking:

"It is impossible for me to pay you, Mr. Gryde, but I implore you not to sell me out. Take this painting. It is the one good piece of work I have done. I have worked it over a hundred times; I have put my heart's blood into it. Even now I realize that it isn't quite finished. There is something lacking still—I can't tell exactly what it is—but I know I shall find out in time, and then I will finish it.

"Take it for this debt which is killing me—and is killing my poor mother!"

Gryde sneered. When he noticed me, he called my attention to a moderately large painting which stood against his bookcase. When I caught sight of it, I started with surprise and admiration. It seemed to me that I had never seen anything so perfect.

It was a life-size nude, a man as handsome as a god, standing out against a vague, cloudy background, a background of tempest, night and flame.

"I don't know yet what I shall call it," said the artist in a voice filled with pain. "That figure you see there—I have been dreaming of it ever since I was a child; it came to me in a dream just as certain melodies came from heaven in the night to Mozart and Haydn."

"You owe me three hundred pounds, Mr. Warton," said Gryde.

The young man clasped his hands together.

"And my painting, Mr. Gryde! It is worth twice that, three times that, ten times that!"

"In a hundred years," assented Gryde. "I shan't live long enough to get the good of it."

But as he spoke I seemed to catch in his face a sort of vacillating glimmer which was different from the steel-hard gaze I had always seen there before. Was it admiration of an artistic masterpiece, or was it the prospect of fabulous profit?

Then Gryde went on:

"I am sorry for you," he said, "and away down in my heart I have a weakness for artists. I will take it and credit you with a hundred pounds on your debt."

The artist opened his mouth to reply. The usurer cut him off.

"You owe me three hundred pounds, payable at the rate of ten pounds a month. I will sign a receipt for ten months. Don't forget to be prompt in your payment eleven months from today, Mr. Warton!"

Warton had covered his face with his beautiful hands.

"Ten months! You are giving me ten months free from worry, ten months of relief for Mother—Mother is sadly nervous and ill, Mr. Gryde—and I can work hard in these ten months—" He took the receipt.

"But," added Gryde, "you admit yourself that there is something still lacking to the picture. You must put the finishing touch to it, and you must find a name for it by the time the ten months are up."

The artist promised all this, and the picture was hung on the wall above old Gryde's desk.

Eleven months went by, and Warton was unable to pay his installment of ten pounds. He begged and implored Gryde to allow him more time, but to no avail. The usurer secured an order for the sale of the poor boy's effects. When the officers came, they found mother and son sleeping the sleep of death in a room filled with asphyxiating fumes from a brazier of live coals.

On the table, there was a letter for Gryde.

"I agreed to furnish you a name for my picture," the artist had written him. "You may call it *Vengeance*. And as for my promise to finish the picture, I will keep that promise, too."

Gryde was very much annoyed.

"The name," he argued "doesn't fit the picture at all. And how can a dead man come back and finish a picture?"

But his challenge to the other world was answered.

One morning I found Gryde terribly worried and excited.

"Look at the painting!" he cried, the moment I entered the room. "Don't you see something strange about it?"

I studied the painting, but I could discover no change in it. My assurance seemed to relieve him greatly.

"Do you know—" he began. He passed his hand over his forehead, and I could see drops of perspiration standing out on his brow. "It was last night, sometime after midnight. I had gone to bed; then all at once I remembered that I had left some very important papers lying on my desk.

"I got up at once to see that they were put away safely. I never have any trouble in finding my way about in the dark in this house, for I know every corner and crevice of it. I came into my office here without taking the trouble to turn on a light. There was really no need for one, for the moonlight fell square on my desk. As I leaned over my papers, I had a feeling that something was moving between the window and me—

"Look at the picture! Look at the picture!" Gryde cried out suddenly in abject terror.

Then, in a moment, he murmured: "I must be imagining things. I have heard of hallucinations but I can't remember ever having had one—I thought I saw the man in the picture move again.

"Well, when I came in here last night, it seemed to me I saw—no, I swear I *did* see that man in the painting reach out his arm to seize me!"

"You're going crazy," said I.

"I wish I could explain it so," said Gryde; "that would be better than—"

"Well, why don't you destroy the painting, if you think all this isn't just imagination?"

Gryde's face brightened. "That hadn't occurred to me," he said; "I suppose because it was too simple."

He opened a drawer and took out a long-bladed dagger with a delicately chiseled handle.

He walked toward the picture with the dagger in his hand. Then, suddenly, he seemed to change his mind.

"No!" he said. "I'm not going to fling a hundred pounds into the fire just because I had a bad dream. You're the one that's crazy, young friend."

And he flung the weapon angrily down on his desk.

When I went back the next day, I did not find the same Gryde. In his stead was a broken old man with the eyes of a tracked beast, shaking with insane terror.

"No," he howled, "I'm not crazy, I'm not an imbecile! I know what I'm talking about. I got up again last night, and came in here to see if the other thing had been a dream. And I tell you—I tell you—*he* came out of the picture," Gryde bellowed, twisting his hands around each other, "and—and—look at the picture, you damned fool! He took my dagger away from me!"

I put my hands up to my head. I felt myself turning as crazy as old Gryde was. The thing was impossible, but it was true. The nude figure in the painting held in his hand a dagger which had not been there the day before, a dagger that I recognized by the artistic carving on the handle. It was the weapon which Gryde had flung down on the desk when I was here last!

I begged Gryde, by all he held sacred, to destroy the painting. But mad with terror though he was, he could not bring himself to wreck an object that had money value.

*He still did not believe that Warton would keep his promise!*

* * *

Gryde is dead.

We found him in his armchair, his body emptied of blood, his throat cut clear across. The murderous steel had slashed into the leather of the chair.

And when I looked at the painting, I saw that the blade of the dagger was red to the hilt.

# The Sinister Painting
## Greye La Spina
### 1934

The taxi drove off, leaving Funk on the Hoddeston lawn, surrounded by valises. Funk was thinking it more than merely odd that Barclay, for whose coaching he had come prepared to spend a month, had not met him as planned. He tried the screen door; it was hooked inside.

"Hello, in there!" he hailed hopefully.

There was no response. The Hoddeston farm lay drenched in a torpid lethargy for which it was obvious more than the July heat must be responsible. Within the house, no one stirred. On the surrounding fields, no one was abroad. Even the usual sounds of the farm animals were hushed.

Funk was unpleasantly affected. Surely the entire household had not gone to meet his train and somehow missed it.

He carried his traps to the stoop, crossed the yard to the barnyard, and halloed again. He knew of old where Barclay's studio was, so he set off down the path toward the grateful shade of the woods.

The gray stone walls of the old building soon glinted through the tree trunks and heavy foliage. A strong conviction possessed Funk that Barclay was not within. In fact, he found the studio door padlocked. He noted that the west window was rudely boarded up. He walked around the studio to the north.

Here the trees had been cut down, and the studio wall was entirely of glass. He peered in with deepening curiosity, but apart from the usual litter of easels, painting paraphernalia and accessories, canvases in serried rows against the walls, his attention was almost immediately drawn to a painting propped against the south wall where the full light from the opposite windows poured in revealingly.

"Rum go!" Funk muttered, puzzled. "That never is Barclay's work. And he would never have let a student perpetrate such a monstrosity of line and crude color."

He pressed his face to the glass, cupping it against the outside light.

"That old man," Funk said aloud, amazed, "may be crudely done, but he's also absolutely horrible. His hands—ugh, they're dead hands. Bloodless—waxen—aaarrrgh! Something about the way he's sitting there—drooping as if he hadn't the strength of himself to sit erect, and was being held by something—something without, that you can't see. . . . I don't like the thing. It's ugly. There's—something wrong with it."

He said this last with conviction, and as he exclaimed became aware of another gaze fixed upon himself. He snapped upright and wheeled quickly. Waiting patiently for him to finish his examination of the studio's interior stood a man in patched, stained blue overalls.

"Well?" snapped Funk sharply, a bit taken aback.

"Mr. Barclay's at the house, sor. You're Mr. Funk? I'm Mulcahy, Hoddeston's hired man."

Funk nodded. "All right. I'm coming. How did Mr. Barclay come to miss my train?"

"We was all down to the police station, sor." Mulcahy fell in behind him.

"Police station?" echoed Funk. "What's been going on here?"

"I found Mr. Oakey dead in the studio this mornin', sor."

"What!" Funk whirled and confronted the Irishman.

"There's somethin' wrong in there, sor. I saw blood on the ould divil's beard." The man's voice quavered.

"Snap out of it, Mulcahy. Are you referring to that— picture?"

"I am that, sor."

"Blood on the old man's beard? Ridiculous! I saw none."

Mulcahy insisted stubbornly: "Blood it was, sor. An' the poor young man's was all drained out av him, sor."

Funk stiffened to deep attention. "Ha! This sounds intriguing. Blood on the old man's beard?"

"An' drippin' from his dead fingers, sor. An' not wan dhrop left in the corpse, sor. Blood—all over the dommed ould divil's whiskers, an' his dead fingers, sor. Mary Mother!" Mulcahy crossed himself with pious haste.

"Who did that painting?" Funk demanded, turning again toward the house.

"A mon be the name av Silva, sor. He's afther bein' a cabinet-maker, but he got to thinkin' he cud paint, so he made that beauty back there, divil fly away wid him!"

"He sure can paint!" muttered Funk cryptically.

"He's mixin' somethin' wid his paint that only divils from the Pit can give him," the Irishman declared darkly. He hesitated, then rushed on: "Sor, the night before the poor lad was murthered, there was a fine canvas of Mr. Barclay's cut into ribbons, and Mr. Oakey's prize picture the same. What might that mean, along with the poor lad's bein' killed the next night? An' Silva only gettin' honorable mention last week, where he was lookin' for first prize?"

"Looks as if Silva had a motive," declared Funk as they walked into the barnyard.

Life was stirring normally about the farm now, as if a ban of enchanted silence had been lifted. Funk could see Barclay's bulky body leaning over the valises on the front stoop. He hailed his friend, then asked Mulcahy hastily: "What do the police say?"

"Anny of us might have done it, sor, but the studio was locked from the inside. An' there's no motive. An' they can't figure where the poor lad's blood wint, sor." Back of the simple words pushed a dark significance of terrible things.

"Looks as if there were more here than appears on the surface."

"Right you are, sor. From now on, Tom Mulcahy wears a blessed medal next his hide, day an' night."

Funk met Barclay's welcoming hand with a heartening grip.

"Sorry to have missed you, Funk, but this ghastly tragedy has dislocated all plans. I—I was fond of the boy," groaned Barclay, his face working. "He had a gift, had Harry. I—I was looking forward to what he would do with color in the not far future. And now—" his voice broke.

"Where's my room, Barclay?" Funk gathered up his bags and followed the other painter up the front stairs.

Both men lighted cigarettes in silence. Barclay stared abstractedly from the window, while Funk unpacked rapidly, puffing clouds of smoke about himself as he tossed shirts, underwear, ties, into the open bureau drawers.

"I want to know how Silva's painting got into your studio," he said at last, with an air of relief as he finished his work.

"So you are taking that attitude?" Barclay asked, his eyes heavy.

Funk did not attempt to evade the implied issue. "Anybody but a crass, materialistic jackass would," he responded quietly.

"I didn't know you went in for that sort of thing. I've no time for anything but painting. Just making a living takes most of my time these days, Funk."

The younger man's eyes snapped. "A very little suffices for me. I'm too fascinated with studying the truths underlying the illusions of material existence. Not that I've gotten very far, but what I know, I know."

"Then perhaps you can say what's unnatural about poor Harry's death? I know there's—something wrong about it."

"Something wrong!" echoed the younger man thoughtfully. "Yes, there's something wrong—and uncanny—about this lad's death. As to its being unnatural, there are many strange and little-known laws operating along lines so new to us—" He broke off there, his expression clearing as if an illuminating idea had suddenly clarified the situation for him. "I believe the poor chap's death is due to an extremely interesting example of the transference of an evil will-to-power."

Barclay wheeled from the window, saying abruptly: "I didn't tell the police what I felt lay behind this tragedy. I have no hankering to live in an insane asylum. Now I have a faint hope that *you* may be able to appreciate the strangeness of my experience. Listen!

"Manuel Silva settled here a few years ago and has been doing well as a cabinetmaker. Recently he learned that I got from three hundred dollars up, for a canvas. He thought this an easy way to get rich, but I refused to teach him. You know, I never take any but advanced students of decided promise. My refusal roused Silva's furious resentment.

"I have instituted an annual art exhibit in town. Silva entered three canvases, to force my hand. They were rather terrible. One was a blacksmith, dark, sullen, sinister; he was hammering viciously at what appeared to be a battered crucifix. Another was a farmer slaughtering a wretched hog that somehow looked like a naked man; the butcher's face wore a too realistic grin of sadistic enjoyment as he wielded his bloody knife. The third—the third was the painting you've just seen in my studio.

"Harry's entry took first prize; this was inevitable. I felt inclined to encourage a couple of young local art-ists, so gave them honorable mention. Not to slight Silva's pride, I included him.

"The night before the canvases were removed, Harry and I were in the gallery, and he pointed out that some-one had deliberately cut the honorable mention ribbon on Silva's canvas so that it hung in dangling strips. Odd, that, eh?"

"You're opening vistas," replied Funk, lighting another cigarette from the one he had been smoking. "You are ab-sorbingly interesting."

"I criticized Silva's painting, observing that Harry was right when he said it gave him the jitters, but that in just that degree it possessed a touch of wild genius. Harry pronounced it ghastly, to paint a hunched-up old man as dead as a doornail, his hands frightful, decomposing—yet sitting up there—ugh! Silva's colors were crude, his draw-ing distorted—just how, it would be difficult to say, but—wrong, you understand—wrong.

"I said I dared not encourage Silva because of a very strange quality in his work—that something wrong. And then we both nearly jumped out of our skins, for in the dusk behind us someone broke into an ugly chuckle, and we turned to see a dark figure slouching out. It was Silva, and I realized that he'd heard me pronounce him an evil genius. Harry made light of my compunctions, but I was disturbed.

"We confronted the old man in the painting once more. As twilight gained the room, a murky dusk seemed creeping into the very canvas. Its shadows deepened. The old man merged into his dark background; all but his pallid face, his grayish beard, the waxen fingers dropping over his angular knees. It *was* wrong. Entirely wrong. And then all at once Harry twitched my sleeve, and exclaimed, 'Let's get out of here!' and we turned and plunged into the street, stricken by some subtle panic so obsessing that it was not until we were back at the Hoddeston farm that we realized how foolish and unreasonable had been our flight."

Funk lighted another cigarette.

"We went sketching next day," Barclay went on, "and Hoddeston brought our canvases back to the studio. That night he told me that Silva had sent me one of his for a gift; so Harry and I went down to see which one. We lighted candles, and really, we got a nasty shock. The flickering, inadequate candle-light made that old man appear more than ever an entity with a horrid existence independent of his painted presentment. Harry said, 'My God!' in a kind of comic dismay.

"I knew instinctively that Silva was up to no good; he bore me malice. His very gift seemed to convey dire menace. In the pale candle-light the old man's beard appeared to rustle stiffly as if his lips were parting under its bushy shelter. Of course, I could not *see* anything, but I *felt* that I was seeing a pale dead tongue flick moisture over dry dead lips. Ugh!"

"That must have been an odd sensation," cogitated Funk aloud, as he expelled a thick cloud of smoke. "You make it very clear."

"Yes? Well, there's more of it, Funk. Oakey and I went over our canvases to check on their return and good condition. We were satisfied. Just remember this point, will you? We padlocked the studio door and went off to bed.

When we went in next morning, the padlock was undisturbed, and all the windows locked on the inside.

"But one of my best canvases had been slit into ribbons. And Harry's, which had taken first prize, was completely demolished, even the frame. That last act of vandalism made me feel bad. I'd been sure the boy could cash in on his work, and he needed the money. He took it like a Spartan, but he told me he was going to sleep in the studio that night, for he felt sure that Silva had done the damage.

"I agreed, although I couldn't figure out how Silva could have gotten inside. So last night I left the boy there. He said he was going to hang something over the old man's gosh-awful face. I offered to stay with him, but he wouldn't have it. This morning—" Barclay broke down, turning back to the window with a suspicious gulp.

"Mulcahy told me," Funk hastened to say, lighting another cigarette.

"It was ghastly, Funk. Mulcahy was howling 'Blood!' at every jump he took. Blood, he yelled, on the old man's beard!"

"H'm. How about the coroner?"

"Harry'd been dead for hours. Finger marks on his throat. Every drop of blood drained from his body," Barclay said with slow emphasis. "Mulcahy had seen him through the north windows. I had to break the west window to get in. The coroner said at first that he'd had a fit but finally decided he'd been killed by a person unknown."

"About the blood?" queried Funk.

"Mulcahy was right about it. Funk—I saw it, too."

"It's not there now," Funk declared.

Barclay nodded. "That's another strange thing. When I rushed over, I found poor Harry sprawling on the floor, his body all twisted in a grotesque, gruesome position. And so terribly white! As I threw myself on the floor beside him, something struck upon my inner ear. It was a sound. But *such* a sound! Even as I heard it, I knew I was hearing what could not be apprehended physically.

"I sprang to my feet and confronted Silva's hideous canvas. God, it was horrible!" He shuddered at the bare recollection. "The painted old man sat there motionless, but it was a sinister restraint, Funk. I stared, stricken by a horror that affected me with nausea, for I saw then that someone had smeared that ancient's deathly pallor with crimson that crawled down the painted gray beard. The dead hands that hung over the angular knees were dripping, every pallid finger-tip, with blood. *Blood,* Funk!"

"How do you know it was blood?" Funk demanded sharply.

"I—I touched it," whispered the old man, distastefully.

"And then?" Funk prompted, not ungently.

"A ghastly thing came to pass. I did not see it. I felt, rather than saw. I became aware with that inner sense of the movement of one of the old man's painted arms. It lifted with the jerking unevenness of an automaton, and passed across the stained gray beard. I say, it moved. I felt it move, yet at the same time I was aware that it was only painted, hence incapable of movement. It was a Something Else behind it that actually moved.

"I find it almost impossible to clarify my intuitions," Barclay deprecated despairingly, "other than to say that while the painted figure did not stir, I was yet inwardly aware that it lifted one arm and wiped away the crimson from its beard. Then it reached out on either side, to drag off that horrible drip from its waxen finger-tips against the painted grass that reddened under them.

"God! It was the more horrible because, although the figure did not show movement to my straining eyes, yet I saw the crimson life-blood of poor Harry disappearing from the canvas as those movements which I felt, rather than saw, took place. Of course this explanation is inadequate," he finished.

Funk pushed the consumed tip of his cigarette to the fresh one he was holding between his thin lips. A cloud of blue smoke enveloped him, out of which his voice pronounced decidedly: "Not inadequate, my dear fellow. On the contrary, it is very enlightening; so clear that I believe we may yet punish the murderer of that poor lad."

Barclay's dreamy eyes burned with sudden fire. "I'd give a year of my life to accomplish that," he exclaimed fiercely.

"I hardly think so much will be required, but you may have to sacrifice one or two of your canvases. We'd better get the rest of Oakey's work over here. And Silva must learn that you are taking steps to protect Harry's work and your own. He must be informed that tomorrow night you yourself will sleep in the studio. That will bring him," Funk predicted darkly.

"You agree that it's Silva!" cried Barclay in relief.

"I've no doubt of it. But not *in propria persona*. He's projecting his astral body through that hideous old man, and he's already made a grave error."

"What do you mean?"

"He's permitted himself to savor human blood. Hence, he can not be permitted to—continue. He's dangerous, now. He will be yet more so, unless checked. I propose to do this in the only permanent way possible."

"We have no proof of his presence in the studio, Funk. Who would believe the intangible evidence of my experience?"

"No one, ordinarily," Funk agreed, adding quickly, "but *I* believe. And there is another person who will not only believe, but will furnish me with the means of putting a stop to Silva's murderous proclivities, without disturbing the authorities unduly," he finished dryly.

"Wouldn't it be wise to return that picture to Silva? Or cut it to bits and burn it?" suggested Barclay uneasily.

"Later," said Funk, queerly. "You see, Silva has somehow learned how to transfer his will-for-evil to that creature of his own making. It is through that same creation that we must reach him and stop his criminal career before it is too late."

Barclay sighed. "You speak as if you knew what you were talking about, Funk. I can't just understand you, but I feel that you are somehow right. What do you wish done?"

"Get Mulcahy—or Hoddeston—to clear out all Oakey's canvases. Leave only a couple of your own that you don't particularly care about, so as not to stir Silva's suspicions overly. He'll imagine you're exhibiting. Then have Hoddeston step in and tell Silva what happened to the canvases in the studio, and ask him to have his moved out of harm's way. That will appear a kindly impulse on your part, and he will reply that he'll send for his canvas in a couple of days. He'll figure on polishing you off by then," finished Funk callously.

"Agreeable thought, that," sighed the older painter.

"Now, you're going to lend me your roadster. I'll be back tomorrow afternoon at the latest. Be sure Silva is given to understand that tomorrow night you'll be sleeping in the studio. Under no circumstances, however, venture in there tonight," Funk warned gravely. "Tonight Silva, or whatever wakens in the studio under the stimulus of his evil purpose, may have free play. But tomorrow night—ah, tomorrow night I shall be there, not you."

"I won't permit your getting into a nasty situation, Funk. This isn't your affair, after all. Harry was my protégé. It's up to me."

"Are you prepared to give effective battle to a painted demon, Barclay?" Funk's laugh was incredulous. "Can you, through that painted thing, silence for ever the intangible, distant malefactor?"

"You can do such things?" said Barclay's hushed murmur.

"I shall know how to, before I return tomorrow afternoon."

"But how?"

"I'm going to someone who knows. I shall demand the secret. She will yield it, I am certain. I'm going to see Gwen Carradorne."

"Where have I heard that name?" puzzled Barclay.

"Possibly in connection with her published brochures. Her *Reality of the Abstract* is fairly well known; it's discussed everywhere."

"Quite likely," sighed Barclay. "I seem to remember it vaguely."

"Now," pursued Funk briskly, "how about your car?"

It was dusk when Funk returned on the following day. The seriousness and abstraction that wove a cloak about him struck Barclay's curious inquiries into silence. A certain high air about the younger artist forbade imperiously any break upon that lofty mood. Funk's first query was, Had Silva been duly informed of the occupation of the studio that night?

"He knows. He told Hoddeston that he would call for his unappreciated masterpiece in a couple of days." The words were significantly emphasized.

"I rather fancied he'd say that. He knows you'll be there tonight?"

"Hoddeston told him, if there were any further trouble, I'd sleep there from tonight on, to protect his painting."

"Excellent!" Funk rubbed his hands together and blew a cloud of thick smoke from the cigarette in one comer of his mouth. "And was there any?"

"Yes. Last night the two canvases I'd left were demolished."

"Good! He'll be expecting you to sleep there tonight. Let's have supper. Then I'll run into town and fetch Miss Carradorne. She insists upon coming out; the time was too brief to prepare me to handle the situation single-handed."

"That's extraordinarily kind of her, Funk. But if she is to be at the studio tonight, why not I?" Barclay insisted.

"She would have handled it alone, only that she—" Funk broke off suddenly,

looking apologetic. "Sorry I can't be more explicit, but she bans discussion of herself unless she decides to come out into the open, which she rarely does. She's—well, wait until you meet her, if she permits it," Funk broke off, in a kind of embarrassment. "You'll understand then. But believe me, she is worthy the highest respect and admiration a human being could expect."

Funk did not have to drive to town. Between dusk and dark a shining dark blue car with a special delivery body slipped into the driveway. From the limousine-like front two uniformed men alighted and walked to the rear of the car. There were wide doors there, which they proceeded to open. They withdrew, with the utmost care, a strange anachronism; a blue-and-black-and-gold decorated sedan chair, small and delicate. They placed themselves between the shafts and started toward the farmhouse.

Funk exclaimed, and sprang down the steps to meet that odd equipage. He bent over what was obviously an extended hand, white in the dusk. Barclay, staring, saw the young artist touch his lips to those extended fingers. A child's high, shrilly sweet voice gave an order, and the chair-bearers carried the sedan chair toward the barnyard. Funk followed, calling back as he went.

"See you tomorrow morning, Barclay." With that, he disappeared after the chair into the soft darkness beyond the barnyard.

Barclay felt that he could not sleep. He was intensely irritated that Gwen Carradorne should have sent a child to take her place in what he felt must be a post of danger. He went down to the shining automobile and walked around it with curiosity. The rear doors had been closed, and nothing marked it as out of the ordinary save, perhaps, the expensive type of shock-absorbers for a delivery body; and of course, what looked very like a periscope set in the top, as much out of place as was a modern child in a sedan chair.

He sat at his window, fell asleep there in his chair, and did not waken until Mrs. Hoddeston tapped at his door, calling that Mr. Funk and the little girl had returned. She volunteered that the little girl was a perfect little French doll.

Barclay took the stairs three at a stride. In the hall Funk sat on a hassock which brought his face slightly below the level of the small oval countenance of the child, who sat sedately on the hall chair.

Barclay noted with an artist's appreciation the bloom on her dazzling cheeks; the straight nose; the richly scarlet mobile lips. He approved the curling black lashes, finely penciled arching eyebrows, sleek black bobbed hair. Her creamy silk dress, rather longer than worn by most children of her age (apparently about six), was smocked in a knowing fashion with bright colors. Her feet were inappropriately encased in high-heeled French slippers.

All this the artist in Barclay captured at a glance, just as he took in the beauty of the slender, tiny hands, of the taper fingers, and the eloquence of every gesture. A strange, an unusual child, this. His leaping footsteps brought upon

him a lifting of fringed eyelids, and what he felt shrink-
ingly was a glance of indifference. He stopped short at the
foot of the staircase, abashed at this disdainful glance.

He knew all at once why this child's frock was longer
than customary; why her tiny feet wore adult-styled foot-
gear; why sophistication animated those taper fingers. The
cobalt blue eyes that regarded him from the child's elf-
in face were the eyes of a grown woman. They were the
informed eyes of one who has passed through the fires
of varied experiences; the eyes of one who has gazed unafraid upon unveiled mysteries. The child was not a child,
but was an exquisite midget, a creature set apart from the
entire world by her miniature proportions.

Funk sprang up, caught the other man's hand and
drew him down to the hassock, himself sinking upon the
floor so that both men's faces were below the level of the
midget's.

"Barclay," Funk said, in a tone of repressed excitement,
"Miss Carradorne permits me to present you."

"Honored, Miss Carradorne," mumbled Barclay, still
confused under the keen gaze of those faintly derisive blue
eyes. He understood it, after a minute; she was touched
with amusement at his discomfiture.

An elfish smile twitched at one corner of her scarlet
lips, and she actually turned away those too-shrewd eyes
as if to spare Barclay's feelings, a kindly gesture which did
not serve to tranquilize him, for there was just a touch of
condescension in her half-smile.

"Mr. Funk has been showing me these canvases from
your studio," she said, slowly, in a shrilly sweet voice. "I
would very much like that snow scene; it is charming. If
you will tell me the price—?"

Barclay's embarrassment vanished. Here he could be
sure of himself.

"I would feel honored if you would accept it as a proof of my gratitude for your having come here," he began, but his eyes questioned Funk.

"You are anxious to learn the outcome of last night's plans?" said Miss Carradorne's high voice lightly.

Suspended in the bosom of her frock by a slender platinum chain was a platinum whistle which she put to her lips and sounded. At once the bearers of the sedan chair came up the steps and into the hall, holding the chair close to their mistress. Like some bright bird, so airy and graceful was her lithe movement, she seemed to fly from her chair into the sedan's shelter. She waved one tiny hand. The bearers took their light burden outside, slid it into place in the rear of the waiting automobile. They mounted into the front, and the car slipped noiselessly away down the road, bespeaking the many-cylindered motor by its very silence and power.

Barclay stared after it, amazed. "So that strange little thing is your wonderful Gwen Carradorne? Why didn't you warn me?"

Funk lighted a cigarette hastily and began surrounding himself with smoke. "Why didn't I? Because she won't be talked about. She's proud and sensitive. She considers her miniature body the ultimate of human perfection, and won't permit its comparison with what she considers our gross bodies. And she's abnormally proud of her brain. She has reason to be. I think it is the most highly developed I have ever known. As an occultist—she's the seventh daughter of a seventh daughter—"

Funk broke off brusquely. "You are anxious to know about last night? She has forbidden me to divulge details, but I may tell you briefly that Silva will never again repeat his evil act."

"He was there, then, last night?" gasped Barclay incredulously.

"Not *in propria persona,* but his familiar was already locked in with us, when I bolted the door behind Gwen and myself."

"What do you mean?"

Funk sighed resignedly. "Let's go down to the studio. It's easier to understand, when you've seen things with your own eyes."

The telephone rang. Mrs. Hoddeston ran out of the kitchen and answered it. An expression of horror settled on her placid face. "Manuel Silva's been found dead, with a knife-wound in his throat," she called, and gave closer attention to the telephone.

Funk beckoned Barclay silently, and the two hurried across the barnyard and into the woods. With the key Barclay had loaned him, Funk unlocked the padlock. He pushed the studio door open. Words seemed superfluous.

Spread on the floor lay a painted canvas figure, pinned down by a knife through its throat. The edges of the canvas were sharply defined as if just cut out of the painting leaning against the south wall with a neatly trimmed vacancy in its center.

Barclay stared, closed his eyes convulsively, then stared again.

"I couldn't have done it alone," Funk kept repeating in a kind of feverish excitement. "*She* furnished the *power.* She'd have done it herself, but she's too—I mean," he corrected himself hastily, "*he* was too tall."

Barclay stared, motionless. He was absorbing the details of a bizarre thing which confirmed him in his hasty resolution to burn Silva's painting without delay.

The empty space in the painting distinctly outlined a drooping, seated figure. The painted canvas shape lying on the floor, pinned down by the knife through its pallid painted throat, could have filled that vacancy twice over.

It was a full length, standing figure. . . .

# The Golgotha Dancers

### MANLY WADE WELLMAN

### 1937

I had come to the Art Museum to see the special show of Goya prints, but that particular gallery was so crowded that I could hardly get in, much less see or savor anything; wherefore I walked out again. I wandered through the other wings with their rows and rows of oils, their Greek and Roman sculptures, their stern ranks of medieval armors, their Oriental porcelains, their Egyptian gods. At length, by chance and not by design, I came to the head of a certain rear stairway. Other habitués of the museum will know the one I mean when I remind them that Arnold Böcklin's *The Isle of the Dead* hangs on the wall of the landing.

I started down, relishing in advance the impression Böcklin's picture would make with its high brown rocks and black poplars, its midnight sky and gloomy film of sea, its single white figure erect in the bow of the beach-nosing skiff. But, as I descended, I saw that *The Isle of the Dead* was not in its accustomed position on the wall. In that space, arresting even in the bad light and from the up-angle of the stairs, hung a gilt-framed painting I had never seen or heard of in all my museum-haunting years.

I gazed at it, one will imagine, all the way down to the landing. Then I had a close, searching look, and a final appraising stare from the lip of the landing above the lower half of the flight. So far as I can learn—and I have been diligent in my research—the thing is unknown even to the best-informed of art experts. Perhaps it is as well that I describe it in detail.

It seemed to represent action upon a small plateau or table rock, drab and bare, with a twilight sky deepening into a starless evening. This setting, restrainedly worked up in blue-grays and blue-blacks, was not the first thing to catch the eye, however. The front of the picture was filled with lively dancing creatures, as pink, plump and naked as cherubs and as patently evil as the meditations of Satan in his rare idle moments.

I counted those dancers. There were twelve of them, ranged in a half-circle, and they were cavorting in evident glee around a central object—a prone cross, which appeared to be made of two stout logs with some of the bark still upon them. To this cross a pair of the pink things— that makes fourteen—kneeling and swinging blocky-looking hammers or mauls, spiked a human figure.

I say *human* when I speak of that figure, and I withhold the word in describing the dancers and their hammer-wielding fellows. There is a reason. The supine victim on the cross was a beautifully represented male body, as clear and anatomically correct as an illustration in a surgical textbook. The head was writhed around, as if in pain, and I could not see the face or its expression; but in the tortured tenseness of the muscles, in the slaty white sheen of the skin with jagged streaks of vivid gore upon it, agonized nature was plain and doubly plain. I could almost see the painted limbs writhe against the transfixing nails.

By the same token, the dancers and hammerers were so dynamically done as to seem half in motion before my eyes. So much for the sound skill of the painter. Yet, where the crucified prisoner was all clarity, these others were all fog. No lines, no angles, no muscles—their features could not be seen or sensed. I was not even sure if they had hair or not. It was as if each was picked out with a ray of light in that surrounding dusk, light that revealed and yet shimmered indistinctly; light, too, that had absolutely nothing of comfort or honesty in it.

"Hold on, there!" came a sharp challenge from the stairs behind and below me. "What are you doing? And what's that picture doing?"

I started so that I almost lost my footing and fell upon the speaker—one of the Museum guards. He was a slight old fellow and his thin hair was gray, but he advanced upon me with all the righteous, angry pluck of a beefy policeman. His attitude surprised and nettled me.

"I was going to ask somebody that same question," I told him as austerely as I could manage. "What about this picture? I thought there was a Böcklin hanging here."

The guard relaxed his forbidding attitude at first sound of my voice. "Oh, I beg your pardon, sir. I thought you were somebody else—the man who brought that thing." He nodded at the picture, and the hostile glare came back into his eyes. "It so happened that he talked to me first, then to the curator. Said it was art—great art—and the Museum must have it." He lifted his shoulders, in a shrug or a shudder. "Personally, I think it's plain beastly."

So it was, I grew aware as I looked at it again. "And the Museum has accepted it at last?" I prompted.

He shook his head. "Oh, no, sir. An hour ago he was at the back door, with that nasty daub there under his arm. I heard part of the argument. He got insulting, and he was told to clear out and take his picture with him. But he must have got in here somehow, and hung it himself." Walking close to the painting, as gingerly as though he expected the pink dancers to leap out at him, he pointed to the lower edge of the frame. "If it was a real Museum piece, we'd have a plate right there, with the name of the painter and the title."

I, too, came close. There was no plate, just as the guard had said. But in the lower left-hand corner of the canvas were sprawling capitals, pale paint on the dark, spelling out the word *GOLGOTHA*. Beneath these, in small, barely readable script:

*I sold my soul that I might paint a living picture.*

No signature or other clue to the artist's identity.

The guard had discovered a great framed rectangle against the wall to one side. "Here's the picture he took down," he informed me, highly relieved. "Help me put it back, will you, sir? And do you suppose," here he grew almost wistful, "that we could get rid of this other thing before someone finds I let the crazy fool slip past me?"

I took one edge of *The Isle of the Dead* and lifted it to help him hang it once more.

"Tell you what," I offered on sudden impulse; "I'll take this *Golgotha* piece home with me, if you like."

"Would you do that?" he almost yelled out in his joy at the suggestion. "Would you, to oblige me?"

"To oblige myself," I returned. "I need another picture at my place."

And the upshot of it was, he smuggled me and the unwanted painting out of the Museum. Never mind how. I have done quite enough as it is to jeopardize his job and my own welcome up there.

It was not until I had paid off my taxi and lugged the unwieldy parallelogram of canvas and wood upstairs to my bachelor apartment that I bothered to wonder if it might be valuable. I never did find out, but from the first I was deeply impressed.

Hung over my own fireplace, it looked as large and living as a scene glimpsed through a window or, perhaps, on a stage in a theater. The capering pink bodies caught new lights from my lamp, lights that glossed and intensified their shape and color but did not reveal any new details. I pored once more over the cryptic legend: *I sold my soul that I might paint a living picture.*

A living picture—was it that? I could not answer. For all my honest delight in such things, I cannot be called expert or even knowing as regards art. Did I even like the Golgotha painting? I could not be sure of that, either. And the rest of the inscription, about selling a soul; I was considerably intrigued by that, and let my thoughts ramble on the subject of Satanist complexes and the vagaries of half-crazy painters. As I read, that evening, I glanced up again and again at my new possession. Sometimes it seemed ridiculous, sometimes sinister. Shortly after midnight I rose, gazed once more, and then turned out the parlor lamp. For a moment, or so it seemed, I could see those dancers, so many dim-pink silhouettes in the sudden darkness. I went to the kitchen for a bit of whisky and water, and thence to my bedroom.

I had dreams. In them I was a boy again, and my mother and sister were leaving the house to go to a theater where— think of it!—Richard Mansfield would play *Beau Brummell*. I, the youngest, was told to stay at home and mind the troublesome furnace. I wept copiously in my disappointed loneliness, and then Mansfield himself stalked in, in full Brummell regalia. He laughed goldenly and stretched out his hand in warm greeting. I, the lad of my dreams, put out my own hand, then was frightened when he would not loosen his grasp. I tugged, and he laughed again. The gold of his laughter turned suddenly hard, cold. I tugged with all my strength, and woke.

Something held me tight by the wrist.

In my first half-moment of wakefulness I was aware that the room was filled with the pink dancers of the picture, in nimble, fierce-happy motion. They were man-size, too, or nearly so, visible in the dark with the dim radiance of fox-fire. On the small scale of the painting they had seemed no more than babyishly plump; now they were gross, like huge erect toads. And, as I awakened fully, they were closing in, a menacing ring of them, around my bed. One stood at my right side, and its grip, clumsy and rubbery-hard like that of a monkey, was closed upon my arm.

I saw and sensed all this, as I say, in a single moment. With the sensing came the realization of peril, so great that I did not stop to wonder at the uncanniness of my visitors. I tried frantically to jerk loose. For the moment I did not succeed and as I thrashed about, throwing my body nearly across the bed, a second dancer dashed in from the left. It seized and clamped my other arm. I felt, rather than heard, a wave of soft, wordless merriment from them all. My heart and sinews seemed to fail, and briefly I lay still in a daze of horror, pinned down crucifix-fashion between my two captors.

Was that a *hammer* raised above me as I sprawled?

There rushed and swelled into me the sudden startled strength that sometimes favors the desperate. I screamed like any wild thing caught in a trap, rolled somehow out of bed and to my feet. One of the beings I shook off and the other I dashed against the bureau. Freed, I made for the bedroom door and the front of the apartment, stumbling and staggering on fear-weakened legs.

One of the dim-shining pink things barred my way at the very threshold, and the others were closing in behind, as if for a sudden rush. I flung my right fist with all my strength and weight. The being bobbed back unresistingly before my smash, like a rubber toy floating through water. I plunged past, reached the entry and fumbled for the knob of the outer door.

They were all about me then, their rubbery palms fumbling at my shoulders, my elbows, my pajama jacket. They would have dragged me down before I could negotiate the lock. A racking shudder possessed me and seemed to flick them clear. Then I stumbled against a stand, and purely by good luck my hand fell upon a bamboo walking-stick. I yelled again, in truly hysterical fierceness, and laid about me as with a whip. My blows did little or no damage to those unearthly assailants, but they shrank back, teetering and dancing, to a safe distance. Again I had the sense that they were laughing, mocking. For the moment I had beaten them off, but they were sure of me in the end. Just then my groping free hand pressed a switch. The entry sprang into light.

On the instant they were not there.

Somebody was knocking outside, and with trembling fingers I turned the knob of the door. In came a tall, slender girl with a blue lounging-robe caught hurriedly around her. Her bright hair was disordered as though she had just sprung from her bed.

"Is someone sick?" she asked in a breathless voice. "I live down the hall—I heard cries." Her round blue eyes were studying my face, which must have been ghastly pale. "You see, I'm a trained nurse, and perhaps—"

"Thank God you did come!" I broke in, unceremoniously but honestly, and went before her to turn on every lamp in the parlor.

It was she who, without guidance, searched out my whisky and siphon and mixed for me a highball of grateful strength. My teeth rang nervously on the edge of the glass as I gulped it down. After that I got my own robe—a becoming one, with satin facings—and sat with her on the divan to tell of my adventure. When I had finished, she gazed long at the painting of the dancers, then back at me. Her eyes, like two chips of the April sky, were full of concern and she held her rosy lower lip between her teeth. I thought that she was wonderfully pretty.

"What a perfectly terrible nightmare!" she said.

"It was no nightmare," I protested.

She smiled and argued the point, telling me all manner of comforting things about mental associations and their reflections in vivid dreams.

To clinch her point she turned to the painting.

"This line about a 'living picture' is the peg on which your slumbering mind hung the whole fabric," she suggested, her slender fingertip touching the painted scribble. "Your very literal subconscious self didn't understand that the artist meant his picture would live only figuratively."

"Are you sure that's what the artist meant?" I asked, but finally I let her convince me. One can imagine how badly I wanted to be convinced.

She mixed me another highball, and a short one for herself. Over it she told me her name—Miss Dolby—and finally she left me with a last comforting assurance. But, nightmare or no, I did not sleep again that night. I sat in the parlor among the lamps, smoking and dipping into book after book. Countless times I felt my gaze drawn back to the painting over the fireplace, with the cross and the nail-pierced wretch and the shimmering pink dancers.

After the rising sun had filled the apartment with its honest light and cheer I felt considerably calmer. I slept all morning, and in the afternoon was disposed to agree with Miss Dolby that the whole business had been a bad dream, nothing more. Dressing, I went down the hall, knocked on her door and invited her to dinner with me.

It was a good dinner. Afterward we went to an amusing motion picture, with Charles Butterworth in it as I remember. After bidding her good-night, I went to my own place. Undressed and in bed, I lay awake. My late morning slumber made my eyes slow to close. Thus it was that I heard the faint shuffle of feet and, sitting up against my pillows, saw the glowing silhouettes of the Golgotha dancers. Alive and magnified, they were creeping into my bedroom.

I did not hesitate or shrink this time. I sprang up, tense and defiant.

"No, you don't!" I yelled at them. As they seemed to hesitate before the impact of my wild voice, I charged frantically. For a moment I scattered them and got through the bedroom door, as on the previous night. There was another shindy in the entry; this time they all got hold of me, like a pack of hounds, and wrestled me back against the wall. I writhe even now when I think of the unearthly hardness of their little gripping paws. Two on each arm were spread-eagling me upon the plaster. The cruciform position again!

I swore, yelled and kicked. One of them was in the way of my foot. He floated back, unhurt. That was their strength and horror—their ability to go flabby and non-re-sistant under smashing, flattening blows. Something tick-led my palm, pricked it. The point of a spike. . . .

"Miss Dolby!" I shrieked, as a child might call for its mother. "Help! Miss D—"

The door flew open; I must not have locked it. "Here I am," came her unafraid reply.

She was outlined against the rectangle of light from the hall. My assailants let go of me to dance toward her. She gasped but did not scream. I staggered along the wall, touched a light-switch, and the parlor just beyond us flared into visibility. Miss Dolby and I ran in to the lamp, rallying there as stone-age folk must have rallied at their fire to face the monsters of the night. I looked at her; she was still fully dressed, as I had left her, apparently had been sitting up. Her rouge made flat patches on her pale cheeks, but her eyes were level.

This time the dancers did not retreat or vanish; they lurked in the comparative gloom of the entry, jigging and trembling as if mustering their powers and resolutions for another rush at us.

"You see," I chattered out to her, "it wasn't a nightmare."

She spoke, not in reply, but as if to herself. "They have no faces," she whispered. "No faces!" In the half-light that was diffused upon them from our lamp they presented the featurelessness of so many huge gingerbread boys, covered with pink icing. One of them, some kind of leader, pressed forward within the circle of the light. It daunted him a bit. He hesitated, but did not retreat.

From my center table Miss Dolby had picked up a bright paper-cutter. She poised it with the assurance of one who knows how to handle cutting instruments.

"When they come," she said steadily, "let's stand close together. We'll be harder to drag down that way."

I wanted to shout my admiration of her fearless front toward the dreadful beings, my thankfulness for her quick run to my rescue. All I could mumble was, "You're mighty brave."

She turned for a moment to look at the picture above my dying fire. My eyes followed hers. I think I expected to see a blank canvas—find that the painted dancers had vanished from it and had grown into the living ones. But they were still in the picture, and the cross and the victim were there, too. Miss Dolby read aloud the inscription:

*"A living picture* . . . The artist knew what he was talking about, after all."

"Couldn't a living picture be killed?" I wondered.

It sounded uncertain, and a childish quibble to boot, but Miss Dolby exclaimed triumphantly, as at an inspiration.

"Killed? Yes!" she shouted. She sprang at the picture, darting out with the paper-cutter. The point ripped into one of the central figures in the dancing semicircle.

All the crowd in the entry seemed to give a concerted throb, as of startled protest. I swung, heart racing, to front them again. What had happened? Something had changed, I saw. The intrepid leader had vanished. No, he had not drawn back into the group. He had vanished.

Miss Dolby, too, had seen. She struck again, gashed the painted representation of another dancer. And this time the vanishing happened before my eyes, a creature at the rear of the group went out of existence as suddenly and completely as though a light had blinked out.

The others, driven by their danger, rushed.

I met them, feet planted. I tried to embrace them all at once, went over backward under them. I struck, wrenched, tore. I think I even bit something grisly and bloodless, like fungoid tissue, but I refuse to remember for certain. One or two of the forms struggled past me and grappled Miss Dolby. I struggled to my feet and pulled them back from her. There were not so many swarming after me now. I fought hard before they got me down again. And Miss Dolby kept tearing and stabbing at the canvas—again, again. Clutches melted from my throat, my arms. There were only two dancers left. I flung them back and rose. Only one left. Then none.

They were gone, gone into nowhere.

"That did it," said Miss Dolby breathlessly.

She had pulled the picture down. It was only a frame now, with ragged ribbons of canvas dangling from it.

I snatched it out of her hands and threw it upon the coals of the fire.

"Look," I urged her joyfully. "It's burning! That's the end. Do you see?"

"Yes, I see," she answered slowly. "Some fiend-ridden artist—his evil genius brought it to life."

"The inscription is the literal truth, then?" I supplied.

"Truth no more." She bent to watch the burning. "As the painted figures were destroyed, their incarnations faded."

We said nothing further, but sat down together and gazed as the flames ate the last thread of fabric, the last splinter of wood. Finally we looked up again and smiled at each other.

All at once I knew that I loved her.

# GALLERY
# (LONG STORIES)

# The Adventure of the Mysterious Picture
## Washington Irving
### 1824

As one story of the kind produces another, and as all the company seemed fully engrossed by the topic, and disposed to bring their relatives and ancestors upon the scene, there is no knowing how many more ghost adventures we might have heard, had not a corpulent old fox-hunter, who had slept soundly through the whole, now suddenly awakened, with a loud and long-drawn yawn. The sound broke the charm; the ghosts took to flight as though it had been cock-crowing, and there was a universal move for bed.

"And now for the haunted chamber," said the Irish captain, taking his candle.

"Aye, who's to be the hero of the night?" said the gentleman with the ruined head.

"That we shall see in the morning," said the old gentleman with the nose: "whoever looks pale and grizzly will have seen the ghost."

"Well, gentlemen," said the Baronet, "there's many a true thing said in jest. In fact, one of you will sleep in a room to-night—"

"What—a haunted room?—a haunted room?—I claim the adventure—and I—and I—and I," cried a dozen guests, talking and laughing at the same time.

"No—no," said mine host, "there is a secret about one of my rooms on which I feel disposed to try an experiment.

So, gentlemen, none of you shall know who has the haunted chamber, until circumstances reveal it. I will not even know it myself, but will leave it to chance and the allotment of the housekeeper. At the same time, if it will be any satisfaction to you, I will observe, for the honor of my paternal mansion, that there's scarcely a chamber in it but is well worthy of being haunted."

We now separated for the night, and each went to his allotted room. Mine was in one wing of the building, and I could not but smile at its resemblance in style to those eventful apartments described in the tales of the supper table. It was spacious and gloomy, decorated with lamp-black portraits, a bed of ancient damask, with a tester sufficiently lofty to grace a couch of state, and a number of massive pieces of old-fashioned furniture. I drew a great claw-footed arm-chair before the wide fire-place; stirred up the fire; sat looking into it, and musing upon the odd stories I had heard; until, partly overcome by the fatigue of the day's hunting, and partly by the wine and wassail of mine host, I fell asleep in my chair.

The uneasiness of my position made my slumber troubled, and laid me at the mercy of all kinds of wild and fearful dreams; now it was that my perfidious dinner and supper rose in rebellion against my peace. I was hag-ridden by a fat saddle of mutton; a plum pudding weighed like lead upon my conscience; the merry thought of a capon filled me with horrible suggestions; and a devilled leg of a turkey stalked in all kinds of diabolical shapes through my imagination. In short, I had a violent fit of the nightmare. Some strange indefinite evil seemed hanging over me that I could not avert; something terrible and loathsome oppressed me that I could not shake off. I was conscious of being asleep, and strove to rouse myself, but every effort redoubled the evil; until gasping, struggling, almost strangling, I suddenly sprang bolt upright in my chair, and awoke.

The light on the mantel-piece had burnt low, and the wick was divided; there was a great winding sheet made by the dripping wax, on the side towards me. The disordered taper emitted a broad flaring flame, and threw a strong light on a painting over the fire-place, which I had not hitherto observed. It consisted merely of a head, or rather a face, that appeared to be staring full upon me, and with an expression that was startling. It was without a frame, and at the first glance I could hardly persuade myself that it was not a real face, thrusting itself out of the dark oaken panel. I sat in my chair gazing at it, and the more I gazed the more it disquieted me. I had never before been affected in the same way by any painting. The emotions it caused were strange and indefinite. They were something like what I have heard ascribed to the eyes of the basilisk; or like that mysterious influence in reptiles termed fascination. I passed my hand over my eyes several times, as if seeking instinctively to brush away this allusion—in vain—they instantly reverted to the picture, and its chilling, creeping influence over my flesh was redoubled.

I looked around the room on other pictures, either to divert my attention, or to see whether the same effect would be produced by them. Some of them were grim enough to produce the effect, if the mere grimness of the painting produced it. No such thing—my eye passed over them all with perfect indifference, but the moment it reverted to this visage over the fire-place, it was as if an electric shock darted through me. The other pictures were dim and faded; but this one protruded from a plain black ground in the strongest relief, and with wonderful truth of coloring. The expression was that of agony—the agony of intense bodily pain; but a menace scowled upon the brow, and a few sprinklings of blood added to its ghastliness. Yet it was not all these characteristics—it was some horror of the mind, some inscrutable antipathy awakened by this picture, which harrowed up my feelings.

I tried to persuade myself that this was chimerical; that my brain was confused by the fumes of mine host's good cheer, and, in some measure, by the odd stories about paintings which had been told at supper. I determined to shake off these vapors of the mind; rose from my chair, and walked about the room; snapped my fingers; rallied myself; laughed aloud. It was a forced laugh, and the echo of it in the old chamber jarred upon my ear. I walked to the window; tried to discern the landscape through the glass. It was pitch darkness, and howling storm without; and as I heard the wind moan among the trees, I caught a reflection of this accursed visage in the pane of glass, as though it were staring through the window at me. Even the reflection of it was thrilling.

How was this vile nervous fit, for such I now persuaded myself it was, to be conquered? I determined to force myself not to look at the painting but to undress quickly and get into bed. I began to undress, but in spite of every effort I could not keep myself from stealing a glance every now and then at the picture; and a glance was now sufficient to distress me. Even when my back was turned to it, the idea of this strange face behind me, peering over my shoulder, was insufferable. I threw off my clothes and hurried into bed; but still this visage gazed upon me. I had a full view of it from my bed, and for some time could not take my eyes from it. I had grown nervous to a dismal degree. I put out the light, and tried to force myself to sleep—all in vain! The fire gleaming up a little, threw an uncertain light about the room, leaving, however, the region of the picture in deep shadow. What, thought I, if this be the chamber about which mine host spoke as having a mystery reigning over it? I had taken his words merely as spoken in jest; might they have a real import? I looked around. The faintly lighted apartment had all the qualifications requisite for a haunted chamber. It began in my infected imagination to assume strange appearances. The old portraits turned paler and paler, and blacker and blacker; the streaks of light and shadow thrown among the quaint old articles of furniture, gave them singular shapes and characters. There was a huge dark clothes-press of antique form, gorgeous in brass and lustrous with wax, that began to grow oppressive to me.

Am I then, thought I, indeed, the hero of the haunted room? Is there really a spell laid upon me, or is this all some contrivance of mine host, to raise a laugh at my expense? The idea of being hag-ridden by my own fancy all night, and then bantered on my haggard looks the next day was intolerable; but the very idea was sufficient to produce the effect, and to render me still more nervous. "Pish," said I, "it can be no such thing. How could my worthy host imagine that I, or any man would be so worried by a mere picture? It is my own diseased imagination that torments me."

I turned in my bed, and shifted from side to side, to try to fall asleep; but all in vain. When one cannot get asleep by lying quiet, it is seldom that tossing about will effect the purpose. The fire gradually went out and left the room in darkness. Still I had the idea of this inexplicable countenance gazing and keeping watch upon me through the darkness. Nay, what was worse, the very darkness seemed to give it additional power, and to multiply its terrors. It was like having an unseen enemy hovering about one in the night. Instead of having one picture now to worry me, I had a hundred. I fancied it in every direction. "There it is," thought I, "and there! and there! with its horrible and mysterious expression, still gazing and gazing on me.

No—if I must suffer this strange and dismal influence, it were better face a single foe, than thus be haunted by a thousand images of it.

Whoever has been in such a state of nervous agitation must know that the longer it continues, the more uncontrollable it grows; the very air of the chamber seemed at length infected by the baleful presence of this picture. I fancied it hovering over me. I almost felt the fearful visage from the wall approaching my face—it seemed breathing upon me. "This is not to be borne," said I, at length, springing out of bed. "I can stand this no longer. I shall only tumble and toss about here all night; make a very spectre of myself, and become the hero of the haunted chamber in good earnest. Whatever be the consequence. I'll quit this cursed room, and seek a night's rest elsewhere—they can but laugh at me at all events, and they'll be sure to have the laugh upon me if I pass a sleepless night and show them a haggard and woe-begone visage in the morning."

All this was half muttered to myself, as I hastily slipped on my clothes, which having done, I groped my way out of the room, and down-stairs to the drawing-room. Here, after tumbling over two or three pieces of furniture, I made out to reach a sofa, and stretching myself upon it determined to bivouac there for the night. The moment I found myself out of the neighborhood of that strange picture, it seemed as if the charm were broken. All its influence was at an end. I felt assured that it was confined to its own dreary chamber, for I had, with a sort of instinctive caution, turned the key when I closed the door. I soon calmed down, therefore, into a state of tranquility; from that into a drowsiness, and finally into a deep sleep; out of which I did not awake, until the housemaid, with her besom and her matin-song, came to put the room in order. She stared at finding me stretched upon the sofa;

but I presume circumstances of the kind were not uncommon after hunting dinners, in her master's bachelor establishment; for she went on with her song and her work, and
took no farther heed of me.

I had an unconquerable repugnance to return to my
chamber; so I found my way to the butler's quarters, made
my toilet in the best way circumstances would permit, and
was among the first to appear at the breakfast table. Our
breakfast was a substantial fox-hunter's repast, and the
company were generally assembled at it. When ample justice had been done to the tea, coffee, cold meats, and
humming ale, for all these were furnished in abundance,
according to the tastes of the different guests, the conversation began to break out, with all the liveliness and
freshness of morning mirth.

"But who is the hero of the haunted chamber?—Who
has seen the ghost last night?" said the inquisitive gentleman, rolling his lobster eyes about the table.

The question set every tongue in motion; a vast deal
of bantering; criticizing of countenances; of mutual accu-
sation and retort took place. Some had drunk deep, and
some were unshaven, so that there were suspicious faces
enough in the assembly. I alone could not enter with ease
and vivacity into the joke. I felt tongue-tied—embarrassed.
A recollection of what I had seen and felt the preceding
night still haunted my mind. It seemed as if the mysterious picture still held a thrall upon me. I thought also that
our host's eye was turned on me with an air of curiosity. In
short, I was conscious that I was the hero of the night, and
felt as if every one might read it in my looks. The joke,
however, passed over, and no suspicion seemed to attach to
me. I was just congratulating myself on my escape, when a
servant came in, saying, that the gentleman who had slept
on the sofa in the drawing-room had left his watch under
one of the pillows. My repeater was in his hand.

"What!" said the inquisitive gentleman, "did any gentleman sleep on the sofa?"

"Soho! soho! a hare—a hare!" cried the old gentleman with the flexible nose.

I could not avoid acknowledging the watch, and was rising in great confusion, when a boisterous old squire who sat beside me, exclaimed, slapping me on the shoulder, "'Sblood, lad! thou'rt the man as has seen the ghost!"

The attention of the company was immediately turned to me; if my face had been pale the moment before, it now glowed almost to burning. I tried to laugh, but could only make a grimace; and found all the muscles of my face twitching at sixes and sevens, and totally out of all control.

It takes but little to raise a laugh among a set of fox-hunters. There was a world of merriment and joking at my expense; and as I never relished a joke overmuch when it was at my own expense, I began to feel a little nettled. I tried to look cool and calm and to restrain my pique; but the coolness and calmness of a man in a passion are confounded treacherous.

"Gentlemen," said I, with a slight cocking of the chin, and a bad attempt at a smile, "this is all very pleasant—ha! ha!—very pleasant—but I'd have you know I am as little superstitious as any of you—ha! ha!—and as to anything like timidity—you may smile, gentlemen—but I trust there is no one here means to insinuate that. As to a room's being haunted, I repeat, gentlemen—(growing a little warm at seeing a cursed grin breaking out round me)—as to a room's being haunted, I have as little faith in such silly stories as any one. But, since you put the matter home to me, I will say that I have met with something in my room strange and inexplicable to me. (A shout of laughter.) Gentlemen, I am serious; I know well what I am saying. I am calm, gentlemen, (striking my fist upon the table)—by heaven I am calm. I am neither trifling, nor do I wish to be trifled with. (The laughter of the company suppressed with ludicrous attempts at gravity.) There is a picture in the room in which I was put last night, that has had an effect upon me the most singular and incomprehensible."

"A picture!" said the old gentleman with the haunted head. "A picture!" cried the narrator with the waggish nose. "A picture! a picture!" echoed several voices. Here there was an ungovernable peal of laughter. I could not contain myself. I started up from my seat—looked round on the company with fiery indignation—thrust both my hands into my pockets, and strode up to one of the windows, as though I would have walked through it. I stopped short; looked out upon the landscape without distinguishing a feature of it, and felt my gorge rising almost to suffocation.

Mine host saw it was time to interfere. He had maintained an air of gravity through the whole of the scene, and now stepped forth as if to shelter me from the overwhelming merriment of my companions.

"Gentlemen," said he, "I dislike to spoil sport, but you have had your laugh, and the joke of the haunted chamber has been enjoyed. I must now take the part of my guest. I must not only vindicate him from your pleasantries, but I must reconcile him to himself, for I suspect he is a little out of humor with his own feelings; and above all, I must crave his pardon for having made him the subject of a kind of experiment. Yes, gentlemen, there is something strange and peculiar in the chamber to which our friend was shown last night. There is a picture which possesses a singular and mysterious influence; and with which there is connected a very curious story. It is a picture to which I attach a value from a variety of circumstances; and though I have often been tempted to destroy it from the odd and uncomfortable sensations it produces in every one that beholds it, yet I have never been able to prevail upon myself to make the sacrifice. It is a picture I never like to look upon myself, and which is held in awe by all my servants. I have, therefore, banished it to a room but rarely used, and should have had it covered last night, had not the nature of our conversation, and the whimsical talk about a haunted chamber tempted me to let it remain, by way of experiment, to see whether a stranger, totally unacquainted with its story, would be affected by it."

The words of the Baronet had turned every thought into a different channel: all were anxious to hear the story of the mysterious picture; and for myself, so strongly were my feelings interested, that I forgot to feel piqued at the experiment which my host had made upon my nerves, and joined eagerly in the general entreaty. As the morning was stormy, and precluded all egress, my host was glad of any means of entertaining his company; so drawing his armchair beside the fire, he began—

### The Adventure of the Mysterious Stranger

Many years since, when I was a young man, and had just left Oxford, I was sent on the grand tour to finish my education. I believe my parents had tried in vain to inoculate me with wisdom; so they sent me to mingle with society, in hopes I might take it the natural way. Such, at least, appears to be the reason for which nine-tenths of our youngsters are sent abroad. In the course of my tour I remained some time at Venice. The romantic character of the place delighted me; I was very much amused by the air of adventure and intrigue that prevailed in this region of masks and gondolas; and I was exceedingly smitten by a pair of languishing black eyes, that played upon my heart from under an Italian mantle; so I persuaded myself that

I was lingering at Venice to study men and manners. At least I persuaded my friends so, and that answered all my purpose.

I was a little prone to be struck by peculiarities in character and conduct, and my imagination was so full of romantic associations with Italy, that I was always on the lookout for adventure. Everything chimed in with such a humor in this old mermaid of a city. My suite of apartments were in a proud, melancholy palace on the grand canal, formerly the residence of a magnifico, and sumptuous with the traces of decayed grandeur. My gondolier was one of the shrewdest of his class, active, merry, intelligent, and, like his brethren, secret as the grave; that is to say, secret to all the world except his master. I had not had him a week before he put me behind all the curtains in Venice. I liked the silence and mystery of the place, and when I sometimes saw from my window a black gondola gliding mysteriously along in the dusk of the evening, with nothing visible but its little glimmering lantern, I would jump into my own zendeletta, and give a signal for pursuit— "But I am running away from my subject with the recollection of youthful follies," said the Baronet, checking himself. "Let me come to the point."

Among my familiar resorts was a cassino under the arcades on one side of the grand square of St. Mark. Here I used frequently to lounge and take my ice on those warm summer nights when in Italy everybody lives abroad until morning. I was seated here one evening, when a group of Italians took seat at a table on the opposite side of the saloon. Their conversation was gay and animated, and carried on with Italian vivacity and gesticulation. I remarked among them one young man, however, who appeared to take no share, and find no enjoyment in the conversation; though he seemed to force himself to attend to it. He was tall and slender, and of extremely prepossessing appearance. His features were fine, though emaciated. He had a profusion of black glossy hair that curled lightly about his head, and contrasted with the extreme paleness of his countenance. His brow was haggard; deep furrows seemed to have been ploughed into his visage by care, not by age, for he was evidently in the prime of youth. His eye was full of expression and fire, but wild and unsteady. He seemed to be tormented by some strange fancy or apprehension. In spite of every effort to fix his attention on the conversation of his companions, I noticed that every now and then he would turn his head slowly round, give a glance over his shoulder, and then withdraw it with a sudden jerk, as if something painful had met his eye. This was repeated at intervals of about a minute, and he appeared hardly to have got over one shock, before I saw him slowly preparing to encounter another.

After sitting some time in the cassino, the party paid for the refreshments they had taken, and departed. The young man was the last to leave the saloon, and I remarked him glancing behind him in the same way, just as he passed out at the door. I could not resist the impulse to rise and follow him; for I was at an age when a romantic feeling of curiosity is easily awakened. The party walked slowly down the Arcades, talking and laughing as they went. They crossed the Piazetta, but paused in the middle of it to enjoy the scene. It was one of those moonlight nights so brilliant and clear in the pure atmosphere of Italy. The moon-beams streamed on the tall tower of St. Mark, and lighted up the magnificent front and swelling domes of the Cathedral. The party expressed their delight in animated terms. I kept my eye upon the young man. He alone seemed abstracted and self-occupied. I noticed the same singular, and, as it were, furtive glance over the shoulder that had attracted my attention in the cassino. The party moved on, and I followed; they passed along the walks called the Broglio, turned the corner of the Ducal Palace, and getting into a gondola, glided swiftly away.

The countenance and conduct of this young man dwelt upon my mind. There was something in his appearance that interested me exceedingly. I met him a day or two after in a gallery of paintings. He was evidently a connoisseur, for he always singled out the most masterly productions, and the few remarks drawn from him by his companions showed an intimate acquaintance with the art. His own taste, however, ran on singular extremes. On Salvator Rosa in his most savage and solitary scenes; on Raphael, Titian, and Correggio in their softest delineations of female beauty. On these he would occasionally gaze with transient enthusiasm. But this seemed only a momentary forgetfulness. Still would recur that cautious glance behind, and always quickly withdrawn, as though something terrible had met his view.

I encountered him frequently afterwards. At the theatre, at balls, at concerts; at the promenades in the gardens of San Georgio; at the grotesque exhibitions in the square of St. Mark; among the throng of merchants on the exchange by the Rialto. He seemed, in fact, to seek crowds; to hunt after bustle and amusement; yet never to take any interest in either the business or gayety of the scene. Ever an air of painful thought, of wretched abstraction; and ever that strange and recurring movement, of glancing fearfully over the shoulder. I did not know at first but this might be caused by apprehension of arrest; or perhaps from dread of assassination. But, if so, why should he go thus continually abroad; why expose himself at all times and in all places?

I became anxious to know this stranger. I was drawn to him by that romantic sympathy that sometimes draws young men towards each other. His melancholy threw a charm about him in my eyes, which was no doubt heightened by the touching expression of his countenance, and the manly graces of his person; for manly beauty has its effect even upon man. I had an Englishman's habitual diffidence and awkwardness of address to contend with; but I subdued it, and from frequently meeting him in the Cassino, gradually edged myself into his acquaintance. I had no reserve on his part to contend with. He seemed on the contrary to court society; and, in fact, to seek anything rather than be alone.

When he found I really took an interest in him he threw himself entirely upon my friendship. He clung to me like a drowning man. He would walk with me for hours up and down the place of St. Mark—or he would sit until night was far advanced in my apartment; he took rooms under the same roof with me; and his constant request was that I would permit him, when it did not incommode me, to sit by me in my saloon. It was not that he seemed to take a particular delight in my conversation; but rather that he craved the vicinity of a human being; and above all, of a being that sympathized with him. "I have often heard," said he, "of the sincerity of Englishmen—thank God I have one at length for a friend!"

Yet he never seemed disposed to avail himself of my sympathy other than by mere companionship. He never sought to unbosom himself to me; there appeared to be a settled corroding anguish in his bosom that neither could be soothed "by silence nor by speaking."

A devouring melancholy preyed upon his heart, and seemed to be drying up the very blood in his veins. It was not a soft melancholy—the disease of the affections; but a parching, withering agony. I could see at times that his mouth was dry and feverish; he almost panted rather than breathed; his eyes were bloodshot; his cheeks pale and livid; with now and then faint streaks athwart them—baleful gleams of the fire that was consuming his heart. As my arm was within his, I felt him press it at times with a convulsive motion to his side; his hands would clinch themselves involuntarily, and a kind of shudder would run through his frame.

I reasoned with him about his melancholy, and sought to draw from him the cause—he shrunk from all confiding. "Do not seek to know it," said he, "you could not relieve it if you knew it; you would not even seek to relieve it—on the contrary, I should lose your sympathy; and that," said he, pressing my hand convulsively, "that I feel has become too dear to me to risk."

I endeavored to awaken hope within him. He was young; life had a thousand pleasures in store for him; there is a healthy reaction in the youthful heart; it medicines its own wounds— "Come, come," said I, "there is no grief so great that youth cannot outgrow it."—"No! no!" said he, clinching his teeth, and striking repeatedly, with the energy of despair, upon his bosom—"It is here—here—deep-rooted; draining my heart's blood. It grows and grows, while my heart withers and withers! I have a dreadful monitor that gives me no repose—that follows me step by step; and will follow me step by step, until it pushes me into my grave!"

As he said this he gave involuntarily one of those fearful glances over his shoulder, and shrunk back with more than usual horror. I could not resist the temptation to allude to this movement, which I supposed to be some mere malady of the nerves. The moment I mentioned it his face became crimsoned and convulsed—he grasped me by both hands:

"For God's sake," exclaimed he, with a piercing agony of voice—"never allude to that again; let us avoid this subject, my friend; you cannot relieve me, indeed you cannot relieve me; but you may add to the torments I suffer;—at some future day you shall know all."

I never resumed the subject; for however much my curiosity might be aroused, I felt too true compassion for his sufferings to increase them by my intrusion. I sought various ways to divert his mind, and to arouse him from the constant meditations in which he was plunged. He saw my efforts, and seconded them as far as in his power, for there was nothing moody or wayward in his nature; on the contrary, there was something frank, generous, unassuming, in his whole deportment. All the sentiments that he uttered were noble and lofty. He claimed no indulgence; he asked no toleration. He seemed content to carry his load of misery in silence, and only sought to carry it by my side. There was a mute beseeching manner about him, as if he craved companionship as a charitable boon; and a tacit thankfulness in his looks, as if he felt grateful to me for not repulsing him.

I felt this melancholy to be infectious. It stole over my spirits; interfered with all my gay pursuits, and gradually saddened my life; yet I could not prevail upon myself to shake off a being who seemed to hang upon me for support. In truth, the generous traits of character that beamed through all this gloom had penetrated to my heart. His bounty was lavish and open-handed. His charity melting and spontaneous. Not confined to mere donations, which often humiliate as much as they relieve. The tone of his voice, the beam of his eye, enhanced every gift, and surprised the poor suppliant with that rarest and sweetest of charities, the charity not merely of the hand, but of the heart. Indeed, his liberality seemed to have something in it of self-abasement and expiation. He humbled himself, in a manner, before the mendicant. "What right have I to ease and affluence," would he murmur to himself, "when innocence wanders in misery and rags?"

The carnival-time arrived. I hoped the gay scenes then presented might have some cheering effect. I mingled with him in the motley throng that crowded the place of St. Mark. We frequented operas, masquerades, balls—all in vain. The evil kept growing on him. He became more and more haggard and agitated. Often, after we had returned from one of these scenes of revelry, I have entered his room, and found him lying on his face on the sofa: his hands clinched in his fine hair, and his whole countenance bearing traces of the convulsions of his mind.

The carnival passed away; the season of Lent succeeded; passion-week arrived. We attended one evening a solemn service in one of the churches; in the course of which a grand piece of vocal and instrumental music was performed relating to the death of our Saviour.

I had remarked that he was always powerfully affected by music; on this occasion he was so in an extraordinary degree. As the peeling notes swelled through the lofty aisles, he seemed to kindle up with fervor. His eyes rolled upwards, until nothing but the whites were visible; his hands were clasped together, until the fingers were deeply imprinted in the flesh. When the music expressed the dying agony, his face gradually sunk upon his knees; and at the touching words resounding through the church, *"Jesu mori,"* sobs burst from him uncontrolled. I had never seen him weep before; his had always been agony rather than sorrow. I augured well from the circumstance. I let him weep on uninterrupted. When the service was ended we left the church. He hung on my arm as we walked homewards, with something of a softer and more subdued manner; instead of that nervous agitation I had been accustomed to witness. He alluded to the service we had heard. "Music," said he, "is indeed the voice of heaven; never before have I felt more impressed by the story of the atonement of our Saviour. Yes, my friend," said he, clasping his hands with a kind of transport, "I know that my Redeemer liveth."

We parted for the night. His room was not far from mine, and I heard him for some time busied in it. I fell asleep, but was awakened before daylight. The young man stood by my bed-side, dressed for travelling. He held a sealed packet and a large parcel in his hand, which he laid on the table.

"Farewell, my friend," said he, "I am about to set forth on a long journey; but, before I go, I leave with you these remembrances. In this packet you will find the particulars of my story. When you read them, I shall be far away; do not remember me with aversion. You have been, indeed, a friend to me. You have poured oil into a broken heart,—but you could not heal it.—Farewell—let me kiss your hand—I am unworthy to embrace you." He sunk on his knees, seized my hand in despite of my efforts to the contrary, and covered it with kisses. I was so surprised by all this scene that I had not been able to say a word. "But we shall meet again," said I, hastily, as I saw him hurrying towards the door. "Never, never, in this world!" said he, solemnly. He sprang once more to my bed-side—seized my hand, pressed it to his heart and to his lips, and rushed out of the room.

Here the Baronet paused. He seemed lost in thought, and sat looking upon the floor and drumming with his fingers on the arm of his chair.

"And did this mysterious personage return?" said the inquisitive gentleman.

"Never!" replied the Baronet, with a pensive shake of the head: "I never saw him again."

"And pray what has all this to do with the picture?" inquired the old gentleman with the nose.

"True!" said the questioner; "is it the portrait of this crack-brained Italian?"

"No!" said the Baronet drily, not half liking the appellation given to his hero; "but this picture was enclosed in the parcel he left with me. The sealed packet contained its explanation. There was a request on the outside that I would not open it until six months had elapsed. I kept my promise, in spite of my curiosity. I have a translation of it by me, and had meant to read it, by way of accounting for the mystery of the chamber, but I fear I have already detained the company too long."

Here there was a general wish expressed to have the manuscript read; particularly on the part of the inquisitive gentleman. So the worthy Baronet drew out a fairly-written manuscript, and wiping his spectacles, read aloud the following story:

## The Story of the Young Italian

I was born at Naples. My parents, though of noble rank, were limited in fortune, or rather my father was ostentatious beyond his means, and expended so much in his palace, his equipage, and his retinue, that he was continually straitened in his pecuniary circumstances. I was a younger son, and looked upon with indifference by my father, who, from a principle of family pride, wished to leave all his property to my elder brother. I showed, when quite a child, an extreme sensibility. Everything affected me violently. While yet an infant in my mother's arms, and before I had learnt to talk, I could be wrought upon to a wonderful degree of anguish or delight by the power of music. As I grew older my feelings remained equally acute, and I was easily transported into paroxysms of pleasure or rage. It was the amusement of my relatives and of the domestics to play upon this irritable temperament. I was moved to tears, tickled to laughter, provoked to fury, for the entertainment of company, who were amused by such a tempest of mighty passion in a pigmy frame—they little thought, or perhaps little heeded the dangerous sensibilities they were fostering. I thus became a little creature of passion, before reason was developed. In a short time I grew too old to be a plaything, and then I became a torment. The tricks and passions I had been teased into became irksome, and I was disliked by my teachers for the very lessons they had taught me. My mother died; and my power as a spoiled child was at an end. There was no longer any necessity to humor or tolerate me, for there was nothing to be gained by it, as I was no favorite of my father. I therefore experienced the fate of a spoiled child in such situation, and was neglected or noticed only to be crossed and contradicted. Such was the early treatment of a heart, which, if I am judge of it at all, was naturally disposed to the extremes of tenderness and affection.

My father, as I have already said, never liked me—in fact, he never understood me; he looked upon me as wilful and wayward, as deficient in natural affection. It was the stateliness of his own manner, the loftiness and grandeur of his own look, that had repelled me from his arms. I always pictured him to myself as I had seen him clad in his senatorial robes, rustling with pomp and pride. The magnificence of his person had daunted my strong imagination. I could never approach him with the confiding affection of a child.

My father's feelings were wrapped up in my elder brother. He was to be the inheritor of the family title and the family dignity, and everything was sacrificed to him—I, as well as everything else. It was determined to devote me to the church, that so my humors and myself might be removed out of the way, either of tasking my father's time and trouble, or interfering with the interests of my brother. At an early age, therefore, before my mind had dawned upon the world and its delights, or known anything of it beyond the precincts of my father's palace, I was sent to a convent, the superior of which was my uncle, and was confided entirely to his care.

My uncle was a man totally estranged from the world; he had never relished, for he had never tasted its pleasures; and he regarded rigid self-denial as the great basis of Christian virtue. He considered every one's temperament like his own; or at least he made them conform to it. His character and habits had an influence over the fraternity of which he was superior. A more gloomy, saturnine set of beings were never assembled together. The convent, too, was calculated to awaken sad and solitary thoughts. It was situated in a gloomy gorge of those mountains away south of Vesuvius. All distant views were shut out by sterile volcanic heights. A mountain stream raved beneath its walls, and eagles screamed about its turrets.

I had been sent to this place at so tender an age as soon to lose all distinct recollection of the scenes I had left behind. As my mind expanded, therefore, it formed its idea of the world from the convent and its vicinity, and a dreary world it appeared to me. An early tinge of melancholy was thus infused into my character; and the dismal stories of the monks, about devils and evil spirits, with which they affrighted my young imagination, gave me a tendency to superstition, which I could never effectually shake off. They took the same delight to work upon my ardent feelings that had been so mischievously exercised by my father's household. I can recollect the horrors with which they fed my heated fancy during an eruption of

Vesuvius. We were distant from that volcano, with mountains between us; but its convulsive throes shook the solid foundations of nature. Earthquakes threatened to topple down our convent towers. A lurid, baleful light hung in the heavens at night, and showers of ashes, borne by the wind, fell in our narrow valley. The monks talked of the earth being honey-combed beneath us; of streams of molten lava raging through its veins; of caverns of sulphurous flames roaring in the centre, the abodes of demons and the damned; of fiery gulfs ready to yawn beneath our feet. All these tales were told to the doleful accompaniment of the mountain's thunders, whose low bellowing made the walls of our convent vibrate.

One of the monks had been a painter, but had retired from the world, and embraced this dismal life in expiation of some crime. He was a melancholy man, who pursued his art in the solitude of his cell, but made it a source of penance to him. His employment was to portray, either on canvas or in waxen models, the human face and human form, in the agonies of death and in all the stages of dissolution and decay. The fearful mysteries of the charnel house were unfolded in his labors—the loathsome banquet of the beetle and the worm. I turn with shuddering even from the recollection of his works. Yet, at that time, my strong, but ill-directed imagination seized with ardor upon his instructions in his art. Anything was a variety from the dry studies and monotonous duties of the cloister. In a little while I became expert with my pencil, and my gloomy productions were thought worthy of decorating some of the altars of the chapel.

In this dismal way was a creature of feeling and fancy brought up. Everything genial and amiable in my nature was repressed and nothing brought out but what was unprofitable and ungracious. I was ardent in my temperament; quick, mercurial, impetuous, formed to be a creature all love and adoration; but a leaden hand was laid on all my finer qualities. I was taught nothing but fear and hatred. I hated my uncle, I hated the monks, I hated the convent in which I was immured. I hated the world, and I almost hated myself, for being, as I supposed, so hating and hateful an animal.

When I had nearly attained the age of sixteen, I was suffered, on one occasion, to accompany one of the brethren on a mission to a distant part of the country. We soon left behind us the gloomy valley in which I had been pent up for so many years, and after a short journey among the mountains, emerged upon the voluptuous landscape that spreads itself about the Bay of Naples. Heavens! How transported was I, when I stretched my gaze over a vast reach of delicious sunny country, gay with groves and vineyards; with Vesuvius rearing its forked summit to my right; the blue Mediterranean to my left, with its enchanting coast, studded with shining towns and sumptuous villas; and Naples, my native Naples, gleaming far, far in the distance.

Good God! was this the lovely world from which I had been excluded! I had reached that age when the sensibilities are in all their bloom and freshness. Mine had been checked and chilled. They now burst forth with the suddenness of a retarded spring. My heart, hitherto unnaturally shrunk up, expanded into a riot of vague, but delicious emotions. The beauty of nature intoxicated, bewildered me. The song of the peasants; their cheerful looks; their happy avocations; the picturesque gayety of their dresses; their rustic music; their dances; all broke upon me like witchcraft. My soul responded to the music; my heart danced in my bosom. All the men appeared amiable, all the women lovely.

I returned to the convent, that is to say, my body returned but my heart and soul never entered there again. I

could not forget this glimpse of a beautiful and a happy
world; a world so suited to my natural character. I had
felt so happy while in it; so different a being from what I
felt myself while in the convent—that tomb of the living.
I contrasted the countenances of the beings I had seen,
full of fire and freshness and enjoyment, with the pallid,
leaden, lack-lustre visages of the monks; the music of the
dance, with the droning chant of the chapel. I had before
found the exercises of the cloister wearisome; they now
became intolerable. The dull round of duties wore away
my spirit; my nerves became irritated by the fretful tin-
kling of the convent bell; evermore dinging among the
mountain echoes; evermore calling me from my repose at
night, my pencil by day, to attend to some tedious and
mechanical ceremony of devotion.

I was not of a nature to meditate long, without putting my thoughts into action. My spirit had been suddenly
aroused, and was now all awake within me. I watched my
opportunity, fled from the convent, and made my way on
foot to Naples. As I entered its gay and crowded streets,
and beheld the variety and stir of life around me, the luxury of palaces, the splendor of equipages, and the panto-
mimic animation of the motley populace, I seemed as if
awakened to a world of enchantment, and solemnly vowed
that nothing should force me back to the monotony of the
cloister.

I had to inquire my way to my father's palace, for I had
been so young on leaving it, that I knew not its situation.
I found some difficulty in getting admitted to my father's
presence, for the domestics scarcely knew that there was
such a being as myself in existence, and my monastic dress
did not operate in my favor. Even my father entertained
no recollection of my person. I told him my name, threw
myself at his feet, implored his forgiveness, and entreated
that I might not be sent back to the convent.

He received me with the condescension of a patron rather than the kindness of a parent. He listened patiently, but coldly, to my tale of monastic grievances and disgusts, and promised to think what else could be done for me. This coldness blighted and drove back all the frank affection of my nature that was ready to spring forth at the least warmth of parental kindness. All my early feelings towards my father revived; I again looked up to him as the stately magnificent being that had daunted my childish imagination, and felt as if I had no pretensions to his sympathies. My brother engrossed all his care and love; he inherited his nature, and carried himself towards me with a protecting rather than a fraternal air. It wounded my pride, which was great. I could brook condescension from my father, for I looked up to him with awe as a superior being, but I could not brook patronage from a brother, who, I felt, was intellectually my inferior. The servants perceived that I was an unwelcome intruder in the paternal mansion, and, menial-like, they treated me with neglect. Thus baffled at every point, my affections outraged wherever they would attach themselves, I became sullen, silent, and despondent. My feelings driven back upon myself, entered and preyed upon my own heart. I remained for some days an unwelcome guest rather than a restored son in my father's house. I was doomed never to be properly known there. I was made, by wrong treatment, strange even to myself; and they judged of me from my strangeness.

I was startled one day at the sight of one of the monks of my convent, gliding out of my father's room. He saw me, but pretended not to notice me; and this very hypocrisy made me suspect something. I had become sore and susceptible in my feelings; everything inflicted a wound on them. In this state of mind I was treated with marked disrespect by a pampered minion, the favorite servant of my father. All the pride and passion of my nature rose in an instant, and I struck him to the earth. My father was passing by; he stopped not to inquire the reason, nor indeed could he read the long course of mental sufferings which were the real cause. He rebuked me with anger and scorn; he summoned all the haughtiness of his nature, and grandeur of his look, to give weight to the contumely with which he treated me. I felt I had not deserved it—I felt that I was not appreciated—I felt that I had that within me which merited better treatment; my heart swelled against a father's injustice. I broke through my habitual awe of him. I replied to him with impatience; my hot spirit flushed in my cheek and kindled in my eye, but my sensitive heart swelled as quickly, and before I had half vented my passion I felt it suffocated and quenched in my tears. My father was astonished and incensed at this turning of the worm, and ordered me to my chamber. I retired in silence, choking with contending emotions.

I had not been long there when I overheard voices in an adjoining apartment. It was a consultation between my father and the monk, about the means of getting me back quietly to the convent. My resolution was taken. I had no longer a home nor a father. That very night I left the paternal roof. I got on board a vessel about making sail from the harbor, and abandoned myself to the wide world. No matter to what port she steered; any part of so beautiful a world was better than my convent. No matter where I was cast by fortune; any place would be more a home to me than the home I had left behind. The vessel was bound to Genoa. We arrived there after a voyage of a few days.

As I entered the harbor, between the moles which embrace it, and beheld the amphitheatre of palaces and churches and splendid gardens, rising one above another, I felt at once its title to the appellation of Genoa the Superb. I landed on the mole an utter stranger, without knowing what to do, or whither to direct my steps. No matter; I was released from the thraldom of the convent and the humiliations of home! When I traversed the Strada Balbi and the Strada Nuova, those streets of palaces, and gazed at the wonders of architecture around me; when I wandered at close of day, amid a gay throng of the brilliant and the beautiful, through the green alleys of the Aqua Verdi, or among the colonnades and terraces of the magnificent Doria Gardens, I thought it impossible to be ever otherwise than happy in Genoa. A few days sufficed to show me my mistake. My scanty purse was exhausted, and for the first time in my life I experienced the sordid distress of penury. I had never known the want of money, and had never adverted to the possibility of such an evil. I was ignorant of the world and all its ways; and when first the idea of destitution came over my mind its effect was withering. I was wandering pensively through the streets which no longer delighted my eyes, when chance led my stops into the magnificent church of the Annunciata.

A celebrated painter of the day was at that moment superintending the placing of one of his pictures over an altar. The proficiency which I had acquired in his art during my residence in the convent had made me an enthusiastic amateur. I was struck, at the first glance, with the painting. It was the face of a Madonna. So innocent, so lovely, such a divine expression of maternal tenderness! I lost for the moment all recollection of myself in the enthusiasm of my art. I clasped my hands together, and uttered an ejaculation of delight. The painter perceived my emotion. He was flattered and gratified by it. My air and manner pleased him, and he accosted me. I felt too much the want of friendship to repel the advances of a stranger, and there was something in this one so benevolent and winning that in a moment he gained my confidence.

I told him my story and my situation, concealing only my name and rank. He appeared strongly interested by my recital; invited me to his house, and from that time I became his favorite pupil. He thought he perceived in me extraordinary talents for the art, and his encomiums awakened all my ardor. What a blissful period of my existence was it that I passed beneath his roof. Another being seemed created within me, or rather, all that was amiable and excellent was drawn out. I was as recluse as ever I had been at the convent, but how different was my seclusion. My time was spent in storing my mind with lofty and poetical ideas; in meditating on all that was striking and noble in history or fiction; in studying and tracing all that was sublime and beautiful in nature. I was always a visionary, imaginative being, but now my reveries and imaginings all elevated me to rapture. I looked up to my master as to a benevolent genius that had opened to me a region of enchantment. I became devotedly attached to him. He was not a native of Genoa, but had been drawn thither by the solicitation of several of the nobility, and had resided there but a few years, for the completion of certain works he had undertaken. His health was delicate, and he had to confide much of the filling up of his designs to the pencils of his scholars. He considered me as particularly happy in delineating the human countenance; in seizing upon characteristic, though fleeting expressions and fixing them powerfully upon my canvas. I was employed continually, therefore, in sketching faces, and often when some particular grace or beauty or expression was wanted in a countenance, it was entrusted to my pencil. My benefactor was fond of bringing me forward; and partly, perhaps, through my actual skill, and partly by his partial praises, I began to be noted for the expression of my countenances.

Among the various works which he had undertaken, was an historical piece for one of the palaces of Genoa, in which were to be introduced the likenesses of several of the family. Among these was one entrusted to my pencil. It was that of a young girl, who as yet was in a convent for her education. She came out for the purpose of sitting for the picture. I first saw her in an apartment of one of the sumptuous palaces of Genoa. She stood before a casement that looked out upon the bay, a stream of vernal sunshine fell upon her, and shed a kind of glory round her as it lit up the rich crimson chamber. She was but sixteen years of age—and oh, how lovely! The scene broke upon me like a mere vision of spring and youth and beauty. I could have fallen down and worshipped her. She was like one of those fictions of poets and painters, when they would express the *beau ideal* that haunts their minds with shapes of indescribable perfection. I was permitted to sketch her countenance in various positions, and I fondly protracted the study that was undoing me. The more I gazed on her the more I became enamoured; there was something almost painful in my intense admiration. I was but nineteen years of age; shy, diffident, and inexperienced. I was treated with attention and encouragement, for my youth and my enthusiasm in my art had won favor for me; and I am inclined to think that there was something in my air and manner that inspired interest and respect. Still the kindness with which I was treated could not dispel the embarrassment into which my own imagination threw me when in presence of this lovely being. It elevated her into something almost more than mortal. She seemed too exquisite for earthly use; too delicate and exalted for human attainment. As I sat tracing her charms on my canvas, with my eyes occasionally riveted on her features, I drank in delicious poison that made me giddy. My heart alternately gushed with tenderness, and ached with despair. Now I became more than ever sensible of the violent fires that had lain dormant at the bottom of my soul. You who are born in a more temperate climate and under a cooler sky, have little idea of the violence of passion in our southern bosoms.

A few days finished my task; Bianca returned to her convent, but her image remained indelibly impressed upon my heart. It dwelt on my imagination; it became my pervading idea of beauty. It had an effect even upon my pencil; I became noted for my felicity in depicting female loveliness; it was but because I multiplied the image of Bianca. I soothed, and yet fed my fancy, by introducing her in all the productions of my master. I have stood with delight in one of the chapels of the Annunciata, and heard the crowd extol the seraphic beauty of a saint which I had painted; I have seen them bow down in adoration before the painting: they were bowing before the loveliness of Bianca.

I existed in this kind of dream, I might almost say delirium, for upwards of a year. Such is the tenacity of my imagination that the image which was formed in it continued in all its power and freshness. Indeed, I was a solitary, meditative being, much given to reverie, and apt to foster ideas which had once taken strong possession of me. I was roused from this fond, melancholy, delicious dream by the death of my worthy benefactor. I cannot describe the pangs his death occasioned me. It left me alone and almost broken-hearted. He bequeathed to me his little property; which, from the liberality of his disposition and his expensive style of living, was indeed but small; and he most particularly recommended me, in dying, to the protection of a nobleman who had been his patron.

The latter was a man who passed for munificent. He was a lover and an encourager of the arts, and evidently wished to be thought so. He fancied he saw in me indications of future excellence; my pencil had already attracted attention; he took me at once under his protection; seeing that I was overwhelmed with grief, and incapable of exerting myself in the mansion of my late benefactor, he invited me to sojourn for a time in a villa which he possessed on the border of the sea, in the picturesque neighborhood of Sestri de Ponenti.

I found at the villa the Count's only son, Filippo: he was nearly of my age, prepossessing in his appearance, and fascinating in his manners; he attached himself to me, and seemed to court my good opinion. I thought there was something of profession in his kindness, and of caprice in his disposition; but I had nothing else near me to attach myself to, and my heart felt the need of something to repose itself upon. His education had been neglected; he looked upon me as his superior in mental powers and acquirements, and tacitly acknowledged my superiority. I felt that I was his equal in birth, and that gave an independence to my manner which had its effect. The caprice and tyranny I saw sometimes exercised on others, over whom he had power, were never manifested towards me. We became intimate friends, and frequent companions. Still I loved to be alone, and to indulge in the reveries of my own imagination, among the beautiful scenery by which I was surrounded. The villa stood in the midst of ornamented grounds, finely decorated with statues and fountains, and laid out into groves and alleys and shady bowers. It commanded a wide view of the Mediterranean, and the picturesque Ligurian coast. Everything was assembled here that could gratify the taste or agreeably occupy the mind. Soothed by the tranquility of this elegant retreat, the turbulence of my feelings gradually subsided, and, blending with the romantic spell that still reigned over my imagination, produced a soft voluptuous melancholy.

I had not been long under the roof of the Count, when our solitude was enlivened by another inhabitant. It was a daughter of a relation of the Count, who had lately died

in reduced circumstances, bequeathing this only child
to his protection. I had heard much of her beauty from
Filippo, but my fancy had become so engrossed by one
idea of beauty as not to admit of any other. We were in
the central saloon of the villa when she arrived. She was
still in mourning, and approached, leaning on the Count's
arm. As they ascended the marble portico, I was struck
by the elegance of her figure and movement, by the grace
with which the *mezzaro*, the bewitching veil of Genoa,
was folded about her slender form. They entered. Heavens!
what was my surprise when I beheld Bianca before me.
It was herself; pale with grief; but still more matured in
loveliness than when I had last beheld her. The time that
had elapsed had developed the graces of her person; and
the sorrow she had undergone had diffused over her countenance an irresistible tenderness.

She blushed and trembled at seeing me, and tears
rushed into her eyes, for she remembered in whose company she had been accustomed to behold me. For my part, I
cannot express what were my emotions. By degrees I overcame the extreme shyness that had formerly paralyzed me
in her presence. We were drawn together by sympathy of
situation. We had each lost our best friend in the world;
we were each, in some measure thrown upon the kindness
of others. When I came to know her intellectually, all my
ideal picturings of her were confirmed. Her newness to the
world, her delightful susceptibility to everything beautiful
and agreeable in nature, reminded me of my own emotions when first I escaped from the convent. Her rectitude
of thinking delighted my judgment; the sweetness of her
nature wrapped itself around my heart; and then her young
and tender and budding loveliness, sent a delicious madness to my brain.

I gazed upon her with a kind of idolatry, as something
more than mortal; and I felt humiliated at the idea of my

comparative unworthiness. Yet she was mortal; and one of mortality's most susceptible and loving compounds; for she loved me!

How first I discovered the transporting truth I cannot recollect; I believe it stole upon me by degrees, as a wonder past hope or belief. We were both at such a tender and loving age; in constant intercourse with each other; mingling in the same elegant pursuits; for music, poetry, and painting were our mutual delights, and we were almost separated from society, among lovely and romantic scenery! Is it strange that two young hearts thus brought together should readily twine round each other?

Oh, gods! what a dream—a transient dream! of unalloyed delight then passed over my soul! Then it was that the world around me was indeed a paradise, for I had a woman—lovely, delicious woman, to share it with me. How often have I rambled over the picturesque shores of Sestri, or climbed its wild mountains, with the coast gemmed with villas, and the blue sea far below me, and the slender Faro of Genoa on its romantic promontory in the distance; and as I sustained the faltering steps of Bianca, have thought there could no unhappiness enter into so beautiful a world. Why, oh, why is this budding season of life and love so transient—why is this rosy cloud of love that sheds such a glow over the morning of our days so prone to brew up into the whirlwind and the storm!

I was the first to awaken from this blissful delirium of the affections. I had gained Bianca's heart: what was I to do with it? I had no wealth nor prospects to entitle me to her hand. Was I to take advantage of her ignorance of the world, of her confiding affection, and draw her down to my own poverty? Was this requiting the hospitality of the Count?—was this requiting the love of Bianca?

Now first I began to feel that even successful love may have its bitterness. A corroding care gathered about my heart. I moved about the palace like a guilty being. I felt as if I had abused its hospitality—as if I were a thief within its walls. I could no longer look with unembarrassed mien in the countenance of the Count. I accused myself of perfidy to him, and I thought he read it in my looks, and began to distrust and despise me. His manner had always been ostentatious and condescending, it now appeared cold and haughty. Filippo, too, became reserved and distant; or at least I suspected him to be so. Heavens!—was this mere coinage of my brain: was I to become suspicious of all the world?—a poor surmising wretch; watching looks and gestures; and torturing myself with misconstructions. Or if true—was I to remain beneath a roof where I was merely tolerated, and linger there on sufferance? "This is not to be endured!" exclaimed I; "I will tear myself from this state of self-abasement; I will break through this fascination and fly—Fly?—whither?—from the world?—for where is the world when I leave Bianca behind me?"

My spirit was naturally proud, and swelled within me at the idea of being looked upon with contumely. Many times I was on the point of declaring my family and rank, and asserting my equality, in the presence of Bianca, when I thought her relatives assumed an air of superiority. But the feeling was transient. I considered myself discarded and contemned by my family; and had solemnly vowed never to own relationship to them, until they themselves should claim it.

The struggle of my mind preyed upon my happiness and my health. It seemed as if the uncertainty of being loved would be less intolerable than thus to be assured of it, and yet not dare to enjoy the conviction. I was no longer the enraptured admirer of Bianca; I no longer hung in ecstasy on the tones of her voice, nor drank in with insatiate gaze the beauty of her countenance. Her very smiles ceased to delight me, for I felt culpable in having won them.

She could not but be sensible of the change in me, and inquired the cause with her usual frankness and simplicity. I could not evade the inquiry, for my heart was full to aching. I told her all the conflict of my soul; my devouring passion, my bitter self-upbraiding. "Yes!" said I, "I am unworthy of you. I am an offcast from my family—a wanderer—a nameless, homeless wanderer, with nothing but poverty for my portion, and yet I have dared to love you—have dared to aspire to your love!"

My agitation moved her to tears; but she saw nothing in my situation so hopeless as I had depicted it. Brought up in a convent, she knew nothing of the world, its wants, its cares; and, indeed, what woman is a worldly casuist in matters of the heart? Nay, more, she kindled into a sweet enthusiasm when she spoke of my fortunes and myself. We had dwelt together on the works of the famous masters. I had related to her their histories; the high reputation, the influence, the magnificence to which they had attained. The companions of princes, the favorites of kings, the pride and boast of nations. All this she applied to me. Her love saw nothing in their greatest productions that I was not able to achieve; and when I saw the lovely creature glow with fervor, and her whole countenance radiant with the visions of my glory, which seemed breaking upon her, I was snatched up for the moment into the heaven of her own imagination.

I am dwelling too long upon this part of my story; yet I cannot help lingering over a period of my life, on which, with all its cares and conflicts, I look back with fondness; for as yet my soul was unstained by a crime. I do not know what might have been the result of this struggle between pride, delicacy, and passion, had I not read in a Neapolitan gazette an account of the sudden death of my brother. It was accompanied by an earnest inquiry for intelligence concerning me, and a prayer, should this notice meet my eye, that I would hasten to Naples, to comfort an infirm and afflicted father.

I was naturally of an affectionate disposition, but my brother had never been as a brother to me. I had long considered myself as disconnected from him, and his death caused me but little emotion. The thoughts of my father, infirm and suffering, touched me, however, to the quick; and when I thought of him, that lofty, magnificent being, now bowed down and desolate, and suing to me for comfort, all my resentment for past neglect was subdued, and a glow of filial affection was awakened within me.

The predominant feeling, however, that overpowered all others was transport at the sudden change in my whole fortunes. A home—a name—a rank—wealth awaited me; and love painted a still more rapturous prospect in the distance. I hastened to Bianca, and threw myself at her feet. "Oh, Bianca," exclaimed I, "at length I can claim you for my own. I am no longer a nameless adventurer, a neglected, rejected outcast. Look—read, behold the tidings that restore me to my name and to myself!"

I will not dwell on the scene that ensued. Bianca rejoiced in the reverse of my situation, because she saw it lightened my heart of a load of care; for her own part she had loved me for myself, and had never doubted that my own merits would command both fame and fortune.

I now felt all my native pride buoyant within me; I no longer walked with my eyes bent to the dust; hope elevated them to the skies; my soul was lit up with fresh fires, and beamed from my countenance.

I wished to impart the change in my circumstances to the Count; to let him know who and what I was, and to make formal proposals for the hand of Bianca; but he was absent on a distant estate. I opened my whole soul to Filippo. Now first I told him of my passion; of the doubts and fears that had distracted me, and of the tidings that had suddenly dispelled them. He overwhelmed me with congratulations and with the warmest expressions of sympathy. I embraced him in the fullness of my heart. I felt compunctious for having suspected him of coldness, and asked him forgiveness for having ever doubted his friendship.

Nothing is so warm, and enthusiastic as a sudden expansion of the heart between young men. Filippo entered into our concerns with the most eager interest. He was our confidant and counsellor. It was determined that I should hasten at once to Naples to re-establish myself in my father's affections and my paternal home, and the moment the reconciliation was effected and my father's consent insured, I should return and demand Bianca of the Count. Filippo engaged to secure his father's acquiescence; indeed, he undertook to watch over our interests, and was the channel through which we were to correspond.

My parting with Bianca was tender—delicious—agonizing.

It was in a little pavilion of the garden which had been one of our favorite resorts. How often and often did I return to have one more adieu—to have her look once more on me in speechless emotion—to enjoy once more the rapturous sight of those tears streaming down her lovely cheeks—to seize once more on that delicate hand, the frankly accorded pledge of love, and cover it with tears and kisses! Heavens! There is a delight even in the parting agony of two lovers worth a thousand tame pleasures of the world. I have her at this moment before my eyes—at the window of the pavilion, putting aside the vines that clustered about the casement—her light form beaming forth in virgin white—her countenance all tears and smiles—sending a thousand and a thousand adieus after me, as, hesitating, in a delirium of fondness and agitation, I faltered my way down the avenue.

As the bark bore me out of the harbor of Genoa, how eagerly my eyes stretched along the coast of Sestri, till it discerned the villa gleaming from among trees at the foot of the mountain. As long as day lasted, I gazed and gazed upon it, till it lessened and lessened to a mere white speck in the distance; and still my intense and fixed gaze discerned it, when all other objects of the coast had blended into indistinct confusion, or were lost in the evening gloom.

On arriving at Naples, I hastened to my paternal home. My heart yearned for the long-withheld blessing of a father's love. As I entered the proud portal of the ancestral palace, my emotions were so great that I could not speak. No one knew me. The servants gazed at me with curiosity and surprise. A few years of intellectual elevation and development had made a prodigious change in the poor fugitive stripling from the convent. Still that no one should know me in my rightful home was overpowering. I felt like the prodigal son returned. I was a stranger in the house of my father. I burst into tears, and wept aloud. When I made myself known, however, all was changed. I who had once been almost repulsed from its walls, and forced to fly as an exile, was welcomed back with acclamation, with servility. One of the servants hastened to prepare my father for my reception; my eagerness to receive the paternal embrace was so great that I could not await his return; but hurried after him. What a spectacle met my eyes as I entered the chamber! My father, whom I had left in the pride of vigorous age, whose noble and majestic bearing had so awed my young imagination, was bowed down and withered into decrepitude. A paralysis had ravaged his stately form, and left it a shaking ruin. He sat propped up in his chair, with pale, relaxed visage and glassy, wandering eye. His intellects had evidently shared in the ravage of his frame. The servant was endeavoring to make him comprehend the visitor that was at hand. I tottered up to him and sunk at his feet. All his past coldness and neglect were forgotten in his present sufferings. I remembered only that he was my parent, and that I had deserted him. I clasped his knees; my voice was almost stifled with convulsive sobs. "Pardon—pardon—oh my father!" was all that I could utter. His apprehension seemed slowly to return to him. He gazed at me for some moments with a vague, inquiring look; a convulsive tremor quivered about his lips; he feebly extended a shaking hand, laid it upon my head, and burst into an infantine flow of tears.

From that moment he would scarcely spare me from his sight. I appeared the only object that his heart responded to in the world; all else was as a blank to him. He had almost lost the powers of speech, and the reasoning faculty seemed at an end. He was mute and passive; excepting that fits of child-like weeping would sometimes come over him without any immediate cause. If I left the room at any time, his eye was incessantly fixed on the door till my return, and on my entrance there was another gush of tears.

To talk with him of my concerns, in this ruined state of mind, would have been worse than useless; to have left him, for ever so short a time, would have been cruel, unnatural. Here then was a new trial for my affections. I wrote to Bianca an account of my return and of my actual situation; painting in colors vivid, for they were true, the torments I suffered at our being thus separated; for to the youthful lover every day of absence is an age of love lost. I enclosed the letter in one to Filippo, who was the channel of our correspondence. I received a reply from him full of friendship and sympathy; from Bianca full of assurances of affection and constancy.

Week after week, month after month elapsed, without making any change in my circumstances. The vital flame, which had seemed nearly extinct when first I met my

father, kept fluttering on without any apparent diminu-
tion. I watched him constantly, faithfully—I had almost
said patiently. I knew that his death alone would set me
free; yet I never at any moment wished it. I felt too glad
to be able to make any atonement for past disobedience;
and, denied as I had been all endearments of relationship
in my early days, my heart yearned towards a father, who,
in his age and helplessness, had thrown himself entirely on
me for comfort.

My passion for Bianca gained daily more force from
absence; by constant meditation it wore itself a deeper
and deeper channel. I made no new friends nor acquaintances; sought none of the pleasures of Naples which my
rank and fortune threw open to me. Mine was a heart that
confined itself to few objects, but dwelt upon those with
the intenser passion. To sit by my father, and administer
to his wants, and to meditate on Bianca in the silence of
his chamber, was my constant habit. Sometimes I amused
myself with my pencil in portraying the image that was
ever present to my imagination. I transferred to canvas
every look and smile of hers that dwelt in my heart. I
showed them to my father in hopes of awakening an
interest in his bosom for the mere shadow of my love; but
he was too far sunk in intellect to take any more than a
child-like notice of them.

When I received a letter from Bianca it was a new
source of solitary luxury. Her letters, it is true, were less
and less frequent, but they were always full of assurances
of unabated affection. They breathed not the frank and
innocent warmth with which she expressed herself in conversation, but I accounted for it from the embarrassment
which inexperienced minds have often to express themselves upon paper. Filippo assured me of her unaltered
constancy. They both lamented in the strongest terms our

continued separation, though they did justice to the filial feeling that kept me by my father's side.

Nearly eighteen months elapsed in this protracted exile. To me they were so many ages. Ardent and impetuous by nature, I scarcely know how I should have supported so long an absence, had I not felt assured that the faith of Bianca was equal to my own. At length my father died. Life went from him almost imperceptibly. I hung over him in mute affliction, and watched the expiring spasms of nature. His last faltering accents whispered repeatedly a blessing on me—alas! how has it been fulfilled!

When I had paid due honors to his remains, and laid them in the tomb of our ancestors, I arranged briefly my affairs; put them in a posture to be easily at my command from a distance, and embarked once more, with a bounding heart, for Genoa.

Our voyage was propitious, and oh! what was my rapture when first, in the dawn of morning, I saw the shadowy summits of the Apennines rising almost like clouds above the horizon. The sweet breath of summer just moved us over the long wavering billows that were rolling us on towards Genoa. By degrees the coast of Sestri rose like a sweet creation of enchantment from the silver bosom of the deep. I behold the line of villages and palaces studding its borders. My eye reverted to a well-known point, and at length, from the confusion of distant objects, it singled out the villa which contained Bianca. It was a mere speck in the landscape, but glimmering from afar, the polar star of my heart.

Again I gazed at it for a livelong summer's day; but oh how different the emotions between departure and return. It now kept growing and growing, instead of lessening on my sight. My heart seemed to dilate with it. I looked at it through a telescope. I gradually defined one feature after another. The balconies of the central saloon where first I met Bianca beneath its roof; the terrace where we so often had passed the delightful summer evenings; the awning that shaded her chamber window—I almost fancied I saw her form beneath it. Could she but know her lover was in the bark whose white sail now gleamed on the sunny bosom of the sea! My fond impatience increased as we neared the coast. The ship seemed to lag lazily over the billows; I could almost have sprung into the sea and swam to the desired shore.

The shadows of evening gradually shrouded the scene, but the moon arose in all her fullness and beauty and shed the tender light so dear to lovers, over the romantic coast of Sestri. My whole soul was bathed in unutterable tenderness. I anticipated the heavenly evenings I should pass in wandering with Bianca by the light of that blessed moon.

It was late at night before we entered the harbor. As early next morning as I could get released from the formalities of landing I threw myself on horseback and hastened to the villa. As I galloped round the rocky promontory on which stands the Faro, and saw the coast of Sestri opening upon me, a thousand anxieties and doubts suddenly sprang up in my bosom. There is something fearful in returning to those we love, while yet uncertain what ills or changes absence may have effected. The turbulence of my agitation shook my very frame. I spurred my horse to redoubled speed; he was covered with foam when we both arrived panting at the gateway that opened to the grounds around the villa. I left my horse at a cottage and walked through the grounds, that I might regain tranquility for the approaching interview. I chid myself for having suffered mere doubts and surmises thus suddenly to overcome me; but I was always prone to be carried away by these gusts of the feelings.

On entering the garden everything bore the same look as when I had left it; and this unchanged aspect of things reassured me. There were the alleys in which I had so often walked with Bianca; the same shades under which we had so often sat during the noontide. There were the same flowers of which she was fond; and which appeared still to be under the ministry of her hand. Everything around looked and breathed of Bianca; hope and joy flushed in my bosom at every step. I passed a little bower in which we had often sat and read together. A book and a glove lay on the bench. It was Bianca's glove; it was a volume of the *Metestasio* I had given her. The glove lay in my favorite passage. I clasped them to my heart. "All is safe!" exclaimed I, with rapture, "she loves me! she is still my own!"

I bounded lightly along the avenue down which I had faltered so slowly at my departure. I beheld her favorite pavilion which had witnessed our parting scene. The window was open, with the same vine clambering about it, precisely as when she waved and wept me an adieu. Oh! how transporting was the contrast in my situation. As I passed near the pavilion, I heard the tones of a female voice. They thrilled through me with an appeal to my heart not to be mistaken. Before I could think, I *felt* they were Bianca's. For an instant I paused, overpowered with agitation. I feared to break in suddenly upon her. I softly ascended the steps of the pavilion. The door was open. I saw Bianca seated at a table; her back was towards me; she was warbling a soft melancholy air, and was occupied in drawing. A glance sufficed to show me that she was copying one of my own paintings. I gazed on her for a moment in a delicious tumult of emotions. She paused in her singing; a heavy sigh, almost a sob followed. I could no longer contain myself. "Bianca!" exclaimed I, in a half-smothered voice. She started at the sound; brushed back the ringlets that hung clustering about her face; darted a glance at me; uttered a piercing shriek and would have fallen to the earth, had I not caught her in my arms.

"Bianca! my own Bianca!" exclaimed I, folding her to my bosom; my voice stifled in sobs of convulsive joy. She lay in my arms without sense or motion. Alarmed at the effects of my own precipitation, I scarce knew what to do. I tried by a thousand endearing words to call her back to consciousness. She slowly recovered, and half opening her eyes—"where am I?" murmured she faintly. "Here," exclaimed I, pressing her to my bosom. "Here! close to the heart that adores you; in the arms of your faithful Ottavio!" "Oh no! no! no!" shrieked she, starting into sudden life and terror—"away! away! leave me! leave me!"

She tore herself from my arms; rushed to a corner of the saloon, and covered her face with her hands, as if the very sight of me were baleful. I was thunderstruck—I could not believe my senses. I followed her, trembling, confounded. I endeavored to take her hand, but she shrunk from my very touch with horror.

"Good heavens, Bianca," exclaimed I, "what is the meaning of this? Is this my reception after so long an absence? Is this the love you professed for me?"

At the mention of love, a shuddering ran through her. She turned to me a face wild with anguish. "No more of that! no more of that!" gasped she—"talk not to me of love—I—I—am married!"

I reeled as if I had received a mortal blow. A sickness struck to my very heart. I caught at a window frame for support. For a moment or two, everything was chaos around me. When I recovered, I beheld Bianca lying on a sofa; her face buried in a pillow, and sobbing convulsively. Indignation at her fickleness for a moment overpowered every other feeling.

"Faithless—perjured—" cried I, striding across the room. But another glance at that beautiful being in distress, checked all my wrath. Anger could not dwell together with her idea in my soul.

"Oh, Bianca," exclaimed I, in anguish, "could I have dreamt of this; could I have suspected you would have been false to me?"

She raised her face all streaming with tears, all disordered with emotion, and gave me one appealing look— "False to you!—they told me you were dead!"

"What," said I, "in spite of our constant correspondence?"

She gazed wildly at me—"correspondence!—what correspondence?"

"Have you not repeatedly received and replied to my letters?"

She clasped her hands with solemnity and fervor—"As I hope for mercy, never!"

A horrible surmise shot through my brain—"Who told you I was dead?"

"It was reported that the ship in which you embarked for Naples perished at sea."

"But who told you the report?"

She paused for an instant, and trembled—"Filippo!"

"May the God of heaven curse him!" cried I, extending my clinched fists aloft.

"Oh do not curse him—do not curse him!" exclaimed she—"He is—he is—my husband!"

This was all that was wanting to unfold the perfidy that had been practiced upon me. My blood boiled like liquid fire in my veins. I gasped with rage too great for utterance. I remained for a time bewildered by the whirl of horrible thoughts that rushed through my mind. The poor victim of deception before me thought it was with her I was incensed. She faintly murmured forth her exculpation.

I will not dwell upon it. I saw in it more than she meant to reveal. I saw with a glance how both of us had been betrayed. "'Tis well!" muttered I to myself in smothered accents of concentrated fury. "He shall account to me for this!"

Bianca overhead me. New terror flashed in her countenance. "For mercy's sake do not meet him—say nothing of what has passed—for my sake say nothing to him—I only shall be the sufferer!"

A new suspicion darted across my mind—"What!" exclaimed I—"do you then *fear* him? is he *unkind* to you—tell me," reiterated I, grasping her hand and looking her eagerly in the face—"tell me—*dares* he to use you harshly!"

"No! no! no!" cried she faltering and embarrassed; but the glance at her face had told me volumes. I saw in her pallid and wasted features; in the prompt terror and subdued agony of her eye a whole history of a mind broken down by tyranny. Great God! and was this beauteous flower snatched from me to be thus trampled upon? The idea roused me to madness. I clinched my teeth and my hands; I foamed at the mouth; every passion seemed to have resolved itself into the fury that like a lava boiled within my heart. Bianca shrunk from me in speechless affright. As I strode by the window my eye darted down the alley. Fatal moment! I beheld Filippo at a distance! My brain was in a delirium—I sprang from the pavilion, and was before him with the quickness of lightning. He saw me as I came rushing upon him—he turned pale, looked wildly to right and left, as if he would have fled, and trembling drew his sword.

"Wretch!" cried I, "well may you draw your weapon!"

I spoke not another word—I snatched forth a stiletto, put by the sword which trembled in his hand, and buried my poniard in his bosom. He fell with the blow, but my rage was unsated. I sprang upon him with the blood-thirsty feeling of a tiger; redoubled my blows; mangled him in my frenzy, grasped him by the throat, until with re-iterated wounds and strangling convulsions he expired in my grasp. I remained glaring on the countenance, horrible in death, that seemed to stare back with its protruded eyes upon me. Piercing shrieks roused me from my delirium. I looked round and beheld Bianca flying distractedly towards us. My brain whirled. I waited not to meet her, but fled from the scene of horror. I fled forth from the garden like another Cain, a hell within my bosom, and a curse upon my head. I fled without knowing whither—almost without knowing why—my only idea was to get farther and farther from the horrors I had left behind; as if I could throw space between myself and my conscience. I fled to the Apennines, and wandered for days and days among their savage heights. How I existed I cannot tell—what rocks and precipices I braved, and how I braved them, I know not. I kept on and on—trying to outtravel the curse that clung to me. Alas, the shrieks of Bianca rung for ever in my ear. The horrible countenance of my victim was for ever before my eyes. The blood of Filippo cried to me from the ground. Rocks, trees, and torrents all resounded with my crime. Then it was I felt how much more insupportable is the anguish of remorse than every other mental pang. Oh! could I but have cast off this crime that festered in my heart; could I but have regained the innocence that reigned in my breast as I entered the garden at Sestri; could I but have restored my victim to life, I felt as if I could look on with transport even though Bianca were in his arms.

By degrees this frenzied fever of remorse settled into a permanent malady of the mind. Into one of the most horrible that ever poor wretch was cursed with. Wherever

I went, the countenance of him I had slain appeared to follow me. Wherever I turned my head I beheld it behind me, hideous with the contortions of the dying moment. I have tried in every way to escape from this horrible phantom; but in vain. I know not whether it is an illusion of the mind, the consequence of my dismal education at the convent, or whether a phantom really sent by heaven to punish me; but there it ever is—at all times—in all places—nor has time nor habit had any effect in familiarizing me with its terrors. I have travelled from place to place, plunged into amusements—tried dissipation and distraction of every kind—all—all in vain. I once had recourse to my pencil as a desperate experiment. I painted an exact resemblance of this phantom face. I placed it before me in hopes that by constantly contemplating the copy I might diminish the effect of the original. But I only doubled instead of diminishing the misery. Such is the curse that has clung to my footsteps—that has made my life a burthen—but the thoughts of death, terrible. God knows what I have suffered. What days and days, and nights and nights, of sleepless torment. What a never-dying worm has preyed upon my heart; what an unquenchable fire has burned within my brain. He knows the wrongs that wrought upon my poor weak nature; that converted the tenderest of affections into the deadliest of fury. He knows best whether a frail erring creature has expiated by long-enduring torture and measureless remorse, the crime of a moment of madness. Often, often have I prostrated myself in the dust, and implored that he would give me a sign of his forgiveness, and let me die—

Thus far had I written some time since. I had meant to leave this record of misery and crime with you, to be read when I should be no more.

My prayer to heaven has at length been heard. You were witness to my emotions last evening at the church, when the vaulted temple resounded with the words of atonement and redemption. I heard a voice speaking to me from the midst of the music; I heard it rising above the pealing of the organ and the voices of the choir—it spoke to me in tones of celestial melody—it promised mercy and forgiveness, but demanded from me full expiation. I go to make it. To-morrow I shall be on my way to Genoa to surrender myself to justice. You who have pitied my sufferings; who have poured the balm of sympathy into my wounds, do not shrink from my memory with abhorrence now that you know my story. Recollect, when you read of my crime I shall have atoned for it with my blood!

When the Baronet had finished, there was an universal desire expressed to see the painting of this frightful visage. After much entreaty the Baronet consented, on condition that they should only visit it one by one. He called his housekeeper and gave her charge to conduct the gentlemen singly to the chamber. They all returned varying in their stories: some affected in one way, some in another; some more, some less; but all agreeing that there was a certain something about the painting that had a very odd effect upon the feelings.

I stood in a deep bow window with the Baronet, and could not help expressing my wonder. "After all," said I, "there are certain mysteries in our nature, certain inscrutable impulses and influences, that warrant one in being superstitious. Who can account for so many persons of different characters being thus strangely affected by a mere painting?"

"And especially when not one of them has seen it!" said the Baronet with a smile.

"How!" exclaimed I, "not seen it?"

"Not one of them!" replied he, laying his finger on his lips, in sign of secrecy. "I saw that some of them were in a bantering vein, and did not choose that the memento of the poor Italian should be made a jest of. So I gave the housekeeper a hint to show them all to a different chamber!"

# The Picture of Dorian Gray
OSCAR WILDE
1890


CHAPTER I

The studio was filled with the rich odor of roses, and when the light summer wind stirred amidst the trees of the garden there came through the open door the heavy scent of the lilac, or the more delicate perfume of the pink-flowering thorn.

From the corner of the divan of Persian saddle-bags on which he was lying, smoking, as usual, innumerable cigarettes, Lord Henry Wotton could just catch the gleam of the honey-sweet and honey-colored blossoms of the laburnum, whose tremulous branches seemed hardly able to bear the burden of a beauty so flame-like as theirs; and now and then the fantastic shadows of birds in flight flitted across the long tussore-silk curtains that were stretched in front of the huge window, producing a kind of momentary Japanese effect, and making him think of those pallid jade-faced painters who, in an art that is necessarily immobile, seek to convey the sense of swiftness and motion. The sullen murmur of the bees shouldering their way through the long unmown grass, or circling with monotonous insistence round the black-crocketed spires of the early June hollyhocks, seemed to make the stillness more oppressive, and the dim roar of London was like the bourdon note of a distant organ.

In the centre of the room, clamped to an upright easel, stood the full-length portrait of a young man of extraordinary personal beauty, and in front of it, some little distance away, was sitting the artist himself, Basil Hallward, whose sudden disappearance some years ago caused, at the time, such public excitement, and gave rise to so many strange conjectures.

As he looked at the gracious and comely form he had so skilfully mirrored in his art, a smile of pleasure passed across his face, and seemed about to linger there. But he suddenly started up, and, closing his eyes, placed his fingers upon the lids, as though he sought to imprison within his brain some curious dream from which he feared he might awake.

"It is your best work, Basil, the best thing you have ever done," said Lord Henry, languidly. "You must certainly send it next year to the Grosvenor. The Academy is too large and too vulgar. The Grosvenor is the only place."

"I don't think I will send it anywhere," he answered, tossing his head back in that odd way that used to make his friends laugh at him at Oxford. "No: I won't send it anywhere."

Lord Henry elevated his eyebrows, and looked at him in amazement through the thin blue wreaths of smoke that curled up in such fanciful whorls from his heavy opium-tainted cigarette. "Not send it anywhere? My dear fellow, why? Have you any reason? What odd chaps you painters are! You do anything in the world to gain a reputation. As soon as you have one, you seem to want to throw it away. It is silly of you, for there is only one thing in the world worse than being talked about, and that is not being talked about. A portrait like this would set you far above all the young men in England, and make the old men quite jealous, if old men are ever capable of any emotion."

"I know you will laugh at me," he replied, "but I really can't exhibit it. I have put too much of myself into it."

Lord Henry stretched his long legs out on the divan and shook with laughter.

"Yes, I knew you would laugh; but it is quite true, all the same."

"Too much of yourself in it! Upon my word, Basil, I didn't know you were so vain; and I really can't see any resemblance between you, with your rugged strong face and your coal-black hair, and this young Adonis, who looks as if he was made of ivory and rose-leaves. Why, my dear Basil, he is a Narcissus, and you—well, of course you have an intellectual expression, and all that. But beauty, real beauty, ends where an intellectual expression begins. Intellect is in itself an exaggeration, and destroys the harmony of any face. The moment one sits down to think, one becomes all nose, or all forehead, or something horrid. Look at the successful men in any of the learned professions. How perfectly hideous they are! Except, of course, in the Church. But then in the Church they don't think. A bishop keeps on saying at the age of eighty what he was told to say when he was a boy of eighteen, and consequently he always looks absolutely delightful. Your mysterious young friend, whose name you have never told me, but whose picture really fascinates me, never thinks. I feel quite sure of that. He is a brainless, beautiful thing, who should be always here in winter when we have no flowers to look at, and always here in summer when we want something to chill our intelligence. Don't flatter yourself, Basil: you are not in the least like him."

"You don't understand me, Harry. Of course I am not like him. I know that perfectly well. Indeed, I should be sorry to look like him. You shrug your shoulders? I am telling you the truth. There is a fatality about all physical and intellectual distinction, the sort of fatality that seems to dog through history the faltering steps of kings. It is better not to be different from one's fellows. The ugly and the stupid have the best of it in this world. They can sit quietly and gape at the play. If they know nothing of victory, they are at least spared the knowledge of defeat. They live as we all should live, undisturbed, indifferent, and without disquiet. They neither bring ruin upon others nor ever receive it from alien hands. Your rank and wealth, Harry; my brains, such as they are,—my fame, whatever it may be worth; Dorian Gray's good looks,—we will all suffer for what the gods have given us, suffer terribly."

"Dorian Gray? is that his name?" said Lord Henry, walking across the studio towards Basil Hallward.

"Yes; that is his name. I didn't intend to tell it to you."

"But why not?"

"Oh, I can't explain. When I like people immensely I never tell their names to any one. It seems like surrendering a part of them. You know how I love secrecy. It is the only thing that can make modern life wonderful or mysterious to us. The commonest thing is delightful if one only hides it. When I leave town I never tell my people where I am going. If I did, I would lose all my pleasure. It is a silly habit, I dare say, but somehow it seems to bring a great deal of romance into one's life. I suppose you think me awfully foolish about it?"

"Not at all," answered Lord Henry, laying his hand upon his shoulder; "not at all, my dear Basil. You seem to forget that I am married, and the one charm of marriage is that it makes a life of deception necessary for both parties. I never know where my wife is, and my wife never knows what I am doing. When we meet,—we do meet occasionally, when we dine out together, or go down to the duke's,— we tell each other the most absurd stories with the most serious faces. My wife is very good at it,—much better, in fact, than I am. She never gets confused over her dates, and I always do. But when she does find me out, she makes no row at all. I sometimes wish she would; but she merely laughs at me."

"I hate the way you talk about your married life, Harry," said Basil Hallward, shaking his hand off, and strolling towards the door that led into the garden. "I believe that you are really a very good husband, but that you are thoroughly ashamed of your own virtues. You are an extraordinary fellow. You never say a moral thing, and you never do a wrong thing. Your cynicism is simply a pose.

"Being natural is simply a pose, and the most irritating pose I know," cried Lord Henry, laughing; and the two young men went out into the garden together, and for a time they did not speak.

After a long pause Lord Henry pulled out his watch. "I am afraid I must be going, Basil," he murmured, "and before I go I insist on your answering a question I put to you some time ago."

"What is that?" asked Basil Hallward, keeping his eyes fixed on the ground.

"You know quite well."

"I do not, Harry."

"Well, I will tell you what it is."

"Please don't."

"I must. I want you to explain to me why you won't exhibit Dorian Gray's picture. I want the real reason."

"I told you the real reason."

"No, you did not. You said it was because there was too much of yourself in it. Now, that is childish."

"Harry," said Basil Hallward, looking him straight in the face, "every portrait that is painted with feeling is a portrait of the artist, not of the sitter. The sitter is merely the accident, the occasion. It is not he who is revealed by the painter; it is rather the painter who, on the colored canvas, reveals himself. The reason I will not exhibit this picture is that I am afraid that I have shown with it the secret of my own soul."

Lord Harry laughed. "And what is that?" he asked.

"I will tell you," said Hallward; and an expression of perplexity came over his face.

"I am all expectation, Basil," murmured his companion, looking at him.

"Oh, there is really very little to tell, Harry," answered the young painter; "and I am afraid you will hardly understand it. Perhaps you will hardly believe it."

Lord Henry smiled, and, leaning down, plucked a pink-petalled daisy from the grass, and examined it. "I am quite sure I shall understand it," he replied, gazing intently at the little golden white-feathered disk, "and I can believe anything, provided that it is incredible."

The wind shook some blossoms from the trees, and the heavy lilac blooms, with their clustering stars, moved to and fro in the languid air. A grasshopper began to chirrup in the grass, and a long thin dragon-fly floated by on its brown gauze wings. Lord Henry felt as if he could hear Basil Hallward's heart beating, and he wondered what was coming.

"Well, this is incredible," repeated Hallward, rather bitterly,—"incredible to me at times. I don't know what it means. The story is simply this. Two months ago I went to a crush at Lady Brandon's. You know we poor painters have to show ourselves in society from time to time, just to remind the public that we are not savages. With an evening coat and a white tie, as you told me once, anybody, even a stock-broker, can gain a reputation for being civilized. Well, after I had been in the room about ten minutes, talking to huge overdressed dowagers and tedious Academicians, I suddenly became conscious that some one was looking at me. I turned half-way round, and saw Dorian

Gray for the first time. When our eyes met, I felt that I was growing pale. A curious instinct of terror came over me. I knew that I had come face to face with some one whose mere personality was so fascinating that, if I allowed it to do so, it would absorb my whole nature, my whole soul, my very art itself. I did not want any external influence in my life. You know yourself, Harry, how independent I am by nature. My father destined me for the army.

I insisted on going to Oxford. Then he made me enter my name at the Middle Temple. Before I had eaten half a dozen dinners I gave up the Bar, and announced my intention of becoming a painter. I have always been my own master; had at least always been so, till I met Dorian Gray. Then—But I don't know how to explain it to you. Something seemed to tell me that I was on the verge of a terrible crisis in my life. I had a strange feeling that Fate had in store for me exquisite joys and exquisite sorrows. I knew that if I spoke to Dorian I would become absolutely devoted to him, and that I ought not to speak to him. I grew afraid, and turned to quit the room. It was not con-science that made me do so: it was cowardice. I take no credit to myself for trying to escape."

"Conscience and cowardice are really the same things, Basil. Conscience is the trade-name of the firm. That is all."

"I don't believe that, Harry. However, whatever was my motive,—and it may have been pride, for I used to be very proud,—I certainly struggled to the door. There, of course, I stumbled against Lady Brandon. 'You are not go-ing to run away so soon, Mr. Hallward?' she screamed out. You know her shrill horrid voice?"

"Yes; she is a peacock in everything but beauty," said Lord Henry, pulling the daisy to bits with his long, ner-vous fingers.

"I could not get rid of her. She brought me up to Royal-ties, and people with Stars and Garters, and elderly ladies with gigantic tiaras and hooked noses. She spoke of me as her dearest friend. I had only met her once before, but she took it into her head to lionize me. I believe some picture of mine had made a great success at the time, at least had been chattered about in the penny newspapers, which is the nineteenth-century standard of immortality. Suddenly I found myself face to face with the young man whose personality had so strangely stirred me. We were quite close, almost touching. Our eyes met again. It was mad of me, but I asked Lady Brandon to introduce me to him. Perhaps it was not so mad, after all. It was simply inevitable. We would have spoken to each other without any introduction. I am sure of that. Dorian told me so afterwards. He, too, felt that we were destined to know each other."

"And how did Lady Brandon describe this wonderful young man? I know she goes in for giving a rapid *précis* of all her guests. I remember her bringing me up to a most truculent and red-faced old gentleman covered all over with orders and ribbons, and hissing into my ear, in a tragic whisper which must have been perfectly audible to everybody in the room, something like 'Sir Humpty Dumpty—you know—Afghan frontier—Russian intrigues: very successful man—wife killed by an elephant—quite inconsolable—wants to marry a beautiful American widow—everybody does nowadays—hates Mr. Gladstone—but very much interested in beetles: ask him what he thinks of Schouvaloff.' I simply fled. I like to find out people for myself. But poor Lady Brandon treats her guests exactly as an auctioneer treats his goods. She either explains them entirely away, or tells one everything about them except what one wants to know. But what did she say about Mr. Dorian Gray?"

"Oh, she murmured, 'Charming boy—poor dear mother and I quite inseparable—engaged to be married to the same man—I mean married on the same day—how very silly of me! Quite forget what he does—afraid he—doesn't do anything—oh, yes, plays the piano—or is it the violin, dear Mr. Gray?' We could neither of us help laughing, and we became friends at once."

"Laughter is not a bad beginning for a friendship, and it is the best ending for one," said Lord Henry, plucking another daisy.

Hallward buried his face in his hands. "You don't understand what friendship is, Harry," he murmured,—"or what enmity is, for that matter. You like every one; that is to say, you are indifferent to every one."

"How horribly unjust of you!" cried Lord Henry, tilting his hat back, and looking up at the little clouds that were drifting across the hollowed turquoise of the summer sky, like raveled skeins of glossy white silk. "Yes; horribly unjust of you. I make a great difference between people. I choose my friends for their good looks, my acquaintances for their characters, and my enemies for their brains. A man can't be too careful in the choice of his enemies. I have not got one who is a fool. They are all men of some intellectual power, and consequently they all appreciate me. Is that very vain of me? I think it is rather vain."

"I should think it was, Harry. But according to your category I must be merely an acquaintance."

"My dear old Basil, you are much more than an acquaintance."

"And much less than a friend. A sort of brother, I suppose?"

"Oh, brothers! I don't care for brothers. My elder brother won't die, and my younger brothers seem never to do anything else."

"Harry!"

"My dear fellow, I am not quite serious. But I can't help detesting my relations. I suppose it comes from the fact that we can't stand other people having the same faults as ourselves. I quite sympathize with the rage of the English democracy against what they call the vices of the upper classes. They feel that drunkenness, stupidity, and immorality should be their own special property, and that if any one of us makes an ass of himself he is poaching on their preserves. When poor Southwark got into the Divorce Court, their indignation was quite magnificent. And yet I don't suppose that ten per cent of the lower orders live correctly."

"I don't agree with a single word that you have said, and, what is more, Harry, I don't believe you do either."

Lord Henry stroked his pointed brown beard, and tapped the toe of his patent-leather boot with a tasseled malacca cane. "How English you are, Basil! If one puts forward an idea to a real Englishman,— always a rash thing to do,— he never dreams of considering whether the idea is right or wrong. The only thing he considers of any importance is whether one believes it one's self. Now, the value of an idea has nothing whatsoever to do with the sincerity of the man who expresses it. Indeed, the probabilities are that the more insincere the man is, the more purely intellectual will the idea be, as in that case it will not be colored by either his wants, his desires, or his prejudices. However, I don't propose to discuss politics, sociology, or metaphysics with you. I like persons better than principles. Tell me more about Dorian Gray. How often do you see him?"

"Every day. I couldn't be happy if I didn't see him every day. Of course sometimes it is only for a few minutes. But a few minutes with somebody one worships mean a great deal.

"But you don't really worship him?"

"I do."

"How extraordinary! I thought you would never care for anything but your painting,—your art, I should say. Art sounds better, doesn't it?"

"He is all my art to me now. I sometimes think, Harry, that there are only two eras of any importance in the history of the world. The first is the appearance of a new medium for art, and the second is the appearance of a new personality for art also. What the invention of oil-painting was to the Venetians, the face of Antinoüs was to late Greek sculpture, and the face of Dorian Gray will some day be to me. It is not merely that I paint from him, draw from him, model from him. Of course I have done all that. He has stood as Paris in dainty armor, and as Adonis with huntsman's cloak and polished boar-spear. Crowned with heavy lotus-blossoms, he has sat on the prow of Adrian's barge, looking into the green, turbid Nile. He has leaned over the still pool of some Greek woodland, and seen in the water's silent silver the wonder of his own beauty. But he is much more to me than that. I won't tell you that I am dissatisfied with what I have done of him, or that his beauty is such that art cannot express it. There is nothing that art cannot express, and I know that the work I have done since I met Dorian Gray is good work, is the best work of my life. But in some curious way—I wonder will you understand me?—his personality has suggested to me an entirely new manner in art, an entirely new mode of style. I see things differently, I think of them differently. I can now re-create life in a way that was hidden from me before. 'A dream of form in days of thought,'—who is it who says that? I forget; but it is what Dorian Gray has been to me. The merely visible presence of this lad,—for he seems to me little more than a lad, though he is really over twenty,—his merely visible presence,—ah! I wonder can you realize all that that means? Unconsciously he defines for me the lines of a fresh school, a school that is to have in itself all the passion of the romantic spirit, all the perfection of the spirit that is Greek. The harmony of soul and body,—how much that is! We in our madness have separated the two, and have invented a realism that is bestial, an ideality that is void. Harry! Harry! if you only knew what Dorian Gray is to me! You remember that landscape of mine, for which Agnew offered me such a huge price, but which I would not part with? It is one of the best things I have ever done. And why is it so? Because, while I was painting it, Dorian Gray sat beside me."

"Basil, this is quite wonderful! I must see Dorian Gray." Hallward got up from the seat, and walked up and down the garden. After some time he came back. "You don't understand, Harry," he said. "Dorian Gray is merely to me a motive in art. He is never more present in my work than when no image of him is there. He is simply a suggestion, as I have said, of a new manner. I see him in the curves of certain lines, in the loveliness and the subtleties of certain colors. That is all."

"Then why won't you exhibit his portrait?"

"Because I have put into it all the extraordinary romance of which, of course, I have never dared to speak to him. He knows nothing about it. He will never know anything about it. But the world might guess it; and I will not bare my soul to their shallow, prying eyes. My heart shall never be put under their microscope. There is too much of myself in the thing, Harry,—too much of myself!"

"Poets are not so scrupulous as you are. They know how useful passion is for publication. Nowadays a broken heart will run to many editions."

"I hate them for it. An artist should create beautiful things, but should put nothing of his own life into them. We live in an age when men treat art as if it were meant to be a form of autobiography. We have lost the abstract sense of beauty. If I live, I will show the world what it is; and for that reason the world shall never see my portrait of Dorian Gray."

"I think you are wrong, Basil, but I won't argue with you. It is only the intellectually lost who ever argue. Tell me, is Dorian Gray very fond of you?"

Hallward considered for a few moments. "He likes me," he answered, after a pause; "I know he likes me. Of course I flatter him dreadfully. I find a strange pleasure in saying things to him that I know I shall be sorry for having said. I give myself away. As a rule, he is charming to me, and we walk home together from the club arm in arm, or sit in the studio and talk of a thousand things. Now and then, however, he is horribly thoughtless, and seems to take a real delight in giving me pain. Then I feel, Harry, that I have given away my whole soul to some one who treats it as if it were a flower to put in his coat, a bit of decoration to charm his vanity, an ornament for a summer's day."

"Days in summer, Basil, are apt to linger. Perhaps you will tire sooner than he will. It is a sad thing to think of, but there is no doubt that Genius lasts longer than Beauty. That accounts for the fact that we all take such pains to over-educate ourselves. In the wild struggle for existence, we want to have something that endures, and so we fill our minds with rubbish and facts, in the silly hope of keeping our place. The thoroughly well-informed man,— that is the modern ideal. And the mind of the thoroughly well-informed man is a dreadful thing. It is like a bric-à-brac shop, all monsters and dust, and everything priced above its proper value. I think you will tire first, all the same. Some day you will look at Gray, and he will seem to you to be a little out of drawing, or you won't like his tone of color, or something. You will bitterly reproach him in your own heart, and seriously think that he has behaved very badly to you. The next time he calls, you will be perfectly cold and indifferent. It will be a great pity, for it will alter you. The worst of having a romance is that it leaves one so unromantic."

"Harry, don't talk like that. As long as I live, the personality of Dorian Gray will dominate me. You can't feel what I feel. You change too often."

"Ah, my dear Basil, that is exactly why I can feel it. Those who are faithful know only the pleasures of love: it is the faithless who know love's tragedies." And Lord Henry struck a light on a dainty silver case, and began to smoke a cigarette with a self-conscious and self-satisfied air, as if he had summed up life in a phrase. There was a rustle of chirruping sparrows in the ivy, and the blue cloud-shadows chased themselves across the grass like swallows.

How pleasant it was in the garden! And how delightful other people's emotions were!—much more delightful than their ideas, it seemed to him. One's own soul, and the passions of one's friends,—those were the fascinating things in life. He thought with pleasure of the tedious luncheon that he had missed by staying so long with Basil Hallward. Had he gone to his aunt's, he would have been sure to meet Lord Goodbody there, and the whole conversation would have been about the housing of the poor, and the necessity for model lodging-houses. It was charming to have escaped all that! As he thought of his aunt, an idea seemed to strike him. He turned to Hallward, and said, "My dear fellow, I have just remembered."

"Remembered what, Harry?"

"Where I heard the name of Dorian Gray."

"Where was it?" asked Hallward, with a slight frown.

"Don't look so angry, Basil. It was at my aunt's, Lady Agatha's. She told me she had discovered a wonderful young man, who was going to help her in the East End, and that his name was Dorian Gray. I am bound to state that she never told me he was good-looking. Women have no appreciation of good looks. At least, good women have not. She said that he was very earnest, and had a beautiful nature. I at once pictured to myself a creature with spectacles and lank hair, horridly freckled, and tramping about on huge feet. I wish I had known it was your friend."

"I am very glad you didn't, Harry."

"Why?"

"I don't want you to meet him."

"Mr. Dorian Gray is in the studio, sir," said the butler, coming into the garden.

"You must introduce me now," cried Lord Henry, laughing.

Basil Hallward turned to the servant, who stood blinking in the sunlight. "Ask Mr. Gray to wait, Parker: I will be in in a few moments." The man bowed, and went up the walk.

Then he looked at Lord Henry. "Dorian Gray is my dearest friend," he said. "He has a simple and a beautiful nature. Your aunt was quite right in what she said of him. Don't spoil him for me. Don't try to influence him. Your influence would be bad. The world is wide, and has many marvelous people in it. Don't take away from me the one person that makes life absolutely lovely to me, and that gives to my art whatever wonder or charm it possesses. Mind, Harry, I trust you." He spoke very slowly, and the words seemed wrung out of him almost against his will.

"What nonsense you talk!" said Lord Henry, smiling, and, taking Hallward by the arm, he almost led him into the house.

## Chapter II

As they entered they saw Dorian Gray. He was seated at the piano, with his back to them, turning over the pages of a volume of Schumann's *Forest Scenes*. "You must lend me these, Basil," he cried. "I want to learn them. They are perfectly charming."

"That entirely depends on how you sit today, Dorian."

"Oh, I am tired of sitting, and I don't want a life-sized portrait of myself," answered the lad, swinging round on the music-stool, in a willful, petulant manner. When he caught sight of Lord Henry, a faint blush colored his cheeks for a moment, and he started up. "I beg your pardon, Basil, but I didn't know you had any one with you."

"This is Lord Henry Wotton, Dorian, an old Oxford friend of mine. I have just been telling him what a capital sitter you were, and now you have spoiled everything."

"You have not spoiled my pleasure in meeting you, Mr. Gray," said Lord Henry, stepping forward and shaking him by the hand. "My aunt has often spoken to me about you. You are one of her favorites, and, I am afraid, one of her victims also."

"I am in Lady Agatha's black books at present," answered Dorian, with a funny look of penitence. "I promised to go to her club in Whitechapel with her last Tuesday, and I really forgot all about it. We were to have played a duet together,—three duets, I believe. I don't know what she will say to me. I am far too frightened to call."

"Oh, I will make your peace with my aunt. She is quite devoted to you. And I don't think it really matters about your not being there. The audience probably thought it was a duet. When Aunt Agatha sits down to the piano she makes quite enough noise for two people."

"That is very horrid to her, and not very nice to me," answered Dorian, laughing.

Lord Henry looked at him. Yes, he was certainly wonderfully handsome, with his finely-curved scarlet lips, his frank blue eyes, his crisp gold hair. There was something in his face that made one trust him at once. All the candor of youth was there, as well as all youth's passionate purity. One felt that he had kept himself unspotted from the world. No wonder Basil Hallward worshipped him. He was made to be worshipped.

"You are too charming to go in for philanthropy, Mr. Gray,—far too charming." And Lord Henry flung himself down on the divan, and opened his cigarette-case.

Hallward had been busy mixing his colors and getting his brushes ready. He was looking worried, and when he heard Lord Henry's last remark he glanced at him, hesitated for a moment, and then said, "Harry, I want to finish this picture today. Would you think it awfully rude of me if I asked you to go away?"

Lord Henry smiled, and looked at Dorian Gray. "Am I to go, Mr. Gray?" he asked.

"Oh, please don't, Lord Henry. I see that Basil is in one of his sulky moods; and I can't bear him when he sulks. Besides, I want you to tell me why I should not go in for philanthropy."

"I don't know that I shall tell you that, Mr. Gray. But I certainly will not run away, now that you have asked me to stop. You don't really mind, Basil, do you? You have often told me that you liked your sitters to have some one to chat to."

Hallward bit his lip. "If Dorian wishes it, of course you must stay. Dorian's whims are laws to everybody, except himself."

Lord Henry took up his hat and gloves. "You are very pressing, Basil, but I am afraid I must go. I have promised to meet a man at the Orleans.—Good-by, Mr. Gray. Come and see me some afternoon in Curzon Street. I am nearly always at home at five o'clock. Write to me when you are coming. I should be sorry to miss you."

"Basil," cried Dorian Gray, "if Lord Henry goes I shall go too. You never open your lips while you are painting, and it is horribly dull standing on a platform and trying to look pleasant. Ask him to stay. I insist upon it."

"Stay, Harry, to oblige Dorian, and to oblige me," said Hallward, gazing intently at his picture. "It is quite true, I never talk when I am working, and never listen either, and it must be dreadfully tedious for my unfortunate sitters. I beg you to stay."

"But what about my man at the Orleans?"

Hallward laughed. "I don't think there will be any difficulty about that. Sit down again, Harry.—And now, Dorian, get up on the platform, and don't move about too much, or pay any attention to what Lord Henry says. He has a very bad influence over all his friends, with the exception of myself."

Dorian stepped up on the dais, with the air of a young Greek martyr, and made a little *moue* of discontent to Lord Henry, to whom he had rather taken a fancy. He was so unlike Hallward. They made a delightful contrast. And he had such a beautiful voice. After a few moments he said to him, "Have you really a very bad influence, Lord Henry? As bad as Basil says?"

"There is no such thing as a good influence, Mr. Gray. All influence is immoral,—immoral from the scientific point of view."

"Why?"

"Because to influence a person is to give him one's own soul. He does not think his natural thoughts, or burn with his natural passions. His virtues are not real to him. His sins, if there are such things as sins, are borrowed. He becomes an echo of some one else's music, an actor of a part that has not been written for him. The aim of life is self-development. To realize one's nature perfectly,—that is what each of us is here for. People are afraid of themselves, nowadays. They have forgotten the highest of all duties, the duty that one owes to one's self. Of course they are charitable. They feed the hungry, and clothe the beggar. But their own souls starve, and are naked.

Courage has gone out of our race. Perhaps we never really had it. The terror of society, which is the basis of morals, the terror of God, which is the secret of religion,—these are the two things that govern us. And yet—"

"Just turn your head a little more to the right, Dorian, like a good boy," said Hallward, deep in his work, and conscious only that a look had come into the lad's face that he had never seen there before.

"And yet," continued Lord Henry, in his low, musical voice, and with that graceful wave of the hand that was always so characteristic of him, and that he had even in his Eton days, "I believe that if one man were to live his life out fully and completely, were to give form to every feeling, expression to every thought, reality to every dream,—I believe that the world would gain such a fresh impulse of joy that we would forget all the maladies of medievalism, and return to the Hellenic ideal,—to something finer, richer, than the Hellenic ideal, it may be. But the bravest man among us is afraid of himself. The mutilation of the savage has its tragic survival in the self-denial that mars our lives. We are punished for our refusals. Every impulse that we strive to strangle broods in the mind, and poisons us. The body sins once, and has done with its sin, for action is a mode of purification. Nothing remains then but the recollection of a pleasure, or the luxury of a regret. The only way to get rid of a temptation is to yield to it. Resist it, and your soul grows sick with longing for the things it has forbidden to itself, with desire for what its monstrous laws have made monstrous and unlawful. It has been said that the great events of the world take place in the brain. It is in the brain, and the brain only, that the great sins of the world take place also. You, Mr. Gray, you yourself, with your rose-red youth and your rose-white boyhood, you have had passions that have made you afraid, thoughts that have filled you with terror, day-dreams and sleeping dreams whose mere memory might stain your cheek with shame—"

"Stop!" murmured Dorian Gray, "stop! you bewilder me. I don't know what to say. There is some answer to you, but I cannot find it. Don't speak. Let me think, or, rather, let me try not to think."

For nearly ten minutes he stood there motionless, with parted lips, and eyes strangely bright. He was dimly conscious that entirely fresh impulses were at work within him, and they seemed to him to have come really from himself. The few words that Basil's friend had said to him—words spoken by chance, no doubt, and with willful paradox in them—had yet touched some secret chord, that had never been touched before, but that he felt was now vibrating and throbbing to curious pulses.

Music had stirred him like that. Music had troubled him many times. But music was not articulate. It was not a new world, but rather a new chaos, that it created in us. Words! Mere words! How terrible they were! How clear, and vivid, and cruel! One could not escape from them. And yet what a subtle magic there was in them! They seemed to be able to give a plastic form to formless things, and to have a music of their own as sweet as that of viol or of lute. Mere words! Was there anything so real as words?

Yes; there had been things in his boyhood that he had not understood. He understood them now. Life suddenly became fiery-colored to him. It seemed to him that he had been walking in fire. Why had he not known it?

Lord Henry watched him, with his sad smile. He knew the precise psychological moment when to say nothing. He felt intensely interested. He was amazed at the sudden impression that his words had produced, and, remembering a book that he had read when he was sixteen, which had revealed to him much that he had not known before, he wondered whether Dorian Gray was passing through the same experience. He had merely shot an arrow into the air. Had it hit the mark? How fascinating the lad was!

Hallward painted away with that marvelous bold touch of his, that had the true refinement and perfect delicacy that come only from strength. He was unconscious of the silence.

"Basil, I am tired of standing," cried Dorian Gray, suddenly. "I must go out and sit in the garden. The air is stifling here."

"My dear fellow, I am so sorry. When I am painting, I can't think of anything else. But you never sat better. You were perfectly still. And I have caught the effect I wanted,—the half-parted lips, and the bright look in the eyes. I don't know what Harry has been saying to you, but he has certainly made you have the most wonderful expression. I suppose he has been paying you compliments. You mustn't believe a word that he says."

"He has certainly not been paying me compliments. Perhaps that is the reason I don't think I believe anything he has told me."

"You know you believe it all," said Lord Henry, looking at him with his dreamy, heavy-lidded eyes. "I will go out to the garden with you. It is horridly hot in the studio.— Basil, let us have something iced to drink, something with strawberries in it."

"Certainly, Harry. Just touch the bell, and when Parker comes I will tell him what you want. I have got to work up this background, so I will join you later on. Don't keep Dorian too long. I have never been in better form for painting than I am today. This is going to be my masterpiece. It is my masterpiece as it stands."

Lord Henry went out to the garden, and found Dorian Gray burying his face in the great cool lilac-blossoms, feverishly drinking in their perfume as if it had been wine. He came close to him, and put his hand upon his shoulder.

"You are quite right to do that," he murmured. "Nothing can cure the soul but the senses, just as nothing can cure the senses but the soul."

The lad started and drew back. He was bareheaded, and the leaves had tossed his rebellious curls and tangled all their gilded threads. There was a look of fear in his eyes, such as people have when they are suddenly awakened. His finely-chiseled nostrils quivered, and some hidden nerve shook the scarlet of his lips and left them trembling.

"Yes," continued Lord Henry, "that is one of the great secrets of life,—to cure the soul by means of the senses, and the senses by means of the soul. You are a wonderful creature. You know more than you think you know, just as you know less than you want to know."

Dorian Gray frowned and turned his head away. He could not help liking the tall, graceful young man who was standing by him. His romantic olive-colored face and worn expression interested him. There was something in his low, languid voice that was absolutely fascinating. His cool, white, flower-like hands, even, had a curious charm. They moved, as he spoke, like music, and seemed to have a language of their own. But he felt afraid of him, and ashamed of being afraid. Why had it been left for a stranger to reveal him to himself? He had known Basil Hallward for months, but the friendship between then had never altered him. Suddenly there had come some one across his life who seemed to have disclosed to him life's mystery. And, yet, what was there to be afraid of? He was not a school-boy, or a girl. It was absurd to be frightened.

"Let us go and sit in the shade," said Lord Henry. "Parker has brought out the drinks, and if you stay any longer in this glare you will be quite spoiled, and Basil will never paint you again. You really must not let yourself become sunburnt. It would be very unbecoming to you."

"What does it matter?" cried Dorian, laughing, as he sat down on the seat at the end of the garden.

"It should matter everything to you, Mr. Gray."

"Why?"

"Because you have now the most marvelous youth, and youth is the one thing worth having."

"I don't feel that, Lord Henry."

"No, you don't feel it now. Some day, when you are old and wrinkled and ugly, when thought has seared your forehead with its lines, and passion branded your lips with its hideous fires, you will feel it, you will feel it terribly. Now, wherever you go, you charm the world. Will it always be so?

"You have a wonderfully beautiful face, Mr. Gray. Don't frown. You have. And Beauty is a form of Genius,— is higher, indeed, than Genius, as it needs no explanation. It is one of the great facts of the world, like sunlight, or spring-time, or the reflection in dark waters of that silver shell we call the moon. It cannot be questioned. It has its divine right of sovereignty. It makes princes of those who have it. You smile? Ah! when you have lost it you won't smile.

"People say sometimes that Beauty is only superficial. That may be so. But at least it is not so superficial as Thought. To me, Beauty is the wonder of wonders. It is only shallow people who do not judge by appearances. The true mystery of the world is the visible, not the invisible.

"Yes, Mr. Gray, the gods have been good to you. But what the gods give they quickly take away. You have only a few years in which really to live. When your youth goes, your beauty will go with it, and then you will suddenly discover that there are no triumphs left for you, or have to content yourself with those mean triumphs that the memory of your past will make more bitter than defeats. Every month as it wanes brings you nearer to something dreadful. Time is jealous of you, and wars against your lilies and your roses. You will become sallow, and hollow-cheeked, and dull-eyed. You will suffer horribly.

"Realize your youth while you have it. Don't squander the gold of your days, listening to the tedious, trying to improve the hopeless failure, or giving away your life to the ignorant, the common, and the vulgar, which are the aims, the false ideals, of our age. Live! Live the wonderful life that is in you! Let nothing be lost upon you. Be always searching for new sensations. Be afraid of nothing.

"A new hedonism,—that is what our century wants. You might be its visible symbol. With your personality there is nothing you could not do. The world belongs to you for a season.

"The moment I met you I saw that you were quite unconscious of what you really are, what you really might be. There was so much about you that charmed me that I felt I must tell you something about yourself. I thought how tragic it would be if you were wasted. For there is such a little time that your youth will last,—such a little time.

"The common hill-flowers wither, but they blossom again. The laburnum will be as golden next June as it is now. In a month there will be purple stars on the clematis, and year after year the green night of its leaves will have its purple stars. But we never get back our youth. The pulse of joy that beats in us at twenty, becomes sluggish. Our limbs fail, our senses rot. We degenerate into hideous puppets, haunted by the memory of the passions of which we were too much afraid, and the exquisite temptations that we did not dare to yield to. Youth! Youth! There is absolutely nothing in the world but youth!"

Dorian Gray listened, open-eyed and wondering. The spray of lilac fell from his hand upon the gravel. A furry bee came and buzzed round it for a moment. Then it began to scramble all over the fretted purple of the tiny blossoms. He watched it with that strange interest in trivial things that we try to develop when things of high import make us afraid, or when we are stirred by some new emotion, for which we cannot find expression, or when some thought that terrifies us lays sudden siege to the brain and calls on us to yield. After a time it flew away. He saw it creeping into the stained trumpet of a Tyrian convolvulus. The flower seemed to quiver, and then swayed gently to and fro.

Suddenly Hallward appeared at the door of the studio, and made frantic signs for them to come in. They turned to each other, and smiled.

"I am waiting," cried Hallward. "Do come in. The light is quite perfect, and you can bring your drinks."

They rose up, and sauntered down the walk together. Two green-and-white butterflies fluttered past them, and in the pear-tree at the end of the garden a thrush began to sing.

"You are glad you have met me, Mr. Gray," said Lord Henry, looking at him.

"Yes, I am glad now. I wonder shall I always be glad?"

"Always! That is a dreadful word. It makes me shudder when I hear it. Women are so fond of using it. They spoil every romance by trying to make it last forever. It is a meaningless word, too. The only difference between a caprice and a life-long passion is that the caprice lasts a little longer."

As they entered the studio, Dorian Gray put his hand upon Lord Henry's arm. "In that case, let our friendship be a caprice," he murmured, flushing at his own boldness, then stepped upon the platform and resumed his pose.

Lord Henry flung himself into a large wicker arm-chair, and watched him. The sweep and dash of the brush on the canvas made the only sound that broke the stillness, except when Hallward stepped back now and then to look at his work from a distance. In the slanting beams that streamed through the open door-way the dust danced and was golden. The heavy scent of the roses seemed to brood over everything.

After about a quarter of an hour, Hallward stopped painting, looked for a long time at Dorian Gray, and then for a long time at the picture, biting the end of one of his huge brushes, and smiling. "It is quite finished," he cried, at last, and stooping down he wrote his name in thin vermilion letters on the left-hand corner of the canvas.

Lord Henry came over and examined the picture. It was certainly a wonderful work of art, and a wonderful likeness as well.

"My dear fellow, I congratulate you most warmly," he said.—"Mr. Gray, come and look at yourself."

The lad started, as if awakened from some dream. "Is it really finished?" he murmured, stepping down from the platform.

"Quite finished," said Hallward. "And you have sat splendidly today. I am awfully obliged to you."

"That is entirely due to me," broke in Lord Henry. "Isn't it, Mr. Gray?"

Dorian made no answer, but passed listlessly in front of his picture and turned towards it. When he saw it he drew back, and his cheeks flushed for a moment with pleasure. A look of joy came into his eyes, as if he had recognized himself for the first time. He stood there motionless, and in wonder, dimly conscious that Hallward was speaking to him, but not catching the meaning of his words. The sense of his own beauty came on him like a revelation. He had never felt it before. Basil Hallward's compliments had seemed to him to be merely the charming exaggerations of friendship. He had listened to them, laughed at them, forgotten them. They had not influenced his nature.

Then had come Lord Henry, with his strange panegyric on youth, his terrible warning of its brevity. That had stirred him at the time, and now, as he stood gazing at the shadow of his own loveliness, the full reality of the description flashed across him. Yes, there would be a day when his face would be wrinkled and wizen, his eyes dim and colorless, the grace of his figure broken and deformed. The scarlet would pass away from his lips, and the gold steal from his hair. The life that was to make his soul would mar his body. He would become ignoble, hideous, and uncouth.

As he thought of it, a sharp pang of pain struck like a knife across him, and made each delicate fibre of his nature quiver. His eyes deepened into amethyst, and a mist of tears came across them. He felt as if a hand of ice had been laid upon his heart.

"Don't you like it?" cried Hallward at last, stung a little by the lad's silence, and not understanding what it meant.

"Of course he likes it," said Lord Henry. "Who wouldn't like it? It is one of the greatest things in modern art. I will give you anything you like to ask for it. I must have it."

"It is not my property, Harry."

"Whose property is it?"

"Dorian's, of course."

"He is a very lucky fellow."

"How sad it is!" murmured Dorian Gray, with his eyes still fixed upon his own portrait. "How sad it is! I shall grow old, and horrid, and dreadful. But this picture will remain always young. It will never be older than this particular day of June. . . . If it was only the other way! If it was I who were to be always young, and the picture that were to grow old! For this—for this—I would give everything! Yes, there is nothing in the whole world I would not give!"

"You would hardly care for that arrangement, Basil," cried Lord Henry, laughing. "It would be rather hard lines on you."

"I should object very strongly, Harry."

Dorian Gray turned and looked at him. "I believe you would, Basil. You like your art better than your friends. I am no more to you than a green bronze figure. Hardly as much, I dare say."

Hallward stared in amazement. It was so unlike Dorian to speak like that. What had happened? He seemed almost angry. His face was flushed and his cheeks burning.

"Yes," he continued, "I am less to you than your ivory Hermes or your silver Faun. You will like them always. How long will you like me? Till I have my first wrinkle, I suppose. I know, now, that when one loses one's good looks, whatever they may be, one loses everything. Your picture has taught me that. Lord Henry is perfectly right. Youth is the only thing worth having. When I find that I am growing old, I will kill myself."

Hallward turned pale, and caught his hand. "Dorian! Dorian!" he cried, "don't talk like that. I have never had such a friend as you, and I shall never have such another. You are not jealous of material things, are you?"

"I am jealous of everything whose beauty does not die. I am jealous of the portrait you have painted of me. Why should it keep what I must lose? Every moment that passes takes something from me, and gives something to it. Oh, if it was only the other way! If the picture could change, and I could be always what I am now! Why did you paint it? It will mock me some day,—mock me horribly!" The hot tears welled into his eyes; he tore his hand away, and, flinging himself on the divan, he buried his face in the cushions, as if he was praying.

"This is your doing, Harry," said Hallward, bitterly.

"My doing?"

"Yes, yours, and you know it."

Lord Henry shrugged his shoulders. "It is the real Dorian Gray,—that is all," he answered.

"It is not."

"If it is not, what have I to do with it?"

"You should have gone away when I asked you."

"I stayed when you asked me."

"Harry, I can't quarrel with my two best friends at once, but between you both you have made me hate the finest piece of work I have ever done, and I will destroy it. What is it but canvas and color? I will not let it come across our three lives and mar them."

Dorian Gray lifted his golden head from the pillow, and looked at him with pallid face and tear-stained eyes, as he walked over to the deal painting-table that was set beneath the large curtained window. What was he doing there? His fingers were straying about among the litter of tin tubes and dry brushes, seeking for something. Yes, it was the long palette-knife, with its thin blade of lithe steel. He had found it at last. He was going to rip up the canvas.

With a stifled sob he leaped from the couch, and, rushing over to Hallward, tore the knife out of his hand, and flung it to the end of the studio. "Don't, Basil, don't!" he cried. "It would be murder!"

"I am glad you appreciate my work at last, Dorian," said Hallward, coldly, when he had recovered from his surprise. "I never thought you would."

"Appreciate it? I am in love with it, Basil. It is part of myself, I feel that."

"Well, as soon as you are dry, you shall be varnished, and framed, and sent home. Then you can do what you like with yourself." And he walked across the room and rang the bell for tea. "You will have tea, of course, Dorian? And so will you, Harry? Tea is the only simple pleasure left to us."

"I don't like simple pleasures," said Lord Henry. "And I don't like scenes, except on the stage. What absurd fellows you are, both of you! I wonder who it was defined man as a rational animal. It was the most premature definition ever given. Man is many things, but he is not rational. I am glad he is not, after all: though I wish you chaps would not squabble over the picture. You had much better let me have it, Basil. This silly boy doesn't really want it, and I do."

"If you let any one have it but me, Basil, I will never forgive you!" cried Dorian Gray. "And I don't allow people to call me a silly boy."

"You know the picture is yours, Dorian. I gave it to you before it existed."

"And you know you have been a little silly, Mr. Gray, and that you don't really mind being called a boy."

"I should have minded very much this morning, Lord Henry."

"Ah! this morning! You have lived since then."

There came a knock to the door, and the butler entered with the tea-tray and set it down upon a small Japanese table. There was a rattle of cups and saucers and the hissing of a fluted Georgian urn. Two globe-shaped china dishes were brought in by a page. Dorian Gray went over and poured the tea out. The two men sauntered languidly to the table, and examined what was under the covers.

"Let us go to the theatre to-night," said Lord Henry. "There is sure to be something on, somewhere. I have promised to dine at White's, but it is only with an old friend, so I can send him a wire and say that I am ill, or that I am prevented from coming in consequence of a subsequent engagement. I think that would be a rather nice excuse: it would have the surprise of candor."

"It is such a bore putting on one's dress-clothes," muttered Hallward. "And, when one has them on, they are so horrid."

"Yes," answered Lord Henry, dreamily, "the costume of our day is detestable. It is so sombre, so depressing. Sin is the only color-element left in modern life."

"You really must not say things like that before Dorian, Harry."

"Before which Dorian? The one who is pouring out tea for us, or the one in the picture?"

"Before either."

"I should like to come to the theatre with you, Lord Henry," said the lad.

"Then you shall come; and you will come too, Basil, won't you?"

"I can't, really. I would sooner not. I have a lot of work to do."

"Well, then, you and I will go alone, Mr. Gray."

"I should like that awfully."

Basil Hallward bit his lip and walked over, cup in hand, to the picture. "I will stay with the real Dorian," he said, sadly.

"Is it the real Dorian?" cried the original of the portrait, running across to him. "Am I really like that?"

"Yes; you are just like that."

"How wonderful, Basil!"

"At least you are like it in appearance. But it will never alter," said Hallward. "That is something."

"What a fuss people make about fidelity!" murmured Lord Henry.

"And, after all, it is purely a question for physiology. It has nothing to do with our own will. It is either an unfortunate accident, or an unpleasant result of temperament. Young men want to be faithful, and are not; old men want to be faithless, and cannot: that is all one can say."

"Don't go to the theatre to-night, Dorian," said Hallward. "Stop and dine with me."

"I can't, really."

"Why?"

"Because I have promised Lord Henry to go with him."

"He won't like you better for keeping your promises. He always breaks his own. I beg you not to go."

Dorian Gray laughed and shook his head.

"I entreat you."

The lad hesitated, and looked over at Lord Henry, who was watching them from the tea-table with an amused smile.

"I must go, Basil," he answered.

"Very well," said Hallward; and he walked over and laid his cup down on the tray. "It is rather late, and, as you have to dress, you had better lose no time. Good-by, Harry; good-by, Dorian. Come and see me soon. Come tomorrow."

"Certainly."

"You won't forget?"

"No, of course not."

"And . . . Harry!"

"Yes, Basil?"

"Remember what I asked you, when in the garden this morning."

"I have forgotten it."

"I trust you."

"I wish I could trust myself," said Lord Henry, laughing.—"Come, Mr. Gray, my hansom is outside, and I can drop you at your own place.—Good-by, Basil. It has been a most interesting afternoon."

As the door closed behind them, Hallward flung himself down on a sofa, and a look of pain came into his face.


CHAPTER III

One afternoon, a month later, Dorian Gray was reclining in a luxurious arm-chair, in the little library of Lord Henry's house in Curzon Street. It was, in its way, a very charming room, with its high-paneled wainscoting of olive-stained oak, its cream-colored frieze and ceiling of raised plaster-work, and its brick-dust felt carpet strewn with long-fringed silk Persian rugs. On a tiny satinwood table stood a statuette by Clodion, and beside it lay a copy of *Les Cent Nouvelles,* bound for Margaret of Valois by Clovis Eve, and powdered with the gilt daisies that the queen had selected for her device. Some large blue china jars, filled with parrot-tulips, were ranged on the mantel-shelf, and through the small leaded panes of the window streamed the apricot-colored light of a summer's day in London.

Lord Henry had not come in yet. He was always late on principle, his principle being that punctuality is the thief of time. So the lad was looking rather sulky, as with listless fingers he turned over the pages of an elaborately-illustrated edition of *Manon Lescaut* that he had found in one of the bookcases. The formal monotonous ticking of the Louis Quatorze clock annoyed him. Once or twice he thought of going away.

At last he heard a light step outside, and the door opened. "How late you are, Harry!" he murmured.

"I am afraid it is not Harry, Mr. Gray," said a woman's voice.

He glanced quickly round, and rose to his feet. "I beg your pardon. I thought—"

"You thought it was my husband. It is only his wife. You must let me introduce myself. I know you quite well by your photographs. I think my husband has got twenty-seven of them."

"Not twenty-seven, Lady Henry?"

"Well, twenty-six, then. And I saw you with him the other night at the Opera." She laughed nervously, as she spoke, and watched him with her vague forget-me-not eyes. She was a curious woman, whose dresses always looked as if they had been designed in a rage and put on in a tempest. She was always in love with somebody, and, as her passion was never returned, she had kept all her illusions. She tried to look picturesque, but only succeeded in being untidy. Her name was Victoria, and she had a perfect mania for going to church.

"That was at 'Lohengrin,' Lady Henry, I think?"

"Yes; it was at dear 'Lohengrin.' I like Wagner's music better than any other music. It is so loud that one can talk the whole time, without people hearing what one says. That is a great advantage: don't you think so, Mr. Gray?"

The same nervous staccato laugh broke from her thin lips, and her fingers began to play with a long paper-knife.

Dorian smiled, and shook his head: "I am afraid I don't think so, Lady Henry. I never talk during music,—at least during good music. If one hears bad music, it is one's duty to drown it by conversation."

"Ah! that is one of Harry's views, isn't it, Mr. Gray? But you must not think I don't like good music. I adore it, but I am afraid of it. It makes me too romantic. I have simply worshipped pianists,—two at a time, sometimes. I don't know what it is about them. Perhaps it is that they are foreigners. They all are, aren't they? Even those that are born in England become foreigners after a time, don't they? It is so clever of them, and such a compliment to art. Makes it quite cosmopolitan, doesn't it? You have never been to any of my parties, have you, Mr. Gray? You must come. I can't afford orchids, but I spare no expense in foreigners. They make one's rooms look so picturesque. But here is Harry!—Harry, I came in to look for you, to ask you something,—I forget what it was,—and I found Mr. Gray here. We have had such a pleasant chat about music. We have quite the same views. No; I think our views are quite different. But he has been most pleasant. I am so glad I've seen him."

"I am charmed, my love, quite charmed," said Lord Henry, elevating his dark crescent-shaped eyebrows and looking at them both with an amused smile.—"So sorry I am late, Dorian. I went to look after a piece of old brocade in Wardour Street, and had to bargain for hours for it. Nowadays people know the price of everything, and the value of nothing."

"I am afraid I must be going," exclaimed Lady Henry, after an awkward silence, with her silly sudden laugh. "I have promised to drive with the duchess.—Good-by, Mr. Gray.—Good-by, Harry. You are dining out, I suppose? So am I. Perhaps I shall see you at Lady Thornbury's."

"I dare say, my dear," said Lord Henry, shutting the door behind her, as she flitted out of the room, looking like a bird-of-paradise that had been out in the rain, and leaving a faint odor of patchouli behind her. Then he shook hands with Dorian Gray, lit a cigarette, and flung himself down on the sofa.

"Never marry a woman with straw-colored hair, Dorian," he said, after a few puffs.

"Why, Harry?"

"Because they are so sentimental."

"But I like sentimental people."

"Never marry at all, Dorian. Men marry because they are tired; women, because they are curious: both are disappointed."

"I don't think I am likely to marry, Harry. I am too much in love. That is one of your aphorisms. I am putting it into practice, as I do everything you say."

"Whom are you in love with?" said Lord Henry, looking at him with a curious smile.

"With an actress," said Dorian Gray, blushing.

Lord Henry shrugged his shoulders. "That is a rather common-place *début*," he murmured.

"You would not say so if you saw her, Harry."

"Who is she?"

"Her name is Sibyl Vane."

"Never heard of her."

"No one has. People will some day, however. She is a genius."

"My dear boy, no woman is a genius: women are a decorative sex. They never have anything to say, but they say it charmingly. They represent the triumph of matter over mind, just as we men represent the triumph of mind over morals. There are only two kinds of women, the plain and the colored. The plain women are very useful. If you want to gain a reputation for respectability, you have merely to take them down to supper. The other women are very charming. They commit one mistake, however. They paint in order to try to look young. Our grandmothers painted in order to try to talk brilliantly. *Rouge* and *esprit* used to go together. That has all gone out now. As long as a woman can look ten years younger than her own daughter, she is perfectly satisfied. As for conversation, there are only five women in London worth talking to, and two of these can't be admitted into decent society. However, tell me about your genius. How long have you known her?"

"About three weeks. Not so much. About two weeks and two days."

"How did you come across her?"

"I will tell you, Harry; but you mustn't be unsympathetic about it. After all, it never would have happened if I had not met you. You filled me with a wild desire to know everything about life. For days after I met you, something seemed to throb in my veins. As I lounged in the Park, or strolled down Piccadilly, I used to look at every one who passed me, and wonder with a mad curiosity what sort of lives they led. Some of them fascinated me. Others filled me with terror. There was an exquisite poison in the air. I had a passion for sensations.

"One evening about seven o'clock I determined to go out in search of some adventure. I felt that this gray, monstrous London of ours, with its myriads of people, its splendid sinners, and its sordid sins, as you once said, must have something in store for me. I fancied a thousand things.

"The mere danger gave me a sense of delight. I remembered what you had said to me on that wonderful night when we first dined together, about the search for beauty being the poisonous secret of life. I don't know what I expected, but I went out, and wandered eastward, soon losing my way in a labyrinth of grimy streets and black, grassless squares. About half-past eight I passed by a little third-rate theatre, with great flaring gas-jets and gaudy play-bills. A hideous Jew, in the most amazing waistcoat I ever beheld in my life, was standing at the entrance, smoking a vile cigar. He had greasy ringlets, and an enormous diamond blazed in the centre of a soiled shirt. ''Ave a box, my lord?' he said, when he saw me, and he took off his hat with an act of gorgeous servility. There was something about him, Harry, that amused me. He was such a monster. You will laugh at me, I know, but I really went in and paid a whole guinea for the stage-box. To the present day I can't make out why I did so; and yet if I hadn't!—my dear Harry, if I hadn't, I would have missed the greatest romance of my life. I see you are laughing. It is horrid of you!"

"I am not laughing, Dorian; at least I am not laughing at you. But you should not say the greatest romance of your life. You should say the first romance of your life. You will always be loved, and you will always be in love with love. There are exquisite things in store for you. This is merely the beginning."

"Do you think my nature so shallow?" cried Dorian Gray, angrily.

"No; I think your nature so deep."

"How do you mean?"

"My dear boy, people who only love once in their lives are really shallow people. What they call their loyalty, and their fidelity, I call either the lethargy of custom or the lack of imagination. Faithlessness is to the emotional life what consistency is to the intellectual life,—simply a confession of failure. But I don't want to interrupt you. Go on with your story."

"Well, I found myself seated in a horrid little private box, with a vulgar drop-scene staring me in the face. I looked out behind the curtain, and surveyed the house. It was a tawdry affair, all Cupids and cornucopias, like a third-rate wedding-cake. The gallery and pit were fairly full, but the two rows of dingy stalls were quite empty, and there was hardly a person in what I suppose they called the dress-circle. Women went about with oranges and ginger-beer, and there was a terrible consumption of nuts going on."

"It must have been just like the palmy days of the British Drama."

"Just like, I should fancy, and very horrid. I began to wonder what on earth I should do, when I caught sight of the play-bill. What do you think the play was, Harry?"

"I should think 'The Idiot Boy, or Dumb but Innocent.' Our fathers used to like that sort of piece, I believe. The longer I live, Dorian, the more keenly I feel that whatever was good enough for our fathers is not good enough for us. In art, as in politics, *les grandpères ont toujours tort.*"

"This play was good enough for us, Harry. It was 'Romeo and Juliet.' I must admit I was rather annoyed at the idea of seeing Shakespeare done in such a wretched hole of a place. Still, I felt interested, in a sort of way. At any rate, I determined to wait for the first act. There was a dreadful orchestra, presided over by a young Jew who sat at a cracked piano, that nearly drove me away, but at last the drop-scene was drawn up, and the play began. Romeo was a stout elderly gentleman, with corked eyebrows, a husky tragedy voice, and a figure like a beer-barrel. Mercutio was almost as bad. He was played by the low-comedian, who had introduced gags of his own and was on most familiar terms with the pit. They were as grotesque as the scenery, and that looked as if it had come out of a pantomime of fifty years ago. But Juliet! Harry, imagine a girl, hardly seventeen years of age, with a little flower-like face, a small Greek head with plaited coils of dark-brown hair, eyes that were violet wells of passion, lips that were like the petals of a rose. She was the loveliest thing I had ever seen in my life. You said to me once that pathos left you unmoved, but that beauty, mere beauty, could fill your eyes with tears. I tell you, Harry, I could hardly see this girl for the mist of tears that came across me. And her voice,—I never heard such a voice. It was very low at first, with deep mellow notes, that seemed to fall singly upon one's ear. Then it became a little louder, and sounded like a flute or a distant hautbois. In the garden-scene it had all the tremulous ecstasy that one hears just before dawn when nightingales are singing. There were moments, later on, when it had the wild passion of violins. You know how a voice can stir one. Your voice and the voice of Sibyl Vane are two things that I shall never forget. When I close my eyes, I hear them, and each of them says something different. I don't know which to follow. Why should I not love her? Harry, I do love her. She is everything to me in life. Night after night I go to see her play. One evening she is Rosalind, and the next evening she is Imogen. I have seen her die in the gloom of an Italian tomb, sucking the poison from her lover's lips. I have watched her wandering through the forest of Arden, disguised as a pretty boy in hose and doublet and dainty cap. She has been mad, and has come into the presence of a guilty king, and given him rue to wear, and bitter herbs to taste of. She has been innocent, and the black hands of jealousy have crushed her reed-like throat. I have seen her in every age and in every costume. Ordinary women never appeal to one's imagination. They are limited to their century. No glamour ever transfigures them. One knows their minds as easily as one knows their bonnets. One can always find them. There is no mystery in one of them. They ride in the Park in the morning, and chatter at tea-parties in the afternoon. They have their stereotyped smile, and their fashionable manner. They are quite obvious. But an actress! How different an actress is! Why didn't you tell me that the only thing worth loving is an actress?"

"Because I have loved so many of them, Dorian."

"Oh, yes, horrid people with dyed hair and painted faces."

"Don't run down dyed hair and painted faces. There is an extraordinary charm in them, sometimes."

"I wish now I had not told you about Sibyl Vane."

"You could not have helped telling me, Dorian. All through your life you will tell me everything you do."

"Yes, Harry, I believe that is true. I cannot help telling you things. You have a curious influence over me. If I ever did a crime, I would come and confide it to you. You would understand me."

"People like you—the wilful sunbeams of life—don't commit crimes, Dorian. But I am much obliged for the compliment, all the same. And now tell me,—reach me the matches, like a good boy: thanks,—tell me, what are your relations with Sibyl Vane?"

Dorian Gray leaped to his feet, with flushed cheeks and burning eyes. "Harry, Sibyl Vane is sacred!"

"It is only the sacred things that are worth touching, Dorian," said Lord Henry, with a strange touch of pathos in his voice. "But why should you be annoyed? I suppose she will be yours some day. When one is in love, one always begins by deceiving one's self, and one always ends by deceiving others. That is what the world calls romance. You know her, at any rate, I suppose?"

"Of course I know her. On the first night I was at the theatre, the horrid old Jew came round to the box after the performance was over, and offered to bring me behind the scenes and introduce me to her. I was furious with him, and told him that Juliet had been dead for hundreds of years, and that her body was lying in a marble tomb in Verona. I think, from his blank look of amazement, that he thought I had taken too much champagne, or something."

"I am not surprised."

"I was not surprised either. Then he asked me if I wrote for any of the newspapers. I told him I never even read them. He seemed terribly disappointed at that, and confided to me that all the dramatic critics were in a conspiracy against him, and that they were all to be bought."

"I believe he was quite right there. But, on the other hand, most of them are not at all expensive."

"Well, he seemed to think they were beyond his means. By this time the lights were being put out in the theatre, and I had to go. He wanted me to try some cigars which he strongly recommended. I declined. The next night, of course, I arrived at the theatre again. When he saw me he made me a low bow, and assured me that I was a patron of art. He was a most offensive brute, though he had an extraordinary passion for Shakespeare. He told me once, with an air of pride, that his three bankruptcies were entirely due to the poet, whom he insisted on calling 'The Bard.' He seemed to think it a distinction."

"It was a distinction, my dear Dorian,—a great distinction. But when did you first speak to Miss Sibyl Vane?"

"The third night. She had been playing Rosalind. I could not help going round. I had thrown her some flowers, and she had looked at me; at least I fancied that she

had. The old Jew was persistent. He seemed determined
to bring me behind, so I consented. It was curious my not
wanting to know her, wasn't it?"

"No; I don't think so."

"My dear Harry, why?"

"I will tell you some other time. Now I want to know
about the girl."

"Sibyl? Oh, she was so shy, and so gentle. There is
something of a child about her. Her eyes opened wide in
exquisite wonder when I told her what I thought of her
performance, and she seemed quite unconscious of her
power. I think we were both rather nervous. The old Jew
stood grinning at the door-way of the dusty greenroom,
making elaborate speeches about us both, while we stood
looking at each other like children. He would insist on
calling me 'My Lord,' so I had to assure Sibyl that I was
not anything of the kind. She said quite simply to me,
'You look more like a prince.'"

"Upon my word, Dorian, Miss Sibyl knows how to pay
compliments."

"You don't understand her, Harry. She regarded me
merely as a person in a play. She knows nothing of life.
She lives with her mother, a faded tired woman who played
Lady Capulet in a sort of magenta dressing-wrapper on the
first night, and who looks as if she had seen better days."

"I know that look. It always depresses me."

"The Jew wanted to tell me her history, but I said it did
not interest me."

"You were quite right. There is always something infinitely mean about other people's tragedies."

"Sibyl is the only thing I care about. What is it to me
where she came from? From her little head to her little
feet, she is absolutely and entirely divine. I go to see her
act every night of my life, and every night she is more
marvelous."

"That is the reason, I suppose, that you will never dine with me now. I thought you must have some curious romance on hand. You have; but it is not quite what I expected."

"My dear Harry, we either lunch or sup together every day, and I have been to the Opera with you several times."

"You always come dreadfully late."

"Well, I can't help going to see Sibyl play, even if it is only for an act. I get hungry for her presence; and when I think of the wonderful soul that is hidden away in that little ivory body, I am filled with awe."

"You can dine with me to-night, Dorian, can't you?"

He shook his head. "To night she is Imogen," he answered, "and tomorrow night she will be Juliet."

"When is she Sibyl Vane?"

"Never."

"I congratulate you."

"How horrid you are! She is all the great heroines of the world in one. She is more than an individual. You laugh, but I tell you she has genius. I love her, and I must make her love me. You, who know all the secrets of life, tell me how to charm Sibyl Vane to love me! I want to make Romeo jealous. I want the dead lovers of the world to hear our laughter, and grow sad. I want a breath of our passion to stir their dust into consciousness, to wake their ashes into pain. My God, Harry, how I worship her!" He was walking up and down the room as he spoke. Hectic spots of red burned on his cheeks. He was terribly excited.

Lord Henry watched him with a subtle sense of pleasure. How different he was now from the shy, frightened boy he had met in Basil Hallward's studio! His nature had developed like a flower, had borne blossoms of scarlet flame. Out of its secret hiding-place had crept his Soul, and Desire had come to meet it on the way.

"And what do you propose to do?" said Lord Henry, at last.

"I want you and Basil to come with me some night and see her act. I have not the slightest fear of the result. You won't be able to refuse to recognize her genius. Then we must get her out of the Jew's hands. She is bound to him for three years—at least for two years and eight months—from the present time. I will have to pay him something, of course. When all that is settled, I will take a West-End theatre and bring her out properly. She will make the world as mad as she has made me."

"Impossible, my dear boy!"

"Yes, she will. She has not merely art, consummate art-instinct, in her, but she has personality also; and you have often told me that it is personalities, not principles, that move the age."

"Well, what night shall we go?"

"Let me see. Today is Tuesday. Let us fix tomorrow. She plays Juliet tomorrow."

"All right. The Bristol at eight o'clock; and I will get Basil."

"Not eight, Harry, please. Half-past six. We must be there before the curtain rises. You must see her in the first act, where she meets Romeo."

"Half-past six! What an hour! It will be like having a meat-tea. However, just as you wish. Shall you see Basil between this and then? Or shall I write to him?"

"Dear Basil! I have not laid eyes on him for a week. It is rather horrid of me, as he has sent me my portrait in the most wonderful frame, designed by himself, and, though I am a little jealous of it for being a whole month younger than I am, I must admit that I delight in it. Perhaps you had better write to him. I don't want to see him alone. He says things that annoy me."

Lord Henry smiled. "He gives you good advice, I suppose. People are very fond of giving away what they need most themselves."

"You don't mean to say that Basil has got any passion or any romance in him?"

"I don't know whether he has any passion, but he certainly has romance," said Lord Henry, with an amused look in his eyes. "Has he never let you know that?"

"Never. I must ask him about it. I am rather surprised to hear it. He is the best of fellows, but he seems to me to be just a bit of a Philistine. Since I have known you, Harry, I have discovered that."

"Basil, my dear boy, puts everything that is charming in him into his work. The consequence is that he has nothing left for life but his prejudices, his principles, and his common sense. The only artists I have ever known who are personally delightful are bad artists. Good artists give everything to their art, and consequently are perfectly uninteresting in themselves. A great poet, a really great poet, is the most unpoetical of all creatures. But inferior poets are absolutely fascinating. The worse their rhymes are, the more picturesque they look. The mere fact of having published a book of second-rate sonnets makes a man quite irresistible. He lives the poetry that he cannot write. The others write the poetry that they dare not realize."

"I wonder is that really so, Harry?" said Dorian Gray, putting some perfume on his handkerchief out of a large gold-topped bottle that stood on the table. "It must be, if you say so. And now I must be off. Imogen is waiting for me. Don't forget about tomorrow. Good-by."

As he left the room, Lord Henry's heavy eyelids drooped, and he began to think. Certainly few people had ever interested him so much as Dorian Gray, and yet the lad's

mad adoration of some one else caused him not the slightest pang of annoyance or jealousy. He was pleased by it.
It made him a more interesting study. He had been always
enthralled by the methods of science, but the ordinary
subject-matter of science had seemed to him trivial and
of no import. And so he had begun by vivisecting himself,
as he had ended by vivisecting others. Human life,—that
appeared to him the one thing worth investigating. There
was nothing else of any value, compared to it. It was true
that as one watched life in its curious crucible of pain
and pleasure, one could not wear over one's face a mask
of glass, or keep the sulphurous fumes from troubling the
brain and making the imagination turbid with monstrous
fancies and misshapen dreams. There were poisons so subtle that to know their properties one had to sicken of
them. There were maladies so strange that one had to pass
through them if one sought to understand their nature.
And, yet, what a great reward one received! How wonderful the whole world became to one! To note the curious
hard logic of passion, and the emotional colored life of the
intellect,—to observe where they met, and where they separated, at what point they became one, and at what point
they were at discord,—there was a delight in that! What
matter what the cost was? One could never pay too high a
price for any sensation.

He was conscious—and the thought brought a gleam
of pleasure into his brown agate eyes—that it was through
certain words of his, musical words said with musical utterance, that Dorian Gray's soul had turned to this white
girl and bowed in worship before her. To a large extent,
the lad was his own creation. He had made him premature.
That was something. Ordinary people waited till life disclosed to them its secrets, but to the few, to the elect, the
mysteries of life were revealed before the veil was drawn
away. Sometimes this was the effect of art, and chiefly of

the art of literature, which dealt immediately with the passions and the intellect. But now and then a complex personality took the place and assumed the office of art, was indeed, in its way, a real work of art, Life having its elaborate masterpieces, just as poetry has, or sculpture, or painting.

Yes, the lad was premature. He was gathering his harvest while it was yet spring. The pulse and passion of youth were in him, but he was becoming self-conscious. It was delightful to watch him. With his beautiful face, and his beautiful soul, he was a thing to wonder at. It was no matter how it all ended, or was destined to end. He was like one of those gracious figures in a pageant or a play, whose joys seem to be remote from one, but whose sorrows stir one's sense of beauty, and whose wounds are like red roses.

Soul and body, body and soul—how mysterious they were! There was animalism in the soul, and the body had its moments of spirituality. The senses could refine, and the intellect could degrade. Who could say where the fleshly impulse ceased, or the psychical impulse began? How shallow were the arbitrary definitions of ordinary psychologists! And yet how difficult to decide between the claims of the various schools! Was the soul a shadow seated in the house of sin? Or was the body really in the soul, as Giordano Bruno thought? The separation of spirit from matter was a mystery, and the union of spirit with matter was a mystery also.

He began to wonder whether we should ever make psychology so absolute a science that each little spring of life would be revealed to us. As it was, we always misunderstood ourselves, and rarely understood others. Experience was of no ethical value. It was merely the name we gave to our mistakes. Men had, as a rule, regarded it as a mode of warning, had claimed for it a certain moral efficacy in the formation of character, had praised it as something that taught us what to follow and showed us what to avoid. But there was no motive power in experience. It was as little of an active cause as conscience itself. All that it really demonstrated was that our future would be the same as our past, and that the sin we had done once, and with loathing, we would do many times, and with joy.

It was clear to him that the experimental method was the only method by which one could arrive at any scientific analysis of the passions; and certainly Dorian Gray was a subject made to his hand, and seemed to promise rich and fruitful results. His sudden mad love for Sibyl Vane was a psychological phenomenon of no small interest. There was no doubt that curiosity had much to do with it, curiosity and the desire for new experiences; yet it was not a simple but rather a very complex passion. What there was in it of the purely sensuous instinct of boyhood had been transformed by the workings of the imagination, changed into something that seemed to the boy himself to be remote from sense, and was for that very reason all the more dangerous. It was the passions about whose origin we deceived ourselves that tyrannized most strongly over us. Our weakest motives were those of whose nature we were conscious. It often happened that when we thought we were experimenting on others we were really experimenting on ourselves.

While Lord Henry sat dreaming on these things, a knock came to the door, and his valet entered, and reminded him it was time to dress for dinner. He got up and looked out into the street. The sunset had smitten into scarlet gold the upper windows of the houses opposite. The panes glowed like plates of heated metal. The sky above was like a faded rose. He thought of Dorian Gray's young fiery-colored life, and wondered how it was all going to end.

When he arrived home, about half-past twelve o'clock, he saw a telegram lying on the hall-table. He opened it and found it was from Dorian. It was to tell him that he was engaged to be married to Sibyl Vane.

CHAPTER IV

"I suppose you have heard the news, Basil?" said Lord Henry on the following evening, as Hallward was shown into a little private room at the Bristol where dinner had been laid for three.

"No, Harry," answered Hallward, giving his hat and coat to the bowing waiter. "What is it? Nothing about politics, I hope? They don't interest me. There is hardly a single person in the House of Commons worth painting; though many of them would be the better for a little whitewashing."

"Dorian Gray is engaged to be married," said Lord Henry, watching him as he spoke.

Hallward turned perfectly pale, and a curious look flashed for a moment into his eyes, and then passed away, leaving them dull. "Dorian engaged to be married!" he cried. "Impossible!"

"It is perfectly true."

"To whom?"

"To some little actress or other."

"I can't believe it. Dorian is far too sensible."

"Dorian is far too wise not to do foolish things now and then, my dear Basil."

"Marriage is hardly a thing that one can do now and then, Harry," said Hallward, smiling.

"Except in America. But I didn't say he was married. I said he was engaged to be married. There is a great difference. I have a distinct remembrance of being married, but I have no recollection at all of being engaged. I am inclined to think that I never was engaged."

"But think of Dorian's birth, and position, and wealth. It would be absurd for him to marry so much beneath him."

"If you want him to marry this girl, tell him that, Basil. He is sure to do it then. Whenever a man does a thoroughly stupid thing, it is always from the noblest motives."

"I hope the girl is good, Harry. I don't want to see Dorian tied to some vile creature, who might degrade his nature and ruin his intellect."

"Oh, she is more than good—she is beautiful," murmured Lord Henry, sipping a glass of vermouth and orange-bitters. "Dorian says she is beautiful; and he is not often wrong about things of that kind. Your portrait of him has quickened his appreciation of the personal appearance of other people. It has had that excellent effect, among others. We are to see her to-night, if that boy doesn't forget his appointment."

"But do you approve of it, Harry?" asked Hallward, walking up and down the room, and biting his lip. "You can't approve of it, really. It is some silly infatuation."

"I never approve, or disapprove, of anything now. It is an absurd attitude to take towards life. We are not sent into the world to air our moral prejudices. I never take any notice of what common people say, and I never interfere with what charming people do. If a personality fascinates me, whatever the personality chooses to do is absolutely delightful to me. Dorian Gray falls in love with a beautiful girl who acts Shakespeare, and proposes to marry her. Why not? If he wedded Messalina he would be none the less interesting. You know I am not a champion of marriage. The real drawback to marriage is that it makes one unselfish. And unselfish people are colorless. They lack individuality. Still, there are certain temperaments that marriage makes more complex. They retain their egotism, and add to it many other egos. They are forced to have more than one life. They become more highly organized. Besides, every experience is of value, and, whatever one may say against marriage, it is certainly an experience. I hope that Dorian Gray will make this girl his wife, passionately adore her for six months, and then suddenly become fascinated by some one else. He would be a wonderful study."

"You don't mean all that, Harry; you know you don't. If Dorian Gray's life were spoiled, no one would be sorrier than yourself. You are much better than you pretend to be."

Lord Henry laughed. "The reason we all like to think so well of others is that we are all afraid for ourselves. The basis of optimism is sheer terror. We think that we are generous because we credit our neighbor with those virtues that are likely to benefit ourselves. We praise the banker that we may overdraw our account, and find good qualities in the highwayman in the hope that he may spare our pockets. I mean everything that I have said. I have the greatest contempt for optimism. And as for a spoiled life, no life is spoiled but one whose growth is arrested. If you want to mar a nature, you have merely to reform it. But here is Dorian himself. He will tell you more than I can."

"My dear Harry, my dear Basil, you must both congratulate me!" said the boy, throwing off his evening cape with its satin-lined wings, and shaking each of his friends by the hand in turn. "I have never been so happy. Of course it is sudden: all really delightful things are. And yet it seems to me to be the one thing I have been looking for all my life." He was flushed with excitement and pleasure, and looked extraordinarily handsome.

"I hope you will always be very happy, Dorian," said Hallward, "but I don't quite forgive you for not having let me know of your engagement. You let Harry know."

"And I don't forgive you for being late for dinner," broke in Lord Henry, putting his hand on the lad's shoulder, and smiling as he spoke. "Come, let us sit down and

try what the new chef here is like, and then you will tell
us how it all came about."

"There is really not much to tell," cried Dorian, as they
took their seats at the small round table. "What happened
was simply this. After I left you yesterday evening, Harry,
I had some dinner at that curious little Italian restaurant
in Rupert Street, you introduced me to, and went down
afterwards to the theatre. Sibyl was playing Rosalind. Of
course the scenery was dreadful, and the Orlando absurd.
But Sibyl! You should have seen her! When she came on
in her boy's dress she was perfectly wonderful. She wore
a moss-colored velvet jerkin with cinnamon sleeves, slim
brown cross-gartered hose, a dainty little green cap with a
hawk's feather caught in a jewel, and a hooded cloak lined
with dull red. She had never seemed to me more exquisite.
She had all the delicate grace of that Tanagra figurine that
you have in your studio, Basil. Her hair clustered round
her face like dark leaves round a pale rose. As for her acting—well, you will see her to-night. She is simply a born
artist. I sat in the dingy box absolutely enthralled. I forgot
that I was in London and in the nineteenth century. I was
away with my love in a forest that no man had ever seen.
After the performance was over I went behind, and spoke
to her. As we were sitting together, suddenly there came
a look into her eyes that I had never seen there before.
My lips moved towards hers. We kissed each other. I can't
describe to you what I felt at that moment. It seemed to
me that all my life had been narrowed to one perfect point
of rose-colored joy. She trembled all over, and shook like
a white narcissus. Then she flung herself on her knees and
kissed my hands. I feel that I should not tell you all this,
but I can't help it. Of course our engagement is a dead
secret. She has not even told her own mother. I don't know
what my guardians will say. Lord Radley is sure to be furious. I don't care. I shall be of age in less than a year, and

then I can do what I like. I have been right, Basil, haven't I, to take my love out of poetry, and to find my wife in Shakespeare's plays? Lips that Shakespeare taught to speak have whispered their secret in my ear. I have had the arms of Rosalind around me, and kissed Juliet on the mouth."

"Yes, Dorian, I suppose you were right," said Hallward, slowly.

"Have you seen her today?" asked Lord Henry.

Dorian Gray shook his head. "I left her in the forest of Arden, I shall find her in an orchard in Verona."

Lord Henry sipped his champagne in a meditative manner. "At what particular point did you mention the word marriage, Dorian? and what did she say in answer? Perhaps you forgot all about it."

"My dear Harry, I did not treat it as a business transaction, and I did not make any formal proposal. I told her that I loved her, and she said she was not worthy to be my wife. Not worthy! Why, the whole world is nothing to me compared to her."

"Women are wonderfully practical," murmured Lord Henry,—"much more practical than we are. In situations of that kind we often forget to say anything about marriage, and they always remind us."

Hallward laid his hand upon his arm. "Don't, Harry. You have annoyed Dorian. He is not like other men. He would never bring misery upon any one. His nature is too fine for that."

Lord Henry looked across the table. "Dorian is never annoyed with me," he answered. "I asked the question for the best reason possible, for the only reason, indeed, that excuses one for asking any question,—simple curiosity. I have a theory that it is always the women who propose to us, and not we who propose to the women, except, of course, in middle-class life. But then the middle classes are not modern."

Dorian Gray laughed, and tossed his head. "You are quite incorrigible, Harry; but I don't mind. It is impossible to be angry with you. When you see Sibyl Vane you will feel that the man who could wrong her would be a beast without a heart. I cannot understand how any one can wish to shame what he loves. I love Sibyl Vane. I wish to place her on a pedestal of gold, and to see the world worship the woman who is mine. What is marriage? An irrevocable vow. And it is an irrevocable vow that I want to take. Her trust makes me faithful, her belief makes me good. When I am with her, I regret all that you have taught me. I become different from what you have known me to be. I am changed, and the mere touch of Sibyl Vane's hand makes me forget you and all your wrong, fascinating, poisonous, delightful theories."

"You will always like me, Dorian," said Lord Henry. "Will you have some coffee, you fellows?—Waiter, bring coffee, and fine-champagne, and some cigarettes. No: don't mind the cigarettes; I have some.—Basil, I can't allow you to smoke cigars. You must have a cigarette. A cigarette is the perfect type of a perfect pleasure. It is exquisite, and it leaves one unsatisfied. What more can you want?—Yes, Dorian, you will always be fond of me. I represent to you all the sins you have never had the courage to commit."

"What nonsense you talk, Harry!" cried Dorian Gray, lighting his cigarette from a fire-breathing silver dragon that the waiter had placed on the table. "Let us go down to the theatre. When you see Sibyl you will have a new ideal of life. She will represent something to you that you have never known."

"I have known everything," said Lord Henry, with a sad look in his eyes, "but I am always ready for a new emotion. I am afraid that there is no such thing, for me at any rate. Still, your wonderful girl may thrill me. I love acting. It is so much more real than life. Let us go. Dorian, you will come with me.—I am so sorry, Basil, but there is only room for two in the brougham. You must follow us in a hansom."

They got up and put on their coats, sipping their coffee standing. Hallward was silent and preoccupied. There was a gloom over him. He could not bear this marriage, and yet it seemed to him to be better than many other things that might have happened. After a few moments, they all passed down-stairs. He drove off by himself, as had been arranged, and watched the flashing lights of the little brougham in front of him. A strange sense of loss came over him. He felt that Dorian Gray would never again be to him all that he had been in the past. His eyes darkened, and the crowded flaring streets became blurred to him. When the cab drew up at the doors of the theatre, it seemed to him that he had grown years older.

## Chapter V

For some reason or other, the house was crowded that night, and the fat Jew manager who met them at the door was beaming from ear to ear with an oily, tremulous smile. He escorted them to their box with a sort of pompous humility, waving his fat jeweled hands, and talking at the top of his voice. Dorian Gray loathed him more than ever. He felt as if he had come to look for Miranda and had been met by Caliban. Lord Henry, upon the other hand, rather liked him. At least he declared he did, and insisted on shaking him by the hand, and assured him that he was proud to meet a man who had discovered a real genius and gone bankrupt over Shakespeare. Hallward amused himself with watching the faces in the pit. The heat was terribly oppressive, and the huge sunlight flamed like a monstrous dahlia with petals of fire. The youths in the gallery had taken off their coats and waistcoats and hung them over the side. They talked to each other across the theatre, and shared their oranges with the tawdry painted girls who sat by them. Some women were laughing in the pit; their voices were horribly shrill and discordant. The sound of the popping of corks came from the bar.

"What a place to find one's divinity in!" said Lord Henry.

"Yes!" answered Dorian Gray. "It was here I found her, and she is divine beyond all living things. When she acts you will forget everything. These common people here, with their coarse faces and brutal gestures, become quite different when she is on the stage. They sit silently and watch her. They weep and laugh as she wills them to do. She makes them as responsive as a violin. She spiritualizes them, and one feels that they are of the same flesh and blood as one's self."

"Oh, I hope not!" murmured Lord Henry, who was scanning the occupants of the gallery through his opera-glass.

"Don't pay any attention to him, Dorian," said Hallward. "I understand what you mean, and I believe in this girl. Any one you love must be marvelous, and any girl that has the effect you describe must be fine and noble. To spiritualize one's age,—that is something worth doing. If this girl can give a soul to those who have lived without one, if she can create the sense of beauty in people whose lives have been sordid and ugly, if she can strip them of their selfishness and lend them tears for sorrows that are not their own, she is worthy of all your adoration, worthy of the adoration of the world. This marriage is quite right. I did not think so at first, but I admit it now. God made Sibyl Vane for you. Without her you would have been incomplete."

"Thanks, Basil," answered Dorian Gray, pressing his hand. "I knew that you would understand me. Harry is so cynical, he terrifies me. But here is the orchestra. It is quite dreadful, but it only lasts for about five minutes.

Then the curtain rises, and you will see the girl to whom I am going to give all my life, to whom I have given everything that is good in me."

A quarter of an hour afterwards, amidst an extraordinary turmoil of applause, Sibyl Vane stepped on to the stage. Yes, she was certainly lovely to look at,—one of the loveliest creatures, Lord Henry thought, that he had ever seen. There was something of the fawn in her shy grace and startled eyes. A faint blush, like the shadow of a rose in a mirror of silver, came to her cheeks as she glanced at the crowded, enthusiastic house. She stepped back a few paces, and her lips seemed to tremble. Basil Hallward leaped to his feet and began to applaud. Dorian Gray sat motionless, gazing on her, like a man in a dream. Lord Henry peered through his opera-glass, murmuring, "Charming! charming!"

The scene was the hall of Capulet's house, and Romeo in his pilgrim's dress had entered with Mercutio and his friends. The band, such as it was, struck up a few bars of music, and the dance began. Through the crowd of ungainly, shabbily-dressed actors, Sibyl Vane moved like a creature from a finer world. Her body swayed, as she danced, as a plant sways in the water. The curves of her throat were like the curves of a white lily. Her hands seemed to be made of cool ivory.

Yet she was curiously listless. She showed no sign of joy when her eyes rested on Romeo. The few lines she had to speak,—

> Good pilgrim, you do wrong your hand too much,
>     Which mannerly devotion shows in this;
> For saints have hands that pilgrims' hands do touch,
>     And palm to palm is holy palmers' kiss,—

with the brief dialogue that follows, were spoken in a thoroughly artificial manner. The voice was exquisite, but from the point of view of tone it was absolutely false. It was wrong in color. It took away all the life from the verse. It made the passion unreal.

Dorian Gray grew pale as he watched her. Neither of his friends dared to say anything to him. She seemed to them to be absolutely incompetent. They were horribly disappointed.

Yet they felt that the true test of any Juliet is the balcony scene of the second act. They waited for that. If she failed there, there was nothing in her.

She looked charming as she came out in the moonlight. That could not be denied. But the staginess of her acting was unbearable, and grew worse as she went on. Her gestures became absurdly artificial. She over-emphasized everything that she had to say. The beautiful passage,—

*Thou knowest the mask of night is on my face,*
*Else would a maiden blush bepaint my cheek*
*For that which thou hast heard me speak to-night,—*

was declaimed with the painful precision of a school-girl who has been taught to recite by some second-rate professor of elocution. When she leaned over the balcony and came to those wonderful lines,—

*Although I joy in thee,*
*I have no joy of this contract to-night:*
*It is too rash, too unadvised, too sudden;*
*Too like the lightning, which doth cease to be*
*Ere one can say, "It lightens." Sweet, good-night!*
*This bud of love by summer's ripening breath*
*May prove a beauteous flower when next we meet,—*

she spoke the words as if they conveyed no meaning to her. It was not nervousness. Indeed, so far from being nervous, she seemed absolutely self-contained. It was simply bad art. She was a complete failure.

Even the common uneducated audience of the pit and gallery lost their interest in the play. They got restless, and began to talk loudly and to whistle. The Jew manager, who was standing at the back of the dress-circle, stamped and swore with rage. The only person unmoved was the girl herself.

When the second act was over there came a storm of hisses, and Lord Henry got up from his chair and put on his coat. "She is quite beautiful, Dorian," he said, "but she can't act. Let us go."

"I am going to see the play through," answered the lad, in a hard, bitter voice. "I am awfully sorry that I have made you waste an evening, Harry. I apologize to both of you."

"My dear Dorian, I should think Miss Vane was ill," interrupted Hallward. "We will come some other night."

"I wish she was ill," he rejoined. "But she seems to me to be simply callous and cold. She has entirely altered. Last night she was a great artist. To-night she is merely a commonplace, mediocre actress."

"Don't talk like that about any one you love, Dorian. Love is a more wonderful thing than art."

"They are both simply forms of imitation," murmured Lord Henry. "But do let us go. Dorian, you must not stay here any longer. It is not good for one's morals to see bad acting. Besides, I don't suppose you will want your wife to act. So what does it matter if she plays Juliet like a wooden doll? She is very lovely, and if she knows as little about life as she does about acting, she will be a delightful experience. There are only two kinds of people who are really fascinating,—people who know absolutely everything, and people who know absolutely nothing. Good heavens, my dear boy, don't look so tragic! The secret of remaining young is never to have an emotion that is unbecoming. Come to the club with Basil and myself. We will smoke cigarettes and drink to the beauty of Sibyl Vane. She is beautiful. What more can you want?"

"Please go away, Harry," cried the lad. "I really want to be alone.—Basil, you don't mind my asking you to go? Ah! can't you see that my heart is breaking?" The hot tears came to his eyes. His lips trembled, and, rushing to the back of the box, he leaned up against the wall, hiding his face in his hands.

"Let us go, Basil," said Lord Henry, with a strange tenderness in his voice; and the two young men passed out together.

A few moments afterwards the footlights flared up, and the curtain rose on the third act. Dorian Gray went back to his seat. He looked pale, and proud, and indifferent. The play dragged on, and seemed interminable. Half of the audience went out, tramping in heavy boots, and laughing. The whole thing was a fiasco. The last act was played to almost empty benches.

As soon as it was over, Dorian Gray rushed behind the scenes into the greenroom. The girl was standing alone there, with a look of triumph on her face. Her eyes were lit with an exquisite fire. There was a radiance about her. Her parted lips were smiling over some secret of their own.

When he entered, she looked at him, and an expression of infinite joy came over her. "How badly I acted to-night, Dorian!" she cried.

"Horribly!" he answered, gazing at her in amazement,—"horribly! It was dreadful. Are you ill? You have no idea what it was. You have no idea what I suffered."

The girl smiled. "Dorian," she answered, lingering over his name with long-drawn music in her voice, as though it were sweeter than honey to the red petals of her lips,—

"Dorian, you should have understood. But you understand now, don't you?"

"Understand what?" he asked, angrily.

"Why I was so bad to-night. Why I shall always be bad. Why I shall never act well again."

He shrugged his shoulders. "You are ill, I suppose. When you are ill you shouldn't act. You make yourself ridiculous. My friends were bored. I was bored."

She seemed not to listen to him. She was transfigured with joy. An ecstasy of happiness dominated her.

"Dorian, Dorian," she cried, "before I knew you, acting was the one reality of my life. It was only in the theatre that I lived. I thought that it was all true. I was Rosalind one night, and Portia the other. The joy of Beatrice was my joy, and the sorrows of Cordelia were mine also. I believed in everything. The common people who acted with me seemed to me to be godlike. The painted scenes were my world. I knew nothing but shadows, and I thought them real. You came,—oh, my beautiful love!—and you freed my soul from prison. You taught me what reality really is. To-night, for the first time in my life, I saw through the hollowness, the sham, the silliness, of the empty pageant in which I had always played. To-night, for the first time, I became conscious that the Romeo was hideous, and old, and painted, that the moonlight in the orchard was false, that the scenery was vulgar, and that the words I had to speak were unreal, were not my words, not what I wanted to say. You had brought me something higher, something of which all art is but a reflection. You have made me understand what love really is. My love! my love! I am sick of shadows. You are more to me than all art can ever be. What have I to do with the puppets of a play? When I came on to-night, I could not understand how it was that everything had gone from me. Suddenly it dawned on my

soul what it all meant. The knowledge was exquisite to
me. I heard them hissing, and I smiled. What should they
know of love? Take me away, Dorian—take me away with
you, where we can be quite alone. I hate the stage. I might
mimic a passion that I do not feel, but I cannot mimic one that burns me like fire. Oh, Dorian, Dorian, you
understand now what it all means? Even if I could do it, it
would be profanation for me to play at being in love. You
have made me see that."

He flung himself down on the sofa, and turned away
his face. "You have killed my love," he muttered.

She looked at him in wonder, and laughed. He made no
answer. She came across to him, and stroked his hair with
her little fingers. She knelt down and pressed his hands to
her lips. He drew them away, and a shudder ran through
him.

Then he leaped up, and went to the door. "Yes," he
cried, "you have killed my love. You used to stir my imagination. Now you don't even stir my curiosity. You simply
produce no effect. I loved you because you were wonderful,
because you had genius and intellect, because you realized
the dreams of great poets and gave shape and substance to
the shadows of art. You have thrown it all away. You are
shallow and stupid. My God! how mad I was to love you!
What a fool I have been! You are nothing to me now. I
will never see you again. I will never think of you. I will
never mention your name. You don't know what you were
to me, once. Why, once . . . . Oh, I can't bear to think of
it! I wish I had never laid eyes upon you! You have spoiled
the romance of my life. How little you can know of love,
if you say it mars your art! What are you without your art?
Nothing. I would have made you famous, splendid, magnificent. The world would have worshipped you, and you
would have belonged to me. What are you now? A third-
rate actress with a pretty face."

The girl grew white, and trembled. She clinched her hands together, and her voice seemed to catch in her throat. "You are not serious, Dorian?" she murmured. "You are acting."

"Acting! I leave that to you. You do it so well," he answered, bitterly.

She rose from her knees, and, with a piteous expression of pain in her face, came across the room to him. She put her hand upon his arm, and looked into his eyes. He thrust her back. "Don't touch me!" he cried.

A low moan broke from her, and she flung herself at his feet, and lay there like a trampled flower. "Dorian, Dorian, don't leave me!" she whispered. "I am so sorry I didn't act well. I was thinking of you all the time. But I will try,—indeed, I will try. It came so suddenly across me, my love for you. I think I should never have known it if you had not kissed me,—if we had not kissed each other. Kiss me again, my love. Don't go away from me. I couldn't bear it. Can't you forgive me for to-night? I will work so hard, and try to improve. Don't be cruel to me because I love you better than anything in the world. After all, it is only once that I have not pleased you. But you are quite right, Dorian. I should have shown myself more of an artist. It was foolish of me; and yet I couldn't help it. Oh, don't leave me, don't leave me." A fit of passionate sobbing choked her. She crouched on the floor like a wounded thing, and Dorian Gray, with his beautiful eyes, looked down at her, and his chiseled lips curled in exquisite disdain. There is always something ridiculous about the passions of people whom one has ceased to love. Sibyl Vane seemed to him to be absurdly melodramatic. Her tears and sobs annoyed him.

"I am going," he said at last, in his calm, clear voice. "I don't wish to be unkind, but I can't see you again. You have disappointed me."

She wept silently, and made no answer, but crept nearer to him. Her little hands stretched blindly out, and appeared to be seeking for him. He turned on his heel, and left the room. In a few moments he was out of the theatre.

Where he went to, he hardly knew. He remembered wandering through dimly-lit streets with gaunt black-shadowed archways and evil-looking houses. Women with hoarse voices and harsh laughter had called after him. Drunkards had reeled by cursing, and chattering to themselves like monstrous apes. He had seen grotesque children huddled upon door-steps, and had heard shrieks and oaths from gloomy courts.

When the dawn was just breaking he found himself at Covent Garden. Huge carts filled with nodding lilies rumbled slowly down the polished empty street. The air was heavy with the perfume of the flowers, and their beauty seemed to bring him an anodyne for his pain. He followed into the market, and watched the men unloading their wagons. A white-smocked carter offered him some cherries. He thanked him, wondered why he refused to accept any money for them, and began to eat them listlessly. They had been plucked at midnight, and the coldness of the moon had entered into them. A long line of boys carrying crates of striped tulips, and of yellow and red roses, defiled in front of him, threading their way through the huge jade-green piles of vegetables. Under the portico, with its gray sun-bleached pillars, loitered a troop of draggled bareheaded girls, waiting for the auction to be over. After some time he hailed a hansom and drove home. The sky was pure opal now, and the roofs of the houses glistened like silver against it. As he was passing through the library towards the door of his bedroom, his eye fell upon the portrait Basil Hallward had painted of him. He started back in surprise, and then went over to it and examined it. In the dim arrested light that struggled through the cream-colored silk blinds, the face seemed to him to be a little changed. The expression looked different. One would have said that there was a touch of cruelty in the mouth. It was certainly curious.

He turned round, and, walking to the window, drew the blinds up. The bright dawn flooded the room, and swept the fantastic shadows into dusky corners, where they lay shuddering. But the strange expression that he had noticed in the face of the portrait seemed to linger there, to be more intensified even. The quivering, ardent sunlight showed him the lines of cruelty round the mouth as clearly as if he had been looking into a mirror after he had done some dreadful thing.

He winced, and, taking up from the table an oval glass framed in ivory Cupids, that Lord Henry had given him, he glanced hurriedly into it. No line like that warped his red lips. What did it mean?

He rubbed his eyes, and came close to the picture, and examined it again. There were no signs of any change when he looked into the actual painting, and yet there was no doubt that the whole expression had altered. It was not a mere fancy of his own. The thing was horribly apparent.

He threw himself into a chair, and began to think. Suddenly there flashed across his mind what he had said in Basil Hallward's studio the day the picture had been finished. Yes, he remembered it perfectly. He had uttered a mad wish that he himself might remain young, and the portrait grow old; that his own beauty might be untarnished, and the face on the canvas bear the burden of his passions and his sins; that the painted image might be seared with the lines of suffering and thought, and that he might keep all the delicate bloom and loveliness of his then just conscious boyhood. Surely his prayer had not been answered?

Such things were impossible. It seemed monstrous even to think of them. And, yet, there was the picture before him, with the touch of cruelty in the mouth.

Cruelty! Had he been cruel? It was the girl's fault, not his. He had dreamed of her as a great artist, had given his love to her because he had thought her great. Then she had disappointed him. She had been shallow and unworthy. And, yet, a feeling of infinite regret came over him, as he thought of her lying at his feet sobbing like a little child. He remembered with what callousness he had watched her. Why had he been made like that? Why had such a soul been given to him? But he had suffered also. During the three terrible hours that the play had lasted, he had lived centuries of pain, aeon upon aeon of torture. His life was well worth hers. She had marred him for a moment, if he had wounded her for an age. Besides, women were better suited to bear sorrow than men. They lived on their emotions. They only thought of their emotions. When they took lovers, it was merely to have some one with whom they could have scenes. Lord Henry had told him that, and Lord Henry knew what women were. Why should he trouble about Sibyl Vane? She was nothing to him now.

But the picture? What was he to say of that? It held the secret of his life, and told his story. It had taught him to love his own beauty. Would it teach him to loathe his own soul? Would he ever look at it again?

No; it was merely an illusion wrought on the troubled senses. The horrible night that he had passed had left phantoms behind it. Suddenly there had fallen upon his brain that tiny scarlet speck that makes men mad. The picture had not changed. It was folly to think so.

Yet it was watching him, with its beautiful marred face and its cruel smile. Its bright hair gleamed in the early sunlight. Its blue eyes met his own. A sense of infinite pity, not for himself, but for the painted image of himself, came over him. It had altered already, and would alter more. Its gold would wither into gray. Its red and white roses would die. For every sin that he committed, a stain would fleck and wreck its fairness. But he would not sin. The picture, changed or unchanged, would be to him the visible emblem of conscience. He would resist temptation. He would not see Lord Henry any more,—would not, at any rate, listen to those subtle poisonous theories that in Basil Hallward's garden had first stirred within him the passion for impossible things. He would go back to Sibyl Vane, make her amends, marry her, try to love her again. Yes, it was his duty to do so. She must have suffered more than he had. Poor child! He had been selfish and cruel to her. The fascination that she had exercised over him would return. They would be happy together. His life with her would be beautiful and pure.

He got up from his chair, and drew a large screen right in front of the portrait, shuddering as he glanced at it. "How horrible!" he murmured to himself, and he walked across to the window and opened it. When he stepped out on the grass, he drew a deep breath. The fresh morning air seemed to drive away all his sombre passions. He thought only of Sibyl Vane. A faint echo of his love came back to him. He repeated her name over and over again. The birds that were singing in the dew-drenched garden seemed to be telling the flowers about her.

## Chapter VI

It was long past noon when he awoke. His valet had crept several times into the room on tiptoe to see if he was stirring, and had wondered what made his young master sleep so late. Finally his bell sounded, and Victor came in softly with a cup of tea, and a pile of letters, on a small tray of old Sèvres china, and drew back the olive-satin curtains, with their shimmering blue lining, that hung in front of the three tall windows.

"Monsieur has well slept this morning," he said, smiling.

"What o'clock is it, Victor?" asked Dorian Gray, sleepily.

"One hour and a quarter, monsieur."

How late it was! He sat up, and, having sipped some tea, turned over his letters. One of them was from Lord Henry, and had been brought by hand that morning. He hesitated for a moment, and then put it aside. The others he opened listlessly. They contained the usual collection of cards, invitations to dinner, tickets for private views, programmes of charity concerts, and the like, that are showered on fashionable young men every morning during the season. There was a rather heavy bill, for a chased silver Louis-Quinze toilet-set, that he had not yet had the courage to send on to his guardians, who were extremely old-fashioned people and did not realize that we live in an age when only unnecessary things are absolutely necessary to us; and there were several very courteously worded communications from Jermyn Street money-lenders offering to advance any sum of money at a moment's notice and at the most reasonable rates of interest.

After about ten minutes he got up, and, throwing on an elaborate dressing-gown, passed into the onyx-paved bath-room. The cool water refreshed him after his long sleep. He seemed to have forgotten all that he had gone through. A dim sense of having taken part in some strange tragedy came to him once or twice, but there was the unreality of a dream about it.

As soon as he was dressed, he went into the library and sat down to a light French breakfast, that had been laid out for him on a small round table close to an open window. It was an exquisite day. The warm air seemed laden with spices. A bee flew in, and buzzed round the blue-dragon bowl, filled with sulphur-yellow roses, that stood in front of him. He felt perfectly happy.

Suddenly his eye fell on the screen that he had placed in front of the portrait, and he started.

"Too cold for Monsieur?" asked his valet, putting an omelette on the table. "I shut the window?"

Dorian shook his head. "I am not cold," he murmured.

Was it all true? Had the portrait really changed? Or had it been simply his own imagination that had made him see a look of evil where there had been a look of joy? Surely a painted canvas could not alter? The thing was absurd. It would serve as a tale to tell Basil some day. It would make him smile.

And, yet, how vivid was his recollection of the whole thing! First in the dim twilight, and then in the bright dawn, he had seen the touch of cruelty in the warped lips. He almost dreaded his valet leaving the room. He knew that when he was alone he would have to examine the portrait. He was afraid of certainty. When the coffee and cigarettes had been brought and the man turned to go, he felt a mad desire to tell him to remain. As the door closed behind him he called him back. The man stood waiting for his orders. Dorian looked at him for a moment. "I am not at home to any one, Victor," he said, with a sigh. The man bowed and retired.

He rose from the table, lit a cigarette, and flung himself down on a luxuriously-cushioned couch that stood facing the screen. The screen was an old one of gilt Spanish leather, stamped and wrought with a rather florid Louis-Quatorze pattern. He scanned it curiously, wondering if it had ever before concealed the secret of a man's life.

Should he move it aside, after all? Why not let it stay there? What was the use of knowing? If the thing was true, it was terrible. If it was not true, why trouble about it?

But what if, by some fate or deadlier chance, other eyes than his spied behind, and saw the horrible change? What should he do if Basil Hallward came and asked to look at his own picture? He would be sure to do that. No; the thing had to be examined, and at once. Anything would be better than this dreadful state of doubt.

He got up, and locked both doors. At least he would be alone when he looked upon the mask of his shame. Then he drew the screen aside, and saw himself face to face. It was perfectly true. The portrait had altered.

As he often remembered afterwards, and always with no small wonder, he found himself at first gazing at the portrait with a feeling of almost scientific interest. That such a change should have taken place was incredible to him. And yet it was a fact. Was there some subtle affinity between the chemical atoms, that shaped themselves into form and color on the canvas, and the soul that was within him? Could it be that what that soul thought, they realized?—that what it dreamed, they made true? Or was there some other, more terrible reason? He shuddered, and felt afraid, and, going back to the couch, lay there, gazing at the picture in sickened horror.

One thing, however, he felt that it had done for him. It had made him conscious how unjust, how cruel, he had been to Sibyl Vane. It was not too late to make reparation for that. She could still be his wife. His unreal and self-ish love would yield to some higher influence, would be transformed into some nobler passion, and the portrait that Basil Hallward had painted of him would be a guide to him through life, would be to him what holiness was to some, and conscience to others, and the fear of God to us all. There were opiates for remorse, drugs that could lull the moral sense to sleep. But here was a visible symbol of the degradation of sin. Here was an ever-present sign of the ruin men brought upon their souls.

Three o'clock struck, and four, and half-past four, but he did not stir. He was trying to gather up the scarlet threads of life, and to weave them into a pattern; to find his way through the sanguine labyrinth of passion through which he was wandering. He did not know what to do, or what to think. Finally, he went over to the table and wrote a passionate letter to the girl he had loved, imploring her forgiveness, and accusing himself of madness. He covered page after page with wild words of sorrow, and wilder words of pain. There is a luxury in self-reproach. When we blame ourselves we feel that no one else has a right to blame us. It is the confession, not the priest, that gives us absolution. When Dorian Gray had finished the letter, he felt that he had been forgiven.

Suddenly there came a knock to the door, and he heard Lord Henry's voice outside. "My dear Dorian, I must see you. Let me in at once. I can't bear your shutting yourself up like this."

He made no answer at first, but remained quite still. The knocking still continued, and grew louder. Yes, it was better to let Lord Henry in, and to explain to him the new life he was going to lead, to quarrel with him if it became necessary to quarrel, to part if parting was inevitable. He jumped up, drew the screen hastily across the picture, and unlocked the door.

"I am so sorry for it all, my dear boy," said Lord Henry, coming in. "But you must not think about it too much."

"Do you mean about Sibyl Vane?" asked Dorian.

"Yes, of course," answered Lord Henry, sinking into a chair, and slowly pulling his gloves off. "It is dreadful, from one point of view, but it was not your fault. Tell me, did you go behind and see her after the play was over?"

"Yes."

"I felt sure you had. Did you make a scene with her?"

"I was brutal, Harry,—perfectly brutal. But it is all right now. I am not sorry for anything that has happened. It has taught me to know myself better."

"Ah, Dorian, I am so glad you take it in that way! I was afraid I would find you plunged in remorse, and tearing your nice hair."

"I have got through all that," said Dorian, shaking his head, and smiling. "I am perfectly happy now. I know what conscience is, to begin with. It is not what you told me it was. It is the divinest thing in us. Don't sneer at it, Harry, any more,—at least not before me. I want to be good. I can't bear the idea of my soul being hideous."

"A very charming artistic basis for ethics, Dorian! I congratulate you on it. But how are you going to begin?"

"By marrying Sibyl Vane."

"Marrying Sibyl Vane!" cried Lord Henry, standing up, and looking at him in perplexed amazement. "But, my dear Dorian—"

"Yes, Harry, I know what you are going to say. Something dreadful about marriage. Don't say it. Don't ever say things of that kind to me again. Two days ago I asked Sibyl to marry me. I am not going to break my word to her. She is to be my wife."

"Your wife! Dorian! . . . Didn't you get my letter? I wrote to you this morning, and sent the note down, by my own man."

"Your letter? Oh, yes, I remember. I have not read it yet, Harry. I was afraid there might be something in it that I wouldn't like."

Lord Henry walked across the room, and, sitting down by Dorian Gray, took both his hands in his, and held them tightly. "Dorian," he said, "my letter—don't be frightened—was to tell you that Sibyl Vane is dead."

A cry of pain rose from the lad's lips, and he leaped to his feet, tearing his hands away from Lord Henry's grasp. "Dead! Sibyl dead! It is not true! It is a horrible lie!"

"It is quite true, Dorian," said Lord Henry, gravely. "It is in all the morning papers. I wrote down to you to ask you not to see any one till I came. There will have to be an inquest, of course, and you must not be mixed up in it. Things like that make a man fashionable in Paris. But in London people are so prejudiced. Here, one should never make one's *début* with a scandal. One should reserve that to give an interest to one's old age. I don't suppose they know your name at the theatre. If they don't, it is all right. Did any one see you going round to her room? That is an important point."

Dorian did not answer for a few moments. He was dazed with horror. Finally he murmured, in a stifled voice, "Harry, did you say an inquest? What did you mean by that? Did Sibyl—? Oh, Harry, I can't bear it! But be quick. Tell me everything at once."

"I have no doubt it was not an accident, Dorian, though it must be put in that way to the public. As she was leaving the theatre with her mother, about half-past twelve or so, she said she had forgotten something up-stairs. They waited some time for her, but she did not come down again. They ultimately found her lying dead on the floor of her dressing-room. She had swallowed something by mistake, some dreadful thing they use at theatres. I don't know what it was, but it had either prussic acid or white lead in it. I should fancy it was prussic acid, as she seems to have died instantaneously. It is very tragic, of course, but you must not get yourself mixed up in it. I see by the *Standard* that she was seventeen. I should have thought she was almost younger than that. She looked such a child, and seemed to know so little about acting. Dorian, you mustn't let this thing get on your nerves. You must come and dine with me, and afterwards we will look in at the Opera. It is a Patti night, and everybody will be there. You can come to my sister's box. She has got some smart women with her."

"So I have murdered Sibyl Vane," said Dorian Gray, half to himself,—"murdered her as certainly as if I had cut her little throat with a knife. And the roses are not less lovely for all that. The birds sing just as happily in my garden. And to-night I am to dine with you, and then go on to the Opera, and sup somewhere, I suppose, afterwards. How extraordinarily dramatic life is! If I had read all this in a book, Harry, I think I would have wept over it. Somehow, now that it has happened actually, and to me, it seems far too wonderful for tears. Here is the first passionate love-letter I have ever written in my life. Strange, that my first passionate love-letter should have been addressed to a dead girl. Can they feel, I wonder, those white silent people we call the dead? Sibyl! Can she feel, or know, or listen? Oh, Harry, how I loved her once! It seems years ago to me now. She was everything to me. Then came that dreadful night—was it really only last night?—when she played so badly, and my heart almost broke. She explained it all to me. It was terribly pathetic. But I was not moved a bit. I thought her shallow. Then something happened that made me afraid. I can't tell you what it was, but it was awful. I said I would go back to her. I felt I had done wrong. And now she is dead. My God! my God! Harry, what shall I do? You don't know the danger I am in, and there is nothing to keep me straight. She would have done that for me. She had no right to kill herself. It was selfish of her."

"My dear Dorian, the only way a woman can ever re-form a man is by boring him so completely that he loses all possible interest in life. If you had married this girl you would have been wretched. Of course you would have treated her kindly. One can always be kind to people about whom one cares nothing. But she would have soon found out that you were absolutely indifferent to her. And when a woman finds that out about her husband, she either becomes dreadfully dowdy, or wears very smart bonnets that some other woman's husband has to pay for. I say nothing about the social mistake, but I assure you that in any case the whole thing would have been an absolute failure."

"I suppose it would," muttered the lad, walking up and down the room, and looking horribly pale. "But I thought it was my duty. It is not my fault that this terrible tragedy has prevented my doing what was right. I remember your saying once that there is a fatality about good resolutions,—that they are always made too late. Mine certainly were."

"Good resolutions are simply a useless attempt to interfere with scientific laws. Their origin is pure vanity. Their result is absolutely nil. They give us, now and then, some of those luxurious sterile emotions that have a certain charm for us. That is all that can be said for them."

"Harry," cried Dorian Gray, coming over and sitting down beside him, "why is it that I cannot feel this tragedy as much as I want to? I don't think I am heartless. Do you?"

"You have done too many foolish things in your life to be entitled to give yourself that name, Dorian," answered Lord Henry, with his sweet, melancholy smile.

The lad frowned. "I don't like that explanation, Harry," he rejoined, "but I am glad you don't think I am heartless. I am nothing of the kind. I know I am not. And yet I must admit that this thing that has happened does not affect me as it should. It seems to me to be simply like a wonderful ending to a wonderful play. It has all the terrible beauty of a great tragedy, a tragedy in which I took part, but by which I have not been wounded."

"It is an interesting question," said Lord Henry, who found an exquisite pleasure in playing on the lad's unconscious egotism,—"an extremely interesting question. I fancy that the explanation is this. It often happens that the real tragedies of life occur in such an inartistic manner that they hurt us by their crude violence, their absolute incoherence, their absurd want of meaning, their entire lack of style. They affect us just as vulgarity affects us. They give us an impression of sheer brute force, and we revolt against that. Sometimes, however, a tragedy that has artistic elements of beauty crosses our lives. If these elements of beauty are real, the whole thing simply appeals to our sense of dramatic effect. Suddenly we find that we are no longer the actors, but the spectators of the play. Or rather we are both. We watch ourselves, and the mere wonder of the spectacle enthralls us. In the present case, what is it that has really happened? Some one has killed herself for love of you. I wish I had ever had such an experience. It would have made me in love with love for the rest of my life. The people who have adored me—there have not been very many, but there have been some—have always insisted on living on, long after I had ceased to care for them, or they to care for me. They have become stout and tedious, and when I meet them they go in at once for reminiscences. That awful memory of woman! What a fearful thing it is! And what an utter intellectual stagnation it reveals! One should absorb the color of life, but one should never remember its details. Details are always vulgar.

"Of course, now and then things linger. I once wore nothing but violets all through one season, as mourning for a romance that would not die. Ultimately, however, it did die. I forget what killed it. I think it was her proposing to sacrifice the whole world for me. That is always a dreadful moment. It fills one with the terror of eternity. Well,—would you believe it?—a week ago, at Lady Hampshire's, I found myself seated at dinner next the lady in question, and she insisted on going over the whole thing again, and digging up the past, and raking up the future. I had buried my romance in a bed of poppies. She dragged it out again, and assured me that I had spoiled her life. I am bound to state that she ate an enormous dinner, so I did not feel any anxiety. But what a lack of taste she showed! The one charm of the past is that it is the past. But women never know when the curtain has fallen. They always want a sixth act, and as soon as the interest of the play is entirely over they propose to continue it. If they were allowed to have their way, every comedy would have a tragic ending, and every tragedy would culminate in a farce. They are charmingly artificial, but they have no sense of art. You are more fortunate than I am. I assure you, Dorian, that not one of the women I have known would have done for me what Sibyl Vane did for you. Ordinary women always console themselves. Some of them do it by going in for sentimental colors. Never trust a woman who wears mauve, whatever her age may be, or a woman over thirty-five who is fond of pink ribbons. It always means that they have a history. Others find a great consolation in suddenly discovering the good qualities of their husbands. They flaunt their conjugal felicity in one's face, as if it was the most fascinating of sins. Religion consoles some. Its mysteries have all the charm of a flirtation, a woman once told me; and I can quite understand it. Besides, nothing makes one so vain as being told that one is a sinner. There is really no end to the consolations that women find in modern life. Indeed, I have not mentioned the most important one of all."

"What is that, Harry?" said Dorian Gray, listlessly.

"Oh, the obvious one. Taking some one else's admirer when one loses one's own. In good society that always whitewashes a woman. But really, Dorian, how different Sibyl Vane must have been from all the women one meets! There is something to me quite beautiful about her death. I am glad I am living in a century when such wonders happen. They make one believe in the reality of the things that shallow, fashionable people play with, such as romance, passion, and love."

"I was terribly cruel to her. You forget that."

"I believe that women appreciate cruelty more than anything else. They have wonderfully primitive instincts. We have emancipated them, but they remain slaves looking for their masters, all the same. They love being dominated. I am sure you were splendid. I have never seen you angry, but I can fancy how delightful you looked. And, after all, you said something to me the day before yesterday that seemed to me at the time to be merely fanciful, but that I see now was absolutely true, and it explains everything."

"What was that, Harry?"

"You said to me that Sibyl Vane represented to you all the heroines of romance—that she was Desdemona one night, and Ophelia the other; that if she died as Juliet, she came to life as Imogen."

"She will never come to life again now," murmured the lad, burying his face in his hands.

"No, she will never come to life. She has played her last part. But you must think of that lonely death in the tawdry dressing-room simply as a strange lurid fragment from some Jacobean tragedy, as a wonderful scene from Webster, or Ford, or Cyril Tourneur. The girl never really lived, and so she has never really died. To you at least she was always a dream, a phantom that flitted through Shakespeare's plays and left them lovelier for its presence, a reed through which Shakespeare's music sounded richer and more full of joy. The moment she touched actual life, she marred it, and it marred her, and so she passed away. Mourn for Ophelia, if you like. Put ashes on your head because Cordelia was strangled. Cry out against Heaven because the daughter of Brabantio died. But don't waste your tears over Sibyl Vane. She was less real than they are."

There was a silence. The evening darkened in the room. Noiselessly, and with silver feet, the shadows crept in from the garden. The colors faded wearily out of things.

After some time Dorian Gray looked up. "You have explained me to myself, Harry," he murmured, with something of a sigh of relief. "I felt all that you have said, but somehow I was afraid of it, and I could not express it to myself. How well you know me! But we will not talk again of what has happened. It has been a marvelous experience. That is all. I wonder if life has still in store for me anything as marvelous."

"Life has everything in store for you, Dorian. There is nothing that you, with your extraordinary good looks, will not be able to do."

"But suppose, Harry, I became haggard, and gray, and wrinkled? What then?"

"Ah, then," said Lord Henry, rising to go,—"then, my dear Dorian, you would have to fight for your victories. As it is, they are brought to you. No, you must keep your good looks. We live in an age that reads too much to be wise, and that thinks too much to be beautiful. We cannot spare you. And now you had better dress, and drive down to the club. We are rather late, as it is."

"I think I shall join you at the Opera, Harry. I feel too tired to eat anything. What is the number of your sister's box?"

"Twenty-seven, I believe. It is on the grand tier. You will see her name on the door. But I am sorry you won't come and dine."

"I don't feel up to it," said Dorian, wearily. "But I am awfully obliged to you for all that you have said to me. You are certainly my best friend. No one has ever understood me as you have."

"We are only at the beginning of our friendship, Dorian," answered Lord Henry, shaking him by the hand.

"Good-by. I shall see you before nine-thirty, I hope. Remember, Patti is singing."

As he closed the door behind him, Dorian Gray touched the bell, and in a few minutes Victor appeared with the lamps and drew the blinds down. He waited impatiently for him to go. The man seemed to take an interminable time about everything.

As soon as he had left, he rushed to the screen, and drew it back. No; there was no further change in the picture. It had received the news of Sibyl Vane's death before he had known of it himself. It was conscious of the events of life as they occurred. The vicious cruelty that marred the fine lines of the mouth had, no doubt, appeared at the very moment that the girl had drunk the poison, whatever it was. Or was it indifferent to results? Did it merely take cognizance of what passed within the soul? he wondered, and hoped that some day he would see the change taking place before his very eyes, shuddering as he hoped it.

Poor Sibyl! what a romance it had all been! She had often mimicked death on the stage, and at last Death himself had touched her, and brought her with him. How had she played that dreadful scene? Had she cursed him, as she died? No; she had died for love of him, and love would always be a sacrament to him now. She had atoned for everything, by the sacrifice she had made of her life. He would not think any more of what she had made him go through, that horrible night at the theatre. When he thought of her, it would be as a wonderful tragic figure to show Love had been a great reality. A wonderful tragic figure? Tears came to his eyes as he remembered her child-like look and winsome fanciful ways and shy tremulous grace. He wiped them away hastily, and looked again at the picture.

He felt that the time had really come for making his choice. Or had his choice already been made? Yes, life had decided that for him,—life, and his own infinite curiosity

about life. Eternal youth, infinite passion, pleasures subtle and secret, wild joys and wilder sins,—he was to have
all these things. The portrait was to bear the burden of his
shame: that was all.

A feeling of pain came over him as he thought of the
desecration that was in store for the fair face on the canvas. Once, in boyish mockery of Narcissus, he had kissed,
or feigned to kiss, those painted lips that now smiled so
cruelly at him. Morning after morning he had sat before
the portrait wondering at its beauty, almost enamored of
it, as it seemed to him at times. Was it to alter now with
every mood to which he yielded? Was it to become a hideous and loathsome thing, to be hidden away in a locked
room, to be shut out from the sunlight that had so often
touched to brighter gold the waving wonder of the hair?
The pity of it! the pity of it!

For a moment he thought of praying that the horrible sympathy that existed between him and the picture
might cease. It had changed in answer to a prayer; perhaps
in answer to a prayer it might remain unchanged. And,
yet, who, that knew anything about Life, would surrender
the chance of remaining always young, however fantastic
that chance might be, or with what fateful consequences it
might be fraught? Besides, was it really under his control?
Had it indeed been prayer that had produced the substi-
tution? Might there not be some curious scientific reason
for it all? If thought could exercise its influence upon a
living organism, might not thought exercise an influence
upon dead and inorganic things? Nay, without thought or
conscious desire, might not things external to ourselves
vibrate in unison with our moods and passions, atom calling to atom, in secret love or strange affinity? But the reason was of no importance. He would never again tempt by
a prayer any terrible power. If the picture was to alter, it
was to alter. That was all. Why inquire too closely into it?

For there would be a real pleasure in watching it. He would be able to follow his mind into its secret places. This portrait would be to him the most magical of mirrors. As it had revealed to him his own body, so it would reveal to him his own soul. And when winter came upon it, he would still be standing where spring trembles on the verge of summer. When the blood crept from its face, and left behind a pallid mask of chalk with leaden eyes, he would keep the glamour of boyhood. Not one blossom of his loveliness would ever fade. Not one pulse of his life would ever weaken. Like the gods of the Greeks, he would be strong, and fleet, and joyous. What did it matter what happened to the colored image on the canvas? He would be safe. That was everything.

He drew the screen back into its former place in front of the picture, smiling as he did so, and passed into his bedroom, where his valet was already waiting for him. An hour later he was at the Opera, and Lord Henry was leaning over his chair.

## CHAPTER VII

As he was sitting at breakfast next morning, Basil Hallward was shown into the room.

"I am so glad I have found you, Dorian," he said, gravely. "I called last night, and they told me you were at the Opera. Of course I knew that was impossible. But I wish you had left word where you had really gone to. I passed a dreadful evening, half afraid that one tragedy might be followed by another. I think you might have telegraphed for me when you heard of it first. I read of it quite by chance in a late edition of the *Globe,* that I picked up at the club. I came here at once, and was miserable at not finding you. I can't tell you how heart-broken I am about the whole thing. I know what you must suffer. But where were you? Did you go down and see the girl's mother? For a moment I thought of following you there. They gave the address in the paper. Somewhere in the Euston Road, isn't it? But I was afraid of intruding upon a sorrow that I could not lighten. Poor woman! What a state she must be in! And her only child, too! What did she say about it all?"

"My dear Basil, how do I know?" murmured Dorian, sipping some pale-yellow wine from a delicate gold-beaded bubble of Venetian glass, and looking dreadfully bored. "I was at the Opera. You should have come on there. I met Lady Gwendolen, Harry's sister, for the first time. We were in her box. She is perfectly charming; and Patti sang divinely. Don't talk about horrid subjects. If one doesn't talk about a thing, it has never happened. It is simply expression, as Harry says, that gives reality to things. Tell me about yourself and what you are painting."

"You went to the Opera?" said Hallward, speaking very slowly, and with a strained touch of pain in his voice. "You went to the Opera while Sibyl Vane was lying dead in some sordid lodging? You can talk to me of other women being charming, and of Patti singing divinely, before the girl you loved has even the quiet of a grave to sleep in? Why, man, there are horrors in store for that little white body of hers!"

"Stop, Basil! I won't hear it!" cried Dorian, leaping to his feet. "You must not tell me about things. What is done is done. What is past is past."

"You call yesterday the past?"

"What has the actual lapse of time got to do with it? It is only shallow people who require years to get rid of an emotion. A man who is master of himself can end a sorrow as easily as he can invent a pleasure. I don't want to be at the mercy of my emotions. I want to use them, to enjoy them, and to dominate them."

"Dorian, this is horrible! Something has changed you completely. You look exactly the same wonderful boy who used to come down to my studio, day after day, to sit for his picture. But you were simple, natural, and affectionate then. You were the most unspoiled creature in the whole world. Now, I don't know what has come over you. You talk as if you had no heart, no pity in you. It is all Harry's influence. I see that."

The lad flushed up, and, going to the window, looked out on the green, flickering garden for a few moments. "I owe a great deal to Harry, Basil," he said, at last,—"more than I owe to you. You only taught me to be vain."

"Well, I am punished for that, Dorian,—or shall be some day."

"I don't know what you mean, Basil," he exclaimed, turning round. "I don't know what you want. What do you want?"

"I want the Dorian Gray I used to know."

"Basil," said the lad, going over to him, and putting his hand on his shoulder, "you have come too late. Yesterday when I heard that Sibyl Vane had killed herself—"

"Killed herself! Good heavens! is there no doubt about that?" cried Hallward, looking up at him with an expression of horror.

"My dear Basil! Surely you don't think it was a vulgar accident? Of course she killed herself It is one of the great romantic tragedies of the age. As a rule, people who act lead the most commonplace lives. They are good husbands, or faithful wives, or something tedious. You know what I mean,—middle-class virtue, and all that kind of thing. How different Sibyl was! She lived her finest tragedy. She was always a heroine. The last night she played—the night you saw her—she acted badly because she had known the reality of love. When she knew its unreality, she died, as Juliet might have died. She passed again into the sphere of art. There is something of the martyr about her. Her death has all the pathetic uselessness of martyrdom, all its

wasted beauty. But, as I was saying, you must not think I
have not suffered. If you had come in yesterday at a particular moment,—about half-past five, perhaps, or a quarter
to six,—you would have found me in tears. Even Harry,
who was here, who brought me the news, in fact, had no
idea what I was going through. I suffered immensely, then
it passed away. I cannot repeat an emotion. No one can,
except sentimentalists. And you are awfully unjust, Basil.
You come down here to console me. That is charming of
you. You find me consoled, and you are furious. How like
a sympathetic person! You remind me of a story Harry
told me about a certain philanthropist who spent twenty
years of his life in trying to get some grievance redressed,
or some unjust law altered,—I forget exactly what it was.
Finally he succeeded, and nothing could exceed his disappointment. He had absolutely nothing to do, almost died
of ennui, and became a confirmed misanthrope. And besides, my dear old Basil, if you really want to console me,
teach me rather to forget what has happened, or to see it
from a proper artistic point of view. Was it not Gautier
who used to write about *la consolation des arts?* I remember picking up a little vellum-covered book in your studio
one day and chancing on that delightful phrase. Well, I
am not like that young man you told me of when we were
down at Marlowe together, the young man who used to say
that yellow satin could console one for all the miseries of
life. I love beautiful things that one can touch and handle.
Old brocades, green bronzes, lacquer-work, carved ivories,
exquisite surroundings, luxury, pomp,—there is much to
be got from all these. But the artistic temperament that
they create, or at any rate reveal, is still more to me. To
become the spectator of one's own life, as Harry says, is
to escape the suffering of life. I know you are surprised
at my talking to you like this. You have not realized how
I have developed. I was a school-boy when you knew me.

I am a man now. I have new passions, new thoughts, new ideas. I am different, but you must not like me less. I am changed, but you must always be my friend. Of course I am very fond of Harry. But I know that you are better than he is. You are not stronger,—you are too much afraid of life,—but you are better. And how happy we used to be together! Don't leave me, Basil, and don't quarrel with me. I am what I am. There is nothing more to be said."

Hallward felt strangely moved. Rugged and straightforward as he was, there was something in his nature that was purely feminine in its tenderness. The lad was infinitely dear to him, and his personality had been the great turning-point in his art. He could not bear the idea of reproaching him any more. After all, his indifference was probably merely a mood that would pass away. There was so much in him that was good, so much in him that was noble.

"Well, Dorian," he said, at length, with a sad smile, "I won't speak to you again about this horrible thing, after today. I only trust your name won't be mentioned in connection with it. The inquest is to take place this afternoon. Have they summoned you?"

Dorian shook his head, and a look of annoyance passed over his face at the mention of the word "inquest." There was something so crude and vulgar about everything of the kind. "They don't know my name," he answered.

"But surely she did?"

"Only my Christian name, and that I am quite sure she never mentioned to any one. She told me once that they were all rather curious to learn who I was, and that she invariably told them my name was Prince Charming. It was pretty of her. You must do me a drawing of her, Basil. I should like to have something more of her than the memory of a few kisses and some broken pathetic words."

"I will try and do something, Dorian, if it would please you. But you must come and sit to me yourself again. I can't get on without you."

"I will never sit to you again, Basil. It is impossible!" he exclaimed, starting back.

Hallward stared at him, "My dear boy, what nonsense!" he cried. "Do you mean to say you don't like what I did of you? Where is it? Why have you pulled the screen in front of it? Let me look at it. It is the best thing I have ever painted. Do take that screen away, Dorian. It is simply horrid of your servant hiding my work like that. I felt the room looked different as I came in."

"My servant has nothing to do with it, Basil. You don't imagine I let him arrange my room for me? He settles my flowers for me sometimes,—that is all. No; I did it myself. The light was too strong on the portrait."

"Too strong! Impossible, my dear fellow! It is an admirable place for it. Let me see it." And Hallward walked towards the corner of the room.

A cry of terror broke from Dorian Gray's lips, and he rushed between Hallward and the screen. "Basil," he said, looking very pale, "you must not look at it. I don't wish you to."

"Not look at my own work! you are not serious. Why shouldn't I look at it?" exclaimed Hallward, laughing.

"If you try to look at it, Basil, on my word of honor I will never speak to you again as long as I live. I am quite serious. I don't offer any explanation, and you are not to ask for any. But, remember, if you touch this screen, everything is over between us."

Hallward was thunderstruck. He looked at Dorian Gray in absolute amazement. He had never seen him like this before. The lad was absolutely pallid with rage. His hands were clinched, and the pupils of his eyes were like disks of blue fire. He was trembling all over.

"Dorian!"

"Don't speak!"

"But what is the matter? Of course I won't look at it if you don't want me to," he said, rather coldly, turning on his heel, and going over towards the window. "But, really, it seems rather absurd that I shouldn't see my own work, especially as I am going to exhibit it in Paris in the autumn. I shall probably have to give it another coat of varnish before that, so I must see it some day, and why not today?"

"To exhibit it! You want to exhibit it?" exclaimed Dorian Gray, a strange sense of terror creeping over him. Was the world going to be shown his secret? Were people to gape at the mystery of his life? That was impossible. Something—he did not know what—had to be done at once.

"Yes: I don't suppose you will object to that. Georges Petit is going to collect all my best pictures for a special exhibition in the Rue de Sèze, which will open the first week in October. The portrait will only be away a month. I should think you could easily spare it for that time. In fact, you are sure to be out of town. And if you hide it always behind a screen, you can't care much abut it."

Dorian Gray passed his hand over his forehead. There were beads of perspiration there. He felt that he was on the brink of a horrible danger. "You told me a month ago that you would never exhibit it," he said. "Why have you changed your mind? You people who go in for being consistent have just as many moods as others. The only difference is that your moods are rather meaningless. You can't have forgotten that you assured me most solemnly that nothing in the world would induce you to send it to any exhibition. You told Harry exactly the same thing." He stopped suddenly, and a gleam of light came into his eyes. He remembered that Lord Henry had said to him once, half seriously and half in jest, "If you want to have an interesting quarter of an hour, get Basil to tell you why he won't exhibit your picture. He told me why he wouldn't, and it was a revelation to me." Yes, perhaps Basil, too, had his secret. He would ask him and try.

"Basil," he said, coming over quite close, and looking him straight in the face, "we have each of us a secret. Let me know yours, and I will tell you mine. What was your reason for refusing to exhibit my picture?"

Hallward shuddered in spite of himself. "Dorian, if I told you, you might like me less than you do, and you would certainly laugh at me. I could not bear your doing either of those two things. If you wish me never to look at your picture again, I am content. I have always you to look at. If you wish the best work I have ever done to be hidden from the world, I am satisfied. Your friendship is dearer to me than any fame or reputation."

"No, Basil, you must tell me," murmured Dorian Gray. "I think I have a right to know." His feeling of terror had passed away, and curiosity had taken its place. He was determined to find out Basil Hallward's mystery.

"Let us sit down, Dorian," said Hallward, looking pale and pained. "Let us sit down. I will sit in the shadow, and you shall sit in the sunlight. Our lives are like that. Just answer me one question. Have you noticed in the picture something that you did not like?—something that probably at first did not strike you, but that revealed itself to you suddenly?"

"Basil!" cried the lad, clutching the arms of his chair with trembling hands, and gazing at him with wild, startled eyes.

"I see you did. Don't speak. Wait till you hear what I have to say. It is quite true that I have worshipped you with far more romance of feeling than a man usually gives to a friend. Somehow, I had never loved a woman. I suppose I never had time. Perhaps, as Harry says, a really

*'grande passion'* is the privilege of those who have nothing
to do, and that is the use of the idle classes in a country.
Well, from the moment I met you, your personality had
the most extraordinary influence over me. I quite admit
that I adored you madly, extravagantly, absurdly. I was
jealous of every one to whom you spoke. I wanted to have
you all to myself. I was only happy when I was with you.
When I was away from you, you were still present in my
art. It was all wrong and foolish. It is all wrong and foolish still. Of course I never let you know anything about
this. It would have been impossible. You would not have
understood it; I did not understand it myself. One day I
determined to paint a wonderful portrait of you. It was to
have been my masterpiece. It is my masterpiece. But, as I
worked at it, every flake and film of color seemed to me to
reveal my secret. I grew afraid that the world would know
of my idolatry. I felt, Dorian, that I had told too much.
Then it was that I resolved never to allow the picture to be
exhibited. You were a little annoyed; but then you did not
realize all that it meant to me. Harry, to whom I talked
about it, laughed at me. But I did not mind that. When
the picture was finished, and I sat alone with it, I felt that
I was right. Well, after a few days the portrait left my studio, and as soon as I had got rid of the intolerable fascination of its presence it seemed to me that I had been foolish
in imagining that I had said anything in it, more than that
you were extremely good-looking and that I could paint.
Even now I cannot help feeling that it is a mistake to think
that the passion one feels in creation is ever really shown
in the work one creates. Art is more abstract than we
fancy. Form and color tell us of form and color,—that is
all. It often seems to me that art conceals the artist far
more completely than it ever reveals him. And so when
I got this offer from Paris I determined to make your
portrait the principal thing in my exhibition. It never

occurred to me that you would refuse. I see now that you were right. The picture must not be shown. You must not be angry with me, Dorian, for what I have told you. As I said to Harry, once, you are made to be worshipped."

Dorian Gray drew a long breath. The color came back to his cheeks, and a smile played about his lips. The peril was over. He was safe for the time. Yet he could not help feeling infinite pity for the young man who had just made this strange confession to him. He wondered if he would ever be so dominated by the personality of a friend. Lord Harry had the charm of being very dangerous. But that was all. He was too clever and too cynical to be really fond of. Would there ever be some one who would fill him with a strange idolatry? Was that one of the things that life had in store?

"It is extraordinary to me, Dorian," said Hallward, "that you should have seen this in the picture. Did you really see it?"

"Of course I did."

"Well, you don't mind my looking at it now?"

Dorian shook his head. "You must not ask me that, Basil. I could not possibly let you stand in front of that picture."

"You will some day, surely?"

"Never."

"Well, perhaps you are right. And now good-by, Dorian. You have been the one person in my life of whom I have been really fond. I don't suppose I shall often see you again. You don't know what it cost me to tell you all that I have told you."

"My dear Basil," cried Dorian, "what have you told me? Simply that you felt that you liked me too much. That is not even a compliment."

"It was not intended as a compliment. It was a confession."

"A very disappointing one."

"Why, what did you expect, Dorian? You didn't see anything else in the picture, did you? There was nothing else to see?"

"No: there was nothing else to see. Why do you ask? But you mustn't talk about not meeting me again, or anything of that kind. You and I are friends, Basil, and we must always remain so."

"You have got Harry," said Hallward, sadly.

"Oh, Harry!" cried the lad, with a ripple of laughter. "Harry spends his days in saying what is incredible, and his evenings in doing what is improbable. Just the sort of life I would like to lead. But still I don't think I would go to Harry if I was in trouble. I would sooner go to you, Basil."

"But you won't sit to me again?"

"Impossible!"

"You spoil my life as an artist by refusing, Dorian. No man comes across two ideal things. Few come across one."

"I can't explain it to you, Basil, but I must never sit to you again. I will come and have tea with you. That will be just as pleasant."

"Pleasanter for you, I am afraid," murmured Hallward, regretfully. "And now good-by. I am sorry you won't let me look at the picture once again. But that can't be helped. I quite understand what you feel about it."

As he left the room, Dorian Gray smiled to himself. Poor Basil! how little he knew of the true reason! And how strange it was that, instead of having been forced to reveal his own secret, he had succeeded, almost by chance, in wresting a secret from his friend! How much that strange confession explained to him! Basil's absurd fits of jealousy, his wild devotion, his extravagant panegyrics, his curious reticences,—he understood them all now, and he felt sorry.

There was something tragic in a friendship so colored by romance.

He sighed, and touched the bell. The portrait must be hidden away at all costs. He could not run such a risk of discovery again. It had been mad of him to have the thing remain, even for an hour, in a room to which any of his friends had access.

## Chapter VIII

When his servant entered, he looked at him steadfastly, and wondered if he had thought of peering behind the screen. The man was quite impassive, and waited for his orders. Dorian lit a cigarette, and walked over to the glass and glanced into it. He could see the reflection of Victor's face perfectly. It was like a placid mask of servility. There was nothing to be afraid of, there. Yet he thought it best to be on his guard.

Speaking very slowly, he told him to tell the house-keeper that he wanted to see her, and then to go to the frame-maker's and ask him to send two of his men round at once. It seemed to him that as the man left the room he peered in the direction of the screen. Or was that only his fancy?

After a few moments, Mrs. Leaf, a dear old lady in a black silk dress, with a photograph of the late Mr. Leaf framed in a large gold brooch at her neck, and old-fashioned thread mittens on her wrinkled hands, bustled into the room.

"Well, Master Dorian," she said, "what can I do for you? I beg your pardon, sir,"—here came a courtesy,—"I shouldn't call you Master Dorian any more. But, Lord bless you, sir, I have known you since you were a baby, and many's the trick you've played on poor old Leaf. Not that you were not always a good boy, sir; but boys will be boys, Master Dorian, and jam is a temptation to the young, isn't it, sir?"

He laughed. "You must always call me Master Dorian, Leaf. I will be very angry with you if you don't. And I assure you I am quite as fond of jam now as I used to be. Only when I am asked out to tea I am never offered any. I want you to give me the key of the room at the top of the house."

"The old school-room, Master Dorian? Why, it's full of dust. I must get it arranged and put straight before you go into it. It's not fit for you to see, Master Dorian. It is not, indeed."

"I don't want it put straight, Leaf. I only want the key."

"Well, Master Dorian, you'll be covered with cobwebs if you goes into it. Why, it hasn't been opened for nearly five years,—not since his lordship died."

He winced at the mention of his dead uncle's name. He had hateful memories of him. "That does not matter, Leaf," he replied. "All I want is the key."

"And here is the key, Master Dorian," said the old lady, after going over the contents of her bunch with tremulous-ly uncertain hands. "Here is the key. I'll have it off the ring in a moment. But you don't think of living up there, Master Dorian, and you so comfortable here?"

"No, Leaf, I don't. I merely want to see the place, and perhaps store something in it,—that is all. Thank you, Leaf. I hope your rheumatism is better; and mind you send me up jam for breakfast."

Mrs. Leaf shook her head. "Them foreigners doesn't understand jam, Master Dorian. They calls it 'compot.' But I'll bring it to you myself some morning, if you lets me."

"That will be very kind of you, Leaf," he answered, looking at the key; and, having made him an elaborate courtesy, the old lady left the room, her face wreathed in smiles. She had a strong objection to the French valet. It was a poor thing, she felt, for any one to be born a foreigner.

As the door closed, Dorian put the key in his pocket, and looked round the room. His eye fell on a large purple satin coverlet heavily embroidered with gold, a splendid piece of late seventeenth-century Venetian work that his uncle had found in a convent near Bologna. Yes, that would serve to wrap the dreadful thing in. It had perhaps served often as a pall for the dead. Now it was to hide something that had a corruption of its own, worse than the corruption of death itself,—something that would breed horrors and yet would never die. What the worm was to the corpse, his sins would be to the painted image on the canvas. They would mar its beauty, and eat away its grace. They would defile it, and make it shameful. And yet the thing would still live on. It would be always alive.

He shuddered, and for a moment he regretted that he had not told Basil the true reason why he had wished to hide the picture away. Basil would have helped him to resist Lord Henry's influence, and the still more poisonous influences that came from his own temperament. The love that he bore him—for it was really love—had something noble and intellectual in it. It was not that mere physical admiration of beauty that is born of the senses, and that dies when the senses tire. It was such love as Michael Angelo had known, and Montaigne, and Winckelmann, and Shakespeare himself. Yes, Basil could have saved him. But it was too late now. The past could always be annihilated. Regret, denial, or forgetfulness could do that. But the future was inevitable. There were passions in him that would find their terrible outlet, dreams that would make the shadow of their evil real.

He took up from the couch the great purple-and-gold texture that covered it, and, holding it in his hands, passed behind the screen. Was the face on the canvas viler than before? It seemed to him that it was unchanged; and yet his loathing of it was intensified. Gold hair, blue eyes, and rose-red lips,—they all were there. It was simply the expression that had altered. That was horrible in its cruelty. Compared to what he saw in it of censure or rebuke, how shallow Basil's reproaches about Sibyl Vane had been!— how shallow, and of what little account! His own soul was looking out at him from the canvas and calling him to judgment. A look of pain came across him, and he flung the rich pall over the picture. As he did so, a knock came to the door. He passed out as his servant entered.

"The persons are here, monsieur."

He felt that the man must be got rid of at once. He must not be allowed to know where the picture was being taken to. There was something sly about him, and he had thoughtful, treacherous eyes. Sitting down at the writing-table, he scribbled a note to Lord Henry, asking him to send him round something to read, and reminding him that they were to meet at eight-fifteen that evening.

"Wait for an answer," he said, handing it to him, "and show the men in here."

In two or three minutes there was another knock, and Mr. Ashton himself, the celebrated frame-maker of South Audley Street, came in with a somewhat rough-looking young assistant. Mr. Ashton was a florid, red-whiskered little man, whose admiration for art was considerably tempered by the inveterate impecuniosity of most of the artists who dealt with him. As a rule, he never left his shop. He waited for people to come to him. But he always made an exception in favor of Dorian Gray. There was something about Dorian that charmed everybody. It was a pleasure even to see him.

"What can I do for you, Mr. Gray?" he said, rubbing his fat freckled hands. "I thought I would do myself the honor of coming round in person. I have just got a beauty of a frame, sir. Picked it up at a sale. Old Florentine. Came from Fonthill, I believe. Admirably suited for a religious picture, Mr. Gray."

"I am so sorry you have given yourself the trouble of coming round, Mr. Ashton. I will certainly drop in and look at the frame,—though I don't go in much for religious art,—but today I only want a picture carried to the top of the house for me. It is rather heavy, so I thought I would ask you to lend me a couple of your men."

"No trouble at all, Mr. Gray. I am delighted to be of any service to you. Which is the work of art, sir?"

"This," replied Dorian, moving the screen back. "Can you move it, covering and all, just as it is? I don't want it to get scratched going up-stairs."

"There will be no difficulty, sir," said the genial frame-maker, beginning, with the aid of his assistant, to unhook the picture from the long brass chains by which it was suspended. "And, now, where shall we carry it to, Mr. Gray?"

"I will show you the way, Mr. Ashton, if you will kindly follow me. Or perhaps you had better go in front. I am afraid it is right at the top of the house. We will go up by the front staircase, as it is wider."

He held the door open for them, and they passed out into the hall and began the ascent. The elaborate character of the frame had made the picture extremely bulky, and now and then, in spite of the obsequious protests of Mr. Ashton, who had a true tradesman's dislike of seeing a gentleman doing anything useful, Dorian put his hand to it so as to help them.

"Something of a load to carry, sir," gasped the little man, when they reached the top landing. And he wiped his shiny forehead.

"A terrible load to carry," murmured Dorian, as he unlocked the door that opened into the room that was to keep for him the curious secret of his life and hide his soul from the eyes of men.

He had not entered the place for more than four years,— not, indeed, since he had used it first as a play-room when he was a child and then as a study when he grew somewhat older. It was a large, well-proportioned room, which had been specially built by the last Lord Sherard for the use of the little nephew whom, being himself childless, and perhaps for other reasons, he had always hated and desired to keep at a distance. It did not appear to Dorian to have much changed. There was the huge Italian *cassone,* with its fantastically-painted panels and its tarnished gilt moldings, in which he had so often hidden himself as a boy. There was the satinwood bookcase filled with his dog-eared school-books. On the wall behind it was hanging the same ragged Flemish tapestry where a faded king and queen were playing chess in a garden, while a company of hawkers rode by, carrying hooded birds on their gauntleted wrists. How well he recalled it all! Every moment of his lonely childhood came back to him, as he looked round. He remembered the stainless purity of his boyish life, and it seemed horrible to him that it was here that the fatal portrait was to be hidden away. How little he had thought, in those dead days, of all that was in store for him!

But there was no other place in the house so secure from prying eyes as this. He had the key, and no one else could enter it. Beneath its purple pall, the face painted on the canvas could grow bestial, sodden, and unclean. What did it matter? No one could see it. He himself would not see it. Why should he watch the hideous corruption of his soul? He kept his youth,—that was enough. And, besides, might not his nature grow finer, after all? There was no reason that the future should be so full of shame. Some love might come across his life, and purify him, and shield him from those sins that seemed to be already stirring in spirit and in flesh,—those curious unpictured sins whose very mystery lent them their subtlety and their charm. Perhaps, some day, the cruel look would have passed away from the scarlet sensitive mouth, and he might show to the world Basil Hallward's masterpiece.

No; that was impossible. The thing upon the canvas was growing old, hour by hour, and week by week. Even if it escaped the hideousness of sin, the hideousness of age was in store for it. The cheeks would become hollow or flaccid. Yellow crow's-feet would creep round the fading eyes and make them horrible. The hair would lose its brightness, the mouth would gape or droop, would be foolish or gross, as the mouths of old men are. There would be the wrinkled throat, the cold blue-veined hands, the twisted body, that he remembered in the uncle who had been so stern to him in his boyhood. The picture had to be concealed. There was no help for it.

"Bring it in, Mr. Ashton, please," he said, wearily, turning round. "I am sorry I kept you so long. I was thinking of something else."

"Always glad to have a rest, Mr. Gray," answered the frame-maker, who was still gasping for breath. "Where shall we put it, sir?"

"Oh, anywhere, Here, this will do. I don't want to have it hung up. Just lean it against the wall. Thanks."

"Might one look at the work of art, sir?"

Dorian started. "It would not interest you, Mr. Ashton," he said, keeping his eye on the man. He felt ready to leap upon him and fling him to the ground if he dared to lift the gorgeous hanging that concealed the secret of his life. "I won't trouble you any more now. I am much obliged for your kindness in coming round."

"Not at all, not at all, Mr. Gray. Ever ready to do anything for you, sir." And Mr. Ashton tramped down-stairs, followed by the assistant, who glanced back at Dorian with a look of shy wonder in his rough, uncomely face. He had never seen any one so marvellous.

When the sound of their footsteps had died away, Dorian locked the door, and put the key in his pocket. He felt safe now. No one would ever look on the horrible thing. No eye but his would ever see his shame.

On reaching the library he found that it was just after five o'clock, and that the tea had been already brought up. On a little table of dark perfumed wood thickly incrusted with nacre, a present from his guardian's wife, Lady Radley, who had spent the preceding winter in Cairo, was lying a note from Lord Henry, and beside it was a book bound in yellow paper, the cover slightly torn and the edges soiled. A copy of the third edition of the *St. James's Gazette* had been placed on the tea-tray. It was evident that Victor had returned. He wondered if he had met the men in the hall as they were leaving the house and had wormed out of them what they had been doing. He would be sure to miss the picture,—had no doubt missed it already, while he had been laying the tea-things. The screen had not been replaced, and the blank space on the wall was visible. Perhaps some night he might find him creeping up-stairs and trying to force the door of the room. It was a horrible thing to have a spy in one's house. He had heard of rich men who had been blackmailed all their lives by some servant who had read a letter, or overheard a conversation, or picked up a card with an address, or found beneath a pillow a withered flower or a bit of crumpled lace.

He sighed, and, having poured himself out some tea, opened Lord Henry's note. It was simply to say that he sent him round the evening paper, and a book that might interest him, and that he would be at the club at eight-fifteen. He opened the *St. James's* languidly, and looked through it. A red pencil-mark on the fifth page caught his eye. He read the following paragraph:

"INQUEST ON AN ACTRESS.—An inquest was held this morning at the Bell Tavern, Hoxton Road, by Mr. Danby, the District Coroner, on the body of Sibyl Vane, a young actress recently engaged at the Royal Theatre, Holborn. A verdict of death by misadventure was returned. Considerable sympathy was expressed for the mother of the deceased, who was greatly affected during the giving of her own evidence, and that of Dr. Birrell, who had made the post-mortem examination of the deceased."

He frowned slightly, and, tearing the paper in two, went across the room and flung the pieces into a gilt basket. How ugly it all was! And how horribly real ugliness made things! He felt a little annoyed with Lord Henry for having sent him the account. And it was certainly stupid of him to have marked it with red pencil. Victor might have read it. The man knew more than enough English for that.

Perhaps he had read it, and had begun to suspect something. And, yet, what did it matter? What had Dorian Gray to do with Sibyl Vane's death? There was nothing to fear. Dorian Gray had not killed her.

His eye fell on the yellow book that Lord Henry had sent him. What was it, he wondered. He went towards the little pearl-colored octagonal stand, that had always looked to him like the work of some strange Egyptian bees who wrought in silver, and took the volume up. He flung himself into an arm-chair, and began to turn over the leaves. After a few minutes, he became absorbed. It was the strangest book he had ever read. It seemed to him that in exquisite raiment, and to the delicate sound of flutes, the sins of the world were passing in dumb show before him. Things that he had dimly dreamed of were suddenly made real to him. Things of which he had never dreamed were gradually revealed.

It was a novel without a plot, and with only one character, being, indeed, simply a psychological study of a certain young Parisian, who spent his life trying to realize in the nineteenth century all the passions and modes of thought that belonged to every century except his own, and to sum up, as it were, in himself the various moods through which the world-spirit had ever passed, loving for their mere artificiality those renunciations that men have unwisely called virtue, as much as those natural rebellions that wise men still call sin. The style in which it was written was that curious jeweled style, vivid and obscure at once, full of argot and of archaisms, of technical expressions and of elaborate paraphrases, that characterizes the work of some of the finest artists of the French school of *Décadents*. There were in it metaphors as monstrous as orchids, and as evil in color. The life of the senses was described in the terms of mystical philosophy. One hardly knew at times whether one was reading the spiritual ecstasies of some mediaeval saint or the morbid confessions of a modern sinner. It was a poisonous book. The heavy odor of incense seemed to cling about its pages and to trouble the brain. The mere cadence of the sentences, the subtle monotony of their music, so full as it was of complex refrains and movements elaborately repeated, produced in the mind of the lad, as he passed from chapter to chapter, a form of revery, a malady of dreaming, that made him unconscious of the falling day and the creeping shadows.

Cloudless, and pierced by one solitary star, a copper-green sky gleamed through the windows. He read on by its wan light till he could read no more. Then, after his valet had reminded him several times of the lateness of the hour, he got up, and, going into the next room, placed the book on the little Florentine table that always stood at his bedside, and began to dress for dinner.

It was almost nine o'clock before he reached the club, where he found Lord Henry sitting alone, in the morning-room, looking very bored.

"I am so sorry, Harry," he cried, "but really it is entirely your fault. That book you sent me so fascinated me that I forgot what the time was."

"I thought you would like it," replied his host, rising from his chair.

"I didn't say I liked it, Harry. I said it fascinated me. There is a great difference."

"Ah, if you have discovered that, you have discovered a great deal," murmured Lord Henry, with his curious smile. "Come, let us go in to dinner. It is dreadfully late, and I am afraid the champagne will be too much iced."

Chapter IX

For years, Dorian Gray could not free himself from the memory of this book. Or perhaps it would be more accurate to say that he never sought to free himself from it. He procured from Paris no less than five large-paper copies of the first edition, and had them bound in different colors, so that they might suit his various moods and the changing fancies of a nature over which he seemed, at times, to have almost entirely lost control. The hero, the wonderful young Parisian, in whom the romantic temperament and the scientific temperament were so strangely blended, became to him a kind of prefiguring type of himself. And, indeed, the whole book seemed to him to contain the story of his own life, written before he had lived it.

In one point he was more fortunate than the book's fantastic hero. He never knew—never, indeed, had any cause to know—that somewhat grotesque dread of mirrors, and polished metal surfaces, and still water, which came upon the young Parisian so early in his life, and was occasioned by the sudden decay of a beauty that had once, apparently, been so remarkable. It was with an almost cruel joy—and perhaps in nearly every joy, as certainly in every pleasure, cruelty has its place—that he used to read the latter part of the book, with its really tragic, if somewhat overemphasized, account of the sorrow and despair of one who had himself lost what in others, and in the world, he had most valued.

He, at any rate, had no cause to fear that. The boyish beauty that had so fascinated Basil Hallward, and many others besides him, seemed never to leave him. Even those who had heard the most evil things against him (and from time to time strange rumors about his mode of life crept through London and became the chatter of the clubs) could not believe anything to his dishonor when they saw him. He had always the look of one who had kept himself unspotted from the world. Men who talked grossly became silent when Dorian Gray entered the room. There was something in the purity of his face that rebuked them. His mere presence seemed to recall to them the innocence that they had tarnished. They wondered how one so charming and graceful as he was could have escaped the stain of an age that was at once sordid and sensuous.

He himself, on returning home from one of those mysterious and prolonged absences that gave rise to such strange conjecture among those who were his friends, or thought that they were so, would creep up-stairs to the locked room, open the door with the key that never left him, and stand, with a mirror, in front of the portrait that Basil Hallward had painted of him, looking now at the evil and aging face on the canvas, and now at the fair young face that laughed back at him from the polished glass. The very sharpness of the contrast used to quicken his sense of pleasure. He grew more and more enamored of his own beauty, more and more interested in the corruption of his own soul. He would examine with minute care, and often with a monstrous and terrible delight, the hideous lines that seared the wrinkling forehead or crawled around the heavy sensual mouth, wondering sometimes which were the more horrible, the signs of sin or the signs of age. He would place his white hands beside the coarse bloated hands of the picture, and smile. He mocked the misshapen body and the failing limbs.

There were moments, indeed, at night, when, lying sleepless in his own delicately-scented chamber, or in the sordid room of the little ill-famed tavern near the Docks, which, under an assumed name, and in disguise, it was his habit to frequent, he would think of the ruin he had brought upon his soul, with a pity that was all the more poignant because it was purely selfish. But moments such as these were rare. That curiosity about life that, many years before, Lord Henry had first stirred in him, as they sat together in the garden of their friend, seemed to increase with gratification. The more he knew, the more he desired to know. He had mad hungers that grew more ravenous as he fed them.

Yet he was not really reckless, at any rate in his relations to society. Once or twice every month during the winter, and on each Wednesday evening while the season lasted, he would throw open to the world his beautiful house and have the most celebrated musicians of the day to charm his guests with the wonders of their art. His little dinners, in the settling of which Lord Henry always assisted him, were noted as much for the careful selection and placing of those invited, as for the exquisite taste shown in the decoration of the table, with its subtle symphonic arrangements of exotic flowers, and embroidered cloths, and antique plate of gold and silver. Indeed, there

were many, especially among the very young men, who
saw, or fancied that they saw, in Dorian Gray the true realization of a type of which they had often dreamed in Eton
or Oxford days, a type that was to combine something
of the real culture of the scholar with all the grace and
distinction and perfect manner of a citizen of the world.
To them he seemed to belong to those whom Dante describes as having sought to "make themselves perfect by
the worship of beauty." Like Gautier, he was one for whom
"the visible world existed."

And, certainly, to him life itself was the first, the greatest, of the arts, and for it all the other arts seemed to be
but a preparation. Fashion, by which what is really fantastic becomes for a moment universal, and Dandyism,
which, in its own way, is an attempt to assert the absolute
modernity of beauty, had, of course, their fascination for
him. His mode of dressing, and the particular styles that
he affected from time to time, had their marked influence
on the young exquisites of the Mayfair balls and Pall Mall
club windows, who copied him in everything that he did,
and tried to reproduce the accidental charm of his graceful, though to him only half-serious, fopperies.

For, while he was but too ready to accept the position
that was almost immediately offered to him on his coming
of age, and found, indeed, a subtle pleasure in the thought
that he might really become to the London of his own day
what to imperial Neronian Rome the author of the "Satyr-
icon" had once been, yet in his inmost heart he desired to
be something more than a mere *arbiter elegantiarum,* to
be consulted on the wearing of a jewel, or the knotting of
a necktie, or the conduct of a cane. He sought to elaborate some new scheme of life that would have its reasoned
philosophy and its ordered principles and find in the spir-
itualizing of the senses its highest realization.

The worship of the senses has often, and with much justice, been decried, men feeling a natural instinct of terror about passions and sensations that seem stronger than ourselves, and that we are conscious of sharing with the less highly organized forms of existence. But it appeared to Dorian Gray that the true nature of the senses had never been understood, and that they had remained savage and animal merely because the world had sought to starve them into submission or to kill them by pain, instead of aiming at making them elements of a new spirituality, of which a fine instinct for beauty was to be the dominant characteristic. As he looked back upon man moving through History, he was haunted by a feeling of loss. So much had been surrendered! and to such little purpose! There had been mad willful rejections, monstrous forms of self-torture and self-denial, whose origin was fear, and whose result was a degradation infinitely more terrible than that fancied degradation from which, in their ignorance, they had sought to escape, Nature in her wonderful irony driving the anchorite out to herd with the wild animals of the desert and giving to the hermit the beasts of the field as his companions.

Yes, there was to be, as Lord Henry had prophesied, a new hedonism that was to re-create life, and to save it from that harsh, uncomely puritanism that is having, in our own day, its curious revival. It was to have its service of the intellect, certainly; yet it was never to accept any theory or system that would involve the sacrifice of any mode of passionate experience. Its aim, indeed, was to be experience itself, and not the fruits of experience, sweet or bitter as they might be. Of the asceticism that deadens the senses, as of the vulgar profligacy that dulls them, it was to know nothing. But it was to teach man to concentrate himself upon the moments of a life that is itself but a moment.

There are few of us who have not sometimes wakened before dawn, either after one of those dreamless nights that make one almost enamored of death, or one of those nights of horror and misshapen joy, when through the chambers of the brain sweep phantoms more terrible than reality itself, and instinct with that vivid life that lurks in all grotesques, and that lends to Gothic art its enduring vitality, this art being, one might fancy, especially the art of those whose minds have been troubled with the malady of revery. Gradually white fingers creep through the curtains, and they appear to tremble. Black fantastic shadows crawl into the corners of the room, and crouch there. Outside, there is the stirring of birds among the leaves, or the sound of men going forth to their work, or the sigh and sob of the wind coming down from the hills, and wandering round the silent house, as though it feared to wake the sleepers. Veil after veil of thin dusky gauze is lifted, and by degrees the forms and colors of things are restored to them, and we watch the dawn remaking the world in its antique pattern. The wan mirrors get back their mimic life. The flameless tapers stand where we have left them, and beside them lies the half-read book that we had been studying, or the wired flower that we had worn at the ball, or the letter that we had been afraid to read, or that we had read too often. Nothing seems to us changed. Out of the unreal shadows of the night comes back the real life that we had known. We have to resume it where we had left off, and there steals over us a terrible sense of the necessity for the continuance of energy in the same wearisome round of stereotyped habits, or a wild longing, it may be, that our eyelids might open some morning upon a world that had been re-fashioned anew for our pleasure in the darkness, a world in which things would have fresh shapes and colors, and be changed, or have other secrets, a world in which the past would have little or no place, or survive, at any rate, in no conscious form of obligation or regret, the remembrance even of joy having its bitterness, and the memories of pleasure their pain.

It was the creation of such worlds as these that seemed to Dorian Gray to be the true object, or among the true objects, of life; and in his search for sensations that would be at once new and delightful, and possess that element of strangeness that is so essential to romance, he would often adopt certain modes of thought that he knew to be really alien to his nature, abandon himself to their subtle influences, and then, having, as it were, caught their color and satisfied his intellectual curiosity, leave them with that curious indifference that is not incompatible with a real ardor of temperament, and that indeed, according to certain modern psychologists, is often a condition of it.

It was rumored of him once that he was about to join the Roman Catholic communion; and certainly the Roman ritual had always a great attraction for him. The daily sacrifice, more awful really than all the sacrifices of the antique world, stirred him as much by its superb rejection of the evidence of the senses as by the primitive simplicity of its elements and the eternal pathos of the human trage-dy that it sought to symbolize. He loved to kneel down on the cold marble pavement, and with the priest, in his stiff flowered cope, slowly and with white hands moving aside the veil of the tabernacle, and raising aloft the jeweled lantern-shaped monstrance with that pallid wafer that at times, one would fain think, is indeed the "panis caeles-tis," the bread of angels, or, robed in the garments of the Passion of Christ, breaking the Host into the chalice, and smiting his breast for his sins. The fuming censers, that the grave boys, in their lace and scarlet, tossed into the air like great gilt flowers, had their subtle fascination for him. As he passed out, he used to look with wonder at the black confessionals, and long to sit in the dim shadow

of one of them and listen to men and women whispering
through the tarnished grating the true story of their lives.

But he never fell into the error of arresting his intellectual development by any formal acceptance of creed or
system, or of mistaking, for a house in which to live, an
inn that is but suitable for the sojourn of a night, or for
a few hours of a night in which there are no stars and the
moon is in travail. Mysticism, with its marvelous power of
making common things strange to us, and the subtle anti-
nomianism that always seems to accompany it, moved him
for a season; and for a season he inclined to the materialistic doctrines of the *Darwinismus* movement in Germany,
and found a curious pleasure in tracing the thoughts and
passions of men to some pearly cell in the brain, or some
white nerve in the body, delighting in the conception of
the absolute dependence of the spirit on certain physical
conditions, morbid or healthy, normal or diseased. Yet, as
has been said of him before, no theory of life seemed to
him to be of any importance compared with life itself. He
felt keenly conscious of how barren all intellectual speculation is when separated from action and experiment. He
knew that the senses, no less than the soul, have their
mysteries to reveal.

And so he would now study perfumes, and the secrets
of their manufacture, distilling heavily-scented oils, and
burning odorous gums from the East. He saw that there
was no mood of the mind that had not its counterpart in
the sensuous life, and set himself to discover their true
relations, wondering what there was in frankincense that
made one mystical, and in ambergris that stirred one's
passions, and in violets that woke the memory of dead
romances, and in musk that troubled the brain, and in
champak that stained the imagination; and seeking often
to elaborate a real psychology of perfumes, and to estimate
the several influences of sweet-smelling roots, and scented

pollen-laden flowers, of aromatic balms, and of dark and fragrant woods, of spikenard that sickens, of hovenia that makes men mad, and of aloes that are said to be able to expel melancholy from the soul.

At another time he devoted himself entirely to music, and in a long latticed room, with a vermilion-and-gold ceiling and walls of olive-green lacquer, he used to give curious concerts in which mad gypsies tore wild music from little zithers, or grave yellow-shawled Tunisians plucked at the strained strings of monstrous lutes, while grinning negroes beat monotonously upon copper drums, or tur-baned Indians, crouching upon scarlet mats, blew through long pipes of reed or brass, and charmed, or feigned to charm, great hooded snakes and horrible horned adders. The harsh intervals and shrill discords of barbaric music stirred him at times when Schubert's grace, and Chopin's beautiful sorrows, and the mighty harmonies of Beethoven himself, fell unheeded on his ear. He collected together from all parts of the world the strangest instruments that could be found, either in the tombs of dead nations or among the few savage tribes that have survived contact with Western civilizations, and loved to touch and try them. He had the mysterious *juruparis* of the Rio Negro Indians, that women are not allowed to look at, and that even youths may not see till they have been subjected to fasting and scourging, and the earthen jars of the Peruvians that have the shrill cries of birds, and flutes of human bones such as Alfonso de Ovalle heard in Chili, and the sonorous green stones that are found near Cuzco and give forth a note of singular sweetness. He had painted gourds filled with pebbles that rattled when they were shaken; the long *clarin* of the Mexicans, into which the performer does not blow, but through which he inhales the air; the harsh *turé* of the Amazon tribes, that is sounded by the sentinels who sit all day long in trees, and that can be heard, it is said, at a distance of three leagues; the *teponaztli,* that has two vibrating tongues of wood, and is beaten with sticks that are smeared with an elastic gum obtained from the milky juice of plants; the *yotl*-bells of the Aztecs, that are hung in clusters like grapes; and a huge cylindrical drum, covered with the skins of great serpents, like the one that Bernal Diaz saw when he went with Cortes into the Mexican temple, and of whose doleful sound he has left us so vivid a description. The fantastic character of these instruments fascinated him, and he felt a curious delight in the thought that Art, like Nature, has her monsters, things of bestial shape and with hideous voices. Yet, after some time, he wearied of them, and would sit in his box at the Opera, either alone or with Lord Henry, listening in rapt pleasure to "Tannhäuser," and seeing in that great work of art a presentation of the tragedy of his own soul.

On another occasion he took up the study of jewels, and appeared at a costume ball as Anne de Joyeuse, Admiral of France, in a dress covered with five hundred and sixty pearls. He would often spend a whole day settling and resettling in their cases the various stones that he had collected, such as the olive-green chrysoberyl that turns red by lamplight, the cymophane with its wire-like line of silver, the pistachio-colored peridot, rose-pink and wine-yellow topazes, carbuncles of fiery scarlet with tremulous four-rayed stars, flame-red cinnamon-stones, orange and violet spinels, and amethysts with their alternate layers of ruby and sapphire. He loved the red gold of the sunstone, and the moonstone's pearly whiteness, and the broken rainbow of the milky opal. He procured from Amsterdam three emeralds of extraordinary size and richness of color, and had a turquoise *de la vieille roche* that was the envy of all the connoisseurs.

He discovered wonderful stories, also, about jewels. In Alphonso's *Clericalis Disciplina* a serpent was mentioned with eyes of real jacinth, and in the romantic history of Alexander he was said to have found snakes in the vale of Jordan "with collars of real emeralds growing on their backs." There was a gem in the brain of the dragon, Philostratus told us, and "by the exhibition of golden letters and a scarlet robe" the monster could be thrown into a magical sleep, and slain. According to the great alchemist Pierre de Boniface, the diamond rendered a man invisible, and the agate of India made him eloquent. The cornelian appeased anger, and the hyacinth provoked sleep, and the amethyst drove away the fumes of wine. The garnet cast out demons, and the hydropicus deprived the moon of her color. The selenite waxed and waned with the moon, and the meloceus, that discovers thieves, could be affected only by the blood of kids. Leonardus Camillus had seen a white stone taken from the brain of a newly-killed toad, that was a certain antidote against poison. The bezoar, that was found in the heart of the Arabian deer, was a charm that could cure the plague. In the nests of Arabian birds was the aspilates, that, according to Democritus, kept the wearer from any danger by fire.

The King of Ceilan rode through his city with a large ruby in his hand, as the ceremony of his coronation. The gates of the palace of John the Priest were "made of sardius, with the horn of the horned snake inwrought, so that no man might bring poison within." Over the gable were "two golden apples, in which were two carbuncles," so that the gold might shine by day, and the carbuncles by night. In Lodge's strange romance *A Margarite of America* it was stated that in the chamber of Margarite were seen "all the chaste ladies of the world, inchased out of silver, looking through fair mirrours of chrysolites, carbuncles, sapphires, and greene emeraults." Marco Polo had watched the inhabitants of Zipangu place a rose-colored pearl in the mouth of the dead. A sea-monster had been enamoured

of the pearl that the diver brought to King Perozes, and
had slain the thief, and mourned for seven moons over his
loss. When the Huns lured the king into the great pit, he
flung it away,—Procopius tells the story,—nor was it ever
found again, though the Emperor Anastasius offered five
hundred-weight of gold pieces for it. The King of Malabar
had shown a Venetian a rosary of one hundred and four
pearls, one for every god that he worshipped.

When the Duke de Valentinois, son of Alexander VI.,
visited Louis XII. of France, his horse was loaded with
gold leaves, according to Brantôme, and his cap had double rows of rubies that threw out a great light. Charles of
England had ridden in stirrups hung with three hundred
and twenty-one diamonds. Richard II. had a coat, valued
at thirty thousand marks, which was covered with balas
rubies. Hall described Henry VIII., on his way to the
Tower previous to his coronation, as wearing "a jacket of
raised gold, the placard embroidered with diamonds and
other rich stones, and a great bauderike about his neck of
large balasses." The favorites of James I. wore ear-rings
of emeralds set in gold filigrane. Edward II. gave to Piers
Gaveston a suit of red-gold armor studded with jacinths,
and a collar of gold roses set with turquoise-stones, and
a skull-cap *parsemé* with pearls. Henry II. wore jeweled
gloves reaching to the elbow, and had a hawk-glove set
with twelve rubies and fifty-two great pearls. The ducal
hat of Charles the Rash, the last Duke of Burgundy of
his race, was studded with sapphires and hung with pear-
shaped pearls.

How exquisite life had once been! How gorgeous in its
pomp and decoration! Even to read of the luxury of the
dead was wonderful.

Then he turned his attention to embroideries, and to
the tapestries that performed the office of frescos in the

chill rooms of the Northern nations of Europe. As he inves-
tigated the subject,—and he always had an extraordinary
faculty of becoming absolutely absorbed for the moment
in whatever he took up,—he was almost saddened by the
reflection of the ruin that time brought on beautiful and
wonderful things. He, at any rate, had escaped that. Summer followed summer, and the yellow jonquils bloomed
and died many times, and nights of horror repeated the
story of their shame, but he was unchanged. No winter
marred his face or stained his flower-like bloom. How different it was with material things! Where had they gone
to? Where was the great crocus-colored robe, on which the
gods fought against the giants, that had been worked for
Athena? Where the huge velarium that Nero had stretched
across the Colosseum at Rome, on which were represented
the starry sky, and Apollo driving a chariot drawn by white
gilt-reined steeds? He longed to see the curious table-nap-
kins wrought for Elagabalus, on which were displayed all
the dainties and viands that could be wanted for a feast;
the mortuary cloth of King Chilperic, with its three hundred golden bees; the fantastic robes that excited the indignation of the Bishop of Pontus, and were figured with
"lions, panthers, bears, dogs, forests, rocks, hunters,—all,
in fact, that a painter can copy from nature;" and the
coat that Charles of Orleans once wore, on the sleeves of
which were embroidered the verses of a song beginning
*"Madame, je suis tout joyeux,"* the musical accompaniment
of the words being wrought in gold thread, and each note,
a square shape in those days, formed with four pearls. He
read of the room that was prepared at the palace at Rheims
for the use of Queen Joan of Burgundy, and was decorated
with "thirteen hundred and twenty-one parrots, made in
broidery, and blazoned with the king's arms, and five hundred and sixty-one butterflies, whose wings were similarly

ornamented with the arms of the queen, the whole worked
in gold." Catherine de Médicis had a mourning-bed made
for her of black velvet powdered with crescents and suns.
Its curtains were of damask, with leafy wreaths and gar-
lands, figured upon a gold and silver ground, and fringed
along the edges with broideries of pearls, and it stood in
a room hung with rows of the queen's devices in cut black
velvet upon cloth of silver. Louis XIV. had gold-embroidered caryatides fifteen feet high in his apartment. The
state bed of Sobieski, King of Poland, was made of Smyrna
gold brocade embroidered in turquoises with verses
from the Koran. Its supports were of silver gilt, beautifully chased, and profusely set with enamelled and jewelled
medallions. It had been taken from the Turkish camp before
Vienna, and the standard of Mohammed had stood under it.

And so, for a whole year, he sought to accumulate the
most exquisite specimens that he could find of textile
and embroidered work, getting the dainty Delhi muslins,
finely wrought, with gold-threat palmates, and stitched
over with iridescent beetles' wings; the Dacca gauzes, that
from their transparency are known in the East as "woven
air," and "running water," and "evening dew;" strange figured cloths from Java; elaborate yellow Chinese hangings;
books bound in tawny satins or fair blue silks and wrought
with *fleurs de lys,* birds, and images; veils of *lacis* worked
in Hungary point; Sicilian brocades, and stiff Spanish
velvets; Georgian work with its gilt coins, and Japanese
*Foukousas* with their green-toned golds and their marvel-
ously-plumaged birds.

He had a special passion, also, for ecclesiastical vest-
ments, as indeed he had for everything connected with the
service of the Church. In the long cedar chests that lined
the west gallery of his house he had stored away many rare
and beautiful specimens of what is really the raiment of
the Bride of Christ, who must wear purple and jewels and

fine linen that she may hide the pallid macerated body that
is worn by the suffering that she seeks for, and wounded
by self-inflicted pain. He had a gorgeous cope of crimson silk and gold-thread damask, figured with a repeating
pattern of golden pomegranates set in six-petalled formal
blossoms, beyond which on either side was the pineapple
device wrought in seed-pearls. The orphreys were divided
into panels representing scenes from the life of the Virgin,
and the coronation of the Virgin was figured in colored
silks upon the hood. This was Italian work of the fifteenth
century. Another cope was of green velvet, embroidered
with heart-shaped groups of acanthus-leaves, from which
spread long-stemmed white blossoms, the details of which
were picked out with silver thread and colored crystals. The
morse bore a seraph's head in gold-thread raised work. The
orphreys were woven in a diaper of red and gold silk, and
were starred with medallions of many saints and martyrs,
among whom was St. Sebastian. He had chasubles, also, of
amber-colored silk, and blue silk and gold brocade, and
yellow silk damask and cloth of gold, figured with repre-
sentations of the Passion and Crucifixion of Christ, and
embroidered with lions and peacocks and other emblems;
dalmatics of white satin and pink silk damask, decorated
with tulips and dolphins and *fleurs de lys;* altar frontals of
crimson velvet and blue linen; and many corporals, chal-
ice-veils, and sudaria. In the mystic offices to which these
things were put there was something that quickened his
imagination.

For these things, and everything that he collected in
his lovely house, were to be to him means of forgetfulness,
modes by which he could escape, for a season, from the
fear that seemed to him at times to be almost too great to
be borne. Upon the walls of the lonely locked room where
he had spent so much of his boyhood, he had hung with
his own hands the terrible portrait whose changing features

showed him the real degradation of his life, and had draped the purple-and-gold pall in front of it as a curtain. For weeks he would not go there, would forget the hideous painted thing, and get back his light heart, his wonderful joyousness, his passionate pleasure in mere existence. Then, suddenly, some night he would creep out of the house, go down to dreadful places near Blue Gate Fields, and stay there, day after day, until he was driven away. On his return he would sit in front of the picture, sometimes loathing it and himself, but filled, at other times, with that pride of rebellion that is half the fascination of sin, and smiling, with secret pleasure, at the misshapen shadow that had to bear the burden that should have been his own.

After a few years he could not endure to be long out of England, and gave up the villa that he had shared at Trouville with Lord Henry, as well as the little white walled-in house at Algiers where he had more than once spent his winter. He hated to be separated from the picture that was such a part of his life, and he was also afraid that during his absence some one might gain access to the room, in spite of the elaborate bolts and bars that he had caused to be placed upon the door.

He was quite conscious that this would tell them nothing. It was true that the portrait still preserved, under all the foulness and ugliness of the face, its marked likeness to himself; but what could they learn from that? He would laugh at any one who tried to taunt him. He had not painted it. What was it to him how vile and full of shame it looked? Even if he told them, would they believe it?

Yet he was afraid. Sometimes when he was down at his great house in Nottinghamshire, entertaining the fashionable young men of his own rank who were his chief companions, and astounding the county by the wanton luxury and gorgeous splendor of his mode of life, he would suddenly leave his guests and rush back to town to see that the door had not been tampered with and that the picture was still there. What if it should be stolen? The mere thought made him cold with horror. Surely the world would know his secret then. Perhaps the world already suspected it.

For, while he fascinated many, there were not a few who distrusted him. He was blackballed at a West End club of which his birth and social position fully entitled him to become a member, and on one occasion, when he was brought by a friend into the smoking-room of the Carlton, the Duke of Berwick and another gentleman got up in a marked manner and went out. Curious stories became current about him after he had passed his twenty-fifth year. It was said that he had been seen brawling with foreign sailors in a low den in the distant parts of Whitechapel, and that he consorted with thieves and coiners and knew the mysteries of their trade. His extraordinary absences became notorious, and, when he used to reappear again in society, men would whisper to each other in corners, or pass him with a sneer, or look at him with cold searching eyes, as if they were determined to discover his secret.

Of such insolences and attempted slights he, of course, took no notice, and in the opinion of most people his frank debonair manner, his charming boyish smile, and the infinite grace of that wonderful youth that seemed never to leave him, were in themselves a sufficient answer to the calumnies (for so they called them) that were circulated about him. It was remarked, however, that those who had been most intimate with him appeared, after a time, to shun him. Of all his friends, or so-called friends, Lord Henry Wotton was the only one who remained loyal to him. Women who had wildly adored him, and for his sake had braved all social censure and set convention at defiance, were seen to grow pallid with shame or horror if Dorian Gray entered the room.

Yet these whispered scandals only lent him, in the eyes of many, his strange and dangerous charm. His great wealth was a certain element of security. Society, civilized society at least, is never very ready to believe anything to the detriment of those who are both rich and charming. It feels instinctively that manners are of more importance than morals, and the highest respectability is of less value in its opinion than the possession of a good *chef*. And, after all, it is a very poor consolation to be told that the man who has given one a bad dinner, or poor wine, is irreproachable in his private life. Even the cardinal virtues cannot atone for cold *entrées,* as Lord Henry remarked once, in a discussion on the subject; and there is possibly a good deal to be said for his view. For the canons of good society are, or should be, the same as the canons of art. Form is absolutely essential to it. It should have the dignity of a ceremony, as well as its unreality, and should combine the insincere character of a romantic play with the wit and beauty that make such plays charming. Is insincerity such a terrible thing? I think not. It is merely a method by which we can multiply our personalities.

Such, at any rate, was Dorian Gray's opinion. He used to wonder at the shallow psychology of those who conceive the Ego in man as a thing simple, permanent, reliable, and of one essence. To him, man was a being with myriad lives and myriad sensations, a complex multiform creature that bore within itself strange legacies of thought and passion, and whose very flesh was tainted with the monstrous maladies of the dead. He loved to stroll through the gaunt cold picture-gallery of his country-house and look at the various portraits of those whose blood flowed in his veins. Here was Philip Herbert, described by Francis Osborne, in his "Memoires on the Reigns of Queen Elizabeth and King James," as one who was "caressed by the court for his handsome face, which kept him not long company." Was it young Herbert's life that he sometimes led? Had some strange poisonous germ crept from body to body till it had reached his own? Was it some dim sense of that ruined grace that had made him so suddenly, and almost without cause, give utterance, in Basil Hallward's studio, to that mad prayer that had so changed his life? Here, in gold-embroidered red doublet, jeweled surcoat, and gilt-edged ruff and wrist-bands, stood Sir Anthony Sherard, with his silver-and-black armor piled at his feet. What had this man's legacy been? Had the lover of Giovanna of Naples bequeathed him some inheritance of sin and shame? Were his own actions merely the dreams that the dead man had not dared to realize? Here, from the fading canvas, smiled Lady Elizabeth Devereux, in her gauze hood, pearl stomacher, and pink slashed sleeves. A flower was in her right hand, and her left clasped an enameled collar of white and damask roses. On a table by her side lay a mandolin and an apple. There were large green rosettes upon her little pointed shoes. He knew her life, and the strange stories that were told about her lovers. Had he something of her temperament in him? Those oval heavy-lidded eyes seemed to look curiously at him. What of George Willoughby, with his powdered hair and fantastic patches? How evil he looked! The face was saturnine and swarthy, and the sensual lips seemed to be twisted with disdain. Delicate lace ruffles fell over the lean yellow hands that were so overladen with rings. He had been a macaroni of the eighteenth century, and the friend, in his youth, of Lord Ferrars. What of the second Lord Sherard, the companion of the Prince Regent in his wildest days, and one of the witnesses at the secret marriage with Mrs. Fitzherbert? How proud and handsome he was, with his chestnut curls and insolent pose! What passions had he bequeathed? The world had looked upon him as infamous. He had led the orgies at Carlton House. The star of the Garter glittered upon his breast. Beside him hung the portrait of his wife, a pallid, thin-lipped woman in black. Her blood, also, stirred within him. How curious it all seemed!

Yet one had ancestors in literature, as well as in one's own race, nearer perhaps in type and temperament, many of them, and certainly with an influence of which one was more absolutely conscious. There were times when it seemed to Dorian Gray that the whole of history was merely the record of his own life, not as he had lived it in act and circumstance, but as his imagination had created it for him, as it had been in his brain and in his passions. He felt that he had known them all, those strange terrible figures that had passed across the stage of the world and made sin so marvelous and evil so full of wonder. It seemed to him that in some mysterious way their lives had been his own.

The hero of the dangerous novel that had so influenced his life had himself had this curious fancy. In a chapter of the book he tells how, crowned with laurel, lest lightning might strike him, he had sat, as Tiberius, in a garden at Capri, reading the shameful books of Elephantis, while dwarfs and peacocks strutted round him and the flute-player mocked the swinger of the censer; and, as Caligula, had caroused with the green-shirted jockeys in their stables, and supped in an ivory manger with a jewel-frontleted horse; and, as Domitian, had wandered through a corridor lined with marble mirrors, looking round with haggard eyes for the reflection of the dagger that was to end his days, and sick with that ennui, that *taedium vitae,* that comes on those to whom life denies nothing; and had peered through a clear emerald at the red shambles of the Circus, and then, in a litter of pearl and

purple drawn by silver-shod mules, been carried through
the Street of Pomegranates to a House of Gold, and heard
men cry on Nero Caesar as he passed by; and, as Elagabalus, had painted his face with colors, and plied the distaff
among the women, and brought the Moon from Carthage,
and given her in mystic marriage to the Sun.

Over and over again Dorian used to read this fantastic
chapter, and the chapter immediately following, in which
the hero describes the curious tapestries that he had had
woven for him from Gustave Moreau's designs, and on
which were pictured the awful and beautiful forms of those
whom Vice and Blood and Weariness had made monstrous
or mad: Filippo, Duke of Milan, who slew his wife, and
painted her lips with a scarlet poison; Pietro Barbi, the
Venetian, known as Paul the Second, who sought in his
vanity to assume the title of Formosus, and whose tiara,
valued at two hundred thousand florins, was bought at
the price of a terrible sin; Gian Maria Visconti, who used
hounds to chase living men, and whose murdered body
was covered with roses by a harlot who had loved him; the
Borgia on his white horse, with Fratricide riding beside
him, and his mantle stained with the blood of Perotto;
Pietro Riario, the young Cardinal Archbishop of Florence,
child and minion of Sixtus IV., whose beauty was equaled
only by his debauchery, and who received Leonora of Aragon in a pavilion of white and crimson silk, filled with
nymphs and centaurs, and gilded a boy that he might serve
her at the feast as Ganymede or Hylas; Ezzelin, whose melancholy could be cured only by the spectacle of death, and
who had a passion for red blood, as other men have for
red wine,—the son of the Fiend, as was reported, and one
who had cheated his father at dice when gambling with
him for his own soul; Giambattista Cibo, who in mockery
took the name of Innocent, and into whose torpid veins
the blood of three lads was infused by a Jewish doctor;

Sigismondo Malatesta, the lover of Isotta, and the lord of Rimini, whose effigy was burned at Rome as the enemy of God and man, who strangled Polyssena with a napkin, and gave poison to Ginevra d'Este in a cup of emerald, and in honor of a shameful passion built a pagan church for Christian worship; Charles VI., who had so wildly adored his brother's wife that a leper had warned him of the insanity that was coming on him, and who could only be soothed by Saracen cards painted with the images of Love and Death and Madness; and, in his trimmed jerkin and jeweled cap and acanthus-like curls, Grifonetto Baglioni, who slew Astorre with his bride, and Simonetto with his page, and whose comeliness was such that, as he lay dying in the yellow piazza of Perugia, those who had hated him could not choose but weep, and Atalanta, who had cursed him, blessed him.

There was a horrible fascination in them all. He saw them at night, and they troubled his imagination in the day. The Renaissance knew of strange manners of poisoning,—poisoning by a helmet and a lighted torch, by an embroidered glove and a jeweled fan, by a gilded pomander and by an amber chain. Dorian Gray had been poisoned by a book. There were moments when he looked on evil simply as a mode through which he could realize his conception of the beautiful.


CHAPTER X

It was on the 7th of November, the eve of his own thirty-second birthday, as he often remembered afterwards.

He was walking home about eleven o'clock from Lord Henry's, where he had been dining, and was wrapped in heavy furs, as the night was cold and foggy. At the corner of Grosvenor Square and South Audley Street a man passed him in the mist, walking very fast, and with the collar of his gray ulster turned up. He had a bag in his hand. He recognized him. It was Basil Hallward. A strange sense of fear, for which he could not account, came over him. He made no sign of recognition, and went on slowly, in the direction of his own house.

But Hallward had seen him. Dorian heard him first stopping, and then hurrying after him. In a few moments his hand was on his arm.

"Dorian! What an extraordinary piece of luck! I have been waiting for you ever since nine o'clock in your library. Finally I took pity on your tired servant, and told him to go to bed, as he let me out. I am off to Paris by the midnight train, and I wanted particularly to see you before I left. I thought it was you, or rather your fur coat, as you passed me. But I wasn't quite sure. Didn't you recognize me?"

"In this fog, my dear Basil? Why, I can't even recognize Grosvenor Square. I believe my house is somewhere about here, but I don't feel at all certain about it. I am sorry you are going away, as I have not seen you for ages. But I suppose you will be back soon?"

"No: I am going to be out of England for six months. I intend to take a studio in Paris, and shut myself up till I have finished a great picture I have in my head. However, it wasn't about myself I wanted to talk. Here we are at your door. Let me come in for a moment. I have something to say to you."

"I shall be charmed. But won't you miss your train?" said Dorian Gray, languidly, as he passed up the steps and opened the door with his latch-key.

The lamp-light struggled out through the fog, and Hallward looked at his watch. "I have heaps of time," he answered. "The train doesn't go till twelve-fifteen, and it is only just eleven. In fact, I was on my way to the club to look for you, when I met you. You see, I shan't have any delay about luggage, as I have sent on my heavy things. All I have with me is in this bag, and I can easily get to Victoria in twenty minutes."

Dorian looked at him and smiled. "What a way for a fashionable painter to travel! A Gladstone bag, and an ulster! Come in, or the fog will get into the house. And mind you don't talk about anything serious. Nothing is serious nowadays. At least nothing should be."

Hallward shook his head, as he entered, and followed Dorian into the library. There was a bright wood fire blazing in the large open hearth. The lamps were lit, and an open Dutch silver spirit-case stood, with some siphons of soda-water and large cut-glass tumblers, on a little table.

"You see your servant made me quite at home, Dorian. He gave me everything I wanted, including your best cigarettes. He is a most hospitable creature. I like him much better than the Frenchman you used to have. What has become of the Frenchman, by the bye?"

Dorian shrugged his shoulders. "I believe he married Lady Ashton's maid, and has established her in Paris as an English dressmaker. *Anglomanie* is very fashionable over there now, I hear. It seems silly of the French, doesn't it? But—do you know?—he was not at all a bad servant. I never liked him, but I had nothing to complain about. One often imagines things that are quite absurd. He was really very devoted to me, and seemed quite sorry when he went away. Have another brandy-and-soda? Or would you like hock-and-seltzer? I always take hock-and-seltzer myself. There is sure to be some in the next room."

"Thanks, I won't have anything more," said Hallward, taking his cap and coat off, and throwing them on the bag that he had placed in the corner. "And now, my dear fellow, I want to speak to you seriously. Don't frown like that. You make it so much more difficult for me."

"What is it all about?" cried Dorian, in his petulant way, flinging himself down on the sofa. "I hope it is not about myself. I am tired of myself to-night. I should like to be somebody else."

"It is about yourself," answered Hallward, in his grave, deep voice, "and I must say it to you. I shall only keep you half an hour."

Dorian sighed, and lit a cigarette. "Half an hour!" he murmured.

"It is not much to ask of you, Dorian, and it is entirely for your own sake that I am speaking. I think it right that you should know that the most dreadful things are being said about you in London,—things that I could hardly repeat to you."

"I don't wish to know anything about them. I love scandals about other people, but scandals about myself don't interest me. They have not got the charm of novelty."

"They must interest you, Dorian. Every gentleman is interested in his good name. You don't want people to talk of you as something vile and degraded. Of course you have your position, and your wealth, and all that kind of thing. But position and wealth are not everything. Mind you, I don't believe these rumors at all. At least, I can't believe them when I see you. Sin is a thing that writes itself across a man's face. It cannot be concealed. People talk of secret vices. There are no such things as secret vices. If a wretched man has a vice, it shows itself in the lines of his mouth, the droop of his eyelids, the molding of his hands even. Somebody—I won't mention his name, but you know him—came to me last year to have his portrait done. I had never seen him before, and had never heard anything about him at the time, though I have heard a good deal since. He offered an extravagant price. I refused him. There was something in the shape of his fingers that I hated. I know now that I was quite right in what I fancied about him. His life is dreadful. But you, Dorian, with your pure, bright, innocent face, and your marvelous untroubled youth,—I can't believe anything against you. And yet I see you very seldom, and you never come down to the studio now, and when I am away from you, and I hear all these hideous things that people are whispering about you, I don't know what to say. Why is it, Dorian, that a man like the Duke of Berwick leaves the room of a club when you enter it? Why is it that so many gentlemen in London will neither go to your house nor invite you to theirs? You used to be a friend of Lord Cawdor. I met him at dinner last week. Your name happened to come up in conversation, in connection with the miniatures you have lent to the exhibition at the Dudley. Cawdor curled his lip, and said that you might have the most artistic tastes, but that you were a man whom no pure-minded girl should be allowed to know, and whom no chaste woman should sit in the same room with. I reminded him that I was a friend of yours, and asked him what he meant. He told me. He told me right out before everybody. It was horrible! Why is your friendship so fateful to young men? There was that wretched boy in the Guards who committed suicide. You were his great friend. There was Sir Henry Ashton, who had to leave England, with a tarnished name. You and he were inseparable. What about Adrian Singleton, and his dreadful end? What about Lord Kent's only son, and his career? I met his father yesterday in St. James Street. He seemed broken with shame and sorrow. What about the young Duke of Perth? What sort of life has he got now? What gentleman would associate with him? Dorian, Dorian, your reputation is infamous. I know you and Harry are great friends. I say nothing about that now, but surely you need not have made his sister's name a by-word. When you met Lady Gwendolen, not a breath of scandal had ever touched her. Is there a single decent woman in London now who would drive with her in the Park? Why, even her children are not allowed to live with her. Then there are other stories,—stories that you have been seen creeping at dawn out of dreadful houses and slinking in disguise into the foulest dens in London. Are they true? Can they be true? When I first heard them, I laughed. I hear them now, and they make me shudder. What about your country-house, and the life that is led there? Dorian, you don't know what is said about you. I won't tell you that I don't want to preach to you. I remember Harry saying once that every man who turned himself into an amateur curate for the moment always said that, and then broke his word. I do want to preach to you. I want you to lead such a life as will make the world respect you. I want you to have a clean name and a fair record. I want you to get rid of the dreadful people you associate with. Don't shrug your shoulders like that. Don't be so indifferent. You have a wonderful influence. Let it be for good, not for evil. They say that you corrupt every one whom you become intimate with, and that it is quite sufficient for you to enter a house, for shame of some kind to follow after you. I don't know whether it is so or not. How should I know? But it is said of you. I am told things that it seems impossible to doubt. Lord Gloucester was one of my greatest friends at Oxford. He showed me a letter that his wife had written to him when she was dying alone in her villa at Mentone. Your name was implicated in the most terrible confession I ever read. I told him that it was absurd,—that I knew you thoroughly, and that you were incapable of anything of the kind. Know you? I wonder do I know you? Before I could answer that, I should have to see your soul."

"To see my soul!" muttered Dorian Gray, starting up from the sofa and turning almost white from fear.

"Yes," answered Hallward, gravely, and with infinite sorrow in his voice,—"to see your soul. But only God can do that."

A bitter laugh of mockery broke from the lips of the younger man. "You shall see it yourself, to-night!" he cried, seizing a lamp from the table. "Come: it is your own handiwork. Why shouldn't you look at it? You can tell the world all about it afterwards, if you choose. Nobody would believe you. If they did believe you, they'd like me all the better for it. I know the age better than you do, though you will prate about it so tediously. Come, I tell you. You have chattered enough about corruption. Now you shall look on it face to face."

There was the madness of pride in every word he uttered. He stamped his foot upon the ground in his boyish insolent manner. He felt a terrible joy at the thought that some one else was to share his secret, and that the man who had painted the portrait that was the origin of all his shame was to be burdened for the rest of his life with the hideous memory of what he had done.

"Yes," he continued, coming closer to him, and looking steadfastly into his stern eyes, "I will show you my soul. You shall see the thing that you fancy only God can see."

Hallward started back. "This is blasphemy, Dorian!" he cried. "You must not say things like that. They are horrible, and they don't mean anything."

"You think so?" He laughed again.

"I know so. As for what I said to you to-night, I said it for your good. You know I have been always devoted to you."

"Don't touch me. Finish what you have to say."

A twisted flash of pain shot across Hallward's face. He paused for a moment, and a wild feeling of pity came over him. After all, what right had he to pry into the life of Dorian Gray? If he had done a tithe of what was rumored about him, how much he must have suffered! Then he straightened himself up, and walked over to the fireplace, and stood there, looking at the burning logs with their frost-like ashes and their throbbing cores of flame.

"I am waiting, Basil," said the young man, in a hard, clear voice.

He turned round. "What I have to say is this," he cried. "You must give me some answer to these horrible charges that are made against you. If you tell me that they are absolutely untrue from beginning to end, I will believe you. Deny them, Dorian, deny them! Can't you see what I am going through? My God! don't tell me that you are infamous!"

Dorian Gray smiled. There was a curl of contempt in his lips. "Come up-stairs, Basil," he said, quietly. "I keep a diary of my life from day to day, and it never leaves the room in which it is written. I will show it to you if you come with me."

"I will come with you, Dorian, if you wish it. I see I have missed my train. That makes no matter. I can go to-morrow. But don't ask me to read anything to-night. All I want is a plain answer to my question."

"That will be given to you up-stairs. I could not give it here. You won't have to read long. Don't keep me waiting."

## Chapter XI

He passed out of the room, and began the ascent, Basil Hallward following close behind. They walked softly, as men instinctively do at night. The lamp cast fantastic shadows on the wall and staircase. A rising wind made some of the windows rattle.

When they reached the top landing, Dorian set the lamp down on the floor, and taking out the key turned it in the lock. "You insist on knowing, Basil?" he asked, in a low voice.

"Yes."

"I am delighted," he murmured, smiling. Then he added, somewhat bitterly, "You are the one man in the world who is entitled to know everything about me. You have had more to do with my life than you think." And, taking up the lamp, he opened the door and went in. A cold current of air passed them, and the light shot up for a moment in a flame of murky orange. He shuddered. "Shut the door behind you," he said, as he placed the lamp on the table.

Hallward glanced round him, with a puzzled expression. The room looked as if it had not been lived in for years. A faded Flemish tapestry, a curtained picture, an old Italian *cassone,* and an almost empty bookcase,—that was all that it seemed to contain, besides a chair and a table. As Dorian Gray was lighting a half-burned candle that was standing on the mantel-shelf, he saw that the whole place was covered with dust, and that the carpet was in holes. A mouse ran scuffling behind the wainscoting. There was a damp odor of mildew.

"So you think that it is only God who sees the soul, Basil? Draw that curtain back, and you will see mine."

The voice that spoke was cold and cruel. "You are mad, Dorian, or playing a part," muttered Hallward, frowning.

"You won't? Then I must do it myself," said the young man; and he tore the curtain from its rod, and flung it on the ground.

An exclamation of horror broke from Hallward's lips as he saw in the dim light the hideous thing on the canvas leering at him. There was something in its expression that filled him with disgust and loathing. Good heavens! it was Dorian Gray's own face that he was looking at! The horror, whatever it was, had not yet entirely marred that marvelous beauty. There was still some gold in the thinning hair and some scarlet on the sensual lips. The sodden eyes had kept something of the loveliness of their blue, the noble curves had not yet passed entirely away from chiseled nostrils and from plastic throat. Yes, it was Dorian himself. But who had done it? He seemed to recognize his own brush-work, and the frame was his own design. The idea was monstrous, yet he felt afraid. He seized the lighted candle, and held it to the picture. In the left-hand corner was his own name, traced in long letters of bright vermilion.

It was some foul parody, some infamous, ignoble satire. He had never done that. Still, it was his own picture. He knew it, and he felt as if his blood had changed from fire to sluggish ice in a moment. His own picture! What did it mean? Why had it altered? He turned, and looked at Dorian Gray with the eyes of a sick man. His mouth twitched, and his parched tongue seemed unable to articulate. He passed his hand across his forehead. It was dank with clammy sweat.

The young man was leaning against the mantel-shelf, watching him with that strange expression that is on the faces of those who are absorbed in a play when a great artist is acting. There was neither real sorrow in it nor real joy. There was simply the passion of the spectator, with perhaps a flicker of triumph in the eyes. He had taken the flower out of his coat, and was smelling it, or pretending to do so.

"What does this mean?" cried Hallward, at last. His own voice sounded shrill and curious in his ears.

"Years ago, when I was a boy," said Dorian Gray, "you met me, devoted yourself to me, flattered me, and taught me to be vain of my good looks. One day you introduced me to a friend of yours, who explained to me the wonder of youth, and you finished a portrait of me that revealed to me the wonder of beauty. In a mad moment, that I don't know, even now, whether I regret or not, I made a wish. Perhaps you would call it a prayer . . . ."

"I remember it! Oh, how well I remember it! No! the thing is impossible. The room is damp. The mildew has got into the canvas. The paints I used had some wretched mineral poison in them. I tell you the thing is impossible."

"Ah, what is impossible?" murmured the young man, going over to the window, and leaning his forehead against the cold, mist-stained glass.

"You told me you had destroyed it."

"I was wrong. It has destroyed me."

"I don't believe it is my picture."

"Can't you see your romance in it?" said Dorian, bitterly.

"My romance, as you call it . . ."

"As you called it."

"There was nothing evil in it, nothing shameful. This is the face of a satyr."

"It is the face of my soul."

"God! what a thing I must have worshipped! This has the eyes of a devil."

"Each of us has Heaven and Hell in him, Basil," cried Dorian, with a wild gesture of despair.

Hallward turned again to the portrait, and gazed at it. "My God! if it is true," he exclaimed, "and this is what you have done with your life, why, you must be worse even than those who talk against you fancy you to be!" He held the light up again to the canvas, and examined it. The surface seemed to be quite undisturbed, and as he had left it. It was from within, apparently, that the foulness and horror had come. Through some strange quickening of inner life the leprosies of sin were slowly eating the thing away. The rotting of a corpse in a watery grave was not so fearful.

His hand shook, and the candle fell from its socket on the floor, and lay there sputtering. He placed his foot on it and put it out. Then he flung himself into the rickety chair that was standing by the table and buried his face in his hands.

"Good God, Dorian, what a lesson! what an awful lesson!" There was no answer, but he could hear the young man sobbing at the window.

"Pray, Dorian, pray," he murmured. "What is it that one was taught to say in one's boyhood? 'Lead us not into temptation. Forgive us our sins. Wash away our iniquities.' Let us say that together. The prayer of your pride has been answered. The prayer of your repentance will be answered also. I worshipped you too much. I am punished for it. You worshipped yourself too much. We are both punished."

Dorian Gray turned slowly around, and looked at him with tear-dimmed eyes. "It is too late, Basil," he murmured.

"It is never too late, Dorian. Let us kneel down and try if we can remember a prayer. Isn't there a verse somewhere, 'Though your sins be as scarlet, yet I will make them as white as snow'?"

"Those words mean nothing to me now."

"Hush! don't say that. You have done enough evil in your life. My God! don't you see that accursed thing leering at us?"

Dorian Gray glanced at the picture, and suddenly an uncontrollable feeling of hatred for Basil Hallward came over him. The mad passions of a hunted animal stirred within him, and he loathed the man who was seated at the table, more than he had ever loathed anything in his whole life. He glanced wildly around. Something glimmered on the top of the painted chest that faced him. His eye fell on it. He knew what it was. It was a knife that he had brought up, some days before, to cut a piece of cord, and had forgotten to take away with him. He moved slowly towards it, passing Hallward as he did so. As soon as he got behind him, he seized it, and turned round. Hallward moved in his chair as if he was going to rise. He rushed at him, and dug the knife into the great vein that is behind the ear, crushing the man's head down on the table, and stabbing again and again.

There was a stifled groan, and the horrible sound of some one choking with blood. The outstretched arms shot up convulsively three times, waving grotesque stiff-fingered hands in the air. He stabbed him once more, but the man did not move. Something began to trickle on the floor. He waited for a moment, still pressing the head down. Then he threw the knife on the table, and listened.

He could hear nothing, but the drip, drip on the threadbare carpet. He opened the door, and went out on the landing. The house was quite quiet. No one was stirring.

He took out the key, and returned to the room, locking himself in as he did so.

The thing was still seated in the chair, straining over the table with bowed head, and humped back, and long fantastic arms. Had it not been for the red jagged tear in the neck, and the clotted black pool that slowly widened on the table, one would have said that the man was simply asleep.

How quickly it had all been done! He felt strangely calm, and, walking over to the window, opened it, and stepped out on the balcony. The wind had blown the fog away, and the sky was like a monstrous peacock's tail, starred with myriads of golden eyes. He looked down, and saw the policeman going his rounds and flashing a bull's-eye lantern on the doors of the silent houses. The crimson spot of a prowling hansom gleamed at the corner, and then vanished. A woman in a ragged shawl was creeping round by the railings, staggering as she went. Now and then she stopped, and peered back. Once, she began to sing in a hoarse voice. The policeman strolled over and said something to her. She stumbled away, laughing. A bitter blast swept across the Square. The gas-lamps flickered, and became blue, and the leafless trees shook their black iron branches as if in pain. He shivered, and went back, closing the window behind him.

He passed to the door, turned the key, and opened it. He did not even glance at the murdered man. He felt that the secret of the whole thing was not to realize the situation. The friend who had painted the fatal portrait, the portrait to which all his misery had been due, had gone out of his life. That was enough.

Then he remembered the lamp. It was a rather curious one of Moorish workmanship, made of dull silver inlaid with arabesques of burnished steel. Perhaps it might be missed by his servant, and questions would be asked. He turned back, and took it from the table. How still the man was! How horribly white the long hands looked! He was like a dreadful wax image.

He locked the door behind him, and crept quietly down-stairs. The wood-work creaked, and seemed to cry out as if in pain. He stopped several times, and waited. No: everything was still. It was merely the sound of his own footsteps.

When he reached the library, he saw the bag and coat in the corner. They must be hidden away somewhere. He unlocked a secret press that was in the wainscoting, and put them into it. He could easily burn them afterwards. Then he pulled out his watch. It was twenty minutes to two.

He sat down, and began to think. Every year—every month, almost—men were strangled in England for what he had done. There had been a madness of murder in the air. Some red star had come too close to the earth.

Evidence? What evidence was there against him? Basil Hallward had left the house at eleven. No one had seen him come in again. Most of the servants were at Selby Royal. His valet had gone to bed.

Paris! Yes. It was to Paris that Basil had gone, by the midnight train, as he had intended. With his curious reserved habits, it would be months before any suspicions would be aroused. Months? Everything could be destroyed long before then.

A sudden thought struck him. He put on his fur coat and hat, and went out into the hall. There he paused, hearing the slow heavy tread of the policeman outside on the pavement, and seeing the flash of the lantern reflected in the window. He waited, holding his breath.

After a few moments he opened the front door, and slipped out, shutting it very gently behind him. Then he began ringing the bell. In about ten minutes his valet appeared, half dressed, and looking very drowsy.

"I am sorry to have had to wake you up, Francis," he said, stepping in; "but I had forgotten my latch-key. What time is it?"

"Five minutes past two, sir," answered the man, looking at the clock and yawning.

"Five minutes past two? How horribly late! You must wake me at nine tomorrow. I have some work to do."

"All right, sir."

"Did any one call this evening?"

"Mr. Hallward, sir. He stayed here till eleven, and then he went away to catch his train."

"Oh! I am sorry I didn't see him. Did he leave any message?"

"No, sir, except that he would write to you."

"That will do, Francis. Don't forget to call me at nine tomorrow."

"No, sir."

The man shambled down the passage in his slippers.

Dorian Gray threw his hat and coat upon the yellow marble table, and passed into the library. He walked up and down the room for a quarter of an hour, biting his lip, and thinking. Then he took the Blue Book down from one of the shelves, and began to turn over the leaves. "Alan Campbell, 152, Hertford Street, Mayfair." Yes; that was the man he wanted.

## Chapter XII

At nine o'clock the next morning his servant came in with a cup of chocolate on a tray, and opened the shutters. Dorian was sleeping quite peacefully, lying on his right side, with one hand underneath his cheek. He looked like a boy who had been tired out with play, or study.

The man had to touch him twice on the shoulder before he woke, and as he opened his eyes a faint smile passed across his lips, as though he had been having some delightful dream. Yet he had not dreamed at all. His night had been untroubled by any images of pleasure or of pain. But youth smiles without any reason. It is one of its chiefest charms.

He turned round, and, leaning on his elbow, began to drink his chocolate. The mellow November sun was streaming into the room. The sky was bright blue, and there was a genial warmth in the air. It was almost like a morning in May.

Gradually the events of the preceding night crept with silent blood-stained feet into his brain, and reconstructed themselves there with terrible distinctness. He winced at the memory of all that he had suffered, and for a moment the same curious feeling of loathing for Basil Hallward, that had made him kill him as he sat in the chair, came back to him, and he grew cold with passion. The dead man was still sitting there, too, and in the sunlight now. How horrible that was! Such hideous things were for the darkness, not for the day.

He felt that if he brooded on what he had gone through he would sicken or grow mad. There were sins whose fascination was more in the memory than in the doing of them, strange triumphs that gratified the pride more than the passions, and gave to the intellect a quickened sense of joy, greater than any joy they brought, or could ever bring, to the senses. But this was not one of them. It was a thing to be driven out of the mind, to be drugged with poppies, to be strangled lest it might strangle one itself.

He passed his hand across his forehead, and then got up hastily, and dressed himself with even more than his usual attention, giving a good deal of care to the selection of his necktie and scarf-pin, and changing his rings more than once.

He spent a long time over breakfast, tasting the various dishes, talking to his valet about some new liveries that he was thinking of getting made for the servants at Selby, and going through his correspondence. Over some of the letters he smiled. Three of them bored him. One he read several times over, and then tore up with a slight look of annoyance in his face. "That awful thing, a woman's memory!" as Lord Henry had once said.

When he had drunk his coffee, he sat down at the table, and wrote two letters. One he put in his pocket, the other he handed to the valet.

"Take this round to 152, Hertford Street, Francis, and if Mr. Campbell is out of town, get his address."

As soon as he was alone, he lit a cigarette, and began sketching upon a piece of paper, drawing flowers, and bits of architecture, first, and then faces. Suddenly he remarked that every face that he drew seemed to have an extraordinary likeness to Basil Hallward. He frowned, and, getting up, went over to the bookcase and took out a volume at hazard. He was determined that he would not think about what had happened, till it became absolutely necessary to do so.

When he had stretched himself on the sofa, he looked at the title-page of the book. It was Gautier's *Émaux et Camées*, Charpentier's Japanese-paper edition, with the Jacquemart etching. The binding was of citron-green leather with a design of gilt trellis-work and dotted pomegranates. It had been given to him by Adrian Singleton. As he turned over the pages his eye fell on the poem about the hand of Lacenaire, the cold yellow hand *"du supplice encore mal lavée,"* with its downy red hairs and its *"doigts de faune."* He glanced at his own white taper fingers, and passed on, till he came to those lovely verses upon Venice:

> *Sur une gamme chromatique,*
> *Le sein de perles ruisselant,*
> *La Vénus de l'Adriatique*
> *Sort de l'eau son corps rose et blanc.*
>
> *Les dômes, sur l'azur des ondes*
> *Suivant la phrase au pur contour,*
> *S'enflent comme des gorges rondes*
> *Que soulève un soupir d'amour.*
>
> *L'esquif aborde et me dépose,*
> *Jetant son amarre au pilier,*
> *Devant une façade rose,*
> *Sur le marbre d'un escalier.*

How exquisite they were! As one read them, one seemed to be floating down the green water-ways of the pink and pearl city, lying in a black gondola with silver prow and trailing curtains. The mere lines looked to him like those straight lines of turquoise-blue that follow one as one pushes out to the Lido. The sudden flashes of color reminded him of the gleam of the opal-and-iris-throated birds that flutter round the tall honey-combed Campanile, or stalk, with such stately grace, through the dim arcades. Leaning back with half-closed eyes, he kept saying over and over to himself,—

> *Devant une façade rose,*
> *Sur le marbre d'un escalier.*

The whole of Venice was in those two lines. He remembered the autumn that he had passed there, and a wonderful love that had stirred him to delightful fantastic follies. There was romance in every place. But Venice, like Oxford, had kept the background for romance, and background was everything, or almost everything. Basil had been with him part of the time, and had gone wild over Tintoret. Poor Basil! what a horrible way for a man to die!

He sighed, and took up the book again, and tried to forget. He read of the swallows that fly in and out of the little café at Smyrna where the Hadjis sit counting their amber beads and the turbaned merchants smoke their long tasseled pipes and talk gravely to each other; of the Obelisk in the Place de la Concorde that weeps tears of granite in its lonely sunless exile, and longs to be back by the hot lotus-covered Nile, where there are Sphinxes, and rose-red ibises, and white vultures with gilded claws, and crocodiles, with small beryl eyes, that crawl over the green steaming mud; and of that curious statue that Gautier compares to a contralto voice, the *"monstre charmant"* that couches in the porphyry-room of the Louvre. But after a time the book fell from his hand. He grew nervous, and a horrible fit of terror came over him. What if Alan Campbell should be out of England? Days would elapse before he could come back. Perhaps he might refuse to come. What could he do then? Every moment was of vital importance.

They had been great friends once, five years before,— almost inseparable, indeed. Then the intimacy had come suddenly to an end. When they met in society now, it was only Dorian Gray who smiled: Alan Campbell never did.

He was an extremely clever young man, though he had no real appreciation of the visible arts, and whatever little sense of the beauty of poetry he possessed he had gained entirely from Dorian. His dominant intellectual passion was for science. At Cambridge he had spent a great deal of his time working in the Laboratory, and had taken a good class in the Natural Science tripos of his year. Indeed, he was still devoted to the study of chemistry, and had a laboratory of his own, in which he used to shut himself up all day long, greatly to the annoyance of his mother, who had set her heart on his standing for Parliament and had a vague idea that a chemist was a person who made up prescriptions. He was an excellent musician, however, as well, and played both the violin and the piano better than most amateurs. In fact, it was music that had first brought him and Dorian Gray together,—music and that indefinable attraction that Dorian seemed to be able to exercise whenever he wished, and indeed exercised often without being conscious of it. They had met at Lady Berkshire's the night that Rubinstein played there, and after that used to be always seen together at the Opera, and wherever good music was going on. For eighteen months their intimacy lasted. Campbell was always either at Selby Royal or in Grosvenor Square. To him, as to many others, Dorian Gray was the type of everything that is wonderful and fascinating in life. Whether or not a quarrel had taken place between them no one ever knew. But suddenly people remarked that they scarcely spoke when they met, and that Campbell seemed always to go away early from any party at which Dorian Gray was present. He had changed, too,—was strangely melancholy at times, appeared almost to dislike hearing music of any passionate character, and would never himself play, giving as his excuse, when he was called upon, that he was so absorbed in science that he had no time left in which to practice. And this was certainly true. Every day he seemed to become more interested in biology, and his name appeared once or twice in some of the scientific reviews, in connection with certain curious experiments.

This was the man that Dorian Gray was waiting for, pacing up and down the room, glancing every moment at the clock, and becoming horribly agitated as the minutes went by. At last the door opened, and his servant entered.

"Mr. Alan Campbell, sir."

A sigh of relief broke from his parched lips, and the color came back to his cheeks.

"Ask him to come in at once, Francis."

The man bowed, and retired. In a few moments Alan Campbell walked in, looking very stern and rather pale, his pallor being intensified by his coal-black hair and dark eyebrows.

"Alan! this is kind of you. I thank you for coming."

"I had intended never to enter your house again, Gray. But you said it was a matter of life and death." His voice was hard and cold. He spoke with slow deliberation. There was a look of contempt in the steady searching gaze that he turned on Dorian. He kept his hands in the pockets of his Astrakhan coat, and appeared not to have noticed the gesture with which he had been greeted.

"It is a matter of life and death, Alan, and to more than one person. Sit down."

Campbell took a chair by the table, and Dorian sat opposite to him. The two men's eyes met. In Dorian's there was infinite pity. He knew that what he was going to do was dreadful.

After a strained moment of silence, he leaned across and said, very quietly, but watching the effect of each word upon the face of the man he had sent for, "Alan, in a locked room at the top of this house, a room to which nobody but myself has access, a dead man is seated at a table. He has been dead ten hours now. Don't stir, and don't look at me like that. Who the man is, why he died, how he died, are matters that do not concern you. What you have to do is this—"

"Stop, Gray. I don't want to know anything further. Whether what you have told me is true or not true, doesn't concern me. I entirely decline to be mixed up in your life. Keep your horrible secrets to yourself. They don't interest me any more."

"Alan, they will have to interest you. This one will have to interest you. I am awfully sorry for you, Alan. But I can't help myself. You are the one man who is able to save me. I am forced to bring you into the matter. I have no option. Alan, you are a scientist. You know about chemistry, and things of that kind. You have made experiments. What you have got to do is to destroy the thing that is upstairs,—to destroy it so that not a vestige will be left of it. Nobody saw this person come into the house. Indeed, at the present moment he is supposed to be in Paris. He will not be missed for months. When he is missed, there must be no trace of him found here. You, Alan, you must change him, and everything that belongs to him, into a handful of ashes that I may scatter in the air."

"You are mad, Dorian."

"Ah! I was waiting for you to call me Dorian."

"You are mad, I tell you,—mad to imagine that I would raise a finger to help you, mad to make this monstrous confession. I will have nothing to do with this matter, whatever it is. Do you think I am going to peril my reputation for you? What is it to me what devil's work you are up to?"

"It was a suicide, Alan."

"I am glad of that. But who drove him to it? You, I should fancy."

"Do you still refuse to do this, for me?"

"Of course I refuse. I will have absolutely nothing to do with it. I don't care what shame comes on you. You deserve it all. I should not be sorry to see you disgraced, publicly disgraced. How dare you ask me, of all men in the world, to mix myself up in this horror? I should have thought you knew more about people's characters. Your friend Lord Henry Wotton can't have taught you much about psychology, whatever else he has taught you. Nothing will induce me to stir a step to help you. You have come to the wrong man. Go to some of your friends. Don't come to me."

"Alan, it was murder. I killed him. You don't know what he had made me suffer. Whatever my life is, he had more to do with the making or the marring of it than poor Harry has had. He may not have intended it, the result was the same."

"Murder! Good God, Dorian, is that what you have come to? I shall not inform upon you. It is not my business. Besides, you are certain to be arrested, without my stirring in the matter. Nobody ever commits a murder without doing something stupid. But I will have nothing to do with it."

"All I ask of you is to perform a certain scientific experiment. You go to hospitals and dead-houses, and the horrors that you do there don't affect you. If in some hideous dissecting-room or fetid laboratory you found this man lying on a leaden table with red gutters scooped out in it, you would simply look upon him as an admirable subject. You would not turn a hair. You would not believe that you were doing anything wrong. On the contrary, you would probably feel that you were benefiting the human race, or increasing the sum of knowledge in the world, or gratifying intellectual curiosity, or something of that kind. What I want you to do is simply what you have often done before. Indeed, to destroy a body must be less horrible than what you are accustomed to work at. And, remember, it is the only piece of evidence against me. If it is discovered, I am lost; and it is sure to be discovered unless you help me."

"I have no desire to help you. You forget that. I am simply indifferent to the whole thing. It has nothing to do with me."

"Alan, I entreat you. Think of the position I am in. Just before you came I almost fainted with terror. No! don't think of that. Look at the matter purely from the scientific point of view. You don't inquire where the dead things on which you experiment come from. Don't inquire now. I have told you too much as it is. But I beg of you to do this. We were friends once, Alan."

"Don't speak about those days, Dorian: they are dead."

"The dead linger sometimes. The man up-stairs will not go away. He is sitting at the table with bowed head and outstretched arms. Alan! Alan! if you don't come to my assistance I am ruined. Why, they will hang me, Alan! Don't you understand? They will hang me for what I have done."

"There is no good in prolonging this scene. I refuse absolutely to do anything in the matter. It is insane of you to ask me."

"You refuse absolutely?"

"Yes."

The same look of pity came into Dorian's eyes, then he stretched out his hand, took a piece of paper, and wrote something on it. He read it over twice, folded it carefully, and pushed it across the table. Having done this, he got up, and went over to the window.

Campbell looked at him in surprise, and then took up the paper, and opened it. As he read it, his face became ghastly pale, and he fell back in his chair. A horrible sense of sickness came over him. He felt as if his heart was beating itself to death in some empty hollow.

After two or three minutes of terrible silence, Dorian turned round, and came and stood behind him, putting his hand upon his shoulder.

"I am so sorry, Alan," he murmured, "but you leave me no alternative. I have a letter written already. Here it is. You see the address. If you don't help me, I must send it. You know what the result will be. But you are going to help me. It is impossible for you to refuse now. I tried to spare you. You will do me the justice to admit that. You were stern, harsh, offensive. You treated me as no man has ever dared to treat me,—no living man, at any rate. I bore it all. Now it is for me to dictate terms."

Campbell buried his face in his hands, and a shudder passed through him.

"Yes, it is my turn to dictate terms, Alan. You know what they are. The thing is quite simple. Come, don't work yourself into this fever. The thing has to be done. Face it, and do it."

A groan broke from Campbell's lips, and he shivered all over. The ticking of the clock on the mantel-piece seemed to him to be dividing time into separate atoms of agony, each of which was too terrible to be borne. He felt as if an iron ring was being slowly tightened round his forehead, and as if the disgrace with which he was threatened had already come upon him. The hand upon his shoulder weighed like a hand of lead. It was intolerable. It seemed to crush him.

"Come, Alan, you must decide at once."

He hesitated a moment. "Is there a fire in the room upstairs?" he murmured.

"Yes, there is a gas-fire with asbestos."

"I will have to go home and get some things from the laboratory."

"No, Alan, you need not leave the house. Write on a sheet of note-paper what you want, and my servant will take a cab and bring the things back to you."

Campbell wrote a few lines, blotted them, and addressed an envelope to his assistant. Dorian took the note up and read it carefully. Then he rang the bell, and gave it to his valet, with orders to return as soon as possible, and to bring the things with him.

When the hall door shut, Campbell started, and, having got up from the chair, went over to the chimney-piece. He was shivering with a sort of ague. For nearly twenty minutes, neither of the men spoke. A fly buzzed noisily about the room, and the ticking of the clock was like the beat of a hammer.

As the chime struck one, Campbell turned around, and, looking at Dorian Gray, saw that his eyes were filled with tears. There was something in the purity and refinement of that sad face that seemed to enrage him. "You are infamous, absolutely infamous!" he muttered.

"Hush, Alan: you have saved my life," said Dorian.

"*Your* life? Good heavens! what a life that is! You have gone from corruption to corruption, and now you have culminated in crime. In doing what I am going to do, what you force me to do, it is not of your life that I am thinking."

"Ah, Alan," murmured Dorian, with a sigh, "I wish you had a thousandth part of the pity for me that I have for you." He turned away, as he spoke, and stood looking out at the garden. Campbell made no answer.

After about ten minutes a knock came to the door, and the servant entered, carrying a mahogany chest of chemicals, with a small electric battery set on top of it. He placed it on the table, and went out again, returning with a long coil of steel and platinum wire and two rather curiously-shaped iron clamps.

"Shall I leave the things here, sir?" he asked Campbell.

"Yes," said Dorian. "And I am afraid, Francis, that I have another errand for you. What is the name of the man at Richmond who supplies Selby with orchids?"

"Harden, sir."

"Yes,—Harden. You must go down to Richmond at once, see Harden personally, and tell him to send twice as many orchids as I ordered, and to have as few white ones as possible. In fact, I don't want any white ones. It is a lovely day, Francis, and Richmond is a very pretty place, otherwise I wouldn't bother you about it."

"No trouble, sir. At what time shall I be back?"

Dorian looked at Campbell. "How long will your experiment take, Alan?" he said, in a calm, indifferent voice. The presence of a third person in the room seemed to give him extraordinary courage.

Campbell frowned, and bit his lip. "It will take about five hours," he answered.

"It will be time enough, then, if you are back at half-past seven, Francis. Or stay: just leave my things out for dressing. You can have the evening to yourself. I am not dining at home, so I shall not want you."

"Thank you, sir," said the man, leaving the room.

"Now, Alan, there is not a moment to be lost. How heavy this chest is! I'll take it for you. You bring the other things." He spoke rapidly, and in an authoritative manner. Campbell felt dominated by him. They left the room together.

When they reached the top landing, Dorian took out the key and turned it in the lock. Then he stopped, and a troubled look came into his eyes. He shuddered. "I don't think I can go in, Alan," he murmured.

"It is nothing to me. I don't require you," said Campbell, coldly.

Dorian half opened the door. As he did so, he saw the face of the portrait grinning in the sunlight. On the floor in front of it the torn curtain was lying. He remembered that the night before, for the first time in his life, he had forgotten to hide it, when he crept out of the room.

But what was that loathsome red dew that gleamed, wet and glistening, on one of the hands, as though the canvas had sweated blood? How horrible it was!—more horrible, it seemed to him for the moment, than the silent thing that he knew was stretched across the table, the thing whose grotesque misshapen shadow on the spotted carpet showed him that it had not stirred, but was still there, as he had left it.

He opened the door a little wider, and walked quickly in, with half-closed eyes and averted head, determined that he would not look even once upon the dead man. Then, stooping down, and taking up the gold-and-purple hanging, he flung it over the picture.

He stopped, feeling afraid to turn round, and his eyes fixed themselves on the intricacies of the pattern before him. He heard Campbell bringing in the heavy chest, and the irons, and the other things that he had required for his dreadful work. He began to wonder if he and Basil Hallward had ever met, and, if so, what they had thought of each other.

"Leave me now," said Campbell.

He turned and hurried out, just conscious that the dead man had been thrust back into the chair and was sitting up in it, with Campbell gazing into the glistening yellow face. As he was going downstairs he heard the key being turned in the lock.

It was long after seven o'clock when Campbell came back into the library. He was pale, but absolutely calm. "I have done what you asked me to do," he muttered. "And now, good-by. Let us never see each other again."

"You have saved me from ruin, Alan. I cannot forget that," said Dorian, simply.

As soon as Campbell had left, he went up-stairs. There was a horrible smell of chemicals in the room. But the thing that had been sitting at the table was gone.

## Chapter XIII

"There is no good telling me you are going to be good, Dorian," cried Lord Henry, dipping his white fingers into a red copper bowl filled with rose-water. "You are quite perfect. Pray don't change."

Dorian shook his head. "No, Harry, I have done too many dreadful things in my life. I am not going to do any more. I began my good actions yesterday."

"Where were you yesterday?"

"In the country, Harry. I was staying at a little inn by myself."

"My dear boy," said Lord Henry smiling, "anybody can be good in the country. There are no temptations there. That is the reason why people who live out of town are so uncivilized. There are only two ways, as you know, of becoming civilized. One is by being cultured, the other is by being corrupt. Country-people have no opportunity of being either, so they stagnate."

"Culture and corruption," murmured Dorian. "I have known something of both. It seems to me curious now that they should ever be found together. For I have a new ideal, Harry. I am going to alter. I think I have altered."

"You have not told me yet what your good action was. Or did you say you had done more than one?"

"I can tell you, Harry. It is not a story I could tell to any one else. I spared somebody. It sounds vain, but you understand what I mean. She was quite beautiful, and wonderfully like Sibyl Vane. I think it was that which first attracted me to her. You remember Sibyl, don't you? How long ago that seems! Well, Hetty was not one of our own class, of course. She was simply a girl in a village. But I really loved her. I am quite sure that I loved her. All during this wonderful May that we have been having, I used to run down and see her two or three times a week. Yesterday she met me in a little orchard. The apple-blossoms kept tumbling down on her hair, and she was laughing. We were to have gone away together this morning at dawn. Suddenly I determined to leave her as flower-like as I had found her."

"I should think the novelty of the emotion must have given you a thrill of real pleasure, Dorian," interrupted Lord Henry. "But I can finish your idyl for you. You gave her good advice, and broke her heart. That was the beginning of your reformation."

"Harry, you are horrible! You mustn't say these dreadful things. Hetty's heart is not broken. Of course she cried, and all that. But there is no disgrace upon her. She can live, like Perdita, in her garden."

"And weep over a faithless Florizel," said Lord Henry, laughing. "My dear Dorian, you have the most curious boyish moods. Do you think this girl will ever be really contented now with any one of her own rank? I suppose she will be married some day to a rough carter or a grinning ploughman. Well, having met you, and loved you, will teach her to despise her husband, and she will be wretched. From a moral point of view I really don't think much of your great renunciation. Even as a beginning, it is poor. Besides, how do you know that Hetty isn't floating at the present moment in some mill-pond, with water-lilies round her, like Ophelia?"

"I can't bear this, Harry! You mock at everything, and then suggest the most serious tragedies. I am sorry I told

you now. I don't care what you say to me, I know I was
right in acting as I did. Poor Hetty! As I rode past the farm
this morning, I saw her white face at the window, like a
spray of jasmine. Don't let me talk about it any more, and
don't try to persuade me that the first good action I have
done for years, the first little bit of self-sacrifice I have
ever known, is really a sort of sin. I want to be better. I am
going to be better. Tell me something about yourself. What
is going on in town? I have not been to the club for days."

"The people are still discussing poor Basil's disappearance."

"I should have thought they had got tired of that by
this time," said Dorian, pouring himself out some wine,
and frowning slightly.

"My dear boy, they have only been talking about it
for six weeks, and the public are really not equal to the
mental strain of having more than one topic every three
months. They have been very fortunate lately, however.
They have had my own divorce-case, and Alan Campbell's
suicide. Now they have got the mysterious disappearance of
an artist. Scotland Yard still insists that the man in the gray
ulster who left Victoria by the midnight train on the 7th
of November was poor Basil, and the French police declare
that Basil never arrived in Paris at all. I suppose in about a
fortnight we will be told that he has been seen in San Francisco. It is an odd thing, but every one who disappears is
said to be seen at San Francisco. It must be a delightful
city, and possess all the attractions of the next world."

"What do you think has happened to Basil?" asked
Dorian, holding up his Burgundy against the light, and
wondering how it was that he could discuss the matter so
calmly.

"I have not the slightest idea. If Basil chooses to hide
himself, it is no business of mine. If he is dead, I don't
want to think about him. Death is the only thing that ever

terrifies me. I hate it. One can survive everything nowadays except that. Death and vulgarity are the only two facts in the nineteenth century that one cannot explain away. Let us have our coffee in the music-room, Dorian. You must play Chopin to me. The man with whom my wife ran away played Chopin exquisitely. Poor Victoria! I was very fond of her. The house is rather lonely without her."

Dorian said nothing, but rose from the table, and, passing into the next room, sat down to the piano and let his fingers stray across the keys. After the coffee had been brought in, he stopped, and, looking over at Lord Henry, said, "Harry, did it ever occur to you that Basil was murdered?"

Lord Henry yawned. "Basil had no enemies, and always wore a Waterbury watch. Why should he be murdered? He was not clever enough to have enemies. Of course he had a wonderful genius for painting. But a man can paint like Velasquez and yet be as dull as possible. Basil was really rather dull. He only interested me once, and that was when he told me, years ago, that he had a wild adoration for you."

"I was very fond of Basil," said Dorian, with a sad look in his eyes. "But don't people say that he was murdered?"

"Oh, some of the papers do. It does not seem to be probable. I know there are dreadful places in Paris, but Basil was not the sort of man to have gone to them. He had no curiosity. It was his chief defect. Play me a nocturne, Dorian, and, as you play, tell me, in a low voice, how you have kept your youth. You must have some secret. I am only ten years older than you are, and I am wrinkled, and bald, and yellow. You are really wonderful, Dorian. You have never looked more charming than you do to-night. You remind me of the day I saw you first. You were rather cheeky, very shy, and absolutely extraordinary. You have changed, of course, but not in appearance. I wish you would tell me your secret. To get back my youth I would do anything in the world, except take exercise, get up early, or be respectable. Youth! There is nothing like it. It's absurd to talk of the ignorance of youth. The only people whose opinions I listen to now with any respect are people much younger than myself. They seem in front of me. Life has revealed to them her last wonder. As for the aged, I always contradict the aged. I do it on principle. If you ask them their opinion on something that happened yesterday, they solemnly give you the opinions current in 1820, when people wore high stocks and knew absolutely nothing. How lovely that thing you are playing is! I wonder did Chopin write it at Majorca, with the sea weeping round the villa, and the salt spray dashing against the panes? It is marvelously romantic. What a blessing it is that there is one art left to us that is not imitative! Don't stop. I want music to-night. It seems to me that you are the young Apollo, and that I am Marsyas listening to you. I have sorrows, Dorian, of my own, that even you know nothing of. The tragedy of old age is not that one is old, but that one is young. I am amazed sometimes at my own sincerity. Ah, Dorian, how happy you are! What an exquisite life you have had! You have drunk deeply of everything. You have crushed the grapes against your palate. Nothing has been hidden from you. But it has all been to you no more than the sound of music. It has not marred you. You are still the same.

"I wonder what the rest of your life will be. Don't spoil it by renunciations. At present you are a perfect type. Don't make yourself incomplete. You are quite flawless now. You need not shake your head: you know you are. Besides, Dorian, don't deceive yourself. Life is not governed by will or intention. Life is a question of nerves, and fibres, and slowly-built-up cells in which thought hides itself and passion has its dreams. You may fancy yourself safe, and think yourself strong. But a chance tone of color in a room or a morning sky, a particular perfume that you had once loved and that brings strange memories with it, a line from a forgotten poem that you had come across again, a cadence from a piece of music that you had ceased to play,—I tell you, Dorian, that it is on things like these that our lives depend. Browning writes about that somewhere; but our own senses will imagine them for us. There are moments when the odor of heliotrope passes suddenly across me, and I have to live the strangest year of my life over again.

"I wish I could change places with you, Dorian. The world has cried out against us both, but it has always worshipped you. It always will worship you. You are the type of what the age is searching for, and what it is afraid it has found. I am so glad that you have never done anything, never carved a statue, or painted a picture, or produced anything outside of yourself! Life has been your art. You have set yourself to music. Your days have been your sonnets."

Dorian rose up from the piano, and passed his hand through his hair. "Yes, life has been exquisite," he murmured, "but I am not going to have the same life, Harry. And you must not say these extravagant things to me. You don't know everything about me. I think that if you did, even you would turn from me. You laugh. Don't laugh."

"Why have you stopped playing, Dorian? Go back and play the nocturne over again. Look at that great honey-colored moon that hangs in the dusky air. She is waiting for you to charm her, and if you play she will come closer to the earth. You won't? Let us go to the club, then. It has been a charming evening, and we must end it charmingly. There is some one at the club who wants immensely to know you,—young Lord Poole, Bournmouth's eldest son. He has already copied your neckties, and has begged me to introduce him to you. He is quite delightful, and rather reminds me of you."

"I hope not," said Dorian, with a touch of pathos in his voice. "But I am tired to-night, Harry. I won't go to the club. It is nearly eleven, and I want to go to bed early."

"Do stay. You have never played so well as to-night. There was something in your touch that was wonderful. It had more expression than I had ever heard from it before."

"It is because I am going to be good," he answered, smiling. "I am a little changed already."

"Don't change, Dorian; at any rate, don't change to me. We must always be friends."

"Yet you poisoned me with a book once. I should not forgive that. Harry, promise me that you will never lend that book to any one. It does harm."

"My dear boy, you are really beginning to moralize. You will soon be going about warning people against all the sins of which you have grown tired. You are much too delightful to do that. Besides, it is no use. You and I are what we are, and will be what we will be. Come round tomorrow. I am going to ride at eleven, and we might go together. The Park is quite lovely now. I don't think there have been such lilacs since the year I met you."

"Very well. I will be here at eleven," said Dorian. "Good-night, Harry." As he reached the door he hesitated for a moment, as if he had something more to say. Then he sighed and went out.

It was a lovely night, so warm that he threw his coat over his arm, and did not even put his silk scarf round his throat. As he strolled home, smoking his cigarette, two young men in evening dress passed him. He heard one of them whisper to the other, "That is Dorian Gray." He remembered how pleased he used to be when he was pointed out, or stared at, or talked about. He was tired of hearing his own name now. Half the charm of the little village where he had been so often lately was that no one knew who he was. He had told the girl whom he had made love him that he was poor, and she had believed him. He had told her once that he was wicked, and she had laughed at him, and told him that wicked people were always very old and very ugly. What a laugh she had!—just like a thrush singing. And how pretty she had been in her cotton dresses and her large hats! She knew nothing, but she had everything that he had lost.

When he reached home, he found his servant waiting up for him. He sent him to bed, and threw himself down on the sofa in the library, and began to think over some of the things that Lord Henry had said to him.

Was it really true that one could never change? He felt a wild longing for the unstained purity of his boyhood,— his rose-white boyhood, as Lord Henry had once called it. He knew that he had tarnished himself, filled his mind with corruption, and given horror to his fancy; that he had been an evil influence to others, and had experienced a terrible joy in being so; and that of the lives that had crossed his own it had been the fairest and the most full of promise that he had brought to shame. But was it all irretrievable? Was there no hope for him?

It was better not to think of the past. Nothing could alter that. It was of himself, and of his own future, that he had to think. Alan Campbell had shot himself one night in his laboratory, but had not revealed the secret that he had been forced to know. The excitement, such as it was, over Basil Hallward's disappearance would soon pass away. It was already waning. He was perfectly safe there. Nor, indeed, was it the death of Basil Hallward that weighed most upon his mind. It was the living death of his own soul that troubled him. Basil had painted the portrait that had marred his life. He could not forgive him that. It was the portrait that had done everything. Basil had said things to him that were unbearable, and that he had yet borne with patience. The murder had been simply the madness of a moment. As for Alan Campbell, his suicide had been his own act. He had chosen to do it. It was nothing to him.

A new life! That was what he wanted. That was what he was waiting for. Surely he had begun it already. He had spared one innocent thing, at any rate. He would never again tempt innocence. He would be good.

As he thought of Hetty Merton, he began to wonder if the portrait in the locked room had changed. Surely it was not still so horrible as it had been? Perhaps if his life became pure, he would be able to expel every sign of evil passion from the face. Perhaps the signs of evil had already gone away. He would go and look.

He took the lamp from the table and crept up-stairs. As he unlocked the door, a smile of joy flitted across his young face and lingered for a moment about his lips. Yes, he would be good, and the hideous thing that he had hidden away would no longer be a terror to him. He felt as if the load had been lifted from him already.

He went in quietly, locking the door behind him, as was his custom, and dragged the purple hanging from the portrait. A cry of pain and indignation broke from him. He could see no change, unless that in the eyes there was a look of cunning, and in the mouth the curved wrinkle of the hypocrite. The thing was still loathsome,—more loathsome, if possible, than before,—and the scarlet dew that spotted the hand seemed brighter, and more like blood newly spilt.

Had it been merely vanity that had made him do his one good deed? Or the desire of a new sensation, as Lord Henry had hinted, with his mocking laugh? Or that passion to act a part that sometimes makes us do things finer than we are ourselves? Or, perhaps, all these?

Why was the red stain larger than it had been? It seemed to have crept like a horrible disease over the wrinkled fingers. There was blood on the painted feet, as though the thing had dripped,—blood even on the hand that had not held the knife.

Confess? Did it mean that he was to confess? To give himself up, and be put to death? He laughed. He felt that the idea was monstrous. Besides, who would believe him, even if he did confess? There was no trace of the murdered man anywhere. Everything belonging to him had been destroyed. He himself had burned what had been below-stairs. The world would simply say he was mad. They would shut him up if he persisted in his story.

Yet it was his duty to confess, to suffer public shame, and to make public atonement. There was a God who called upon men to tell their sins to earth as well as to heaven. Nothing that he could do would cleanse him till he had told his own sin. His sin? He shrugged his shoulders. The death of Basil Hallward seemed very little to him. He was thinking of Hetty Merton.

It was an unjust mirror, this mirror of his soul that he was looking at. Vanity? Curiosity? Hypocrisy? Had there been nothing more in his renunciation than that? There had been something more. At least he thought so. But who could tell?

And this murder,—was it to dog him all his life? Was he never to get rid of the past? Was he really to confess? No. There was only one bit of evidence left against him. The picture itself,—that was evidence.

He would destroy it. Why had he kept it so long? It had given him pleasure once to watch it changing and growing old. Of late he had felt no such pleasure. It had kept him awake at night. When he had been away, he had been filled with terror lest other eyes should look upon it.

It had brought melancholy across his passions. Its mere memory had marred many moments of joy. It had been like conscience to him. Yes, it had been conscience. He would destroy it.

He looked round, and saw the knife that had stabbed Basil Hallward. He had cleaned it many times, till there was no stain left upon it. It was bright, and glistened. As it had killed the painter, so it would kill the painter's work, and all that that meant. It would kill the past, and when that was dead he would be free. He seized it, and stabbed the canvas with it, ripping the thing right up from top to bottom.

There was a cry heard, and a crash. The cry was so horrible in its agony that the frightened servants woke, and crept out of their rooms. Two gentlemen, who were passing in the Square below, stopped, and looked up at the great house. They walked on till they met a policeman, and brought him back. The man rang the bell several times, but there was no answer. The house was all dark, except for a light in one of the top windows. After a time, he went away, and stood in the portico of the next house and watched.

"Whose house is that, constable?" asked the elder of the two gentlemen.

"Mr. Dorian Gray's, sir," answered the policeman.

They looked at each other, as they walked away, and sneered. One of them was Sir Henry Ashton's uncle.

Inside, in the servants' part of the house, the half-clad domestics were talking in low whispers to each other. Old Mrs. Leaf was crying, and wringing her hands. Francis was as pale as death.

After about a quarter of an hour, he got the coachman and one of the footmen and crept up-stairs. They knocked, but there was no reply. They called out. Everything was still. Finally, after vainly trying to force the door, they got on the roof, and dropped down on to the balcony. The windows yielded easily: the bolts were old.

When they entered, they found hanging upon the wall a splendid portrait of their master as they had last seen him, in all the wonder of his exquisite youth and beauty. Lying on the floor was a dead man, in evening dress, with a knife in his heart. He was withered, wrinkled, and loathsome of visage. It was not till they had examined the rings that they recognized who it was.

# HORTUS
## DIABOLICUS

*Further Twisting Tales of
Menacing Flora and
Malignant Fungi*

Edited by Chad Arment

TRAVELS THROUGH
LOST WORLDS
THE LIVING DEATH
IN AMUNDSEN'S TENT
DROME

JOHN MARTIN LEAHY

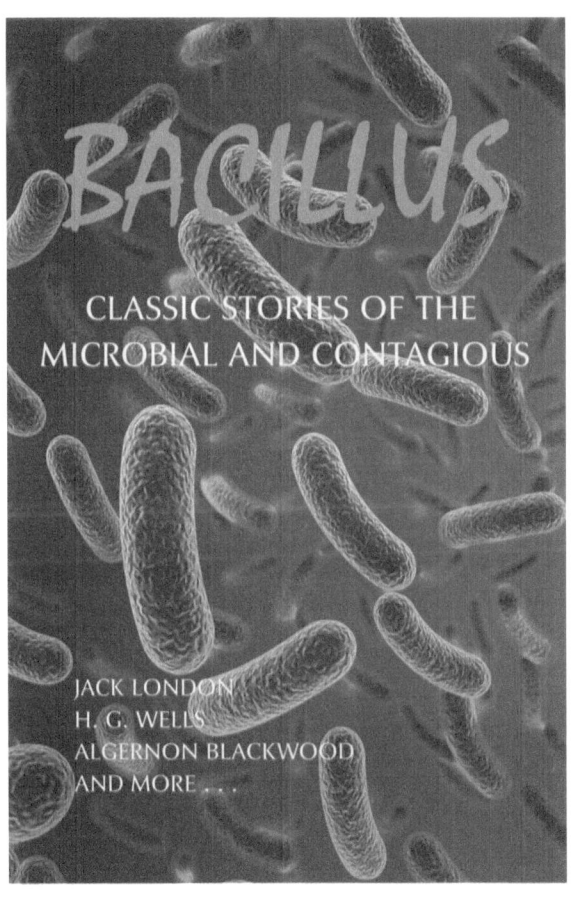

COACHWHIPBOOKS.COM (PRINT)
COACHWHIP.COM (EPUB)

COACHWHIPBOOKS.COM (PRINT)
COACHWHIP.COM (EPUB)

CATS OF SHADOW,
CLAWS OF DARKNESS

Stories of Were-Cats, Ghost Cats,
and Other Supernatural Felines